Twisted Dreams, Fatal Wishes

Lee F. Snyder

1563 Alhambra Way S.
Saint Petersburg, FL 33705

Copyright 2014 Lee Snyder

ISBN 978-1500-4360-49

To Mark, Alva, Dorothy for their valued advice.

For Diane, who has always been there.

For Cheryl, my best critic and love.

CHAPTER 1

Twisted Dreams

I'm going to kill Robert Whitney. But I can only kill him once. That point eats at me. So I kill him in my sleep, my daydreams, and my personal conversations. I kill him every chance I get. I kill him every waking moment. It still isn't enough.

I know now that I missed my best opportunity. The reality, the one chance I had to resolve my hatred I saw as a game instead of a mission. I was too meek, too forgiving, and cautious. When I failed, it wasn't because I lacked effort. I lacked direction and that failure dropped me lower than I already was. I won't make that mistake again.

Albemarle was the Virginia state hospital in Richmond. Attendance there was a requirement for the treatment of all types of complaints. The core of the fading hospital campus was limited to several overcrowded, sixty-year old Kennedy era buildings ignored within an otherwise conscious city. Necessity was all that allowed the facility to remain in use. Paint and neglect hid most of the structural problems just as daily education promoted the inmates' passive behavior.

As the bus with *Albemarle State Hospital* tattooed to the side pulled to a stop, three bearish male orderlies in white gathered near the bus door waiting for David and his companions from the county jail. A tall, slender man with closely cropped graying hair wearing a dark suit and green bow tie waited in the shade of ancient oak trees near the admissions entrance. Beside the man was a much shorter contradiction. The mousy young woman in light blue business attire repeatedly tossed her head against the spring breeze. Her wispy brown hair covered her gold-rimmed glasses. David and the four new additions to the hospital population lined up outside the vehicle depending on the bright white Bluebird bus for back support. They were flanked by the orderlies, there for muscle in case the drugs and the thick, black plastic electric cable ties clasping their wrists weren't enough. The young woman took several steps toward the men and into the sunshine. "Hello and welcome. My name is Dr. Wilson. I am the Head of Psychiatric Services here at Albemarle." She had a weak but pleasant voice. "You have all come here fearing everything. You are probably burrowing into yourselves for protection. Fear has forced you into your own quiet world." Her welcoming speech was intended to comfort and soothe, but its canned delivery exposed her inexperience. "Our job here at Albemarle," she continued, "is to bring you back."

The male suit abruptly stepped forward. As he walked past her, he held his hand up looking back and forth at the five hospital additions plastered to the side of the bus. The man stopped in front of her. Clearly, this was the guy in charge.

Dr. Wilson watched as the man took his position in front of her. "We are here to help you find yourselves once again," she said as her voice faded to silence. She sheepishly smiled and stepped back into the shade.

He opened his suit jacket and casually slid a hand into his pants pocket. "Is that it? Is that really what you're thinking?" he said staring at David. "Guess again," he worked his way past each of the other three additions. "I am Dr. Phillips, the chief administrator of this state facility. Dr. Wilson," he gestured looking briefly over his shoulder at the woman, "has a different philosophy than I have. Don't ever forget that I know why you are here and what each and every one of you has done to earn your place here." He paused to drill his stare into the new recruits, one after the other. "It is my responsibility to see to it that you are in your beds when the lights go out," he paused again with the sentence hanging above them, "and in your beds when the lights go on again in the morning. Unlike Dr. Wilson, I am not here to listen to your whining. I am simply the man with the checklist. Your job, as far as I am concerned, is to serve your time. Fuck up and you get to see my bad side." Again, there was a pause as he looked down the line and then added, "Don't-fuck-up." The words fell like rocks bouncing on a metal roof. "You won't like the consequences.

"Dr. Wilson will meet with each of you over the next few days. She will assign you a therapist." Dr. Wilson smiled meekly. Phillips turned to the head orderly and nodded. The five new patients were sandwiched between the other two men in white. "Let's go," Phillips said coarsely as they shuffled after their leader.

The next day was Monday. It was 8 a.m. and David was sitting on a green, wooden bench in the pale yellow hallway outside Dr. Wilson's door. He had just finished breakfast when he was snatched for his meeting. A new orderly hovered over him as they waited for the door to open. There were some muffled words of a woman's voice and the sound of a telephone being hung up. Moments later Dr. Wilson stepped into the hall and turned toward David. "Good morning, Mr. Gere." Her words echoed off the empty hallway's twelve foot ceilings and naked walls. Turning to the orderly, she said, "Thank you, James. I can handle it from here."

James wasn't buying it. "No ma'am, I'm supposed to stay right here in case . . ." She interrupted and repeated herself in the same soft voice, "No James. It's all right. Thank you."

James reluctantly agreed, stopping for a brief instant to stare a warning in David's direction. David figured the orderly also knew the "Don't fuck up" speech. It applied to him as well. David understood James's glare and had no intention of testing the threat.

"Come in Mr. Gere and please sit down."

Her office was small. Nine by nine, at best, with the same twelve foot ceilings as the hallway making the room appear like a converted elevator shaft. There was one bookcase shoved into a corner against the pale green wall. The doctor covered the shelves with plastic flowers and a few framed bits of childlike crayon art adjacent to several clinical books. Her ancient, over-sized, institutional, gray metal desk was out of place for such a small room. She was able to squeeze one wooden, straight-backed chair with a narrow-legged table wobbling beside it in front of her desk. With all elements in place, it required she enter the room stepping close to the bookshelf before closing the door and attempting the weave through to her chair.

"Please sit down, Mr. Gere. How is everything so far?"

"Fine. No complaints," David said passively, keeping his real thoughts to himself.

She began shuffling a few papers looking for her pen. Finding the long-stemmed red ballpoint, she scribbled on her desk pad; shook it; and scribbled some more. The pad was bathed in red scribbles. Her movements showed tension. "Our purpose here, today, is to introduce you to the curriculum for the next several months," she explained looking for an empty space on the pad to test the pen once more. Again she scribbled.

"It is extremely important that you adhere to these simple rules. To do otherwise . . . , well, we'll deal with that later, if we need to." She stopped scribbling, looked up at him, and smiled. "Tell me something about yourself, Mr. Gere; something I can't find out by reading your file."

David immediately reminded himself that, though she might be easy to manipulate, the threat of the goons in the white outfits and their fearless leader with the bow tie was a very different story. He had to be careful. He suspected she was being watched. He could bend her rules. But bend them too much and his crooked behavior would be noticed by those watching her.

"I don't belong here," he told her. "I'll stay for a while, but just until I think it's safe for me to leave."

"Safe," she said as if trying to understand the meaning. David nodded and said nothing more. "Well, good! That's a start. We've broken the ice. Perhaps, we can pursue this further in a few days after you've had a chance to express yourself in group," she said as if dusting her hands off after digging in his garden.

"My tool for success is simple," she said confidently. "Group therapy," she told him, "is a measure of how far from the burrow we have emerged. How much we trust the room, the people, the hospital and ultimately, the world. You will only get out of it as much as you put in." She smiled. "I've scheduled you for your first group session. We'll begin tomorrow," she said checking the pages of the bleeding appointment book on the desk in front of her. She picked up the pen and added one more pin prick of red ink to the page. "I like to think of it the way the Beatles did, you know, 'the love you take is equal to the love you make.'" She smiled again raising her eyebrows as if asking for recognition. "Try to remember, the benefit you receive is equal to the contribution you make." She smiled, clearly pleased with herself. He was certain he wasn't the first to hear her attempt at paraphrasing *Abbey Road,* though David may have been the first to laugh out loud when she said it. Her smile quickly dissolved and her face burned a bright ink red.

"Well, I think that will be all for now," she said looking down at her pad once more. She scribbled something to make it appear official and reached for the phone. "Yes. Please tell James that Mr. Gere is finished. Thank you." She hung up the phone and without looking at David, stood and went for the door. He injured her. This was his ally. His first and quite probably the only one he would find here and he embarrassed her. David tried to heal the situation. He thought he should begin humming something by the Beatles. Maybe she would think his chuckle was in appreciation of her reference. All he could come out with was *Yellow Submarine*. David thought it better to remain silent. She opened the door and briefly looked up at him forcing a grin. "Please have a seat in the hall, Mr. Gere. James will be here momentarily to take you back to your ward."

"Sure," David said. The door closed and he sat on the green bench against the yellow walls and began unconsciously whistling that damn song. She heard him and his laughter.

Tuesday at noon, the orderly issued his series of daily commands in the day room just after the *Price is Right* wrapped and the TV was silenced. This was David's first time. He had no idea of what to expect. As the light of the TV screen shrunk and disappeared, the rest of the inmates began hurriedly moving their chairs to invisible spots on the floor. The movement abruptly stopped. The group's chaired semi-circle was complete except for David's addition. He followed suit grabbing a spot at the left end. The participants promptly fit themselves into the orange, bucketed fiberglass chairs, nestling in while consciously reserving an invisible perimeter around their positions. No one encroached on that space. It was communally understood. Once settled, they looked from face-to-face waiting, anticipating.

6

"You are preparing for group," the orderly said as if there was more to the chair adjustment than just placing them this way. So, there they sat. This was to be their therapy. Fourteen heavily medicated, mush-minded, middle-aged males waited, barely conscious, for the terror to begin. David had no idea of the power that could be concentrated in one hand until that day.

Seated to his right was Malcolm. He didn't need a last name, even if he had one. He was a kind of know-it-all. He *always* had answers usually to questions he would supply. He *always* sat there and *always* had something to say to whoever squeezed in beside him. But he *never* spoke to more than that one person. It was David's error to fill in the circular void with his chair next to Malcolm's.

Malcolm leaned toward David while looking straight ahead thinking no one would notice him speaking if he didn't turn in David's direction. "Have they asked you what problem sent you here, yet?"

David was startled and annoyed. He turned to look at Malcolm.

"He's going to ask you. He asks everyone. You should be ready," Malcolm suggested.

"What are you talking about?

"He'll have an answer for you. He'll say: 'Maybe the real problem is the personal obsession that keeps us focused on our lost lives.'" The stock explanation was thrown at the group daily as part of every therapy summation. "What do *you* think David?" Malcom smiled, pleased with his mock analysis.

"How did you know my name?" David had never spoken to Malcolm. He saw him wandering through the day room. But now, Malcolm was talking; calling David by name.

Malcolm didn't answer.

David turned away. "Yeah, maybe," he said. "Obsession sounds right. Maybe not." Turning once more toward Malcolm, he said, "You been reading my file?"

Malcolm smiled. "You mean the part Dr. Wilson wrote about your being a psychologically displaced, nearly-fit, fortyish fool with a *need* to accomplish?" There was a broad smile on Malcolm's face as he continued his forward stare.

David leaned toward him. "Yeah, sure. Laugh if you want. There is 'need.' But the Doc's got it wrong," David told him. "It is not about becoming socially accepted. Wanna know my need? My need you can call "getting even . . . and a little more." David's shoulders were tightening. He began rubbing his sweating palms against his legs. His voice got louder. "I see myself in training. I'm looking to regain my life. But, it might take some time. Sometime in the future—a week, month or maybe a couple of years." Again, David looked at Malcolm. Malcolm nervously glanced back shifting in his chair. "I'm going to balance the world's wrongs by killing the man who put me here." David spoke too loudly. A few of the bobble heads that made up the semi-circle perked up. Any raised voice increased the group's excitement level like gasoline on a smoldering fire.

Malcolm waited until the fire cooled once more. He wasn't through. He wanted more answers, so he shared. "Buddha," he said in a soft voice, "said, free your mind from the personal and you free yourself from problems."

"Buddha wants me to forget about Robert. That's probably great advice somewhere. But it's bullshit in here," David said. Tell your friend Buddha he can kiss my ass." David was broadcasting his words into Malcolm's ear in a near yell. He had everyone's attention including the orderly that walked up behind him and placed a heavy hand on his shoulder.

"Let's calm down, Mr. Gere. You'll get your chance to speak when Mr. Simmons gets here." He patted David's right shoulder, then, placed his second hand on the left and squeezed until David relaxed. "That's good, sir," he said and walked back to his corner chair.

"Yeah, Mr. Simmons will let me speak," David mumbled sarcastically. "I heard the talk about him."

Floyd Armand Simmons was the group therapist's name. That shouldn't matter since he seldom remembered anyone else's. He was an asshole—a nearly-interested, state worker with problems bigger than anyone's in the circle. This day Floyd arrived precisely at 10:05, as expected. He stopped briefly upon entering the room to speak with the orderly. Words were exchanged and the orderly turned to look at David. Some more words were exchanged. Floyd nodded and the orderly moved back to his corner while Floyd came closer to the circle. He dressed all in white, down to his matte white shoes and white nylon socks. His vertical image was sliced in half by the horizontal addition of a brown calf-skin belt with a gold buckle. Floyd's red beard was neatly trimmed giving the illusion that it never grew. He simply glued a new one in place every morning and removed it at night. His tightly curled red hair sprang as he walked exposing a right-sided earlobe pierced with two colored stones and a small gold hoop. His stride was accompanied by the music of three copper bracelets on his limply swinging right wrist. The clipboard was nestled tightly under his left arm and against his body. Floyd projected an image. He wanted you to know that he was organized from the moment he woke to the moment he slept. He was a contradiction to all the lifestyles of the people he pursued that day. He was the less than refreshing slap in the face that confronted the population each morning.

Floyd willingly inserted himself among the group's faces like the bloody thorn that he was. And they willingly listened as Floyd tore into their passive flesh. And he opened the wounds. They told themselves they understood that this was his job. They all just

9

wished he didn't enjoy it so much. "It's good for you to face your fears," he gloated. Some took comfort in the order as the beginning of their day. Others found it entertaining to listen to the fairy tales about to unfold. Still others, like David, contemptuously wondered why they were wasting their time at sixty minutes of overindulged self-absorbance. First day in group and David was bored and ready to leave.

"The high road," David whispered to himself. "Take the high road." To his way of thinking the group sessions looked to be one of the tangible offerings the hospital made toward his departure. Floyd was one of the doors, he told himself. Floyd was a key to the outside—David's key to Robert. Get through Floyd's tests and the world was his once again. And, of course, Floyd knew. David quickly learned that Floyd, like Robert, was attempting to rearrange the world to his definition of order.

Floyd took his seat at the center of the semicircle. Malcolm was surprised. "That's not right," he whispered. "Where's his water? He always has a clear plastic bottle of blue-labeled, Zephyrhills water."

Today, the water was replaced by a shapely glass bottle of Fanta orange soda. The long necked bottle was placed tightly against Floyd's leg on the floor near his chair. Glass was not allowed on the wards. Glass was dangerous. Sharp. But Floyd was above that. Floyd had control. The glass bottle, David reasoned, was Floyd's way of saying so.

He went to work immediately. He picked up the bottle and took a sip, and shifted his eyes quickly over the day's notes attached to the aluminum clipboard. Without removing his analytical gaze, he replaced the bottle to its position by his side. The injured minds all watched as if hypnotized by his movement. They swallowed when he sipped. They leaned forward as he placed the bottle on the floor. Then, looking at them all to be certain he had their attention; Floyd began the day's attacks by surgically singling out the most

10

vulnerable biography. Looking down at his meticulously typed notes, never raising his head to look at the victim's expressionless face, he asked, "Tell us . . . about the mutilations." Glancing at the top of the sheet for a name he said, "Mark." He still wasn't certain who Mark was or where he was sitting but other relieved faces knew and they turned toward the slender, paling, squirming form melting into the bucket-shaped chair. Floyd glanced up from the chart and quickly scanned the circle following the thirteen faces that turned toward the victim. Seeing their chosen offering, Floyd leaned forward like a dragon about to bar-b-q its sacrificial virgin prey with an exhaled blast of flame and painful truth.

"What did they mean to you?"

You have to understand, *meaning* was not the real point. *Healing* was not the point, either. *Pain* was the point and *meaning* elicited the pain. That was what Floyd wanted to see. That was his overriding goal. Floyd elicited pain and watched it ooze from the wounded mind in all its slimy, green memory. It smelled of screaming. It squirmed to the floor and gathered in a pool around the victim's feet. It filled up the void around him until it gagged him from the lack of oxygen. And then, the crippled reply spewed like verbal vomit followed by more squirming. All the uncontrollable, convulsive twists pulled more of the green, oily memories from the mind. And all the while, Floyd sat there without emotion staring at the victim engulfed in his terror and offered no comfort. Floyd just glanced back and forth between the clipboard and the tortured soul. These were minutes for Floyd. They were the crush of hours for his victim.

"Mark," he said questioning, "Mark, I have asked you a question. I expect a reply. Tell us what you were thinking when you were slicing the animals—the cats, and the dogs. Tell us how you felt."

Floyd's question dripped with acid on Mark's ears burning the words through to his graying scalp and burrowed deeply into his

11

brain. The room was dead still. No cleared throats. No nervous coughs. It was as if all of them were holding their breath. Mark's reply was the only magic that broke the spell. But Mark never lifted his head and long hair from his hunched shoulders and slender frame. His bleached white cloth robe was crumpled tightly in his lap. The white cotton, general-issue slippers sat on top of the pile neatly aligned with the toes pointed in. His slender folded arms grabbed at his ribs as if trying to keep the anxiety unidentified. He bent at the waist, rocking with an increasing tempo and then, he whispered, "Fuck you, Floyd." The slippers fell noiselessly to the floor covered by the disheveled robe.

There was the first chuckle of the session from the group mixed with sudden coughing and chair shifting—a kind of congratulatory recognition of both Mark's independence and the beginning of the day. A way to shout, "It's on and we are united against Floyd!" But, it was early in the game and it was clear that creativity was not one of Mark's hallmarks. Fear has a way of prioritizing goals. Clever is easily usurped by the threat of discovery. After taking another sip from his bottle, Floyd began reading out loud from his legal-sized, collection of papers. He carefully checked each item from his menu as he ran down the column of atrocities.

"We understand you began with cats and dogs at first," Floyd said as if reading a grocery list. "Later," he thumbed through the pages of his pad, "as you aged, you became less selective." Still thumbing. "It appears whatever was near you when the mood struck was fair game. Is that right?" He didn't expect an answer. He continued. "Even, apparently, if you were alone." Floyd held the preceding paper up to read the final page beneath. He dropped it and flipped all the others over. Placing the clip board on his lap, he shifted his direction toward Mark.

Mark had only one ear hidden under his shaggy, graying mane. There were only three fingers on one of his wrinkled hands.

Oh yes, and Mark, according to Floyd's pad, didn't have a mother anymore.

"I had to warm up to the thought of killing her," Mark whispered, as he lifted his head and smiled. Mark broke through his fear and the cloud of drugs swimming through his brain for a moment and laughed softly with several sympathetic members of the group.

But with Floyd there was no laughter. Not even a polite smile of congratulations for Mark's life-long accomplishments. As the injured prisoner glanced around the circle collecting his approving smiles, he caught Floyd's block-faced stare—the one that stopped the merry-go-round and the happy, spinning, comforting, hollow-headed balloon blessings. Understand that Floyd believed he sold the air that inflated those balloons. If the floating minds strayed, as Mark's just had while looking for approval, Floyd quickly pulled the wandering balloons back to the circle's inner center where he held all the strings. So, Mark's string was yanked back in. Mark's whiplash caused him to quickly drop his gaze back to the floor. He began playing with the two stumps on his left hand.

"Do you think about why you hurt your mother? Why you hurt yourself, Mark?" Floyd took another sip of the magic orange liquid from the Fanta bottle. It gave him strength. His attack was slow and methodical. Each of Floyd's words was weighed and directed in syllabic punches toward Mark. Mark blinked and cringed after each sentence Floyd threw in his direction.

Here we depart for a brief chemical lesson—it's a way to understand Mark's condition at the time. Mark was drugged. Specifically, Mark was enjoying the benefits of Thorazine. Thorazine is brain candy to slow electrons. Thorazine is the absolute zero of the psychiatric chemical world. There is nothing colder. Space and time exist but on a different level. It is half time or less. The consumer hears, speaks, breathes and pisses in slow motion while everyone else speeds past in a calculated blur measured in milligrams.

Despite the chemical handicap, Mark emerged from his defensive cower and started softly as if talking to himself. He never looked up from his floor-directed stare. The hesitation and stammering of the injured mind dissolved with a cruel determination. Mark's well-outlined jaw flexed as his teeth gnashed and the blank stare became directed at his mind's re-enactment of the butchery the prescribed chemicals couldn't wash from his memory. "I feel better whenever I cut something. It helps me. It relaxes me." His voice was subdued but his anger enunciated each word. They were pronounced as if trying to sound them out for a fifth grade spelling bee. "But," Mark explained, "I don't believe in getting angry. It's all about control," he said. "Control is an admirable human quality."

Mark's control wasn't always exact. "I worked at making the cuts straight and clean. I take pride in my work," he said. "There is the blood and the cold for them," he shifted his head slightly to his left, "and for me there is warmth." He shifted his head to the right. It was all a simple comparison.

Mark wrapped himself in his arms, again. "The act gains a life. It has a sense all its own. It surrounds and envelops me." Mark stopped. He was visiting past moments. His eyes were wide as he stared at the dayroom floor. After years in various jails and hospitals, too numerous to count, Mark's problems became more obvious. When he spoke, he didn't hide them anymore. He freely admitted that his myriad mutilations were standard fare. Floyd must have known that.

Mark's Mother was unrecognizable after he did her. He said he lost his temper for the first time, the only time in his life, he claimed. "There were always demands and distractions living with mother," Mark explained. "But as she got older, she got meaner and the distractions required all of my free time. She always had to know

14

what I was doing and when I was doing it. She was always asking questions. It was becoming more difficult for me to gather the things I needed. Then, I lost my temper when she discovered my collection of meats drying in my room. She began shouting and tearing down the drying lines that crisscrossed over my bed."

So, Mark killed her; restrung the drying lines formerly filled with neighborhood pets, and dried her the same way he made strips of the stray animals. It was that simple. Even then, Mark assured everyone, that the Oscar Meyer presentation made of his mother was not the reason for his hospital attendance. "It has to do with the way I treated my mother afterwards that has kept me away from home," Mark said with his eyes squinting and head tipping to the side as if looking at an invisible display. "If I had been neater, there would be no need for my presence here today." He truly believed that if he remained calm as he slashed the old lady, there would have been a consensus opinion excusing the act.

Floyd lifted his bottle and emptied the last swallow. He placed the long-necked, glass bottle on the floor and switched his attention to the papers on the clipboard. Floyd readjusted his seated position; cleared his throat, and began again. "Were you angry with your mother when you killed the animals, Mark?"

Mark was yanked back to reality, such as it was, by Floyd's question. Like a turtle retracting its head, Mark reentered his shell. Looking down, once more, he quietly mumbled: "Fuck you, Floyd." There was a quiet, automatic laugh with some hesitation from a few balloons and Mark looked up with a sheepish smile collecting his minimal accolades before sending his stare back to the floor.

This exercise with Mark was a contradiction to reason! Reason? There was none! This was sandpaper on a baby's ass, a packed elevator with the door jammed. This was tension rising to a scream that seeped through every man's dream. This was Floyd's joy. The group squirmed; moved uneasily and simmered in the heat Floyd generated. They gasped for air fighting the imagined plastic bags over their heads. Floyd ignored them. He continued studying his pad's typed message and doodled notes.

Mark looked to be the mother lode, a jack-pot. But Floyd was unimpressed. Then, David realized Floyd read it all, or heard it all before. Mark was Floyd's way of priming the pump. He knew Mark's story got others to talk. Floyd was playing a terrifying game. He must extract the truth where the group's fear of discovery forced each of them to stuff their problems deeply, darkly inside—too far for treatment.

You must remember that the entertainment, as great as it was, wasn't free. When Floyd finished with Mark someone else squirmed; paid for his ticket. Someone else carried the "Fuck you, Floyd" shield and Floyd, the dragon, melted it with his exhaled fire. If asked, David was certain that the entire hospital would help Mark dry Floyd's stripped flesh in the sun or over the radiator in the day room.

"Let's talk about you," Floyd hesitated looking for a name and a note, ". . . Kirby." Still reading, "Why do you think you're here?"

Kirby didn't answer. Chairs were being readjusted as the asses leaking from the loosely tied hospital gowns kissed the sticky plastic searching for comfort that wasn't there. The chairs seemed to know this story and the riders tried to hold onto their positions. Floyd was the wizard waving his staff above his head creating a storm that would move them all. This was Floyd's *Fantasia*. Brooms and mops escaped from the closet and began dancing. Barred windows gaped open gulping mystic-free air. Doors shut with crashing emphasis. Floyd was pulling out all the stops.

"Do you think masturbating in church is proper behavior?" He looked up searching for a face to associate with the accusation as though the question was harmless; no more important than asking to borrow a pen to sign a death warrant. But Floyd knew it had value.

16

Apparently, Kirby was a favorite target. Attacking Kirby helped Floyd regain the edge over them all.

Kirby was likeable and completely harmless. At five-four, his stature was as slight as his position within the ward community. His pale Irish complexion altered whenever he was addressed by staff or fellow clients attaining a red flush with chameleon-like speed. With an overgrown abundance of dark black hair, he resembled a plump puppy. His instant tail-wagging smile showed grateful affection for even the slightest attention. Because Kirby was not a threat, Floyd saw him as the perfect victim—a tool for the way the wizard reclaimed his hold on the recently discovered confidence in the room.

Kirby's problems were still undiscovered. When they originally found Kirby, just before bringing him to Albemarle, he was sitting in a city church carving into the maple pew with his right hand. Oh yeah, his left hand gripped his crank and Kirby's pants were in the aisle. That didn't look good either. The cops said he mumbled something about the priest. So, they figured: knife, priest, spaced-out. This guy was a prime candidate for . . . Albemarle! Somehow no one got to asking Kirby about the carving or the priest. The therapists were hung up on the sexual aspect of his problem suggesting their interests were a reflection of their own puerile curiosities. So, the questions usually started with the chubby in Kirby's left hand.

"It says you were naked and behaving inappropriately in church." Floyd spoke slowly, disconnected, like reading a sign he passed on his way to and from work for the last hundred years. His pacing and tone soothed—a direct contradiction to the bombs going off in Kirby's head.

The red-faced puppy's tail was wagging very slowly as if grateful for the attention while wisely questioning the motive. There was pain in Kirby's desperate reply. It sounded more like a question. There was no defiance in the declaration. "Fuck you, Floyd?" It was weak and questioning and easily waved away by the sorcerer. There was no resistance in the remark. There was no laughter, either. Score one for Floyd. The circle was his once again. When one fell, they all fell like a pyramid of partially crushed, empty, aluminum Budweiser cans diving for the floor. The noise that echoed with each repeated bounce and collision was a vote for Floyd. They all felt the pain. They all heard the deafening noise of the landslide, except Floyd.

"Tell me, Kirby. Tell me about the carving in the church. It's time we understood what you were doing. This is the time for you to let us inside to understand."

Kirby redirected his gaze from the floor and looked directly at Floyd. It was easy to sense his anger. "My father," he said, "collected souls." That was enough to break the tension. There were a few giggles and then, complete laughter from everyone in the room except for Floyd. After a moment's hesitation and a quick look around the circle, Kirby was smiling. The plump little puppy's tail was gratefully wagging once more. Then, realizing the sudden power of his apparently senseless remark, Kirby laughed too. Floyd looked at his clip board. He slowly dragged the pen from its position beneath the clip. Looking up at Kirby and the circle of laughing comrades, he began writing on his pad. Floyd was moving on but there was a renewed fear that remained on Kirby's face.

Floyd began flipping through his chart once more. He must have learned enough about Kirby. His note pad had few written lines under David's name. He was willing to correct that. After listening to him dissect Mark and Kirby, David knew some of what to expect. He decided to use Floyd. Hate Floyd. Destroy Floyd. Practice on Floyd for when he got out. In that instant, David made Floyd his surrogate Robert.

"David, you have said you wanted to kill someone. Is that why you're here?"

David looked up and turned toward the orderly in the corner. That was what the conversation was about when Floyd came into the room. The orderly filled him in. Now, David saw he was singled out. The rest was just the diversion before Floyd came at him. David wasn't shy. He replied immediately in a soft voice, "I'm here because I *didn't* kill someone." There was a chuckle or two from the circle. "If I had, the world would have thanked me." Again, a few more chuckles. "I'm here because HE was able to put me here. HE has more power than anyone else and HE uses it against me because HE knows when I have the chance *I will kill him.*"

"And that is why you are here? Because . . ." he glanced at his pad, "Robert put you in here. It is Robert, isn't it?" Floyd was still digging while the rest of the minds in the room moved their attention toward the conversation. David saw the smiles on the faces as he quickly scanned the circle.

"Yes," he said, "but you knew that all along didn't you?" This was a fact that had to be said. "You work for him too don't you?" A revelation for some brought a dull murmuring chatter to the room.

Floyd was scratching on his typed notes. Without looking up, he said, "I work for the hospital David I'm here to help you. *Maybe the real problem is the personal obsession that keeps us focused on our lost lives.*" Floyd pulled it out from his collection of pre-packaged diversions. It took no thought to deliver; just throw it out as a minor road block to an on-rushing train. Floyd was concentrating on his clip board. It demanded his attention, not David or the group. Forced into an unexpected corner, Floyd was nervously searching for a new dance step—one that was seldom used, hid among the orderly lessons typed in front of him. It was probably listed under: "In Case of Inexperience or Ineptitude."

The canned reply was recognized by the empty heads for what it was as the murmur increased in volume.

"Help me? You wanna help? Get out of my way. Let me back at the son of a . . ."

Floyd suddenly recognized the disruption. He tried to regain some lost control by interrupting him. "David, David. Let's talk about your anger."

David was on a roll and sensed the backing of the group. He was going to put this son of a bitch in his place. All the David held for Robert was quickly transferred to Floyd. He was the gate between being locked up and being outside to get Robert.

Floyd searched the room beyond the circle for the orderly in the corner chair. He nodded and the orderly quickly rose for the door; disappearing into the hallway; scurrying off to the left and out of sight. Floyd redirected his attention toward the group as a whole. He raised his hands trying to calm the circle.

"You keep all of us in here," David yelled. We are the mirror of your problems. We are the little evils that occupy your mind." David had Floyd and the entire group was with him. It was time to destroy Floyd.

"Working on our problems is really a personal exercise for you isn't it, Floyd? You're the one who spends his time counting the loose change that spills from our heads like little, pink piggy banks cracked open with your therapeutic thumping." There was some clapping and shouting with every word David directed at Floyd.

"You're the one that takes our words and searches the fecal matter for yourself. You sift through this jabber hoping you won't recognize anything personal in our descriptions." Chairs were moved and several of David's compatriots were standing.

"You consider us all disposable people but you still believe the cure for your own insecurities must be within us. Group is a grand, shiny, gilded mirror for you, Floyd. It is your closet therapy.

20

You're the one who's afraid to see what is really inside of us all. You are the real problem here!" There was a raucous slapping of backs and cheers and chairs moving. Now, the circle had substance and the anger was clearly toward Floyd who stumbled, mumbled and grasped the files in his lap as if looking for a shield to ward off the swarming hive of bees being thrown at *him*. A new dragon entered the circle. Now, *David was breathing fire!* The circle was alive. Blank faces became enraged. Mumbles turned to shouts. Fists pumped in the air. David turned to look at what he had done and for the first time he feared for the group. There was no control. All the hatred David helped channel against Floyd was boiling over in the hands, fists and cries of men who hated, feared and destroyed too many parts of their own lives. Now, they channeled that hatred toward one man. Floyd. As he looked at them, the sounds of their shouts mixed with chairs banging on the floor pushed from the neat balance of an ordered circle to the random chaos that fed the moment. David watched them. The sound of breaking glass startled them all.

And then, it stopped.

There was silence except for the bubbling sound. The group's eyes were transfixed in one direction. Everyone stared at Floyd. No one moved. David turned to see Floyd drop to the floor at Kirby's feet. Kirby stood over Floyd holding the broken Fanta bottle in his hand, as the jagged edge dripped with Floyd's blood. Wrapped around his neck where Kirby plunged the broken bottle, Floyd's hands fumbled to stop the bleeding. The artery weakly spurted waves of crimson between Floyd's frantically grasping fingers. The terrifying dye spread across Floyd's white shirt adding to the pool forming beneath him. Floyd gurgled while Kirby looked down at him and said in a very soft voice, "My *father* collected souls." Kirby turned his head and looked at his compatriots and chuckled once before dropping the bottle and walking back to his position in the disheveled circle. Finding his chair, he sat down, smiled, and waited as the orderlies rushed into the room.

CHAPTER 2
Redesigned for Success

Before his hospital presence, David worked for nearly two years at GrowVest International, a realty investment corporation. He was the vice president in charge of acquisitions. GrowVest acquired commercial real estate, both land and buildings, with investor capital.

In the better part of those two years, David was part of a two-man team that took a stale idea and reworked it into a multi-million dollar corporation. They were a functioning power house whose efforts made a small operation one of the largest capital investment firms in the South. David's position with GrowVest was very similar to what he did for years, but on a much larger scale. Where previously his largest investors might represent a quarter million dollars, GrowVest investors placed millions. Often one investor assigned 30 to 40 million into David's care. Among his responsibilities were organizational tasks—finding the right architect, clearing government hurdles and finding tenants for entire projects. The title was, just that, a title, because the truth was even more involved. David was the functioning backbone.

Allen Nguyen was a Vietnamese immigrant and GrowVest's creator—a financial whiz kid. David knew Allen for several years before taking the job at GrowVest. A man several years his junior, Allen's short stocky frame filled out his Brooks Brothers wardrobe giving him the appearance of a muscular martial arts master. His shaggy black hair suggested a comb was always an afterthought. Allen always looked like he was in deep thought. A cavernous furrow between his eyebrows enhanced the pensive truth. But as David's friend and coworker the look softened whenever he was with David. They were comfortable with each other. They enjoyed each other's company enough that Allen began referring to David as his brother. Never having had one through his parent's lack of biological efforts, it was an honor David relished. Theirs was a strong relationship built on trust and mutual respect.

Before the GrowVest adventure, Allen invited David to monthly luncheon meetings whenever he was in town. That was where, above the din of clanging dishes and idle office jabber from adjoining tables, Allen described a project he was working on in his somewhat broken English and asked David what he thought. For the next hour or more they brainstormed, bouncing ideas off of each other, building on Allen's original concept. While David considered his contributions to the conversations minimal, Allen believed there was a positive grounding affect to his suggestions.

Two days after their latest monthly luncheon, David got a call from Allen. "Hey David, can you make it to lunch today?"

David laughed. "It's too soon. We have at least three more weeks before the next scheduled visit."

"Well, I've got something special I want to discuss."

"All right, I'll see you at Phil's at noon."

Phil's was a small café in the heart of Richmond. The neighborhood had the flavor of an upscale renovation. Post-Civil War era brick architecture mixed with individual construction portfolios that reflected the apartment owner's personality. The old buildings had a new, pleasantly confused look as blisters of glass windows and wrought iron porches popped out from condos above small shops lining the street. Book stores, small family markets, flower stalls and lawyer's offices fed the bustle.

David arrived moments before Allen wearing jeans and an Atlanta Braves t-shirt. Allen walked into Phil's business-ready, dressed in an expensive blue suit with an open collared white shirt and sunglasses. He greeted David at their usual table. The brightly lit room was crowded with lunchtime office help; shoppers stuffing bags beneath their chairs; and the occasional lawyer listening to a prospective client over a cup of soup and a salad.. Its buzz fostered anonymity. Alan could come here and not worry about meeting anyone who might know him. He could use the time to concentrate on the conversation without interruption and hope the outcome rejuvenated his day.

As Allen reached the table with one hand grasping the back of a chair, he asked, "Have you ordered?"

"Nope. Just walked in."

Before Allen could sit, Rita was beside their table. Though her years of working tables should have slowed her by now, the waitress was a master at weaving through the crowded room. She carried several menus tucked beneath her left arm while scribbling notes on the green order pad. "Rita" was embroidered on her striped uniform above her left breast. She smiled, "Okay guys, the usual?"

Allen turned to the stocky, middle-aged waitress who knew them as regulars. "Great. That'll be fine, Rita," Allen said and turned to David with his hands out and eyebrows raised as if asking for his order. David nodded and Allen waved to Rita that the same was fine. Rita disappeared into the scurrying mass of the restaurant. Now, Allen wasted no time. As he pulled his chair from the table and sat, he told David of his latest plan. "I've decided to resurrect an old idea," he explained. "I'm not here to ask advice or bounce anything off of you." That was clear from the enthused look and his wide eyes. Allen was making an excited presentation. "I don't think I ever mentioned this idea to you. It ended up causing me more problems than it was worth. Funding and personnel always fell through," he said trying to be heard above the noise. "My previous attempts at hiring a managerial team failed. After four years, I gave up. The team I hired was great at drawing paychecks and not much else. When I came back from vacation last month, I walked in and fired them all." Allen explosively waved his hands in the air. "The company was useless, as far as I could see. I canned the whole bunch of them and stood there waiting while they walked out the door. Then, I turned off the lights and closed the doors on the business and the whole idea." Allen waved a hand in the air again dismissing the company's worth. "The bitch of it all is that I am certain the idea is workable. I'm convinced that the right people could turn GrowVest into the success it should be."

"Is that it?" David laughed. "Are you asking for my advice on an idea that already failed?"

"No. No advice needed. This is something a whole lot better. I want you to work *with* me on putting this together the way it should be. It would mean giving up what you've got. But maybe you could bring some of your clients with you. It would be a step up for them. They'd have to drop a whole lot more than a couple hundred thousand each time—but, small investment means small return. This is big investment . . ." Allen smiled. We can do this. Just the two of us. We can do this.

"Yeah, and it sounds like a step down for me. What are we talking here?"

"I'll throw in a couple of hundred thousand shares and an appropriate salary. Let's say about $100 thousand to start—just until we get this thing moving."

That was enough. David believed in Allen and clearly his faith was reciprocated. David wasted no time. The next morning he moved into his new glass-walled offices located on the 34th floor of one of Richmond's newest uptown constructions. It was a fitting bit of irony that the city's newest building was one David helped sell to investors.

CHAPTER 3
Robert

Early on in GrowVest's resurrection, Allen began meeting with Mac, his accountant, on an irregular basis—more often than before the current GrowVest obsession. Norman MacVickery was the accountant's name. He liked being called "Mac." Small wonder. It was a relatively new identity for him. One he relished. Mac was the typical high school geek that everyone made fun of—too intellectual for his own good. Skinny, tall and pasty faced with a high forehead that, even at 12, looked like a receding hair line. He was socially awkward and athletically inept—the perfect target for every bully throughout his school life. The geek label remained through an uneventful college career until the ugly duckling grew into a successful swan. With a few hard-working years and old family friends as clients, he became a wealthy and respected Corvette-driving professional with a genuinely receding hairline. That's where Mac was and he had no intention of being mistaken for Norman—the class target—whenever he ran into classmates twenty years later.

Mac prepared taxes for a large number of wealthy people who were always asking him for ways to invest or hide some of their profit. Mac became an official member of Allen's lunch and dinner corps. The accountant used his position of trust with his clients to shill them into GrowVest. Deals were consummated over a cob salad and sweetened iced tea with Mac nodding, smiling and "making nice" for the large checks that followed. Mac helped Allen find investors, but he dumped a sizeable chunk of cash into the program too. Part of it was a requirement Allen insisted upon. Mac became a partner and the searching for future investors became his personally designated task.

Financial growth gave GrowVest something new. Allen and David added Mac. The "we" made three. Allen was still looking for a fourth.

Putting in as many hours each week as he did, Mac had few friends. He was far too busy to cultivate card-playing drinking buddies, and his past relationships were better forgotten. So, the few acquaintances he acquired were from his business. That's pretty much how Robert Whitney came into the story.

Robert's success as a corporate real estate lawyer made him reasonably wealthy. Robert wasn't originally from Virginia. A graduate of a less-than prestigious university in western Tennessee, he came to Richmond and opened a legal practice during the last real estate boom. That it coincided with the development of several business parks and a flourishing economy made demands on Robert's time very lucrative. He had a beautiful home, an expensive car or three, a trophy wife with the best tits and nose his money could buy, and corporate clients throughout the metro Richmond area. Mac did Robert's taxes for several years seeing Robert's business grow year after year and suddenly, without apparent reason, it was failing.

Mac got monthly financial reports from Robert's in-house bookkeeper. It was a standard thing that allowed Mac to keep Robert's finances ready for April 15. The receipts showed Robert was partying pretty heavily. Though Robert claimed it was all business related, Mac didn't believe it and was certain the federal tax dogs were ready to lift a leg and piss on this pile of red ink without hesitation. Mac warned Robert, "Keep better records or none at all. A paper trail like this one usually leads to court."

Robert's partying didn't stop with Mac's warning or with the daily sunrise. Richard Pryor once said cocaine is God's way of telling you that you are making too much money. Robert wasn't listening to Mac, much less God, or Richard Pryor. Within a year of his change in social habits, Robert was disappearing for days at a time. He came home without explanation as to where he had been or what he was doing. His wife knew better and didn't need an explanation. So, while Robert entered into his next marathon sleep adventure after days on the loose, Robert's wife packed up and left. That arrangement lasted until Robert woke up and received papers from her divorce lawyer. Then, Robert moved out and she moved back in.

Mac seldom saw Robert except in April. So, he was surprised when Robert showed up in tears at his office in July. The office was located in one of the city's older uptown areas near the war memorial overlooking the James River. It housed a reception area where, from her desk, Mac's secretary, Lisa soothed anxious client's grasping files and checkbooks. Two, overly tall, matching maple doors designed to impress, guarded the entrance to Mac's inner office. These were Mac's concession to prestige. He fondly looked at the doors and his Corvette as jewelry—something that added to his image. A large picture window bathed the inner room in natural light offering a view of the river and city.

Lisa, quietly knocked on the open maple door and leaned in. "You have a guest, sir."

"A guest?" Mac didn't receive guests. Appointments were a polite standard. He looked up from his numbers at Lisa with an annoyed, questioning look. Lisa jerked her head to the side toward Robert who pushed past the woman and into Mac's office. Mac stood not recognizing Robert at first. Astonished at what he finally identified, he looked back at Lisa. "Thank you, Lisa. Close the door for me, please." Lisa grabbed the door handles and slowly pulled the double maple doors shut as she watched Robert stumble past boxes of client files toward a waiting blue and white-striped armchair. He plunked himself down and sighed as he looked up at Mac's puzzled face.

Mac came to know Robert during his success. Not a tall man, Robert always looked taller, dressing well and looking fit—his light, brown hair complemented a perpetual, country club tan. But the man with the tear-stained face sitting in the blue-striped chair this day was pale, disheveled, in need of a shave and haircut and thinner than Mac remembered him.

"Robert?" Mac was cautious. "Robert, how are you?" Mac, standing beside his cluttered, expansive maple desk, slowly made his way back to his chair and sat. He cleared several stacks of papers allowing him a better view of Robert.

"Fine, fine. I'm fine," Robert said dismissively, hurrying his reply. "I need some help, though."

Mac had no idea what prompted the visit. Robert was both hyperactive and exhausted at the same time. Robert began pouring it all out.

"My wife," he said, "is out to get me for everything I own— all that I've built."

Mac made a quick note on a pad near his desk phone: *Robert is getting a divorce.*

"I gotta save the money. Hide the assets. Keep it all from her," he whispered to Mac. "We gotta hide it. We gotta hide the assets," he repeated. "What can I do?" Robert wanted Mac to come through with some of that mythical bookkeeping magic. But, there was no magic because there were no assets.

30

"What assets?" Mac was incredulous. He believed Robert must have known. The reports were sent out in a timely fashion. Mac did his job. Robert, clearly, didn't. Mac had a bad feeling.

Robert hesitated, "What do you mean? What assets?"

"Have you been in a fog for seven months? I started seeing the assets dissolving back in December at the height of your party season. I warned you at least three times—even left a message for you to call me when you got in." Mac was amazed and now, a bit angry. Was Robert setting him up? Was he about to make an accusation that Mac was somehow shirking *his* responsibilities? "Allen you've been pissing it away." Mac swiveled his chair toward files stacked on the floor. He pushed some boxes piling a few to the right and then the left. He was looking for something. There. There it was. The black marker scrawled on the white box's side said "Whitney." "Here. These are your papers. There's another box here too but let's just look at this." Mac rose from his chair and slammed the box on his desk. He began pushing through the files. "Within a couple of months after your last filing," Mac yanked a three inch stack from the box and threw it on the desk, "15 clients dropped to five. Then, one. Then, none. You have *no* business assets," Mac explained emphasizing his own frustration. He took several more files from the box and threw them onto the desk. Robert watched and said nothing.

"You can't make me believe you didn't know this." Mac was looking at a destroyed human being. This was going to be like denying the existence of Santa Claus to a wide-eyed five-year-old. He saw this one before with other clients that went under. The eyes wide open part was happening.

Robert stared at Mac for a moment and asked, "What are you talking about?" "Look, I know. It's been hard since she kicked me out. I've been staying at a motel. I've missed a few appointments. Even had a few pissed-off clients. But that always turns around." Denial was becoming an art form in Robert's repertoire. "This is only temporary. The business is my asset." Robert raised his voice as he leaned forward in the soft, striped chair across from Mac searching for eye contact through the piles of August-extended returns and volumes of revisions to last year's tax codes.

Mac said nothing. He moved back to his chair. He let his previous words, and now, his lack of them, soak in.

Robert slumped back into the high-backed chair. He lifted his hands from his lap and turned them so the empty palms blotched with excitement were in front of him. "I have the house," he blurted, "and the cars?" He again searched for a reassuring face through the number-filled papers on Mac's desk.

"No," was all Mac said.

"The entire financial debacle is a direct result of that greedy, conniving, blood-sucking bitch." For the next seven minutes Robert continued his tirade aimlessly wandering through Mac's office. With his back to Mac and tears once more streaming down his face, he shouted at the office view of the river through the large plate glass window, "She wants it all!"

It was time for Mac to interrupt. "Robert, you're going to have to excuse me. I've got another appointment that should be here at any time." Mac looked down at his watch and rose from his chair. He made no attempt to hide his dismissive tone. "Tell you what, give me a call once you've got some things in order and we'll talk again. How's that?" Mac rounded his desk's massive wooden platform and was at Robert's side. He gently grabbed Robert's arm and helped him toward the door. Robert reluctantly took the hint.

Annoyed, Robert said. "I'll call you." He hurriedly walked from the inner office leaving the door open. Lisa stood as Robert stormed past her desk through the outer office door and into the hallway. Lisa followed to catch the door and gently closed it.

It took days before Robert's misery touched Mac. He knew there was nothing he could do. If ever there was a definition of black-and-white, this was it. But, after that July visit, things began changing. Robert survived. He started visiting business contacts—people who used to send their work to him. Leads were slim. Court appearances were being avoided ever since he was warned about his questionable hygiene by a judge. It appeared shaving and showering were second thoughts for Robert. Complaints from colleagues put Robert's professional ethics into question, too. The bar association sent a letter. Robert had to clean up his act or lose whatever hope he had of resurrecting himself from the nightmare.

It was clear he couldn't live on the desiccated mess he called his practice. He started looking for another place that might need his services—another firm. One by one he checked off the names of local competitors after a visit produced no interest. Robert tried traveling out of town and, finally, found a firm less than a hundred miles away in Charlottesville. Robert knew Felker & Felker as a rapidly expanding super group with media savvy. They were saturating every medium-to-large population center with television, radio, newspapers, and billboards that promised personalized service from an overstuffed figurehead for whom the firm was named—Ellis Felker. The less than sincere, folksy commercials promised concern for the little man and the ads were working. The truth, however, should have been obvious. Like the tooth fairy, Felker's puffy face couldn't be everywhere at once taking each case that walked through the many office doors scattered throughout Virginia. Instead, clients wandered into a satellite office and discovered it was manned by "colleagues" who professed equivalent interest in the bleeding client's case. The only mention of Ellis Felker was the firm's name and the smiling portrait hanging behind the office desk.

Felker & Felker wasn't unique in its application of an old idea, just far more efficient. But, it became a corporate legal giant with ties to Washington and a revolving door. Legal bodies were always needed to fill the plush leather chairs of empty desks in each new office. Lawyers that came to work at the firm usually fit two forms: newbies just out of law school or those without business acumen—like Robert.

After several weeks of awaiting the outcome of a brief telephone interview and the submission of his *curriculum vitae*, Robert was granted an interview. Charlottesville was an hour or more from Richmond in the eastern foothills of the Blue Ridge Mountains. Its country flavor leaned more toward the Founding Fathers than Richmond's preoccupation with the Civil War. The result was a less hurried lifestyle where people enjoyed horse farms, multi-colored trees in autumn, and mountain views. Robert was already feeling out of place.

Felker leaned back in his boardroom chair—one of 15 that gathered around the massive, black onyx table. He occasionally changed direction without ever looking at Robert. Comfortably situated three feet to the left and in back of Jeremy Meek, his negotiator, Felker showed little interest in the interview. Meek, a noticeable opposite to the rotund Felker, did all the work. Though as short in stature, his full head of black hair was neatly trimmed. His gold rimmed glasses slid to the tip of his nose whenever he looked down at Robert's file. Each time he looked up he mindlessly pushed them back into place with the middle finger of his right hand. There was abbreviated efficiency in each question Meek asked. They were simple, straight, and to the point like a man who had done this a hundred times before. Felker awakened from his impartial state when he heard Meek ask, "Questions, Mr. Whitney?" The interview was one-sided and brief.

"Uh, no. Nothing." Robert made no attempt at extending it.

"Nothing?" The room was quiet. Meek was surprised and gave an astonished look toward Ellis Felker who had swiveled back to stare out of the board room window at the mountains in the near distance and the Turkey Vultures that floated in circles on the late summer air. There was no response from the boss. Meek shifted gears. Without the expected interplay from Robert, Meek would have to dig for answers. He glanced back at his notes and restarted his canned interview procedure. "Mr. Whitney, it is clear from what we have seen that you are an experienced arbiter." Meek looked up from Robert's file and smiled as he pushed his glasses back into place. "However, we do have a concern with the manner in which your business failed." Once more Meek buried his nose in the file. "How do you see yourself fitting into this firm?"

That failure had a written history easily traced. Robert couldn't deny it. He shifted his weight crossing, then recrossing his legs. "It is an unfortunate fact of business that I am a lawyer and not a businessman," Robert told Meek, hoping to avoid this line of questioning before Meek went any deeper.

"Wait." The deep, vibrating voice was Felker's. "Law *is* business." The strength of the accented voice surprised Robert. "We are a law firm," Felker said as he turned his chair back toward the room. "How do you think we became the largest firm in the Southeast?" Felker didn't wait for the answer. "*Business,*" he boomed again. "And I expect the people who work for me know that from the start." Felker left his chair and began slowly pacing the length of the table behind Meek for Robert to see.

Meek attempted a restart of the questioning. "Mr. Felker is trying to point out the value . . ."

Felker had enough. He interrupted, ". . . the value of a man who can do both. I expect it." Felker stopped his pacing and gazed at Robert. "I've read your file, Whitney. Meek charted your decline. That wasn't bad business," he said. "Whatever it was, we're willing to look the other way, if you think your contacts and client list still have any value." Robert said nothing. He couldn't speak if he wanted to. Every dodge he configured for this interview was out the window. Felker's mind was already made up. "Think you learned anything from your failure, Mr. Whitney? Think you can handle a position where business is foremost? Think you are capable enough to work for me?"

Robert knew there was no strength in his demands for remuneration. He grabbed at whatever crumbs were thrown at him. Just the same he tried. "Mr. Felker," he started in a soft but firm voice, "I am certain my experiences have taught me a great many things—not the least of which is the value of a business mind."

"Good. That's the most intelligent thing you've said here today. It's the only thing you've said that comes close to supporting what's written on your CV." Felker approached the table still standing behind Meeker. "Son, get it right this time. I'll be watching," Felker said. He turned to Meek who was studying Robert's file while Felker carried the load of the conversation. Meek looked up turning to Felker as he pushed his glasses into place. Felker nodded to Meek and walked out of the room.

Meek waited for the boss to leave before starting the final negotiations. "It's because of your experience and familiarity with the Richmond community that we would like you to spearhead the new office opening back in Richmond," Meek told Robert. "It will be our sixth in that city."

Whoa! What just happened? He did it! This had meaning beyond employment. It meant Robert was back and on his way up once again. The joy was short-lived and heavily tempered by the one-man storefront office located in a strip mall in south Richmond. The broad window with fourteen-inch-tall, red, decaled letters stuck to the glass announced "Felker & Felker Law Office" while offering the receptionist interrupted views of the occasional shopper floating by. Robert's cubicle was a pale yellow shabby enclosure. The three makeshift, eight-foot-high walls failed to reach the ceiling creating a two foot gap above them. Privacy was impossible. And because the walls attached to the concrete divider that separated Felker & Felker from the Dollar General Store next door, sale days meant speaking louder than usual for the client to hear.

CHAPTER 4
The Deal

Allen and Mac's lunches with prospective investors were successful. Backers poured several million into the company coffers. It was time for Allen to make his expected exit—at least part of the way. Allen wanted someone to run the company. He hit his managerial limit. He was getting bored. At least that's what he claimed. More than likely, Allen realized the monster grew and he couldn't control its daily activities. Allen wouldn't let control of the company go completely after the experience with his last failed managerial crew. But, he wanted someone responsible for the day-to-day activities— someone with a reputation as a successful businessman. The credentials would allow Allen to move ahead to look for more funding if that person could be sold to the investors as a major player. Allen wanted Steve Jobs or Bill Gates. He settled for Robert.

"I think I have the perfect candidate for president," Mac told Allen over lunch at Phil's. "He's a successful lawyer," Mac waited while Allen shoveled in a bite of coleslaw, "and a former client."

"What? Really?" Allen finished with a surprised grunt while still crunching through the cabbage.

"His name is Robert Whitney," again Mac paused as Allen put down his fork and reached for his napkin. "He ran one of the largest legal firms in the state." That was a gross exaggeration but it rang like triumphant wedding bells in Allen's ears. Mac knew that at its best, Robert's failed practice grossed a couple hundred thousand a year. It was nothing to sneeze at, but still, far from the top of anyone's legal heap.

Allen caught up. He placed the crumpled paper napkin next to his plate and with a quizzical look on his face leaned in toward Mac. "If he's doing so well, why would you think he'd be interested in GrowVest?"

"He's just gone through a messy divorce. I advised him to close the business down so he could better manage his assets and keep them from the divorce lawyers." In other words, Mac was claiming to Allen that Robert's business failed by design to allow Robert to hide his money. Mac was lying with a straight face. It was something Allen should have been able to detect but his personal needs were outweighing his reason. He only saw this as a way out for himself—a way to have GrowVest's daily problems taken care of.

Allen was interested. "It sounds possible." Allen had more. "But I want some assurances that this guy will invest. That's important. I don't want him walking out with some over-billowing golden parachute as soon as he senses his wife's lawyers have moved on to some other fresh pile of shit. If your man has a stake in the company," Allen wisely reasoned, "he'll work as if the company is his own. His investment in GrowVest must be part of the deal," Allen insisted.

"Yes, I understand and agree." Mac made the sale.

Robert received the news from Mac's cell phone as soon as Mac left the restaurant. "Hey, are you sitting down? It's a go!"

Robert was delighted with the news. "Fantastic! I owe you big time, brother. Whatever I can do for you, just let me know. It's done." They arranged to meet Allen for lunch the next day.

Robert showed up at Phil's well-dressed and looking confidant. Mac was relieved to see that Robert was able to put himself together so well. He was considerably thinner than when Mac last saw him—almost gaunt by comparison. But it also gave Robert a more energetic look like a man constantly on the go and ready for anything. Allen was clearly pleased with Robert's appearance and looked toward Mac with a smile and a nod as Robert approached their table. At lunch, Allen was impressed with Robert's demeanor and continued confidence. Mac recognized the old Robert—the one that had a thriving business whose life was in order. The sweaty, paranoid shell that visited Mac only a few months before dissolved and restored—or nearly so—the man Mac believed Allen would hire. Mac naively reasoned that the divorce, though taxing, was a good thing for Robert and that he was a perfect choice for the job.

Ultimately, Allen agreed. "We would love to have you join the team," Allen told Robert. "There are a few conditions, you understand. To acquire the job, Robert," Allen explained, "you will have to invest $350,000 for the position." Mac was uneasy as the terms unfolded. Robert never blinked. "In return Robert, you will receive 1.5 million shares of the company—about 10%—and a salary of $200,000 per year." Allen hadn't discussed the terms with Mac. It came as a surprise until he realized it was the same deal he received less the initial investment of cash.

Robert saw this as a dream come true but knew the dream could fade fast. He used his verbal skills as a legal snake to squirm around Allen. "There is one problem, and I think Mac will verify this for me," Robert explained.

Mac held his breath.

"I have no cash, as I think Mac has explained to you," he said loudly. He leaned across the table toward Allen lowering his voice to a whisper. "The divorce," Robert said apologetically. "I have nothing." Robert smiled and looked at Mac. "Isn't that right, Mac?" The implication was clear. While Robert told the truth, he was implying that Mac had hidden the divorce assets.

Allen looked at Mac. Mac grinned weakly and shrugged.

"I can come up with the cash," Robert said, "but I'll have to wait until after the divorce is final. It could take six months or more." Robert appeared to open his personal history for Allen. Mac knew the history was contrived. "Meanwhile, I need a cash loan from the company to help me set up house away from my wife's oversight." Robert's palms were up and extended—a kind of, "I'm-at-your-mercy, what-can-you-do?" sort of plea. Allen looked at Mac. Mac shrugged again, then, looked away. There was the dodge.

Allen hesitated. Something wasn't quite right. "How much?" Mac saw Allen's guarded withdrawal and quickly jumped in. "I think we can work out a three-month business loan of say, $60,000. Just for the quarter. Would that work?" Mac looked to Robert and then, to Allen. Mac was giving Robert his safety line while letting Allen see Robert's willingness to proceed.

"Well, if the moneyman sees the fiscal sense in this proposal, it's okay with me," Allen agreed. "Now someone else can handle the daily problems and I can go on without distraction."

Everyone was happy. Allen was free of the weight that came with command; Robert weaseled his way into a new job; Mac tried not to look too eager. The set-up worked. Allen realigned the company giving himself the CEO title. Robert received the presidency, and Mac became Chief Financial Officer—a position he already claimed but now had the title to accompany his name on a business card.

It should have been the start of a great thing. The three of them made a strong looking team on paper. Their bios were slapped up on the new web site. Investors read about the success of the new president. Most of them knew and trusted Mac and Allen's reputation in business circles. They were always success stories. It was done and David's nightmare was just beginning.

CHAPTER 5
You've Got a Friend

The consoling, court-sponsored conversations that brought David to accept his attendance at the state hospital were a designed and elaborate ultimatum, a production calculated to ease him into Albemarle. The procedure and legal wrangling during the commitment trial were politely presented requirements.

Maybe it was more of a hearing than a trial. David couldn't remember much except that there was no need for physical restraints. The hallucinogenic drugs proved hazy, confining and efficient. He later remembered the events as like trying to breathe after putting a brown paper lunch bag over his head. There was the imagined smell of tuna sandwiches and apples accompanied by loud muffled voices and the occasional rustling of the paper bag. Still, the imagined bag let in the trial's shouting, crying, boringly long statements and some gavel-banging. There were indistinct complaints about the threat David posed and the messages he left. There was something about "owning Robert's ass," and "removing his heart with a pickle fork." That sounded like something David might say. But, shit, that sounded like everyone who hated Robert. "I can't be the only one with a pickle fork," he murmured.

The scent of Robert's paranoia tainted everything. David saw him clearly as the villain in his scenario. He was the object of David's directed hatred. As should be expected, the hatred was reciprocated and consumed Robert and David equally. Throughout the courtroom nightmare, when Robert wasn't scribbling something in his notebook, he was moaning about not getting what he wanted from David's misery. For the most part, the 15 minutes of judicial exposure David was pressured into were an incoherent rambling along a confused path. The judge asked David numerous times to repeat himself so the court could hear him. Robert said *he* was in danger. But, David loudly interrupted. Through clenched, teeth never lifting his head he blurted out, "I am more of a danger to myself than I am to Robert." The interruption came across as one more drooled and unintelligible sputtering that was ignored by all but the judge. "What was that? Counselor, what did he say?" The judge shook her head trying to rearrange the sounds into a coherent sentence. David's court-appointed lawyer looked on helplessly. "Never mind," the judge said dismissively. She looked directly at David. He lifted his head to see her staring into his eyes. "Mr. Gere, do you know why you are here today, in court?"

Ah, the judge. She was the best part of David's drug-authored, dream-like state. She was the leading lady. She loomed over the court like a giant black bird and flew from her perch to reprimand the state and silence Robert's objections. Her robes billowed around her as she hovered over him surrounded by glowing clouds. Then she floated to David and gently asked him what he thought.

"Mr. Gere," he heard her say softly, "do you know why you are here today, in court?" He looked up at her and smiled. Her words were slow and soothing. She sounded every syllable and enunciated every consonant. She seemed to be sitting next to him whispering the question into his ear. Warm chocolate dripped from every noise she made. David felt her hand gently rubbing the back of his neck. Her black satin robes brushed his face as her breasts pushed firmly

43

against him. His eyes closed as he swayed with the sound of ocean waves pulsating through his head. She was wonderful, soft, and gentle, and David wanted her. He would tell her anything. Go anywhere with her. David became Ulysses, and she was his Siren. He was certain that he could drown in her arms and not care.

David turned his head and stared through the fog at the people surrounding him. All was quiet as heads turned to David expecting some revelation that might put things back into order. David hung his drug-heavy head once more smiling and nodding in apparent self-agreement. His mind was under chemical control and the only thing the court heard when it addressed him was a mumbled "OK." All they could understand were single words that were audibly incongruous to the court's questions. But the lone words made volumes of sense to David.

"Your honor," the court's examining psychiatrist stood to address the court from behind the state's table. "Mr. Gere's true intention was suicide." The doctor flipped a page on his clipboard and read, "He began falling into himself in an attempt to shut out his problems." He put the clip board down and theatrically walked toward David who kept his head low while he rocked in his chair. As the doctor stood looking at David, he continued, "When his attempt at reasonably solving his problems failed, he withdrew further and concluded that suicide was logical and possible."

David heard little. His reality bordered on the other—the one shared by the rest of the world. David was sifting through points along a semi-conscious road. A word was taken here and another there. But through it all the judge commanded his attention and the drugs tempered his reality. Suddenly, she was a hundred yards away, down a long white corridor bathed in bright sunlight. She sat behind a shiny, massively tall, black marble desk. The robe was gone. Instead, she dressed in a black, tight, low-cut evening gown. She wore diamonds on her hands and in her black hair. Her breasts bubbled out of the top of the black lace covered in a broadly fanned necklace of heavy, glittering gems. Her lips were wet, a sparkling, fiery-red; and she exhaled spring blossoms. There was a message of dominance mixed with a heavy dose of desire. David loved the drugs.

Outside of David's dream—in the reality of the courtroom, the judge was annoyed. She looked at David and then directed her matter-of-fact question to the doctor, "Would you say hospitalization is advised?"

"Your honor, if the court doesn't find the solution; if the patient doesn't receive help now; he will find his own answer."

The judge's irritation increased. "I understand doctor. But before this can be a proper committal, I need your official recommendation on the court's record. I ask you again, would you say hospitalization is advised?"

"Yes, your honor. It is advised."

"Thank you. Now tell me doctor, in your opinion, is Mr. Gere aware of today's proceedings?"

David listened and upon the shrink's conclusion, he smiled and kept rocking. The good doctor said exactly what David needed him to say. The next task was to convince the judge. The judge had the commitment key to the front gate—the final decree. But with judges, you need an ally because they don't have the training of a psychiatrist. Their decisions are more emotionally based. So, David knew he had to capture *her* emotions. He had to appeal to *her* personal sense of guilt. Capture the judge and *she* would consider her decision as a favor to an old friend.

Her hollow voice came at David slowly and echoed down the hall to reach him. "David," she said, "I have to determine if you are a danger to yourself."

David was chemically bombed back thirty years to his adolescence but still saw the opportunity. He babbled something about turning the page in hopes of waking up from this bad dream. "I'm afraid," he told her in the same incoherent mumbles, "there is nothing on the next page." David said it and smiled while he stared at her seeing nothing else.

Unable to understand his reply, she used her best shrink-wrapped theories. Addressing the court participants she said, "This is a plea for help. Suicide," she suggested, "is his intention."

This is where David tried to help some more. He interrupted her summation. "Your honor, I *am* sincere. I meant *every* word," he shouted. But the words came out like a loud, prolonged groan that proved more effective than the original thought.

"There are too many people who cry for help but no one listens." she said, "Then when the decision *is* made, they all scratch their heads in disbelief and ask one another why they didn't see it, or hear it, or care." She loved it. Everyone loved it. Hell, David loved it. "I can assure you that the court is listening, hoping to understand," she told David.

Robert won the battle that brought David to court, but David won the war. He was going to be packed away from Robert's threat into the state hospital. There was a moment of silence—as long as a heartbeat, and just as suddenly the world began turning again. Heads were shaking piteously and everyone was reminding themselves of their parts in this comedy.

CHAPTER 6
Secrets from Across the Bridge

July tenth was the first day David met Robert. Robert came into the office to begin his day as president of the newly named GrowVest International Corporation. He exited the elevator at the 34th floor and walked toward the thick glass doors with GROWVEST INTERNATIONAL newly painted in large black letters. The image of a globe sat behind the words. He liked the logo. It suggested BIG. Robert wanted BIG. He wanted to shout it for all of Richmond to hear.

As Robert walked through the doors into the lobby, his shoes clicked on the polished marble floor. He approached the reception desk and presented himself to Martha, the receptionist, an attractive but older woman —not Robert's idea of BIG. "I am Mr. Whitney. You have been expecting me," he announced.

"Yes, Mr. Whitney. Good morning. You have arrived before Mr. Nguyen and Mr. MacVickery. I don't expect them earlier than ten o'clock today."

Robert made no secret of his being inconvenienced by the news. He dropped the empty leather legal briefcase he was carrying. He brought it thinking it an appropriate accessory intended to impress. This was followed by an annoyed sigh; unbuttoning his suit jacket, and shifting his stance. The stance was something he tried once during a trial where he hoped to intimidate an unruly witness. He called it his "Superman look." It had the same effect then as now. Martha was unshaken.

"Mr. Gere is here. He is usually the first to arrive. Would you like me to call him for you?"

"No. Don't bother. Show me where my office is,"

Martha opened her desk drawer and pulled out a set of keys with a white tag attached. She looked at the keys to be certain they were Robert's then smiled and handed them to him. "Your office, sir, is directly down that hallway behind you. If I can help you further, you will find a directory of all the telephones beside your phone. Welcome aboard, sir," Martha smiled quickly then lost it just as rapidly as Robert picked up his briefcase and turned toward his office.

Within five minutes Robert used the phone. "Martha, please ask Gere to come to my office."

"Sir, you will find Mr. Gere's number beside the phone."

"Yeah," Robert said dismissively, "tell him I've got ten minutes and would like to see him now." Robert hung up the phone. "I'm going to have to do something about her," he muttered.

Allen explained David's abilities to Robert days before in well deserved, glowing terms. Robert was expectedly suspicious. This is the best time to meet, he thought. Establish the hierarchy now and there will be less to correct in the future.

Robert's office was several doors away from David's in the opposite corner of the 34th floor. It faced out toward the river with an unblocked view of much of Richmond. The oversized office had a wall of black enameled bookshelves tightly crammed with volumes of law books and other personal artifacts Robert shipped to the office the previous week. Though the books were relevant in his former life, they had little to do with Robert's new one except as an intimidation factor—or so he believed. A black enameled wet bar, not too near Robert's desk, matched the book shelves. There was a plush, white Italian leather couch, glass coffee table and two adjacent white leather chairs in a far corner. A broad, low antique chestnut cabinet behind his desk held a picture of a much younger, college aged Robert beside a classic 1955 Thunderbird. There were also several images of a sunburned-faced Robert dockside hugging a trophy billfish. In each of the four trophy pictures Robert was pictured with one other less-than-enthusiastic person. That each of the people differed in the four photos suggested they were not friends but the various ship's captains. At the far end of the cabinet, a silver tray held two glasses and a sweating aluminum water carafe.

When David arrived the office door was open. He stuck his head inside and with a smile said, "Busy? I just got the message you wanted to see me."

"No. Come in, please." Robert sat at his desk, twelve feet from the office door. As David approached the desk he realized there were no chairs. He turned and quickly scanned the office noticing the two white leather chairs tucked into the corner. David continued walking toward the seated Robert. David put out his hand expecting to welcome Robert at this first encounter. When Robert saw the hand come up, he immediately looked down at the paper on the desk in front of him.

"There are chairs over there," he said pointing without looking up.

David turned to retrieve one of the chairs while Robert began asking him a series of promotion and advertising related questions—all items David handled daily.

"Tell me something about the contacts we have for funding the Mason project." Robert projected his voice with authority as David walked toward the desk pushing the chair. Robert was asking for financial specifics about one of the many properties currently on the acquisition table.

"Sure," David told him as he positioned the chair in front of the desk. "I'm impressed. First day and you know about the Mason project. That suggests you spent your weekend studying. Great. It's good to have an eager person ready to dive in." With the chair arranged, David sat and smiled as he looked at Robert.

David dismissed Robert's pushy exterior as first day jitters. "We will probably hold off a bit longer on the promotional end of the deal," David said. "At least until financing has cleared." The answer did not directly address Robert's question so, David quickly added, "You might want to ask Mac about it though, since he is the CFO and I have nothing to do with the financial end."

Robert was visibly annoyed and made no attempt to hide it. He appeared to be suffering from a hang-over. His face had a disturbed frown as though he had just awakened and discovered himself in the wrong bed, house, or country. Robert knew he fucked-up his life to this point and wanted to recapture his success badly enough to destroy anyone who wasn't willing to get out of his way. Anyone not falling in line behind him qualified as an obstacle. He was a part-owner in this business. The business was a major element in his proposed rebirth.

David thought his answer about the finances should have been obvious to Robert before he asked it. He assumed Robert's projected annoyance was with himself. He was wrong. This was to be David's first lesson about dealing with Robert. If you disagreed or appeared to disagree with Robert, you became his enemy. By paranoid default, you became part of the legion out to get him. That lesson would make its way around the office to every employee very soon.

50

Robert continued with his questions and then pulled a stapled bunch of papers from a manila folder stacked with others on his desk. Looking at the first page, he was quiet. Then he flipped to the second page and followed along with the reading pointing to each line with his index finger. He stopped and looked up at David. "I have been reviewing production expenses and have decided that I will have to speak with some people about revising their costs."

"All right," David said nodding slowly. "But are you aware that the prices have been bid out through several outlets as is our standard procedure?"

"All right Gere, you have already said you know nothing about finances. That's been established, so your input here is meaningless." Robert saw this as a skirmish in a much bigger war. Every battle was important to him. All or nothing was how he saw this. Not winning was unacceptable. So, Robert schemed to make his point and prove, not only that he was in charge but, that he was far better prepared than any adversary life could put in his way. Robert controlled and David would have to put up with his shit. David left the room shaking his head and chuckling.

Paranoia eats away at the mind. It's like the demon that sits on your shoulder encouraging bad behavior or the guard dog that barks convinced of an intruder when it's only the wind. In the coming months, Robert's paranoid quirk would quickly earn him a reputation with everyone GrowVest did business with. Robert knew nothing of the business but he was certain he knew what was best on all fronts—in every case. There was no need for a protracted learning curve. Robert hit the ground running. As it turned out, the direction didn't matter to him—like the way he decided non-disclosures had to be signed by all employees and especially those suppliers involved in the financial end. The papers were repeatedly revised as Robert brushed against some newly imagined fear. In all, revisions accounted for six repeated signings in three weeks. David realized there was a problem outside of the office a month later after a brief visit to a suppliers meeting from GrowVest's three principles, Allen, Mac, and Robert. Alone with the suppliers, David overheard a reference to Robert by one of the remaining visitors. It included a remark about "that paranoid idiot running the show is more interested in the part he plays than in production." This was a dangerous remark because it came from outside the confining corporate walls. The effect could be as deleterious as telling the world GrowVest had a bad product. GrowVest was making more enemies than working partners. Their reputation in an industry whose threshold they only recently crossed was still thin, at best.

Within six weeks, unshakeable Martha, the corporate receptionist and secretary, came to David's office and closed the door. "I've had all I can take of that son-of-a-bitch," she told David as she plunked herself into one of the plush chairs that faced his desk.

"Why? Who? What's going on?"

"He is rude. Superior. And usually wrong."

"Oh. Robert giving you a hard time?"

"He makes decisions and then changes them without remembering or conveniently forgets what he has told me, sometimes, only minutes before." Martha's voice quavered at the point of tears.

"Martha," David said gently. He got up from his desk and walked toward Martha sitting beside her in the adjacent chair. "I have learned several things about Robert and his personality. First, I have a base belief that, in general, lawyers are snakes manipulating the system and corrupting it at the same time."

Martha chuckled. David smiled and continued. "As kids, they were the smarmy creatures that had to be first, pushing and shoving anyone smaller or meeker out of the way while pleading injustice to the teacher when someone stood up to them. As a human being, Robert is gutless and without a spine. As a lawyer," he therefore reasoned, "Robert *cannot* be termed a snake." David hesitated. Martha looked at him quizzically. "Robert is a worm. And from now on that is exactly how I will refer to him."

Though David tried hard to work with the worm, Robert always had an annoyed edge. Whenever they spoke or interacted on any level there was a never-look-me-in-the-eye kind of thing with Robert. His laughing was always forced and nervous meant to lighten the situation or risk giving his uneasiness an identity. But it really got bad after *the visit*.

Marley was an extraordinary, tall beauty with Cherokee black satin hair that flowed more than half-way down her back in a luxurious braid. Her visit sucked the energy from every male whose office she passed on her way to David's. Promises made in imagined daydreams pulled them from their desks floating on her scent. Fantasies that drew them from their work suddenly took realistic form.

Marley was a dear friend of David's. She came to visit one day to take him to lunch. Wrapped in a form-fitting blue blouse and flowing yellow and pastel green, silk skirt she knew how great she looked and walked with the confidence of a general out to conquer the world. From the minute she stepped off the elevator, work stopped in every male's office as she passed. Eyes, then limbs followed her to David's small but well lit office. She sat in one of the plush chairs at David's desk turned so her back was to the door.

Very quickly David was introducing her to every semi-flaccid member in the place. The worm came by too with his slick smile and hand held out to greet her. "Robert." He insisted it was Robert. Not "Bob" or "Rob." Just a stick up his ass for a backbone, but he was still Robert. Call him Bob after being corrected by him ("No, it's Robert"), and the paranoia took over. He was convinced you mutilated his name to annoy him. You must have something against him. Here he was: an evasive, elusive, vindictive fuck-up with no flare and an inflated conviction of his personal worth versus everyone else. But, he was right; he could never be a "Bob."

Marley turned and smiled that melting look that had most men seeing her face for the next several romantic episodes with anyone else—but not Robert. When she turned to greet him, Robert's smile faltered into a weak grin and the color drained from his face. Robert's pasty visage quickly nodded to David, then back to Marley and said "Nice to meet you" and was gone. Marley turned back to David and looked down to adjust her dress. David was at a loss. He looked at her. "What just happened?" She smiled some more and shrugged. They left for lunch.

The lunch was uneventful. Nothing memorable was discussed. David enjoyed Marley's company and delightedly watched the men stumbling into chairs as they walked by staring at her. He returned to the office alone from lunch but before David could get around his desk to sit, Robert was in the doorway of the office. "What's her name?" He was being cagey. Something was up and it wasn't his libido. He continued. "How do you know her?"

"Marley?" David knew who he meant but wanted to play just a bit. "She's an old friend. I've known her for years—since she was a teenager. Why?"

Robert was clearly upset and very nervous. He closed the office door and walked the few remaining feet to a position behind David's desk standing over him as he sat in his chair. David pushed back and tried to gain some space.

"I know her." Robert said. He was certain that David knew it too. "Has she said anything about me?"

"You?" David couldn't believe this. He tried to suppress a smile and turned to his desk to rearrange some papers to prevent

Robert from seeing his amused response. Where was Robert going with this and why? David looked back to Robert. The worm looked panicked.

Robert wandered from the desk toward the door. And then, in an excited whisper said, "She's a good friend of my ex-wife. If *your friend,*" (he stressed the relationship and let it hang before continuing), "tells her I work here, that I'm the president of the company, the bitch will want more from me." Robert was picking up speed. He blurted out the rest in a rapid gunfire delivery. "She's already milking me for everything I've got." The rest was lost. David didn't hear a word. It was a lot like Charley Brown's teacher giving directions. Robert thought David was taking notes. Actually, he was scribbling some abstract design on the corner of his note pad. But to Robert, it appeared that what he was saying meant something and for Robert that was all that mattered.

Robert was claiming this was all about a potential argument with his soon-to-be ex-wife. The threat of a discovery about his current worth—the company loan, the 1.5 million shares of stock, and the overtly extravagant salary—might destroy any hope of the quickie divorce he counted on. At least that was David's initial impression from the line Robert was spouting.

Robert paused his tirade. The look on his face said that he wanted an answer to a question David never heard. David shifted in his chair and mentally replayed the syrup-laden voice from his memory. No good. There was nothing there. He missed that last part of Robert's bitching. Taking a stab at a possible non-answer, he decided to shrug. When Robert's facial expression changed to disappointment, David added a series of nods to the shrug. It worked. Robert pressed on.

"You have to keep her out of here and don't talk to her again." The eyes bulged a bit and his face flushed. There was far more to this than a question of blood money. Far more at stake and David knew he had to find out what it was.

55

Robert was quiet again as he stared at David from the office door's jamb. David had to be gentle but firm. "First, Robert, she is an old friend. A very old friend," he said. "I have no intention of not speaking to her because of your fear of your wife." Robert stepped forward and straightened up. David quickly realized that might not have been the most supportive choice of words. The fear that forced the urgency of Robert's previous comments was replaced by a rapidly brewing anger.

"Secondly, I know her to be a trustworthy person who has shown no interest in you at all."

Still in his aggressive whisper, Robert asked, "She didn't talk about me at lunch?"

"No! You have *nothing* to be concerned about!" David waited for him to relax but it wasn't happening. "She isn't going to run to tell your ex-wife, even if she did know you." David waited again and smiled. Robert, once more, backed into the office doorway fumbling for the lost door jamb. He stared at David, then turned and left the office. The battle line was drawn. David saw it. He was clearly the enemy. Destruction was Robert's only line of sight and David was in the way.

Having brought Robert to Allen and therefore, into the company, Mac felt a sense of power in his alliance with Robert. He thought of Robert as someone who owed him something—at the very least an overwhelming sense of gratitude. Robert's life was back on the road and Mac correctly assumed he was the catalyst. Mac thought his new "best buddy" was a needed ally should any difficulties arise with Allen. Meanwhile, Mac became Robert's flunky. Robert was described by his ex-wife as having difficulty making friends. It was a polite way of saying he had no trouble making enemies. Nonetheless, Robert found Mac's personality a good fit for his sycophantic association. Whatever Robert said, Mac bought. Whatever Robert complained about, Mac took care of. Robert knew he never wanted to confront adversaries—real or imagined. It was better to have someone else make the accusations and deal with the problem. Robert decided he never *needed* a backbone as long as he could use someone else's. Robert had always been a settle-out-of-court kind of guy.

Mac wandered to David's office, a kind of straight-line, tunnel vision wandering without stopping for his usual glazed donut at the snack tray in the lobby. In a moment he appeared at the office door. One hand was to his face while the elbow rested in the other hand. He waited for David to look up from his desk.

"You know, Robert is in his office right now squirming like you wouldn't believe," Mac said with a chuckle. "He really believes this woman knows him and is going to tell his ex-wife."

David continued looking looked down at his work and smiled. "He's got nothing to worry about. I already told him that."

Mac crawled into a chair by David's desk sitting with his legs crossed. "Yeah, but that doesn't matter. He says if she finds out, she'll be all over him. That was one of the reasons he came here. It's a different town, a different business and nobody knows him." Mac was letting a little bit more out about Robert than Robert would want anyone to know. Robert was hiding. Twelve miles from his past, across a bridged river and Robert thought that was enough? He didn't know Richmond.

This only reinforced David's suspicion that Robert had something more to hide than from an ex-wife no matter how bloodthirsty she might be. David told Robert's messenger boy not to worry. "I won't say anything to Marley about the business and certainly won't mention Robert to her."

Over the next several months Robert was responsible for a series of complaints brought to Allen about projects David led. The complaints were always the same: David did something that hurt the company and should be replaced. Each time Allen came to David and asked about the problem and each time the explanation either proved Robert wrong or simply misinformed. While it was clear David became a thorn in Robert's side, it wasn't clear to others why. Allen recognized it and the illogical behavior Robert was bringing with each complaint. After one of Robert's angry bitch sessions, Allen came to David's office and closed the door. There was a weak smile on his face as he sat down in front of David's desk. "Robert," Allen apologetically explained, "clearly dislikes you."

"I know but I can't figure out what I've done to earn it. The only thing I can figure is that he wants my office." David laughed and watched for a reaction. Allen smiled, again.

"Do you think I should be worried?" David was still smiling, though the question was sincere.

Without hesitation Allen dismissed the idea. "This is still my company and you are one of its most valuable assets," he told him.

"Yeah, but at what point do you throw your hands in the air and decide his bitching can only be stopped by getting rid of me?" Allen stood and turned toward the door waiving off the suggestion as meaningless. He turned again toward David, smiled and left.

Three months passed since Marley's visit. She called David's house to ask a favor and suggested she would buy lunch. It was Saturday, so the lunch had no time constraints. She arrived at the restaurant looking like she just came from the gym. She was wearing a multi-colored wrap over black tights and a short shirt that exposed her midriff. Marley was carrying a Louis Vuitton bag with a water bottle extending from its side pocket. Even dressing down she had everyone staring as she weaved through the tables to the booth where David was standing. She looked like a super hero with her black hair fanning out cape-like behind her head. She hugged him while giving him a peck on the cheek. All he could do was smile.

The lunch was mostly uneventful. She asked her favor—something insignificant. David said "yes," then he hesitated. "I've gotta ask you something," he leaned toward her. "Do you remember coming to the office a few months ago and meeting our president?"

"You mean Robert?"

David leaned back onto the booth bench with his head against the smooth, brown, padded plastic and smiled. "You do know him!"

"Sure," she grinned. "I recognized him immediately. He's the former husband of a friend of a friend. I can't remember her name but she is a bank manager. I met her at a party where we talked about her handling the mortgage on a house I was looking to buy." Marley shifted her purse to her lap and rummaged through the Vuitton bag. "But after watching Robert stuff cocaine up his nose for an hour or more, I decided it probably wasn't a very good idea to be associated with her. I think I have her card in here somewhere."

So, Marley wasn't close friends with Robert's ex-wife as Robert claimed. In fact, they barely knew each other. It all made sense. Robert wasn't hiding from her. He was hiding from a reputation and suddenly seeing Marley meant the reputation was about to cross the river and follow him to his new identity. His attempt at covering up by discounting Marley hadn't worked. That was why he was working on discrediting the other link—David. Get rid of David and any news from his mouth was dismissed as the ranting of a disgruntled *former* employee. David suddenly realized he was exposed. He had been in a war and didn't know it.

Marley continued looking through the large chocolate bag. She went on to say she ran into Robert and his wife at two other parties. "The pattern was the same at all three," she told him. "They arrived. The wife headed for the bar. Robert dove into the nearest dark corner with the same group of nose hounds that attended all their gatherings; stuffing powder into their noses as fast as anyone could produce it," she said. "The habit ruined Robert's legal practice and busted him financially." She was dead on. "I'm sure there was an arrest somewhere along the way," she said still rummaging through the calfskin bag, "but because he was so well known and knew as much about important people with pull, the arrest record was either sealed or expunged. It had to be if Robert was still a member of the bar." It was logical and she was certain but, "I doubt there is any way to find out," she concluded. "I don't know where that card is," she said closing the purse. "I'll look for it at home and get back to you."

David was lost in thought. The news Marley gave him was opening his eyes to a multitude of explanations as to Robert's behavior. "No. Don't bother with the card," he told her.

David said nothing to anyone about Robert's supposed problem. If the information were to get out, it could hurt the company at a time when investors and potential buyers were sniffing around. Estimated stock values were ranging from 90-100 dollars. Allen claimed he was offered $500 million for the company and refused it. But with Allen you never knew whether it was actual or devised promotion. They all expected hundreds of millions and it was looking more and more reasonable every day. A rumor that GrowVest was on the verge of selling to a bidder could spur even more activity. But just as true, the smell of a rotting company could be triggered with the news of a drugged out president running the show. Allen, Mac, Robert and David all had sizeable stakes in the company's future. David decided. Robert's skeleton had to remain in the closet.

Days passed. David harbored Robert's secret wondering when or even if he would share it. The daily meetings between Allen and David continued as before. That hadn't changed since day one. It was their way of keeping the core of the company intact. David watched Allen's back and Allen watched his. It was David's opportunity to let Allen know what was happening in his absence, while Allen let him know behind the scenes negotiations and new ideas that never ceased spawning in Allen's head. On that day, Allen and David discussed extended company plans and directions. Allen looked tired. "Local party," he explained and waved off the rest as unimportant. The meeting continued. Good feelings. Good friends. Here, when others couldn't hear it, Allen still called David his brother.

As David was about to leave, Allen asked if there was anything else. "How are things going? Are there any problems?"

"No. It's good right now."

"Listen. Robert's been all over me about you," Allen said. "His complaints are getting more frequent. It's clear Robert has a grudge of some kind. What do you think?"

David was quiet. He was trying to decide if the time was right to let Allen in on Robert's secret. He considered his answer for a moment. "Robert may have a problem he doesn't want anyone to know about," David said as he looked directly into Allen's eyes. When he broke the news, he wanted to see Allen's reaction. "And he thinks I either know about it or may learn about it through a mutual acquaintance."

"Any idea what the problem is?" Allen asked.

"The thing is," David told him, "I *have* learned about it. He doesn't know it, yet."

"Is the problem cocaine?"

David was startled. Allen had a reputation for being able to see through walls and he was proving it. David simply said an astonished, "Yes!"

"This explains a lot," Allen said. "His behavior at times is very erratic and the drugs would explain it all. I suspected something like this but couldn't be sure. How did you find out?"

David told Allen the entire story and then stressed that this came from only one source. "Supposedly he has been seen by several people," David told him. "It is no secret at these parties."

"Okay," Allen said and hesitated as if forming the proper words for his next comment. "As the CEO, I'm asking you to investigate further and get back to me." That was it. David was given an official assignment. It was coming from the business and was Allen's way of saying that it was about the business and nothing more. "Any information you are able to acquire that confirms Robert's drug involvement will be enough for GrowVest to proceed with replacing him."

David worried about having said anything at all. He placed himself in the middle, exactly where Robert thought he was. After three days, David went back to Allen, "This investigation is not a good idea," he told Allen. "If we go any further it must be through an outside source. If the company's in jeopardy, we should hire an agency." Allen agreed. David said nothing more about it.

CHAPTER 7
On the Hook

The holiday season arrived. The evening before David's important meeting with Allen, Robert decided to throw a party at his newly acquired custom-built home. It was a spur-of-the-moment attempt at announcing his recently acquired social position,

Built in an exclusive gated community surrounded by trees and opulent houses, it didn't have the overgrown comfort of well-manicured lawns or his neighbor's bonsai-like attention to shrubs. There were no oaks with swooping limbs that trailed over flower gardens. Even the walkway from the driveway was simple; made of concrete squares that appeared to have been placed in the ground just before the guests arrived. The pale yellow house was unfinished except for the large mahogany door and glass entryway trimmed in white. Colors flickered through the paneled glass as the guests' bodies moved. Inside the house the foyer stairway wound its way along a wall to the upstairs landing that looked out over the guests through a crystal chandelier. To the right of the foyer, tiled marble floors ended at the entry to Robert's study where the walls swelled with books packed onto neat lines of shelves. Except for his desk, there was very little furniture. A few chairs and a pair of couches in the living area opposite the study finished his attempt at making the place look homey. It didn't matter. Furniture would have made less room for his crowd of guests. It was clear Robert wasn't hiding. He no longer feared the bridge and the history on the other side of the river that once haunted him.

Among his guests, Robert invited the local core of social climbers: neighbors familiar with his questionable social history who shunned him a very short time before. Most guests realized that acceding to Robert's increased social position meant the hors d'oeuvres would taste like crow but refusing his invitation could mean social death. Robert gloated with every embarrassed party greeting he collected.

Allen arrived with his beautiful wife, Sherry: a dazzlingly elegant, slender prize with long black hair and deep black eyes. Allen won her over while visiting relatives in Viet Nam. Tonight, the modestly cut, body-hugging black dress and white pearls complemented her assets. She was spectacular on Allen's arm; there to be seen. Allen was justifiably proud of his possession.

Moments after entering the room, Robert saw Allen and began racing toward him, waving his hand above the noisy crowd. He pushed past everyone and immediately grabbed Allen. Then, with a drink in his hand and another arm wrapped around Allen's shoulder, Robert loudly welcomed him. "There you are. I knew you would make it. Oh, and you must be Sherry" Robert said as an afterthought attempting to give Sherry a quick hug. Her reaction was to pull back splashing Robert's drink on her dress without his notice or concern. Robert pulled Allen to a corner and hanging on him, excitedly gushed, "Can you believe this crowd? They're comin' out of the fuckin' woodwork!" Words slurred as they spilled from Robert's mouth. His glossed eyes wandered through the room counting his guests. Sherry was left to catch up. She took a white cloth napkin from a tray of drinks floating on the hands of a waiter as he jockeyed his way among the crowd of thirsty guests. She began sopping the liquid from her dress while trying to part the closing path of bodies in Allen and Robert's wake.

Allen was amused to see Robert so out of character. The usual business-minded aloofness was lost in a flush of alcohol. Robert was clearly blitzed out of his mind. Sherry reconnected and quickly reached for Allen's hand. Robert began working the crowd being certain to drag Allen along with Sherry holding onto Allen's hand with both of her own. Robert plowed through, making off-handed introductions while remembering few names. Most were introduced by Robert as his neighbors or friends of friends. Robert never described any of them as one of his friends. Allen remained gracious, smiling and nodding slightly as he was pulled by Robert through the bodies. The crush of the crowd caused Allen to lose his grip on Sherry's hand but as he glanced behind, he made eye-contact as she tried to keep up. The crowd was too thick in the small room and Sherry was too polite to force her way through.

It was obvious to Allen that Robert did not know these people well. He was proving it with each introduction. At one point, between intros, Robert leaned in to loudly declare to Allen above the din, "Some of these guests are neighbors and old acquaintance," he stumbled and tried once more, "acquaintances of my former wife's." Robert threw a waving hand into the air suggesting they meant nothing. The lie was irrelevant to anyone but Robert. Those in shouting distance heard. A few turned away.

Robert wrapped Allen under his left arm once more while gesturing with his drink-filled right. "This is a very high-end, exclusive neighborhood," he proclaimed above the crowd noise. "It's packed with the city's financial elite." Robert sounded like he was making a sale. "The subdivision is a who's who of local money—part of the upper one percent of the city's population that control greater than 80 percent of the key investments." Robert hesitated. "It's a kind of super Pareto principle." Robert reassessed his description, and then gave a loud, satisfied "Hah!" before resuming his subterranean push through the fleshy tunnel. Most of Robert's story sounded like another lie, but the financial end was close to the truth. Robert turned to be sure Allen was close by. He smiled, and raised his eyebrows, then stumbled farther into the crowd.

Robert was clearly overplaying his position. Each guest politely acknowledged him as he approached and enthusiastically accepted the introduction to Allen. The enthusiasm and lack of the same toward Robert was not lost on Allen. Allen's impression of Robert, the man, and his corporate value were being revised by the moment.

Continuing his purposeful push through the crowd, Robert headed for a lone table in the corner where several people eagerly talked and laughed. They were clearly enjoying themselves. As Robert, Allen, and a flustered Sherry approached, they moved out of Robert's way exposing the closed bedroom door and a path for Robert's hand to the handle. One turn showed it was locked. Robert hit the door loudly, several times. "Hey. Open up. It's me," he shouted. It was barely audible above the party noise but the knob turned and the door opened a crack. Robert slid in quickly. Then he turned to grab Allen's jacket and pulled him in. Robert quickly closed the door isolating a surprised Sherry on the other side shocked until one of the women in the group near the door grabbed her arm and pulled her gently near. "This always happens at every party, dear" she said. "I've been to too many and the only reason I come is because my husband insists. He's in there too. You know," she said and then sniffed and wiped her nose. "Come on over here and join us. What's your name? I'm Gerry. This is Amy . . . ." She continued introducing the snow-widowed group.

On the other side of the door, Robert entered his element. Though surprised by the obvious isolation of the people in there versus the guests in the other room, Allen wasn't surprised by its activity. The room was poorly lit. A small, 60 watt lamp in each corner were the only light sources. The air was stuffy with tobacco and marijuana smoke. Most of the talk was subdued. In the shadows Allen could see several couples wrapped around one another in various states of undress. Nearby, a woman with her dress pooling at her feet knelt before a man seated in a large soft chair while she actively tugged at his groin. He appeared unconscious. Both arms hung motionless at his side in spite of his partner's eager attacks. Another man, pressed against a wall, covered a woman whose left leg was lifted high around his waist. Her pleasure was expressed by her hands as they dug into his shoulders with each push of the man's stiffened body against hers. There were 15 people in the room. All but the lovers were gathered around a small table seated or standing and watched as several others continued chopping and scraping the white powder across the table's glass surface. "Great stuff. You won't believe this shit," Robert told Allen shouting as if still in party mode and unaccustomed to the whispers in their new surroundings. "This is Rocco," he said more softly. "Rocco is responsible for this wonderful get-together and the party supplies," he said as he leaned in offering his hand toward the slumped, rotund man in the corner. Rocco smiled briefly and looked past Robert and his hand continuing his scrutiny of the room. Robert laughed, pulled back his hand slightly embarrassed, straightened up and turned to go to the table leaving Allen face-to-face with Rocco.

"Have a seat. You a friend of Robert's?"

"Uh, yeah, we work together at GrowVest."

Rocco hesitated, assessing Allen's description of his relationship to Robert. He noted Allen's avoidance of declaring Robert a friend. Suddenly a memory jumped to his forebrain and he blurted, "Oh, wait. You're his partner, aren't you?"

Allen was surprised by the description. PARTNER! "Yeah. Well, okay." Allen did not acknowledge Robert as a partner. Never had. In Allen's mind, Robert was an investor and a co-worker. Maybe even an integral part of Allen's plans, but partner was an elevated status in Allen's eyes that he shared with few.

"Known Robert long?" Allen was changing the subject. He had no intention of allowing this "partner" thing to go any farther.

"Well, I knew him eight years ago when he had his own practice. He blew that. Didn't take long." Rocco smirked and tipped his head as if to say Robert's failure was expected. "Then, I knew him a couple of years later when his world began falling apart and he wanted to borrow some money," Rocco said. "After that, we didn't know each other at all, if you know what I mean, not until about two months ago when he suddenly showed up looking like a million bucks," Rocco raised an eyebrow. "And now, tonight, I'm seeing either the beginning of a new wealth or just another dive from a height he really can't handle." Rocco began shaking his head from side to side as if weighing his next remark before making it public. "Personally, he's always been one of my best customers. I kinda hate to see him keep throwing everything away." Rocco chuckled as a measure of his insincerity. "He just doesn't know how to handle himself. But maybe that's something I shouldn't be sharing with you, eh; you being his partner and all?"

Too late. Allen already saw and heard enough. There was no reason to what Robert did. Allen met Mr. Hyde after working with Dr. Jekyll. It was early and this night already took numerous unexpected turns. Allen just didn't know yet that it was going to end in a very bad way.

CHAPTER 8
Time Off, Time Out

It was Christmas Eve and the last day of the work-year for David—a short day. On Christmas Day, he would be vacationing on a Virgin Island in the Caribbean with his wife, Laura, without GrowVest or anyone else to structure his life. This was a necessary vacation for many reasons. The most important reason, he told himself, was the needed repairs to his marriage. He blamed himself for the distance from his wife. His preoccupation with GrowVest paralleled his home struggles; every time a problem arose at work, a problem presented itself at home. He wasn't handling any of it very well. The problems didn't carry enough weight to trigger complaints from Laura. She was dismissing conflicts on a regular basis; walking away from them without comment. Her interests were with her "hobbies," the gym and a collection of girlfriends David never met. She was away from home as much as he was and often wasn't there when he returned late in the evening. Yeah, he needed the vacation. They both did.

The early afternoon GrowVest Christmas party was ten minutes out of the day and the last thing on the agenda after a company lunch. The employees all gathered in the GrowVest lobby with a plastic cup of white wine from a cardboard box and the uneasiness that comes from sharing time with people they didn't really know. As far as anyone figured, none of them had anything to do with the other on a social basis and it showed. As soon as the staff gathered, Robert announced a general "thanks for a fine year." The clouded plastic was raised and quickly drained. Then, the party began breaking up. Everyone had somewhere to go. So did David. "Merry Christmas, everyone. I won't see any of you for 12 days," David announced. "It is my first vacation since I began working here almost two years ago," he said, "and I intend to forget you all." The few remaining in the rapidly emptying room that heard his declaration laughed. David burnt out weeks before and this was to be a recharging hiatus.

The flight to St. Croix was uneventful. Laura slept most of the way while David drank and thought about GrowVest. After checking into the Carambola Bay Resort late in the afternoon, Laura immediately headed for the shower. "God, I hate travelling," she told David as she walked into the bathroom. "I always feel so dirty after sitting on a plane for four hours." David could barely hear her as she turned the shower on and closed the door. The rest of the evening was a couple of sandwiches from room service and an early bed time in a massively wide bed where the emptiness between them was enough for three more people.

Scheduled habits don't change just because your body is on vacation. The mind still awakens with work the primary purpose of consciousness. David was awake at six. "Going somewhere?" Laura said as David sat at the edge of the king size bed.

"Sorry, I didn't think I'd wake you when you're so far away."

"What is that supposed to mean?" There was an edge to her voice. David shook his head. Not an argument already, he thought. "It's too early in the day and in the vacation to start with an argument," he mumbled. "What I meant was that you are far on the other side of the bed," he said gently. "I didn't think my movement would disturb you. I'm sorry if it did."

Laura said nothing then rolled over to look at David. "I'm sorry. I think I need some unwinding."

"Okaaaay," he said tentatively. "How about we take a walk on the beach before the other tourists decide to spoil it by being there?"

Laura smiled. It was the first time in months he saw her even attempt a smile. She rolled back over and threw the sheet from her naked body. "Mmm, you are still a beautiful woman," he told her. She smiled. Laura was five years younger than David. She worked out daily, and it showed. As she emerged from the bed she stood with her back to him stretching with her hands raised high. She reached for the flowered thin cotton robe on the chair beside the bed and covered herself. As she turned with her back to the open balcony, the sun passed through the robe creating a shapely silhouette. David watched her as she walked toward the bathroom and closed the door. He believed this attempt at repairing the relationship might be easier than he originally thought. With a little tenderness and kindness on his part, Laura might melt before the week ended.

Carambola Bay could be delightfully empty at times. At six a.m., the early morning sun was warm without burning as it did by ten o'clock each day. Sounds carried over the water, bouncing off of the bay's surrounding mountain walls unimpeded by tourist competition. Two sun-darkened, bare-chested fishermen were pulling their traps from the bottom of the clear, aquamarine water thirty yards from the limestone outcrop where David and Laura stood watching. Their small rowboat had Christmas decorations hanging from the bow. The morning sounds were limited to the Caribbean washing onto the beach and the flapping on the boat's wooden deck of freshly caught fish pulled from the traps.

The morning walks remained a part of their daily ritual for the next several days. Laura's body was acquiring a slow roasting, coffee-tinted darkness that contrasted with her bright yellow bikini. David looked more like the bark of the red, peeling gumbo limbo, the tree locals called "the tourist tree." But the walks meant something special to them both. David found himself making silent promises that nothing would jeopardize the loss of this again. He knew GrowVest had to be weighed for what it was—a means to supply his life and wife with happiness. In his recent quest for the best, GrowVest had become a wedge—his new lover—pushing Laura away. He promised himself that would end.

Being with Laura rekindled emotions David welcomed. Laura sensed the same things when one morning walking the quiet beach, she reached out and held his hand. "These last few days have given us something we lost over the past few years. I feel like we've rediscovered each other. This is the way it should be," she said glancing up from watching her feet disappear beneath the warm waves.

"What? Wet and sandy with the smell of dead fish?"

"No," Laura said laughing. "Just the two of us," she said squeezing his hand. "You've come back."

"Yeah, well, maybe." David was embarrassed by her comment.

"Life is easy, simple and so are we. No complications. No outside stress," she hesitated and looked down again at the water rushing to meet her toes. "No invaders to our privacy. Just the two of us sharing each other. That's all."

David sensed a veiled confession in her comment, but let it go. This was the moment David would remember. This was the closest they would be. This was his opportunity to hold her and tell her she was all he ever wanted. But he didn't. This was his glimpse at the lost relationship he would never see again.

"We can't abandon reality," he told her.

"But, this is reality. This is what we said we wanted when we first met," she said pleading for a return to a lost moment.

"What, a beachside resort on an island," he said sarcastically.

"No, the two of us . . ."

David interrupted. There was an edge to his voice. "The two of us cannot be without a means of support. Everything we do . . . Everything *I* do is intended so that we can have a couple of weeks like this—all the paradise money can buy. Make no mistake it's the money that brought us here. It's the money that gives us this artificial moment. And it's the money that gives us everything *you* have." David's last words echoed against the bay's mountain walls and mixed to silence as the waves crushed in.

"I hoped there was another reason than money that brought us here," she said softly.

"You *know* what I mean."

"You're not really here, are you?" Laura suddenly realized David never came back. "This David is borrowed, isn't he? Just a reflection of what used to be." She looked into David's eyes hoping for some light, a flame that might still be there. "This David," she said, "is here only for the allotted vacation time." She knew then that the other David would resurface before they boarded the plane home.

CHAPTER 9
Betrayed

With the vacation over and his burn turned to a deep tan, David was ready to dive into the GrowVest mix once again. He returned on schedule and was surprised to find his office unlocked, and open with Mac seated waiting for him. David greeted Mac with a smile and an offer of his hand as a greeting. Mac limply returned the greeting and turned in the seat to face David's desk.

"We have a problem," he announced to David.

"This is nothing new," David said with a chuckle. "Robert is constantly complaining about something I've done," David said, "real or imagined."

The usual procedure was for Robert to complain either in his office with Mac present or to wait for a meeting with Allen. Both the CEO and David became accustomed to Robert's ranting and realized his complaints were driven by his embedded paranoia, often loudly bordering on the irrational.

David shook his head and threw himself into the padded, black swiveling desk chair. "Wow, back five minutes and we have a problem, huh? So, what's the bitch-de-jour," David said while casually pulling the accumulated pile of mail that had spent two weeks awaiting his attention. He took the top letter and reached into his desk drawer for a silver letter opener. Looking at Mac with a devilish grin on his face he pulled the opener through the letter with a clean slicing motion. "Just wanted you to see how a couple of weeks without a pain in the ass can build character," he said broadening his smile.

Mac showed no interest in David's game. Mac was usually straight-to-the-point. Though he hesitated for a moment, he was still ready to present his case. "Robert," he said, "received a phone call from his wife on Christmas day."

"That's nice," David said slicing open another letter. "It's good to know they're finally getting along—even if it took the birth of God to accomplish it."

"She told him that she learned that a manager at his company was spreading rumors about him."

Uh-oh, this was not good. David stopped slicing envelopes and looked at Mac. The wide grin lessened. Mac had David's attention. David knew where this was going but the CEO, Allen, was not in on this meeting. David reminded himself to listen and not give anything away until he was certain Mac revealed everything he knew. The facts were going to be important. If Mac mentioned that Robert's wife said the employee was investigating Robert, David would have to call Allen in and open the whole thing up.

"You are the only person she could have been talking about—the only one that could be," Mac waited for a response.

"Me?" David feigned surprise. "Wow, I'll bet that made old Robert's tree wilt a bit." Mac didn't smile. "Look, Mac," David said, "I don't know Robert's wife. Don't know her name. Have never, as far as I know, spoken with her about anything and I certainly have never spread any rumors about Robert. Why would I?" David said the obvious knowing there was much more to come.

"Her name is Dierdre. She says the information came from a good friend who happens to be your good friend, Marley." Mac paused again. Mac wasn't looking for an explanation. He was searching for body language or some kind of response in David's face, some kind of telling self-admission. His confidence was saying that this was all decided. The confrontation was just a formality before the final move. There were no questions to be asked. Robert gave Mac everything he needed for a conviction. But Mac was just the messenger. He lacked the killer instinct that, as a lawyer, Robert should have had.

"All right," David told Mac. "What are these rumors? What am I supposed to be saying about Robert, indirectly to his wife?" David was trying to emphasize the absurdity of the accusation. It was going to take a very long talk to convince Mac of anything other than the opinion he came into David's office with.

"She told him you were claiming he was skimming money from the company; demanding personal loans from the company; having an affair with the secretary, and that he was into drugs. Those are just some of the things she said."

Now David's jaw dropped for real. He knew Marley and knew her asking questions couldn't possibly have gotten into any of those areas except for the drugs. Marley said she saw Robert at three parties and that at least three other people with whom she attended those parties saw the same. One of those people was Robert's wife.

It suddenly occurred to David that Robert may have actually received the call he was claiming. But, his wife may only have mentioned the questions being asked about his drug problem. Knowing, now, that the secret of his drug use was out, Robert had to discredit David before David had a chance to let anyone know the truth. So, Robert invented the content of the call hoping to hide the drug knowledge among several other obviously untrue charges. As absurd as these invented ones were, they made the drug charge ludicrous by association.

David still had the problem of protecting the CEO from the situation. Mac and David walked to Allen's office. Mac renewed his story noting it was more than a week since Robert received the call and that in that time Robert only shared the accusations with him. It was clear Allen was unaware of Robert's fanciful phone call. It was also clear Allen had no intention of admitting his own involvement in the mess. No one else was going to know about the investigation into Robert's drug use except David.

With waves of his hand and dismissive looks in Mac's direction, Allen laid the entire fantasy on Robert's wife trying to convince Mac that she was pulling Robert's chain out of spite and nothing more. For a few minutes it worked. Mac left the office smiling. David stayed with Allen.

"What do you know about this?"

"Nothing more than what you know," David told him. "It appears Robert has discovered that his secret is no longer exclusive knowledge and is attempting to discredit the messenger." Allen agreed and said he would talk to Robert. As was the case whenever difficulties arose, the worm was nowhere to be found.

Two days later, at the start of another day, Mac and Allen entered David's office. This was very unusual—both present, at the start of the day and neither man looked very pleased. Mac's lips were pursed together as he glared at David. Without removing his stare he found a chair and sat in front of David's desk. Allen was somber. He looked at David and when David returned the glance, Allen shifted the direction of his stare to the floor and sat down in a chair next to Mac.

Apparently Mac was to do all of the talking. He carried a folder and placed it on the corner of the desk near his chair. "We regret to inform you that your position with this company has been terminated," he began. "Cost cutting measures have forced us to reconsider all employee positions. Yours appears superfluous and expensive and for that reason we feel it wise to dissolve the position." Then as an afterthought to the script, Mac looked at David and said, "We regret that you are no longer employed by GrowVest as of this day."

That was it. Done. The employee roster was trimmed and David was at the top of the list. Truth was David was the list. David was genuinely startled by the news. It was obvious that Robert was twisting the knife all the time that David was gone. David's friend, "brother," confidant, and partner in the investigation sold him out to the opposition. Worse yet, Allen must have been instructed to attend the meeting to give the reading the weight of the betrayal. Of course, again, the worm was nowhere to be found.

"I want a moment alone with Allen," David said looking directly at Allen. Mac hesitated and turned to look to Allen for direction. Mac was thrown. He was unsure what to do next. He leaned toward Allen, "We never discussed . . . This was not an option we reviewed." He spoke hurriedly in a soft voice as if he expected David wouldn't hear. The dress rehearsals that probably included Robert never accounted for this contingency. Allen looked at Mac and nodded. "Go on. Go."

Mac left closing the door behind him.

"What the hell is going on here?" David was still in shock over what just happened. Anger hadn't taken its place. Betrayal was not part of the conversation, yet.

"I have no choice," Allen stammered as he watched his trembling hands folded in his lap.

"You are my friend," David said, clearly hurt by Allen's actions. "If there is going to be a problem, you are supposed to have my back like I have always had yours. Why would you do this to me when you know the truth behind all of this?"

"I have no choice," Allen mumbled. Then after a brief pause, still looking at his hands, Allen began. "The company has several potential buyers looking us over," Allen said with a sing-song delivery that made it sound as if he was reciting his own prepared statement. Then he stopped and slowly raised his head. Quietly, as if the secret was to remain in the room between the two of them Allen began, "If I were to fire Robert, I would have to give a reason. I could not accuse him of cocaine use. The stock value would plummet. I couldn't accuse him of mismanagement, either." Allen was giving David the rationalizations he collected the night before as he went over this event in his mind time and again. He waited. David had no reaction. Allen said to him, "You have to go. The company will be sold very soon and this will all be forgotten."

That was it. It was decided and Robert now controlled everything. In spite of his controlling stock interest, title as CEO, and previous insistence that this was his company, Allen just gave everything to Robert.

Allen relaxed a bit. David said nothing. Perhaps David would go quietly, he thought. "I hope you will forgive this decision," he said. Allen should have stopped there. Maybe David would have gone quietly but Allen's next comment lit the fuse for a much bigger bang. "You should be grateful for having worked with me," Allen said.

David's pain instantly turned to rage. "Grateful?" Stunned by the comment, David was shouting. "Grateful? I helped build this company to what it is. I have done the work of five valued employees. I have covered your ass whenever it was needed and was your eyes and ears to things you couldn't or wouldn't hear or see. You want *me* to be grateful?" David paused. He was waiting for an answer that never came. "Grateful? Not in my lifetime," David sneered. "I trusted you. I covered for you. Now, you want me to take the hit. I don't care what your explanation is for this. No, I won't forgive you but I can tell you this, I will destroy Robert for this and rub your face in it at the same time." David left his office yelling. He was out of control. "*I will finish this*," he said pounding a fist on a lobby table as he walked past. "You will feel this shame," he said stopping to point at Allen who was standing in the doorway of David's office watching David's exit. "I will see to it that everyone knows the truth about Robert. Let him keep the humiliation and loss." David's screaming pulled people from their offices as they watched him rant. Then David said something he never should have said. "That son-of-a-bitch is mine from now on," he announced. As he turned to make his way to the elevator, he muttered, "I swear I will kill him."

CHAPTER 10
. . . we all fall down.

The next several weeks through January David spent alone locked inside his home office sleeping on the floor or in the chair in front of the computer. Meals were late night raids on a darkened kitchen that glowed when the refrigerator door opened to show stacks of dirty dishes and bits of stale food piled around the sink. Laura didn't care. Any hope at a reconciled marriage ended in St. Croix. They were both just waiting for an opportunity to end it. David's withdrawal into himself after being fired became her opportunity. She took whatever material elements she wanted and left. David reasoned that he had more room now and the echoes of his angry tirades in the empty space were all the company he needed.

Robert became David's purpose—his obsession. Every waking hour was spent cruising the internet. He was looking for information about Robert, his past, and anyone whose name was mentioned along with the worm's. David's demeanor changed along with his appearance. He talked to himself swearing, spitting out insults at Robert's memory. There were moments when a one-sided argument would burst from his lips as he walked through the house yelling with his hands clenched. The screaming continued until the fists disappeared and tears streamed down his face melting into the graying stubble of his unshaven face. His sunken eyes and cheeks reflected his personal neglect. He seldom dressed or showered. He had only one purpose. He had to know his enemy from every angle before he could identify his weaknesses and attack. He was never concerned that his behavior might be less than normal.

Harassment was the beginning of the process. Several times during the later weeks of his self-imposed isolation he slipped out of his stuffy dungeon to roam in Robert's neighborhood. He made maps and personally verified them not wanting to trust any other source. Always in the dark and alone, he paced through every escape scenario. The maps were memorized. He was certain that he knew Robert's neighborhood better than Robert. Even though he never met or saw his neighbors, he learned about them too. The internet was a wonderful tool for revenge.

He began charting Robert's daily activities. First, just as a view of his home—the time he left, arrived, shopped. He followed him to work and spent the day in a cafeteria across from the office. He noted Robert's haste as he ran out for meetings. If anyone noticed David, they never recognized him as more than a street bum. David was delighted to think that the worm had no idea he was being watched.

David decided to start by vandalizing Robert's car. He wanted to unnerve Robert—work on his paranoia. The garage where Robert parked near the office was easy to access. The lone guard showed little enthusiasm for his work. There were several floors to canvas and no video monitoring. Shortly after the guard began his casual morning walk through the levels, David entered the structure and headed for the street level reserved section where Robert's car was parked. "Walk boldly like you belong here," he told himself. "If anyone sees you, just move on and try it another day."

The garage was a cavernous concrete spiral that echoed with each step David took. Sounds amplified as they bounced off of the concrete floors, walls and ceiling. David could hear the muffled squeals of tires from several floors above as a car slid down the corkscrew platform. He walked toward one of the monolithic supporting columns with an exit sign posted on its exposed side and waited for the vehicle to pass before continuing his walk.

Each of the reserved spaces on the garage's ground floor was numbered in large, yellow, block letters on the wall in front of the vehicle. An extra double row of spaces was set in the middle of the private area where the space numbers were painted on the floor. A banner of white paint covered the entrance that designated the spaces were for "Reserved Monthly Parking." Here too, the spaces were roomy—an extra two feet between the cars. David weaved his way between a red Porsche Boxster and powder blue Mercedes C-class then slid in between Robert's shiny, new, black Lexus and a metallic green custom pickup that looked out of place among the thoroughbreds. This was it—space "14." The car's vanity plate read "ALL – MINE," Robert's way of declaring this item was never a part of his recent divorce.

David pushed against the Lexus with his hand sheathed in his shirt to see if a motion detector would sound an alarm. There was nothing. David moved to the first wheel and quickly removed the chromed valve cap, inverted and reinserted it. A couple of quick twists and the valve stem came out with the sudden hiss of escaping air. He threw the stem beneath the adjacent vehicle and replaced the cap watching as the tire softened. By the time David finished the other three tires they were all showing a spreading bulge at their base. Four flats. Four major annoyances. Four counts of mischief to Robert's car and no other.

Robert discovered the problem later that evening as he left his office. He was certain the tires were slashed. The fluorescent lights that flickered overhead couldn't help him define the problem. He pulled out his cell phone and called triple-A. Forty-five minutes later, the AAA driver took a quick look at all four tires and declared, "Looks like the air has been let out." He pulled the air hose from the service truck's bed and unscrewed the first stem cap. He attached the hose to the valve and began the pump. The pumps loud chugging echoed off the concrete walls. It continued pushing out air until the first tire was inflated. But as soon as the driver pulled the hose free, there was that beautiful hissing of a thousand angry snakes. Robert took the news badly. Every one of the reptiles bit him in the ass. He immediately claimed that as the vandal's lone victim, this was no random prank. He was targeted he told the driver and continued the serial complaint throughout the next day. Everyone knew Robert and dismissed the event as vandalism. The rest of his complaint, they assumed, was driven by Robert's uniformly established paranoia.

Nine days passed. A good number, David thought. Then, on a Wednesday night around 2 a.m., David attacked again. Robert's neighborhood was a collection of custom homes. Of course, no two were alike. Every effort was made toward individuality. Each lot was immaculately landscaped. Live oaks with dipping limbs swept across manicured lawns that felt the weekly touch of gardeners and the monthly spray of lawn food mixed with insecticides to kill the mole crickets, chinch bugs and foraging birds. A few of the home owners needed to name their properties. So, a collection of wrought iron or cast bronze signs hung from street side mail boxes. They were embedded in the thick sod lawns. Each name declared their owner's property vision: "Heaven's Gate," "Limerock," and "The Maples."

Robert's home had no name. In fact, it lacked any creative touch other than the builder's original concept. It was a pale colored, bland, yellow. Windows, soffit and fascia were trimmed in white as was the garage door. The mail box, at the end of the driveway, one hundred feet from the house, simply said "Whitney." The house number, 14, was painted in black at the foot of his brick trimmed, neutral gray driveway. It was certainly no coincidence that this was the same number as Robert's parking space in the garage at work. Robert was nothing, if not consistent. There were no trees on the lawn despite its lengthy run from the street to the winding sidewalk that led to his heavy wooden front door. A wall of hip high, variegated shrubs encircled the house. Other than that, the sterile home gave every impression of having been recently built even though the neighborhood was much older. If it had to be given a name, it would have been called "Vanilla."

Robert never parked his car in his garage. It was always in the driveway hugging the house and walkway. There was no room in the garage for the Lexus. The garage interior was cluttered from floor to ceiling with heavy cardboard boxes. Most of Robert's belongings filled the boxes as collections of items he brought from his past life. They remained stacked and separated with proposed room designations scrawled in black marker on the tops and sides. There was no time or need to move them into the house.

That night, Robert's car was in its expected spot in the driveway of his home. The neighborhood was dead quiet except for the soothing whinny of a screech owl in the oaks across the street. It was 3 a.m. Any noise, even the sound of David's feet shuffling up the concrete drive was unnecessarily loud. He removed his shoes. With the cats he borrowed from his neighborhood squirming in the pillow case in his left hand, he walked within fifty feet of the car and garage. "There might be, should be a car alarm," he whispered to the cat-filled bag, "one of those directional things that goes off when you get close to it." He looked around once more, certain he was alone. "Or maybe the lights in the driveway are linked to motion detectors." David was overly cautious. He was thinking this might be too far. This was an unquestioned attack—as benign as it may be. The bottom line was that Robert would freak out. That, of course was what David wanted but attacking Robert's home could bring more heat down on David than he anticipated.

There were no street lights. The exclusive community collectively determined they were unnecessary because of the custom lighting that surrounded all the properties. It gave the neighborhood the desired look of individual estates. The only light on Robert's property was one illuminating the front entrance. It offered enough light to clearly see the car—David's primary interest.

"Close enough," he whispered. Laying the pillow case on the concrete, David untied the top releasing the three panicked felines. The sterility of Robert's yard, he was sure, would force the cats to hide under the nearest and only cover, the car. The cats had other ideas. Two split for cover in the house's nearby bushes. But, the third headed right for the car and hid beneath it. No other yard lights! No car alarm! David was giddy at Robert's error.

Realizing that this time he couldn't wait to remove the tire's valve stems, David decided the ice pick was easier. He performed four quick jabs and made a rapid exit after scrawling "thief" with the pick's point and then dragged the pick through the car's multiple layers of pristine black paint. Watching from the shadows across the street, he chuckled as the height of the Lexus hissed down. "Done," he declared. "Well planned." Certainly, this was a minor skirmish but enough that, given Robert's mental health, it would become a magnified distraction.

David was invigorated. The next morning he waited at the cafeteria across from the office grabbing a seat near the window where he was able to face the street. The window position also gave him the opportunity to continue his thoughts without alarming the other customers. David's musings were taking the form of audible conversations. The stress was entering a new phase for David. There were scales tipping in several directions: one for Robert's paranoia, and another for David's sanity. Nursing several cups of Mountain Blue, he waited for Robert to show up. "10:30," he said glancing at his watch. "The worm hasn't made it in." David giggled between gulps of coffee and glanced at the patron who decided to occupy an adjoining window seat. "Is it obvious," he whispered, "Robert is hiding at home? He is convinced there is a stalker out to get him." Again, David chuckled. The patron retrieved his cup and morning newspaper glancing at David and the available seats as if measuring a safe distance between the two before moving to choose one.

David should have been high on Robert's list of suspects. Though Robert was hated by most everyone that knew him, they all had more at stake than to screw with a man's car. They were more inclined to hire a hit man. David was playing games designed to elevate Robert's sense of victimization. He wanted the added pressure to confuse and cause Robert to panic. David's plans required a far slower process than an easy splat from a silenced 22-caliber hand gun. He wanted Robert running away from GrowVest faster than he ran from his wife. And he wanted him going farther away than just a bridge-distance from his past.

The policeman told Robert, "Sir, this is nothing more than a prank by some neighborhood kids. This might not have happened if you had motion detectors on your exterior lights and maybe a custom car alarm. If you do that, it should prevent this sort of thing from happening again."

"Alarms!" The obvious only enraged Robert. "No intellectual defect in a uniform is going to lecture me with 20-20 hindsight." The startled cop stiffened as Robert came closer. "That won't stop them," Robert was shouting directly into the officer's face. "That will only let me know they are already here, you idiot."

The officer dropped his pad to his side and stuffed his pen into his breast pocket. He placed both hands on his hips and leaned into Robert. "Sir, I'm going to ask you to calm down. I understand you are upset but attempting to intimidate a police officer will only get you a spot in the back seat of that squad car," he said pointing at the vehicle without losing eye contact with an unbending Robert.

"Is that the best you can do? Is that what I pay taxes for?" Robert ignored the cop's threat and returned with one of his own. "I know people. I can have this taken care of at a higher level and make your life miserable in the process," Robert sneered. "I want protection. I want these people caught." Turning to the collecting crowd of neighbors wandering up his lawn, Robert waved his arms, "It isn't safe here. You know how many important people live in this neighborhood?" Robert again waved his arms—this time toward his neighbors as he looked for community support for his problem. He pointed at the cop. "You have to take care of this."

Robert's rant awarded him one more police concession. Recognizing a bad situation and unsure of how much of what Robert was saying was true, the officer said, "I will request an increase neighborhood patrol at night, sir. There's nothing else we can do."

And the cops did come for about two weeks.

Robert's personal police profile was not making him any friends with the local law. His abusive screaming against the patrolmen earned him their contempt. There was a police consensus that future responses to Robert's home would require more than the expected 3-6 minutes.

David knew he had to hit Robert's house once more. It had to be something mild enough to prevent the police from suddenly taking interest in Robert's complaints, but annoying enough to cost Robert some money, sleep, or sanity. So far the cops trivialized Robert's complaints about being stalked and assured him it was an unfortunate prank by some kids out past their bedtime. David believed the deed had to be simple enough to fit the cops' description so it could be dismissed once more, but annoying enough to frost Robert.

Combing the internet became David's primary, daily preoccupation. The time yielded some ideas and pointers that came in handy. Porn sites were as common as freckles on a redhead. One of those talented, naked redheads gave David the idea. Robert, he decided, was about to become a common name on porn email lists. Robert's business email address was still in David's files. He found thirty sites within three hours and took the time to register Robert on each of them after disconnecting their ability to drop an internet cookie that could trace the activity back to his own computer. If asked for money—and most did—David simply broke off communication. Often, that remnant registration containing the email address could be picked up by the site and used to contact the person, asking them to complete their application. There was enough of a ghost registration, David was certain, for Robert to get inquiries from the sites and anyone they sold his address to. The problem was that David didn't know how many emails Robert would get or even *if* he would. For that matter, Robert could set up fire wall blocks that would filter out many of the sites. With nothing but time, David figured he would give it a try anyway.

For many web surfers who have sampled the internet's varied menu, it should come as no surprise that David was able to find the pornographic sites that he needed so quickly. Novices who have yet to sample the sexual deviations available on the web should understand that if it can be imagined by a person, it's there. It is even more likely there is a whole lot more that that person can't imagine that someone else has. It's there too. It is all, no matter how tame or perverse, condemned by social convention. David planned to make Robert the neighborhood's dirty old man.

Most of what was on the internet was legal except maybe in Arkansas where the couple had to be closely related. But he also knew there was an awful lot more that wasn't legal. That was where David slipped. His scam was intended to embarrass and annoy. But it ended up leading a local sting operation to Robert's front door. It was David's blunder, but he wished he thought of it just the same.

Cruiser lights flashed as uniformed and plain-clothed cops rushed Robert's house with guns drawn. Robert answered the door and was pushed aside as the first wave of combat ready cops swarmed inside. Robert was pushed against a wall; pivoted so his face was embedded against the floral wallpaper and cuffed with delightful efficiency.

They confiscated his computer, threw him in a cruiser and drove away. Neatly done. Whisked away like one of Vladimir Putin's adversaries. David wasn't there when it happened. He missed it all. But there was a ten-minute, in-depth report on the local Fox news that night with an appropriately pained, shoulder-length blonde female anchor rolling her eyes before throwing it back to her indignant male counterpart. A little unprofessional shake of the head in disgust and they moved on. It was Jerry-Springer-priceless.

The next day, the police showed up at David's front door—early. The lead officer wanted to know if David could tell them anything about internet porn. It didn't look good. He knew he fucked up somewhere. They must have figured out who set Robert up. David decided denial wouldn't work, so he simply slammed the door in their faces and yelled at them to "fuck off." As he turned his back on the door, he succeeded in gaining four, maybe five steps back to the gloom of his office when the door burst open and David was thrown to the floor.

"Take it easy. Take it easy," David shouted as blood spurted from the ridge above his eyebrow.

"You son-of-a-bitch," was the last thing David recalled hearing the bully on his back saying. The bandages David later sported on his head were a tribute to his apparent resistance and the policeman's need to slam David's head repeatedly in the direction of the polished cherry wood floor to get his attention.

The trial was brief. We've already seen how that went. Just know that Robert testified about David stalking him since losing his job. Allen said David claimed he would kill Robert, if given the chance. Mac was uncharacteristically quiet. There were neighbors who claimed David's presence was a regular thing in the neighborhood. The woman across the street used the word "nightly." Either David was less careful than he thought or Robert's neighbors were looking for TV face-time. David remembered little of the trial,

90

but there was a lot more to it than the declaration by the court of a prolonged hospital stay.

Never believe that time flies—fun or not. David spent six months, three weeks, four days and several hours hiding on his crowded court-ordered hospital ward and nearly every moment that wasn't spent trying to count the minutes was spent trying to understand Allen and why he folded for Robert.

For several weeks after the Fanta bottle incident, the days followed a predictable pattern. Predictability was measured in dosages. The drugs were designed to keep everything as expected. They regulated the time a patient took to relieve himself in the morning to the time it took to tuck him in at night. But sometimes the chemicals couldn't drown the root cause of a patient's disturbance. Sometimes the root cause forgets predictability and bubbles to the surface despite the constricting presence of the medication. The agitated bubbles float into the air and burst releasing their scent. The scent permeates everything like a warning for those sniffing the walls and floors. The patients smell it and remain agitated. The hospital's guardians don't.

"It's because I still believe in Allen," David declared to the hollow eyes around the crowded day room that stared back. Through his tearing eyes, he told the blurred faces, "Allen was just trying to save the company." David continued his daily shuffle around the room. It was part of his routine fostered by the ritualized introduction of the pills. David bubbled most every day. This day the agitation was growing. Many of his ward buddies recognized the pattern even if those in charge didn't smell it yet. Despite the scattering bodies that flowed to different zones as David floated through the room telling his story, their collective presence was sympathetically pleased. There was some laughter, slaps on the back and shuffled hiding in corners by a few as a result of the uncomfortable odor of bubbles bursting.

David made his way and sat down in his own corner pulling his feet onto the enveloping soft chair so that his chin came close to resting on his knees. The one-sided conversation continued at a whisper. "He did it because he had to; because it was about saving me as much as it was about himself." At this level David appeared to his captors like all the other isolated minds whispering their own stories. "That's what I tell myself," he whispered. "That's what I believe," he said trying to convince himself while still holding onto the last vestige of a missing friendship. There was hesitation. The legs became untangled as the feet found their way to the floor. David's hands were grasping the soft chair's arms. His fingers dug into the fabric. His facial expression changed from confused hurt to anger. "Fat fucking chance!" David's voice was louder. The heads watching David's were alarmed by his voice. It was clear anger was building to rage. "Fire Robert!" David was standing and the loud voice now yelled for more attention. "Everything Allen built falls!" The room was David's. All eyes and ears had found him. "Allen loses GrowVest. Allen loses his reputation." Three burly day room attendants hurriedly headed toward David while frightened patients stuck to the walls or hid under tables covering their faces trying to become invisible. David saw the men coming to him. He continued his screaming swinging his arms with hands curled into fists that appeared directed toward the men in the white uniforms. "You don't see it because you don't want to!" With arms flailing with windmill-like force, David tried to push his attackers away striking each with a fist. Two of the white-clad mercenaries tackled him forcefully pushing him back into the soft chair where each man grabbed an arm. "You can't stop me. I will get him." His legs were still free. David kicked one bloodied soldier to the floor holding his jaw. Through clenched teeth David shouted, "I will kill that son-of-a-bitch. You can't stop me!" As the white starched nurse injected David with sleep, his foot found its final mark doubling a second attacker in half with both hands cupping his balls.

CHAPTER 11
Powdered Flowers and Dead Kittens

Hospital administration received an overhauling after the Fanta incident. Shortly after the change the new administration comfortably occupied their freshly painted offices. Copies of a memo from the hospital's newest administrator were posted on nearly every wall. The memo was written on hospital stationary and bore the official seal with the phrase, *"pro populo,"*—for the people. The memo declared that "effective immediately," there was a change in hospital policy. It addressed the manner in which staff treated their "clients." "With some exceptions," it noted, "a respectful community of employees must realize their positions are to assist in the care and well-being of those for whom they care." It went on to declare how this new "quality workplace" was going to improve "quality care" and make life for everyone more pleasant. It also contained an obligatory warning against glass bottles on the ward.

Days passed. Since the memo, things had changed. David was calmer. His behavior in the dayroom was adjusted. David was transferred to a ward for "non-violent" patients. The joke wasn't lost on David or his captors. His concocted recipe for happiness was reevaluated daily to maintain his balanced chemical state. It took the edge off of David's world leaving violence out of the equation.

Now, an introduced cloud fogged his mind that promoted a peaceful merging with the fanciful atmosphere the other inmates floated through.

At 8 a.m., David smiled waiting patiently in the day room's medication-line with the other likeminded men shuffling through Albemarle's sanitary days. The institution chairs that lined the sunlit dayroom walls emptied as the men enthusiastically joined the morning procession. The attendants who held David days before for the nurse's needle walked past each man in the line. Their job was to move the leaden feet forward toward the nurse with the stainless steel tray of white paper cups filled with multicolored pills.

David maintained his smile and began speaking in a soft voice. Others heard but ignored him. The chatter in line was normal. Personal conversations were common. The aids never listened—but the inmates usually did.

"Appearances aren't what they seem," David mumbled. "Albemarle is only a hospital," he assured the others shuffling with him. "This is not confinement. We can leave if we want to," he nodded reassuringly while maintaining his smile. "This is not the prison Robert hoped it would be," he told them. Though he may have believed otherwise, it was clear. David was a prisoner. The realization of his forced isolation slowly progressed through David's mind as he voiced his denials. The memo, he believed, was his assurance against captivity. Albemarle was there to help him, it said. It was a slogan that became a part of the personal fantasy he layered over reality.

In truth, the blanketing memo changed very little except to deflate the employees' impression of their own value. Reducing the patient to a faceless schedule became the norm. Doctors, nurses, and aids had schedules and quotas to meet. It all presided over procedures. Patients became faceless bodies included within time lines. Workers came and went and did their jobs with minimally required efficiency. What most visitors to the hospital saw as finely tuned, those that worked there saw as an interruption to their lives. Employee passivity hid boredom. Instead of affirming anyone's value, the memo removed the humanity—good and bad.

For David and the other inmates the "quality initiative" came with unexpected benefits. People spoke in normal voices. There appeared to be a pleasant underlying hum to the day. Life became easy at Albemarle—soothing and uneventful. If asked, everyone said they liked it that way. David continued to deny his capture. It didn't matter. The hospital's recognition of who he was got lost in the flow of the quality work day. It took weeks but David recognized that the new attitude created an opportunity. He would use it to alter his position.

The psychiatric ward at Albemarle had requirements, but the procedures were loosely scheduled and so was the security. Once-a-week David saw the ward's doctor alone in his pretty blue room with pictures of yellow flowers and baskets of kittens on the pastel walls. The weekly sessions helped David sort through the rubbish cluttering the fuzzy wool floors of the shiny, red enamel rooms in his subconscious. The therapist was the light in each space illuminating the dark corners so David could reach forward to sweep out the dust, the dry, powdered, flowers, and dead kittens. With his doctor's help David glided through the rooms a therapeutic hour at a time. He was told the psychiatrist was the mechanism that showed him how to rescue his mind. David saw him as an extension of the steady diet of chemicals they fed him to be certain his edge was properly dulled. The doctor, he was told, was his friend, his guide. The man who would lead him back to a healthy world. So, that first day, the doctor listened to his stories and when David was finished, for a moment, there was silence. Then, in soft even tones, using ever-lengthening sentences, the doctor politely explained that David's mind was trashed. "But," he explained to David, "you shouldn't worry because, I am here to help you."

"Sure you are," David said. Seeing the doctor scribble something on his notepad David quickly added, "No, really, you *are*

95

here to help me. I believe that." David nodded long enough to catch the doctor's eye.

"It requires that you work at this," the doctor said. "You will have to search within yourself for the answers."

And so, David searched and unwittingly tried. In one of his therapeutic sessions, David was encouraged to rework the entire nightmare that cast him into his hell. He began by describing a series of recurring nightmares that nightly built on one another.

"It's a dream," David said. "I know that but, it doesn't matter. Every night I start the dream over again. I try ratting Robert out to the police. The scene plays out in *film noire* with heavy shadows — black and white. They corner Robert coming out of an alley; trip him on the wet street and slam him to the pavement." David smiled and told the doctor, "I'm delighted. They drag Robert away bloodied and screaming. But that doesn't satisfy. No. This is too easy," he said. "Frustration and hatred created expediency—not reality. The scene dissolves.

"I concoct an IRS scenario. A group of men in cheap suits with lapels wider than their ties and fedoras pulled low over their eyes carrying Thompson submachine guns break through the door to Robert's office. Robert, who looks strangely like James Cagney, reaches for the desk drawer and pulls out an absurdly long-barreled pistol. The G-men fire and the wall is plastered with bullets and Robert . . . or Jimmy."

"These dreams are pushing you farther away from reality," the doctor said. "Do you believe an unreasonable solution is all you're left with?"

David didn't hear him. Lost in thought he said, "Calm down. Think!" David lay back in his chair relaxing as he let his body ease into the next attempt. He said nothing to the doctor. This daydream remained his.

96

He imagined long, reasonable explanations about GrowVest in Allen's voice broadcast over a microphone accompanied by French accordion music at a green, palm-shaded afternoon luncheon by the pool with friends he didn't recognize. The voice told stories of how valuable David was. The stories were filled with apologies excusing the pain David experienced as necessary.

Waiters roamed by the pool wearing red bow ties and dressed in short, white jackets and black, pleated pants. Their hair was heavily waxed clinging to their heads as if painted in place. Shapely women wore large, broadly-brimmed, white hats with veils shading them from the bright Mediterranean sun and reflections off of the white adobe walls. They drank mint green martinis and dipped strawberries in silver gravy boats filled with liquid white chocolate and honey. Their French accents covered unheard comments made to their large white, long-legged dogs on white leather leashes. All the men were older. They tried to hide their overweight bellies behind broad, tightly fitted, red cummerbunds beneath open, white dinner jackets. Cigar smoke plumes puffed from the tops of their balding heads. They looked important and had hundred dollar bills scattered on the ground beneath their chairs. All the while Allen's voice broadcast over the microphone made excuses for David's pain. Allen was sobbing.

David climbed a high white tower with a diving board. The stainless steel, metal ladder rungs were cold on his feet. He looked down to see a hundred pairs of Wayfarer sunglasses staring up at him from beneath the white table umbrellas. Dressed in a tight, bulging, black Speedo, olive oil glistened over his imaginary tanned, muscular body. He bounced once on the end of the board and dove entering the water without a splash. There was the crushing impact of the water and the sudden rushing wave of cold bathing his body. He rose unnoticed from the deep water and glided to the pool's ladder emerging from the water completely dry dressed in a white dinner jacket with a red carnation in the lapel. His hair was straight, long, and pulled back in a short pony-tail. He walked toward the group and stopped to remove an unnoticed fish from his jacket pocket as if a magic trick. David placed the fish on the silver drink tray of a passing waiter who served it to delighted guests at an adjacent table. Still, David remained unnoticed by the crowd. Then, between moments of self-indulgent laughter, the crowd turned and redirected its attention to him. They listened as Allen's voice mutated to Robert's.

"It's no good. You can't win," Robert said.

The women raised their veils; the men lowered their cigars and in unison, they all recited a pledge that they would help David destroy Robert.

That dream dissolved too. These were great drugs— instigators to self-affirming dreams that had no other purpose than to feed his hatred. He heard the doctor in midsentence. ". . . eventually, I hope, something will make sense," he said.

"Yeah, me too."

The session ended with David realizing that he needed a plan, any detail that he could convert from dream to reality. Meanwhile, the prescription world kept him in a functioning state. Hospital chemistry kept him dreaming night and day. He knew he had to wake up—not just from the dreams that visited him nightly, but from the constricting daytime dreams that detained him from reaching his goal. A need for satisfaction was the chemical that provoked the solution. But, for a short time, he told himself, the plan must be altered. "For the short term," he mumbled while walking back to his room, "I have to loosen the grip my captors possess. For the short term I have to free myself from this drug shit. I have to regain my edge. Before I leave this hospital, I will be on a first name basis with doctors, nurses, patients and the lady that spoons out the apple sauce at lunch time." But this day, David forgot all that and focused on one hate-filled plan. Get out. Get Robert!

CHAPTER 12
Upset, Confused, and Afraid

The Albemarle hospital shifts changed at 8 a.m., 5 p.m., 1 a.m. and again at 8. It was the schedule standard. But the hospital also staggered that schedule with a second schedule for half of the staff—four hours off of those times. It was designed to keep everyone looking fresh and gave the hospital the appearance of being constantly busy. It offered David his chance.

The hospital schedule had a new, recently graduated nurse on the floor. Nurse Lisa was an attractive, naïve, 21-year-old who still wore her class ring. That, David decided, was a sure sign that pride overrode practicality. Her enthusiasm cheered from every pore. Her uniform was whiter than anyone else's. There was so much starch in her blouse that it shined where her proudly erect nipples pressed against it. Her blonde hair was pulled tightly back, tucked beneath the winged cap worn at her nursing school graduation. She was bright, perky and very green.

State regulations demanded that a newbie was always supervised. But a foul-up in the evening schedule had Lisa's supervision showing up at 9 p.m., four hours later than expected. Lisa was a bit flustered at first, but after a visit from Margaret Clay, the harried unit supervisor, Lisa was assured there was little to be concerned about. Margaret blew through the ward hallways, inspecting as she hurried past closed doors. "If you need anything," Margaret said dismissively, "you can call the next ward . . . and get rid of that cap."

Lisa reached for the cap as she tagged behind the rushing supervisor. She began pulling the pins from her hair that anchored it to her head. "We stopped wearing those damned things twenty years ago," Margaret mumbled.

"I thought . . ."

"Yeah, I know. You probably had a doll when you were a kid," Margaret said as she mechanically jiggled door handles while walking past locked rooms. "Well, that's the only place they wear them anymore. There and graduation," she said, her voice fading. "*This* is your graduation. You *work* for a living now." Margaret's voice was louder and echoed off the shiny floor and yellowed hallway walls. "Take the cap and put it in your locker," she told Lisa. "If you feel the need for a reminder why you chose this profession, you can go stare at it on your break."

Supervisor Clay had been at her job for nearly thirty years. Lisa's confusion reminded her of her own insecurities when she first arrived at the hospital. Back then, things were somewhat different. Then, the population on her ward included lobotomized zombies wandering aimlessly and Margaret was the sheep dog that barked at their heels to keep them in line. With her hair turned white, Margaret had learned every in-and-out the job could throw at her. Now, Supervisor Clay was a short-timer ready to retire and took the survival "sink-or-swim" attitude with Nurse Lisa. It was all she had the energy to do.

After throwing a departing wave over her shoulder toward the uncomforted nurse-ling, Clay left Lisa to put out more administrative fires somewhere else. "There are several clients leaving AMA," she said. Against Medical Advice was a privilege reserved for the self-committed. "There are a few more," Margaret said, "We'll throw them away like an undersized cod fish on a good day of fishing. Oh, and one more thing," Margaret stopped walking and turned to Lisa as she stumbled to a stop in front of the supervisor. "Do not," she said, "let them see you are upset, confused, afraid, or any other thing you can think of that will give them the upper hand. Retain control at all times," she said pointing a finger between Lisa's breasts. "Got it?" Lisa nodded slowly and said nothing. The supervisor dropped her hand. She looked at Lisa and said, "So young," then shook her head and turned. The squeaking noises of Margaret Clay's rippled soles faded outside the ward entry as she was consumed by the intersecting rush of laundry and food carts, coded intercom announcements and wandering clients.

David watched the two nurses walk down the long empty hall from his soft corner chair in the day room. The television sounds were white noise. Big Norman had the remote control and a very short attention span. Bigger than any two other people, Norman controlled the remote as soon as he entered the room. When fully staffed, someone was assigned "Big Norman duty." The first order of business was to rescue the television. But personnel were spread thinly tonight so Big Norman simply added to the growing chaos as he flipped through the channels finding the salt and pepper flicker of non-stations as entertaining as any other offering.

Opportunities for creative thoughts in the hospital were few, for patients or staff. There was little doubt that the stage just set was the confusing opportunity David required. He had to move immediately to take advantage of the moment. Nurse Lisa didn't know anything about David. She didn't know why he was there or where he wanted to be. She could find out but David's intention was to give her information that discouraged her curiosity. He would be conspicuous and get close to her. Maybe engage her in a conversation that would last long enough to allow the rest of the nuts to get out of hand and distract her. David could slip out of the

101

ward. He knew there was a long walk before he could be outside. The long walk made it a long shot that he could escape without being seen.

There was a city bus stop not far from the hospital—a block, maybe two. David hadn't seen it but visitors mentioned it. The bus was the easiest transportation. And there was no problem moving from one ward to the next when things were busy. Making it to the hospital's exit door meant blending in with the departing visitors. A change in hospital policy had most of the clients wearing street clothes by mid-day. This was his best chance to leave. David decided to take it.

"That's it? That is the best escape plan you can come up with?" David was whispering to himself as a wave of uncertainty came over him. "Nearly eight months in this place," he said softly with a disgusted dismissal of his ability, "and the best you can imagine is to walk out of the ward and wander the halls until you can make a line-drive move for the door?" David looked around the room seeing men playing checkers. Others were talking softly to equally disinterested counterparts or themselves. He stopped his wandering glance on Big Norman sitting in a small wooden chair less than six feet from the 50 inch TV screen as the channels floated past him.

"This may be my only chance," David said. "It has to work."

Hurriedly walking back to his room, he grabbed what little cash he had—a couple of quarters a dime and two singles, $2.60. It was enough for the bus and a request for a song from a street musician. "No one said this was easy," he said. He stuffed the cash in his pocket and hurried back to the dayroom. Lisa was wandering through the dayroom like a child rummaging across a country meadow looking for four-leaf clovers. From the lost look on her face, it was a safe bet against her having discovered anything. The accumulating disappointments were beginning to color her view of her newly chosen profession.

David walked toward her. "Hi, you're new here, aren't you?" Lisa was startled, at first. Her hand went to her mouth and quickly changed to brushing her hair from her forehead. She tried to regain some of her authority. "Retain control at all times," she heard Margaret Clay echoing in her head.

Nurse Lisa was a sweet and attractive creature — as fresh as the white tiles of the ward's communal bathroom after a good hosing. It wasn't hard for David to get her talking. "I came to the hospital because I'm interested in continuing my studies," she said nodding then added, "to become a psychologist."

David had already dismissed her story as a load of crap even before she spewed it on the floor for analysis. She saw herself selflessly helping the poor, confused clients. "Mommy and daddy must have been paying the school bills," David mumbled. But David remained plastically sympathetic as she recited her recent past and future plans. "Well, congratulations on your new position. I don't think you can underestimate the importance of what you do." David was laying the butter on thick and she was sliding her pretty tongue across the bread loving every millimeter of praise. She smiled and drifted into a self-congratulatory daydream for a moment while twisting her class ring on her finger.

"Tell me something about yourself," Lisa said.

David thought it must be time to practice the *twenty questions a good psychologist asks her patients.* "That's a graduate level class," he muttered. "Maybe she'll tell me I have lockjaw or something equally interesting." David decided to play. "Me? Oh, well, I've been here for a while after suffering from extreme pressure and subsequent confusion," he told her. That was true.

"A rest," she said excusing him, her big brown eyes filling with attempted understanding. "That's all you needed, then?"

"Yep, absolutely," David told her with a cheery smile. "I expect to be rejoining my family sometime this week," That, of course, was not true. Then, as a way of reassuring her, he said, "If there's anything you need to make your adjustment easier, just let me know."

Lisa tipped her head as if ready to ask a question. David answered it before she was able to ask. "Lisa," David called her by first name to encourage her trust and make her feel more at ease, "I'm very familiar with the clients and the schedules here and where most everything is kept," he explained. "For instance, stay clear of Ben, over there," he said, "until there's another man on the floor to help. He tends to be violent around women." Another lie. Ben was usually too spaced out on drugs to stay awake and his placid stare in their direction was through them, not at Lisa. But it was a way to add a little more confusion to the moment and David gladly dispensed it. As a result, sweet Lisa was clearly concerned as she watched Ben eye her from his chair in front of the large barred window in the corner.

"But if you're worried, I'm here." David smiled and patted her shoulder. "He listens to me. If I weren't here on my own business," he said, "I'd probably have your job."

Nurse Lisa looked at David as if she thought he was serious, not really certain if David was kidding or suffering from a delusion about wanting to be the ward nurse. A quick smile and a chuckle was all it took. Lisa returned the grin with an embarrassed giggle of her own. She was uneasy. A sense of panic was growing in her. She had to make a move before giving her emotions away. "I have to make a quick check of the population," she said. "Would you excuse me?"

"Of course," David assured her. A nod, a smile, and she was on her way. David was again talking softly to himself as Lisa walked on studying her clipboard. "Just head on out of here, Lisa and into everyone's rooms making sure no one's climbed through a barred window or swallowed someone's shoes. I'll just wait a moment and then walk right through these doors and into the hall."

Lisa was busy with the rounds for at least 20 minutes. It would take a while before she realized she never checked David's name off of her list. With any luck the error wouldn't be discovered for another two hours when she did the rounds again.

It was about 6:15. Visiting hours should have wrapped an hour ago but there were still family members wandering toward the exits. Here was David's chance. Maybe his last. He picked a group with at least two families. Neither group was certain which family David was with. His constant smiles and pleasant jabber put them all at ease as they headed for the door. David squeezed in closer to one of the families—Elmer and Louise. They were visiting Louise's father. He was a permanent resident who believed he was Napoleon or MacArthur or Judy Garland. David wasn't listening very closely. The escape had most of his attention and blood flow. David looked at Elmer. Bald and lanky with a pleasant smile, his oversized ears looked like they needed little encouragement to begin flapping like his namesake's, Mr. Fudd. Elmer looked confidant as he held Louise's hand—a kind of "salt-of-the-earth" serenity.

David nervously scanned the halls for any sign of charging men in white coats coming for him as he listened to Elmer's explanation of how he rebuilt a two-cycle engine for his brother-in-law. Each of Elmer's sentences ended with a question-like rising inflection so, David kept his head moving like an affirming bobble doll. That was all it took to keep Elmer's attention and make David look like part of the group. David's new friends easily bought his story about being a hospital visitor.

The middle-aged rent-a-cop seated by the door made a quick glance at all of them and then reentered the world created by his tattered copy of *People*. There was the sound of the automatic doors gushing open and the rush of fresh air that hit David's face as his legs reacted with a rubbery stumble. David was careful not to look

105

too hurried as he walked with the families toward the parking garage though his impulse was to run. Once inside the garage, David said goodbye to his security blankets, Elmer and Louise, and hurriedly walked straight through to the street. Now, with the garage between him and the hospital, David began to relax until he suddenly realized he didn't know which way to turn. An ancient, blue, two-door Chevy pulled up beside him. It was Elmer and Louise. The quizzical look on Elmer's face sent a jolt through David. Had Elmer figured it out? Standing there lost on the street did David suddenly look like he belonged under wraps? Panic was welling up inside David's throat. He was standing there like a lost patient. Five-hundred steps from the front door and he was lost. "Think," he mumbled. "I can't blow my cover." Alternatives mixed with panic flooded his brain. Should he run and confirm their suspicion or wait for them to tell him the staff was on its way? But now Elmer was rolling down his window while David stood there like an idiot and the old Chevy sputtered out puffs of white smoke from the tail pipe.

"Hey, somebody leave you without a ride?"

"What?" Oh, how perfect! David wanted to kiss old Elmer. "Now, think quickly," he told himself. Then, loudly, "Yeah, my son was supposed to be here to pick me up," David stammered. "But I was running a little late." David let his voice trail off as he looked down the street as if expecting a car, then, turned back to Elmer, "Maybe he figured I got a ride or something."

"Well, we've got room here. Can I drop you off somewhere?" Elmer—a gift from God. David was ecstatic. "This is great," he said "I really appreciate this." David jogged toward the back of the car making his way through the tail pipe's clouds of oil-soaked smoke to the passenger side. "Maybe I'll name my first child after you. Most likely not," he said softly as Louise opened the door and slid forward to allow David room to squeeze into the back seat. "What was that? We couldn't hear you."

"Oh, I was just saying first born, you know, we tend to be harder on them than the others."

"That's the truth," Louise said as David settled in behind her.

David sank low into the seat safely hidden from hospital view. Elmer once again explained that he was a mechanic. "I got this car in a trade for services," he told David with pride. "Eighteen miles per gallon. That's pretty good for a car this old," he said.

Somewhere between Elmer's explanation of the miles-per-gallon and Louise's professed love of Jesus, ("He's always with us, you know."), they arrived at a McDonald's by the interstate. Elmer navigated the land yacht through the narrow drive-through lanes. "How 'bout we buy you dinner?" Elmer said as he pulled up to the menu board. Louise turned toward David with a big smile.

"Well, I appreciate that very much," David said realizing his two dollars weren't going to get him very far without a little help.

As the car filled with the odor of cheeseburgers and hydrogenated oil, Elmer found a spot in the parking lot and pulled in. Assuming he was safer hiding in the car than wandering the parking lot, David remained in Elmer's back seat. There was no way of knowing how soon it was before the hospital staff figured that David left the building.

It was nearly dark when Elmer said, "Well, is this gonna be all right for you if we drop you here?" David hurriedly stuffed the last of his fries into his mouth and washed it down with the rest of a root beer, then crammed a pair of cheeseburgers into his jacket pocket. "Yeah, sure. I live a few miles from here. I'm supposed to meet my son here by 7:30, if we didn't connect at the hospital," David explained while he squeezed between Louise's seat and the open door. "Thanks again for the ride and dinner," he said waving goodbye to Elmer, Louise and Jesus. David toasted them with the ice remaining in the paper cup as he backed into the shadow of a landscaped tree.

"He is certainly a nice man," Louise told Elmer. "Good man," Elmer agreed. "Knows a lot about cars too."

It worked. David was out and alone. "Just an interstate artery away from Robert," David said. The chances were good that the hospital and Lisa knew he was gone by now. True or not, David had to believe it. Chances were too, that they figured he was heading home. "I can't call anyone, visit anyone, or be conspicuous in any way."

CHAPTER 13
Thanks, Ralph

Ward Supervisor Margaret Clay was on the phone frantically alerting the guards at each exit to look for David. A string of curses followed every response to questions from the phone's other end. "Look at your fucking computer screen," Margaret screamed. "His face is the one staring back at you, for Chrissake."

Standing in front of her, nervously twisting the class ring on her finger, Nurse Lisa stood with tear-stained cheeks. "It's my fault. I know it's all my fault," she whined. Her tightly pinned hair was loosened on one side sending curls cascading to her shoulders. Margaret barked a few more directions into the phone to one more outpost before returning to her frail charge. Margaret knew there was hell to pay. "Yeah, well, I expected too much from you," she generously told the newbie, when she knew the real reason was that she didn't care enough to be cautious. Margaret was tired and this was one more bit of bullshit.

"Never, never listen to these bastards," she sternly reminded Lisa. "They're fucking nuts, for Chrissake!"

Lisa's sobbing stopped as she looked wide-eyed at Margaret. "There just sick," Lisa softly corrected a bristling Margaret.

"Sick, my ass!" Supervisor Clay realized things were out of her control. There was nothing she could do. She turned from Lisa and walked toward the ward exit. Without looking back she shouted, "If you can keep track of these animals for ten more minutes, I'll have some extra orderlies sent in until the next nurse joins you on duty. Pull it together, dear," she barked with mock concern. "If they sense fear, they'll eat you alive and right about now, I'd say they're planning the hors d'oeuvres." The comment startled Lisa. She began fixing her hair and turned to count the inmates for the seventh time in five minutes while measuring distances between herself and the nearest banquet attendee.

"Hard lessons are the best kind," Margaret shouted. Then mumbled to herself, "The hardest ones come late in life strong enough to crush you." Margaret was still hoping the mutilated schedule would carry enough of the blame to help her retain her impending retirement pension.

David spent the next twenty minutes wandering through the McDonald's parking lot shadows hoping to pick up some transportation. Once he decided that truckers were his best bet for a ride, David approached a promising candidate as he walked out of the restaurant carrying a bag of burgers and munching on an apple pie. It looked as if the trucker's twisted, felt cowboy hat was sat on more than once. He was wearing jeans with an enormous, rectangular Texas longhorn silver belt buckle with "Jake" scrawled across the steer. There were colorful enameled pins advertising every state he had driven across randomly stuck through a fringed, thin, black leather vest. Beneath the vest a red shirt did its best to cover an expansive belly. Insurance, supplied by two Velcro tabs, promised a connection across an impossible four inch gap that otherwise prevented the vest's closing. The back of the vest sported a hand-painted mural of a fire-spewing 18-wheeler crushing a bright yellow school bus. "Killer" was etched on the truck's side. Despite the driver's intimidating size and the artwork's declaration, David decided to ask for the ride. At least, he told himself, he knew the big guy wasn't hungry any more.

Being careful not to startle him, David came up from behind and once instep alongside the man cautiously made his pitch. "I need to get to Arcadia," David told him.

The trucker stopped and turned toward David. Expecting a deep, hoarse voice with a western drawl, David was amused to hear the reply in a surprisingly high voice and heavy New England accent. "That's 'bout 200 miles nawth of heeya and well past Richmon'," Jake squeaked.

"Any chance I can bum a ride?"

After twenty minutes on the road listening to Jake's overstuffed mouth choke out too many country songs, David knew he was closer to his real goal, David interrupted Jake's burger binge. "Oh shit," he said, "I have to go back." The trucker gave David a startled look. "What's wrong?"

"I think I left my wallet back there." David was feverishly fishing through his pockets feeling them all repeatedly then searching on the truck's floor. "Oh SHIT!" David stopped searching and looked up at Jake who returned an annoyed glance toward David. Jake popped the burger between his teeth using his mouth like a third hand while he flipped the signal once more to the right and began downshifting the overweight vehicle. The air brakes hissed then belched out a gush of air. Horns of passing cars blared warnings to the slowing 18-wheeler as it rolled to a stop. David flung open the passenger door. "I'm sorry man, but thanks for the ride," he said as he climbed from the truck's cab. Jake said nothing still grasping the dangling burger between his lips. He looked at David then disappeared behind the closing door. Another gasp of the brakes and the truck shifted through its first few gears while merging with the traffic and the renewed horn blasts from oncoming traffic.

Only a mile from his exit David knew he could slip into the woods and work his way home. He had to be careful. David was walking the roadside with the traffic at his back. The noise from the oncoming cars mixed with the occasional car horn competed with David's thoughts. He began speaking out loud, yelling at the cars as they passed him. "Home is the first place they'll stake out," he shouted. "Just the same, I doubt there is more than one cruiser in the neighborhood." David kicked a piece of roadside retread. "My escape has to be a fairly low priority," he said hopefully as another car blew past. "Hey, you son-of-a-bitch." Head down he continued past the sweeping aluminum guide rail and onto the grass fringe that sloped toward the woods. "Once inside the house, I can hit the safe for the extra ATM card and the little cash that's there," he said. There was no need to shout any longer. The interstate hum was absorbed by the trees as he weaved into the woods. "That's the plan." No more talking. The faint traffic hum was replaced by the snapping of twigs beneath his feet. David stopped walking, looked up at the stars and smiled. "Clear night," he said. Pushing through the undergrowth, David remembered that the safe also held the gun—a Smith & Wesson, .38-caliber, snub-nosed, "Chief's Special" he owned for years and never fired. David began chuckling to himself. He still hadn't decided how to kill Robert. The gun was his best resource, but would probably be his last resort.

When David got to the house, it was still locked tight. He remembered that the back window by the porch was always unlocked. It was painted shut years ago. David grabbed an old screwdriver he kept outside by the pool pump. It was stuck handle-deep into the ground disguised by the proliferation of weeds that had taken over the yard. A little convincing from the rusty screwdriver's blade beneath the window and it squeaked softly open—enough for him to wedge a hand beneath it. He lifted the window and squeezed his body through the narrow opening flopping to the porch floor.

Though it was dark outside, it was considerably darker inside. David crawled to his feet and smelled a garbage-like odor coming from the kitchen a few feet ahead. He could see through the shadows that a few dishes were still in the kitchen sink. He turned to walk toward the front hallway pawing his way in near-total darkness. In an instant, David slammed his left foot into a kitchen chair and tumbled forward taking the wooden chair with him. There was a loud thud as David hit the floor followed by the snapping sounds of the chair runners breaking and the final crack of the chair back separating from the seat then slamming against the wall. For a long moment David lay still with his legs intertwined with pieces of the old chair. He could feel the throbbing in his foot and the bruise on his left leg but was more concerned that the sound of his fall mixed with the cracking of the wooden chair might bring a curious neighbor to investigate. David got up with the aid of the hallway wall and encouragement from his four-letter vocabulary and gently moved pieces of the chair from his way. "No more fucking noise," he whispered. He knew he couldn't turn any lights on as he limped down the hallway to the front entry where he saw the street lights casting shadows through the glass surrounding the front door. The blood on the cherry wood floor convinced him that no one had been in the house since the day it was invaded. An old electric bill in a bright red envelope resting on top of the cascading pile of letters near the front door's mail slot was a warning that the power was about to be shut off for non-payment.

"Ah yes, *eau de* rotten fridge. That explains that mystery."

David made his way to the bedroom and the closet safe. He rummaged through sweaters on the closet's top shelf for the emergency flashlight that he knew was there. He shook it several times before he saw a faint glow like the dyeing embers of a campfire. It was enough to identify the safe's dial. A right, left, and right turn opened the door as the light finally died. Fumbling through the safe's contents, he located a wad of cash wrapped in an elastic band, a few credit cards and the pistol. The pistol was never loaded and without ammunition was of little value except as a threat. He tucked it into his belt and decided to leave the ATM and credit cards. Their use would leave a trail for Robert to follow.

After collecting all he needed, David decided to spend the night in his own bed. First, he checked to see if there was still water. There was and even though it was no warmer than a puddle he might have chosen in the park—it was clean.

Drying off after the quick shower, David heard a loud conversation outside. There were two, maybe three, men and the red flashing lights of a police cruiser. "One of the neighbors said something about a noise that came from inside the house," David heard one of the voices say. It must have been the chair and toe incident or the muffled scream and adjacent swearing that accompanied the chair's relocation. The cops assured the neighbor that they would search the outside for any signs of entry.

Grabbing his clothes and shoes, David cautiously crawled downstairs forgetting the .38. No matter. For the moment his attention was focused on where to go. He decided that if the cops were going to come in, he would have to make a break through whatever exit was available. David considered leaving through the cellar and then realized, "Oh shit! The back window is still open. That'll be the only reason the cops need to enter the house."

David rushed to the back door avoiding the dismantled kitchen chair as the light from the cop's flashlight rounded the house into the back yard. The cop yelled something to his partner but the muffled message made no sense to David. Crouching as low as he could beneath the window, David reached up; grabbed the window bottom, and tried to pull it shut but the paint that had sealed it so completely for so many years, wasn't ready to give up its new position.

The cops were at the side of the house but getting closer. "Hey, check this out. I think I got a footprint," one cop said shining his light into the flower bed.

"Oooo, great clue!" the second cop sarcastically told his partner as he came closer. "And if you shine your light just right, you can see Mickey sucking on a Fudgsicle. Gee, I hope that's a Fudgsicle." he said moving his light back-and-forth over the garden dirt.

"Mickey? What the fuck are you . . ."

"Yeah Mickey Mouse. Can't you see? Right there are the ears. . ."

"Shut the fuck up."

The distraction gave David the time to stand up and force the window down with a thud loud enough that both cops should have come running. But they were too busy to hear much other than each other. David figured the next move was his and it had to be quick. He eased open the door and with most of his clothes and shoes in his arms, quietly walked outside shutting the door behind and gently pulling it until he heard the lock engage. As David turned to run for the woods bordering the back yard, he came face-to-face with Ralph, the neighbor's brown and white Brittany spaniel. Ralph and David were good buddies once. But Ralph hadn't seen David in a while and had never seen him naked with his hair so long. To Ralph's credit and David's luck, he seldom barked. David knew he couldn't say anything—not even a whisper. Toody and Muldoon were just around the corner analyzing another creative swirl in the dirt. David bent over slowly toward the dog. It was the trigger for Ralph. Suddenly, the dog's entire ass-end was wagging and a soft whine of recognition for his old friend was coming from inside the pooch. Ralph often showed up late at night to leave presents that the next morning David would shovel up and fling back into Ralph's yard for his owner to step in. But six months of non-flung returns had turned

115

David's back yard into a mine field. Any soldier stupid enough to risk it was bound to be destroyed numerous times before crossing the yard.

Patting the dog on the head and sides, David made a quick break for the woods feeling a mixture of crust and mush pushing up between the toes of his bare feet. Ralph was slower to follow and as the cops came in the back yard, one of them saw enough of Ralph to decide he saw someone. Both cops rushed after the dog until Ralph turned in the long grass and began growling in their direction. Both men turned in panic. Ralph took the cue and chased the cops back in the direction of their cruiser. At least, that was the idea. The retreating men in blue hadn't counted on the yard mines. Both men slipped and fell. They quickly got to their feet to resume the retreat only to slip again.

David's way out was easier now. The brown-stained cop's report concluded that the neighbor simply heard or saw a neighbors pet.

CHAPTER 14

That's Brewkowski with an I

Clear of the neighborhood and on the run again, David needed an identity. Making up a name wouldn't work. If he tried to interact with any part of society, there would come a time when a license or social security card had to be produced. The thought ate away at him for several days. Unless the problem was solved, he knew hiding would become his way of life. Being permanently lost would prevent him from ever getting back. In the end, it meant Robert won.

David's immediate choice was limited to living in the woods at camps on the edge of reality and the rest of society. He was never the first wherever he stayed. This wasn't like a Holiday Inn and nobody ever left the lights on for him. He was wandering, just trying to survive. The camps were hidden along the borders of malls and grocery store parking lots. They were the outparcels covered with bushes, brush and small trees. These were refuse-lined earthen chunks too small for realty development but just right for the creation of a small social fringe. Once David learned to recognize the lightly trodden walkways and bent, overgrown grasses as paths into the woods, he saw there was refuge. There was an entire community of unnoticed lost souls wandering through these camps. They roamed in and out of the sight of the "haves." To call them

117

"have-nots" was to fail to recognize them for whom and what they were. These were self-proclaimed rejects refusing reality. They chose to be isolated by time and social position. What they *have* was a unique independence. What they *have-not* might include themselves.

Too many preferred solitary conversations—not much different from Albemarle. People were what they rejected. In fact, David seldom saw more than three of them together at a time without a fight breaking out. These were social misfits with a fine edge that kept them teetering on the fence. A fall to one side immersed them in violence; a fall to the other side encased them in a world where the body left the mind behind. Whenever the violence began, David followed the consensus advice and took it as a cue to move on.

Like those lost souls, David was playing the same game—rejecting people. Sitting on a log beside a small campfire in the bushes near a shopping mall, he wondered if the occasional audible thought was the next step in a walk toward permanently solo conversation. Was he getting too close to this side-step of his problems?

"I have to remind myself of my purpose," he said reassuring himself. "I'm hiding, not escaping reality. Still, I have to keep my identity to myself. I need to stay below the radar. These people are so far below the radar that no one will look for me here," he said waving an arm to show the entire camp to his fictitious audience. "I also know I have to remain unseen and hide the other part of my world from them. I have to be unnoticed. I have to be one of them." From then on, David kept his money hidden and subsisted on what he found.

Over several weeks David ran into one particular soul. The man never told David his name. He seldom looked up at David's face to acknowledge his presence. He spoke to himself in low mumbles. The man was gentle, almost sheepish and covered in

118

layers of filthy clothing with a face so completely hidden by beard, hair, and a fraying, black, knitted hat, that his eyes were rarely visible. Like so many of the others in his community, the sheep dog was in his own world and preferred not to share it.

On an evening when the chill couldn't be lost, sitting beside the man's fire, David began talking. He realized the conversation was one sided, still David needed to direct the words toward his silent partner. The speech was simple. David knew the questions deserved answers but an answer was something he couldn't expect. After several minutes of his one-sided ramblings, David said, "I'm gonna call you Mike, if that's all right with you. I think you look like a Mike, if there is such a thing." After that, whenever David spoke to him, Mike responded with a jerk of the head or wave of the hand. David began to believe that was his real name.

After a few intermittent and thoroughly accidental days in Mike's presence, David decided to change things and make his presence intentional. "After all, you know where to go and how to survive," he told Mike. "And you don't seem to mind my being near." He became David's survival guide. When following his mentor at night through the dumpsters and behind the bakeries and grocery stores looking for food and the occasionally needed slab of fresh cardboard, David kept several feet back. Though Mike never said a word, getting too close might elicit the same growls they encountered from the stray cats and dogs that competed for the same discarded bits of garbage.

Each night the procedure was repeated like going to an open market. After a night of hunting, they dragged the food and cardboard back to the nearby woods where the food was sorted. The more likely bits were tossed into a pot of boiling water or wrapped in newspaper and pushed into a plastic bag for safekeeping. The less edible portions were tossed into the adjacent field. Mike usually said a few unintelligible words after each sacrificial toss. David assumed the words were something ritualistic. It may have been part of

119

Mike's religion, a way of thanking the only holy man Mike had come to trust—Saint Refuse. Later, sitting across from Mike near the campfire, David watched as Mike eagerly deposited the day's collection of vegetables and discarded luncheon meat into a pot of boiling water. "You know," David said, "I find it hard to believe that we eat as well as we do. I'm beginning to acquire a fondness for stale bread and overripe fruit." David chuckled and looked up to see if there was any reaction from Mike who said nothing and kept stirring the mixture. "Give you 150 pounds of flesh and a bath and you might be mistaken for some famous bearded chef," David tried once more for recognition. His voice faded into the darkness, ". . . or not."

Though camp fires were common, they were low-heat affairs. Intended to warm some food or heat some water, they seldom got very big. Camp fires large enough to dry rain-soaked clothes were a rare treat. They burned hot for the first few minutes to keep smoke from revealing the camper's position to outsiders. Then, the embers were fed sparingly—just enough to keep the heat available without a noticeable glow from more than a few feet away.

After dinner there were house chores that must be considered. Mike analyzed a collected piece of cardboard for size and strength. "I think I see what you're doing there," David mumbled. "You like the larger, stronger pieces. They make better replacement walls for the house." David watched the procedure Mike followed. "Yeah. After three days that wall looks a bit weathered."

David spent several days in Mike's company. He spoke to Mike as though he expected a reply but knew an audible one wouldn't come. Just the same, Mike's decisions seemed conversational. When David explained the next move of a task to Mike, Mike would make the move without acknowledging David's contribution. It didn't matter. David sensed the words Mike should have said. David believed Mike's moves were the accepted response. They became like an old married couple.

"That wall is looking kinda swollen and weak. They're bowing in," David said contributing his mumbling as half of a required conversation. 'It'd be a good idea to prop it up," he said. "It might fall during the night or sooner if the wind decides to push it." Mike grabbed a sturdy chunk of a "Charmin" box and slid it into place without removing the faulty wall that became a peeling outer skin. Mike stood back for a moment as if admiring a layer of paint he had applied to his home.

Both men roughed up smaller pieces of cardboard; folded it or tore it to reveal the undulating corrugations under the covering surface. These became bedding material. The rougher surface prevented sliding off the cardboard bed at night acting as insulation against the cold ground.

It took David days to adjust to Mike's stench. Really, it took that long for David to catch up to Mike's level of filth. There was no sharing odors. One warded off the other like a defensive mixing of reeking atmospheres. There was no regular bathing or changing of clothes. In this society, "clean" was a word reserved for referencing a man's personal life—as in drug activity or his police record. Most of their momentary camp visitors were clean and filthy. The rare baths, if unavoidable, were at night in rubbish-strewn urban streams of questionable purity where broken bottles, tires, overturned shopping carts and bicycle frames were more common than fish. Mike was as low on the sanitation totem pole as he could get without qualifying as a pile of shit. The filth that caked onto Mike's body gave him a head start on his ultimate ground-dwelling position.

"You know, Mike," David told him one evening as they pawed through a dumpster behind a Pizza Hut, "I have little doubt, Mike, that you will be found in one of these dumpsters someday." Mike grabbed a crust from a discarded pizza box chewing on it while he folded the box and tossed it into the collection pile. "Your filthy, stiffened, cold body will be served up on a used piece of retrieved cardboard," David said while he searched through the trash bin hoping to find his own treasure box of stale crusts. "And I'll probably be the one to find you."

Two days later, David's prophesy came true. Mike was in the habit of falling asleep each night just before sunset and, like the raccoons he chased from the dumpsters, he did his picking later at night. But tonight, Mike wasn't moving. After several hours of waiting, David overcame his fear and decided to wake him. Mike stank. Mike always had a uniquely offensive odor. But now, Mike clearly missed an appointment with the trees and fowled himself in the process. His final bed was soaked with urine. The mud from his body pooled beside him blocking the printed letters on the flattened cardboard. The blue letters of "Kleen" and "oom Tissue" were all David could see in the campfire embers' low light.

He pushed Mike gently with his foot. Then again, harder. Each time David called out to him. Mike was dead. In all the kindness David could collect, he concluded this was a good thing. Mike's corpse laying on the cardboard was unrecognizable as human. The amorphous shape was wrapped in gray and brown rags. Mike's hands were softly clenched; his arms were pulled in toward his chest. David stared at him and wondered what to do. "If I leave, as fast as I can," he told the pile of rags softly, "it may take days or longer before anyone discovers you." David silently stared without seeing anything. There was defeat in the way he stood over the body—a genuine sorrow came over him. "If I leave you like this, the raccoons will find you and take from you some of what you took from them each night. Your competitors will have won the final victory." There were lines of muddy tears on David's face. "I think you deserve more than to become a chew toy for raccoons." Standing over him in the dim light, David realized his fear of Mike's corpse was greater than when he was alive. "I have to bury you. I have to be quick while it remains dark," he told the body. "I have to bury you deeply enough that I don't fear you'll be found anytime soon. They can't tie me to your death," he said grabbing the corner of Mike's cardboard bed. "Deep means I'll have enough time to evaporate before your body's found. They may call me nuts," David whispered, "but I'm not going to be called a murderer too. Not yet."

David managed a hole in the field that separated the woods from the neighboring shopping mall. In the darkness and between security police patrolling the stores' rear side, he carved out something deep enough to cover Mike with a foot or two of dirt. With only an old aluminum cooking pan, it took several sweat-filled hours to complete the grave. When finished, he dragged Mike to the hole on his cardboard sled, picked up the cardboard edge and rolled him in. David scraped in the excavated dirt and covered Mike and the rest of the hole. As a final thought, David placed Mike's cardboard bed over the grave. He figured the urine-soaked panel might repel curious animals and any kids that wandered through the field. It would furnish David time to leave all this behind.

Near dawn, as the light crept above the horizon and through the camp's surrounding bushes, David began rummaging through Mike's plastic garbage bags. Mike carried two, replenishing their torn presence whenever the opportunity arose. Both bags smelled of Mike, that unavoidable stench of garbage, urine and campfire dirt. The first bag had nothing David needed—some rags and a few, aluminum, Coke cans. But, in the bottom of the second bag was a wad of newspaper wrapped around something. The outer side of the package was rough. The paper was worn and torn and appeared to be a rat's nest in the way it fluffed around the corners of the object it protected. David stripped off the outer layers and found the paper was tighter, more carefully folded as he got closer to the packaged contents. The excitement was growing. Carefully unwrapping the package deteriorated to impatience as the layers of paper fell to the ground. He ripped off the final bits and found a wallet and a small framed picture of a young man and woman. David turned the frame over and saw "Happy Birthday, all my love, Cheryl" written in blue ink. He didn't recognize the guy but expected it must have been

Mike. David pulled the wallet open. There was no cash. There was a driver's license from Wisconsin. The license had a picture of the same guy as the one in the picture with Cheryl. The name was Brewkowski. Wayne Brewkowski. "Mike was a Wayne or a "ski." At least in this package he was," David said. But in the same way Wayne wrapped that identity, he wrapped the memories of who he was. In that way, Wayne became whatever others wanted him to be. It didn't matter. To himself, he existed—nothing more. More than likely, this death was what he was seeking. Wayne died years before. Last night was Mike's turn. For a very brief moment David considered finding Mike's Cheryl, to let her know of Wayne's death. Then he realized that, if Cheryl was still alive, she buried Wayne years before. "Any memories of their love left this earth last night when Mike died," David told himself

David tossed the picture and empty wallet onto the glowing embers of the campfire and watched as the photograph heated, became discolored, and burst into a small flame. In the light of the flame David looked once more at the license. The date on the license said that Wayne was roaming parking lots and their adjacent wooded sanctuaries for six years and more than 600 miles. He pawed through the small stack of wallet papers. There was nothing else except a social security card. "Whoa, wait a minute! Bingo! A freakin' social security card!" This was the golden ticket. Mike left David his key to the outside world. "Thank you Mike or Wayne . . . whatever!"

Wayne was reborn. This Wayne had different baggage to carry and a desire to live—and bathe! This Wayne had a driving purpose and had just been given a chance to resurrect a fading goal! David stuffed the card and license into his ragged jeans and headed for the open road as Wayne Brewkowski.

CHAPTER 15
A Very Long Time

The sign in the front passenger window of the lime green, 1970 Plymouth Duster said "low mileage." That wasn't possible considering the rust that consumed most of the rocker panels and a good portion of the chrome area on the left side of the front bumper. But for five-hundred bucks, this was David's ticket away from any threat that might still be wandering behind him. With the money he was able to rescue from the home safe, David convinced the high school senior that two-fifty was the key to his prom plans. The kid agreed and Wayne Brewkowski was one pink slip happier and on his way.

A week later, David was tired of driving and found himself somewhere north, just east of the Rockies. A couple of days off the highway were fine, he figured. The beard he shaved off after acquiring his new identity was showing signs of resurrection. He needed a shower and some time to consider if he was wandering or had a point to all of this. If he hopped into the Duster to earn some time to think, maybe the time had arrived.

David pulled off at the next exit that promised a place to sleep. The motel's nearly empty parking lot was for truckers. Early

125

afternoon heat waves bounced off the wide expanse of softened tar creating distorted images of the local lifeless scenery.

"Motel needs a good painting," David muttered.

A small white rectangular sign hung down from the soffit at one end of the building with an arrow and "OFFICE" blocked in black paint pointing to a compact, well-lighted, room enclosed in glass. An electronic bell chanted David's arrival as he opened the glass door.

The shaved head of a high school teenager popped up from behind the counter leaving his chair and heavily read copy of Hustler magazine. He leaned against the front desk with his sleeves rolled up on his dark blue t-shirt. There was a silk-screened message fading across the shirt's front that shouted something about a two-year-old local music festival.

"Yes sir, how can I help?"

"Just a single," David said as he dug into his jeans for the cash.

"How many nights?" The clerk wrote something in a ledger and then moved to a drawer for the room key.

"Just the one."

Some more ledger writing and then . . . "All right, sign here." He turned the ledger and pushed it in David's direction. David began signing his own name and then caught himself after the first letter. "Uh, I think . . . this pen isn't working. Got another?" As the clerk reached beneath the counter, David scribbled over the "D" he had begun. "Oh, maybe this one is all right. Must have skipped," David told him. Looking at the ledger, the disinterested teen shrugged. David started again, this time writing his new name with confidence.

"Mr. Brekopski," the boy stumbled over the scratching.

"Brewkowski," David said as he turned the ledger toward the clerk. "Wayne Brewkowski."

"Yeah, right. Well, it's twenty-seven dollars and three dollars for the key deposit." Tossing the key onto the desk as he reached for the ledger, the clerk looked up at David with a half-smile.

David handed the cash to the kid, took the key and walked toward the door. As the door slowly closed behind him, David heard him say, "Bar next door's the 'Watering Hole.' It's got some great food, if you're hungry."

Outside, David stopped for a minute trying to take in where he was. He had forgotten to ask. Somehow it didn't matter. He could see he was in the middle of somewhere, going somewhere else. And all this was just temporary. Just the same, David looked around hoping to gain some bearings. Most of the plates said Colorado. There were a few from Montana and one from Alabama. "God loves the interstate," was scrawled in the dirt covering the side of a red Peterbilt cabover chugging next to a metallic blue Kenworth with an equally prominent dirt message of "Fuck this job." A dusty decal slapped to both truck bumpers declared the drivers were "Trucking for Jesus."

"Time to head toward the bar," he told himself. "The next several hours," he said, smiling, "will be an attempt to get lost in a place I know nothing about and my only concern is the amount of Scotch I use to get there." He stuck his hands in his pocket and casually walked toward the Watering Hole sign.

The "Hole" had the sweet smell of Coke and sawdust mixed with stale Budweiser and a touch of vomit. The daylight reached about half-way down the bar before the darkness swallowed it. Yellow incandescent sconces covered the dark walls every eight feet spaced between small neon signs that advertised Heineken, Guinness, and Coor's. As David got closer to the bar, the music got louder. A framed dollar bill hung over the cash register near the collection of liquor bottles. A second sign closer to the large mirror behind the bottles said "Jerry is in." David sat on the first stool that lost the window daylight and swiveled it toward the bartender. "You Jerry?"

Jerry was leaning on the bar closest to the stage. It was too loud to hear much of anything except for the unmusical moaning of the big-haired, blonde, thirtyish woman with a beer-soaked, heavy Texas drawl. Whining into the karaoke microphone singing something with unintelligible lyrics, she was wearing jeans and a yellow blouse covered by an open western shirt several sizes too large. It belonged to the shirtless guy near the stage. The spotlight made her feel good and from the number of silhouetted cowboy hats crowding the tables near her, David figured this was either a great place to get laid or a local party that ended several days ago but nobody knew it yet.

Jerry snapped his head back toward David and gave a quick wave as he started walking toward David who shouted, "Johnny Black, rocks." The bar tender nodded then turned once more toward the stage to watch the singer. Shaking his head, he reached down for a glass and threw a few cubes into it. He turned toward the mirrored back bar with the neatly stacked bottles and reached for the Scotch. David could see the smile on his face in the mirror as he poured the liquid over the ice cubes. He was still smiling as he approached David and shouted over the music, "You know they got the fucking words right there in front of 'em. But for the last three hours she's made up her own lyrics for every single, Goddamn song." He put the drink on the bar in front of David. "Gonna be here long?" David nodded as he tipped the glass toward his lips. "Good. I'll start you a tab." The bar tender knocked twice on the bar and headed back to his spot at the other end.

For the next several hours David concentrated on emptying and re-filling the glass while watching the shape of the ice cubes change. At some point an attractive red-haired woman in a dark green dress sat down next to him and smiled.

"You look like you need a friend," she slurred as she leaned toward him brushing her hand across his lap.

"Now, I have nothing against working girls," David said to her. "Especially since you are so pretty and look like you might have graduated from high school the same year I did. But . . ." The high school reference was a polite way of saying he knew she wasn't new to this. David made some quick calculations about the state of his funds and then respectfully declined her invitation. "I want you to know," He told her, "with the price of gas I couldn't possibly afford your companionship, right now. So, don't blame me. Blame the guy in the parking lot kissing the camel."

She smiled as her hand gently moved from David's lap to his chest. "Then it's lucky for you," she slowly said, "that there are only two things I need from you at the moment." She leaned in toward David nearly falling into his grateful lap. "First, I would like you to tell Tony to fill up my glass," she looked at Jerry and swayed slightly raising her empty glass. Jerry came over, chuckled a bit and shook his head as he poured straight Jack Daniels into the tumbler. "And then when I've emptied it a couple more times," she said, "take me somewhere and fill *me*. How's that?" The bartender walked away holding up two fingers while mouthing, "Two drinks."

It was decision time for David. "Do I need this right now?" he asked himself. "Then again, have I ever needed it this much?"

"What did you say?" She looked at David while readjusting the dress strap that slipped from her shoulder.

David kept the conversation going but the noise was so loud from the karaoke that he couldn't hear what he was saying. It was also unlikely that his new best friend heard any of it. "See, that's the absurdity of questioning this kind of event," he told her. "First, this kind of situation occurs about as often as an apology from the IRS. So, the answer whether or not I am going to respond to this hand roaming across my body is always 'yes,'" he said while reaching for his glass. "Well, almost always. If the flames from the burning furniture are getting too close to the bed and the fire department hasn't even made use of their sirens, then maybe I might have to redefine 'quickie.'"

The redhead looked at David and tipped her head, "What?"

David continued without raising his voice. These were oral comments intended only for his consumption. The words were coming from David's mouth but it was really that little guy sitting on his shoulder doing the talking. "Right now, however, any decision other than where-have-you-been-all-my-life is a lie." He was committed. All systems go. The blood was rushing from one head to the other and David was feeling very suave. "Nice tits."

She laughed and said, "Yeah, that's what they tell me."

David reached over and cupped one measuring its weight. "You know, as you get older, these puppies are gonna start looking . . . longer. What are you going to do then?"

She smiled and took his other hand pressing it to the other breast. "I'll probably have them removed and mounted on a plaque to hang in my office—a memento of better times."

A couple of refills passed the time and then David realized it was a long time since he had been with a woman. A very long time. But the time wasn't what mattered now. In spite of the glow from the booze, he was nervous and suddenly aware of the eager lust that, just ten minutes before, caused him to ask the green dress to his room. The same lust that had him outside, in the dark staggering toward the room with a very attractive and very drunk, red-haired woman whose name he would never care to know.

Funny thing about lust, if it gets to the point where sex is inevitable, it controls everything you think, do, or say. But as the hormones taper off to the point where reason is reawakened your mind sits at a crossroads. It asks you whether you want to think about this some more or just let the lust take over again and handle it for you. Lust easily persuades in its favor.

David was panting like a wire-haired terrier eager to fetch a Lamborghini for her if she wanted one. He was also convinced that he was playing the part of the liquor-smoothed stud. But enough foolishness leaked its way from his brain inviting a semblance of sobriety to replace it. David imagined how ridiculous he must look. He certainly felt that way. That was not to say he was changing his mind.

David's one arm held hers draped over his shoulder while the other wrapped around her waist. He could feel her chest expand and contract through the green polyester with each short breath. The liquor and his newly acquired "give-a-fuck" attitude convinced him she still looked great, even in the pallor of the parking lot's green glowing mercury vapor lamps. Better yet, David was convinced she was every bit as eager to get laid now as she was when he helped her little ass off the adjoining bar stool. David smiled when he realized she probably looked even more foolish than he did. Maybe not. But for the moment, they were a pair that deserved each other. Even so, it was a long time. A very long time.

Outside the door there was the musty odor of a repeatedly wet carpet and stale cigarette smoke. He reminded himself that the glowing white and red sign towering over the interstate simply said "Sleep Cheap." It made no promises against the constant hum of the hi-speed traffic droning a few hundred yards from the bed's pillow or the arguments between drunken patrons rattling disgruntled heads against chugging diesels in the parking lot.

David propped his willing friend against the white, peeling paint on the wall outside the room door and began fumbling for the key. The key elicited a grateful click from the lock. Her experienced hand reached past the opened door. A flick of the light switch and she pushed past him into the room. Both beds showed definite sways to their platforms as a testament to the repeated thumping of hourly guests. David chose the one she collapsed on and began shedding his clothes as he stood over her. Kicking off the shorts that strangled his ankles, he headed, naked, for the bathroom to take a leak and splash some water on his face and other enthusiastic body parts.

When David walked out of the bathroom he was pleased to see his guest was sitting up. The dress top was down around her waist. She removed the straps of her bra from her shoulders and turned the back around to unhook the clasps. A pair of delightfully free breasts kept getting in the way of the hands wrestling with the bra's clasps. As she looked up at David and smiled, he realized he was not drunk enough anymore but she was. Her smile melted to a grin as gravity pushed her head back to the clasps.

"Ta-dah. I got it." She tossed the bra toward the wall and held both arms open with the presentation. David just stood there swaying in rhythm with the rest of the room and looked at her. She lowered her gaze to his middle and then wandered back to his face and pronounced the situation "perfect." It was just as likely a stiff road kill would have received the same approval.

"I have made up my mind," he slurred. "I am either going to enjoy this," logic was telling him she had to pass some portion of a sobriety test, "or I am going to pull the dress back up around those gorgeous tits and lead you to the door." David weighed the options for about five seconds before realizing "gorgeous tits" was the deal-maker.

Offering his hands to her outstretched arms, he got closer to help her up. The dress fell easily to the floor. No panties. Nothing else. Not even a landing swatch to guide a blind pilot.

132

The redirection of blood from David's head was having the appropriate result and now with a secure three-point attachment, he leaned in to kiss her.

She eagerly wrapped herself around him. Both arms and lips grabbed the torso while a lifted leg grasped David's hip. The move exposed an opening for his penis that slid past her belly into the void created by the lifted leg. In an instant his member slapped upward against her wet lips evoking a long deep groan of pleasure muffled by the fact that her mouth was pressed hard against his.

Pushing her forward, they fell onto the bed. He positioned himself above her and slid higher up on her body. At the instant he touched her she stiffened and stopped breathing waiting for complete insertion. As David slowly entered she began exhaling. She was in a hurry. She moved her hands from his shoulders and grabbed his buttocks pushing hard against him demanding he go deeper. David pulled out. As he looked at her, he could see the question on her face. "What are you doing? Don't be so cruel." He teased her once more inserting and then pulling out only as deeply as the head. Then in one rapid thrust David slid in all the way. He closed his eyes and arched his back feeling the years of waiting melting away.

Now, the rhythm began on its own. No thought. No intention. David was moving gently in and out of this woman he had only met an hour before. His hands were pressed hard against the bed for balance while his toes burned against the synthetic rug for traction. Her breasts spilled to either side of her body and swirled in waves of circles as David pushed against her. Settling his knees onto the bed and cupping her ass in his lap, he continued the motion without losing a stroke. Looking down at her startled wide open eyes, he felt her nails dig into his waist. The look was pure pleasure about to burst. She arched her back and tightened her grip on him as her legs lifted higher. He couldn't keep up with her squirming. This was it. So fast. He had wondered if it would be over quickly but he believed he would be the one to end it!

Suddenly, she stopped moving. Her grip relaxed as her legs fell to David's side. "Oh, yeah. That's what I wanted. Just like that." She slowly brushed her hair from her face. "Want to go again?"

"I can't believe what I'm hearing," David said staring at her. "What the hell just happened?"

"You didn't cum, did you?" She didn't wait for an answer. "I didn't think so. But you know what? I'll bet you've pumped enough bullets into that gun of yours to shoot a hole in the ceiling if I squeeze it just right." And with that she reached between her legs and grabbed his scrotum. She bent forward and kissed him then slid slowly past his chest and belly to come head-to-head with David's re-energized penis.

David's mind was as open as his eyes were shut. He could feel the pleasure of all the women he had known: eighteen years old and swimming naked with eager partners; holding the soft, firm breasts of so many beautiful, smiling, young lovers; feeling their skin and hearing their moans. So many, but never enough. He forgot how to enjoy simple, emotionless lust. Hatred ate his soul, depriving him of years and with it his ability to enjoy this sweetest part of living.

She was still stroking David when he felt the surge from deep within his groin and the electric shock that started at her mouth and climbed in an instant to the base of his skull. He grunted as he thrust into her head. David sat up supported by his elbows and watched as her hand stroked and her cheeks filled with the moment. Again an uncontrolled pump or two and David was floating. His head was bursting with cotton. With eyes closed, David was falling backward without concern. She continued tugging as he collapsed on the bed with his mouth wide open gasping for air.

Several hours later David awoke from a sound sleep. The room was partially lit by the car parked in front of the window. The headlights burned through the curtains leaving the pattern of the window's frame on the opposite wall. There were low, bass tones of two men speaking outside above the hum of a car's engine and the dull country beat of the radio.

David got up and worked his way through the discarded clothes and shoes toward the curtains. From the side of the window, hiding behind the door, he could hear the discussion between what looked like two out-for-the-night truckers. One was counting his change and a few other assorted pocket-sized objects while the second placed his arm on the counter's shoulder and reassured him. There was a woman in the front seat. It was the lady crooner from the bar. She was still wearing the western shirt but neither of the guys was large enough to be the original owner. Her head leaned against the car door as she slept off her evening's efforts—or was it early morning?

David walked toward the bathroom scratching his belly and pushing his long black hair back. The guest lay on her side, mouth open and legs spread for balance. One arm hung off the bed. She had had enough after several more events that included nearly suffocating David while she straddled his face and grabbed the headboard for support. To his credit, he never complained. Even better, David was dubbed "the best in more than a week." That was high praise and probably a professional opinion.

After a quick shower, David got dressed; threw his things in the car and left. Sleeping beauty would awake to find a few bucks next to her purse and a note that said: "For breakfast. Thanks."

"Next stop: Canada," he said as he slid into the car's torn front seat. He hadn't decided where he was or where he was going but the farther away from Richmond he got, the less likely he would be found. Getting as far away as possible was a strong part of the healing process.

135

CHAPTER 16
The Greed Muscle

Party night was something special for Robert before it all crashed down around him the year before. The parties and the party favors crept through his skin invading and infecting his social consciousness. With each event, Robert sank more deeply into his hell. It was the crash and lack of funds that helped him up. He escaped but learned little. Now, his recently reacquired standing put him back into the fold where strangers called him friend and salesmen wandered through the partiers peddling their powder.

Simon was a friend from Robert's past life. When the phone rang at the office, his secretary told him someone named Simon wanted a moment of his time. "He says he's an old friend, sir. Do you want me to tell him you've gone to lunch and take a message?'

"No, no I'll take it. Give me about a minute then ring it through." Robert was flexing. Making Simon wait was his way.

A minute later the phone rang. Robert let it ring several times before picking up. "Simon," Robert greeted him with a feigned surprise. "How are you? It's been a while." Robert hurried through the assorted greetings covering as many clichés as possible before giving Simon the chance to say hello. "You'll have to excuse me, I've only got a minute between meetings, but it's really good to hear your voice."

Hear his voice? Simon was only able to stutter through Robert's machinegun delivery. "Ah, well, hi!" Simon finally said something even if it was nothing more than an attempt at recovery.

"How can I help you Simon? Hey, how's your beautiful wife? Roxy, is it?" In truth, Robert didn't remember if Simon even had a wife. Clearly, he didn't care.

"No, it's Barbara. She's fine. No, wait." Simon was about up to Robert's speed now and trying to get his message out. "Look, I'm having a little get-together Friday night. I thought you might like to join us."

"Us?" Robert was interested. He imagined he must still be on the A-list with other connected partiers.

"Yes. Just a few of the old crowd. I think you might like to see some of them again—and I know they want to see you. You've been the subject of more than one conversation over the past few months."

Robert felt the negative twang that accompanied his paranoia. "The past several months," he thought, may be code for the divorce and financial problems. Robert didn't reply immediately. The war in his head had already begun. He was rubbing faces in the dirt at his feet and stepping on heads. Simon continued talking trying to get in as much information as possible about Robert and his personal recovery before Robert broke in to monopolize the conversation once more. But Robert said nothing else and Simon noticed. Simon paused. "Robert? Think you might make it?"

Again silence, then, "Yes, I'll be able to stop by. Friday you said, right?" His reply was slow and measured lacking the car salesman delivery that began the conversation. "Should I bring anything . . . party favors," his voice dropped slightly. It was code for cocaine.

"Not to worry. It's all taken care of," Simon excitedly told him. "I've got a new acquaintance. He has the best connections and will bring everything," Simon assured him.

"The way you're describing this party, it sounds like a wine tasting or a high end Tupperware swap meet." Robert was fishing for more information. His suspicions exceeded his ego. He liked the idea that he had value to Simon and his group. But the suddenness of the invitation begged for an answer.

"I can promise you the menu is varied and top-of-the-line," Simon boasted. Robert's stomach churned with the promise of a welcome visit from an old dusty-white companion. If all went as Robert hoped, he would remember little of the event and would only have to worry about whose bed he was in the next morning.

"Yeah. Sure I'll be there," if for no other reason than to rub his success in their faces. "I'll be there. I look forward to it."

"Great!" Simon said. "This is great. We'll look forward to seeing you."

Robert hung up the phone without saying another word. Simon wasn't finished with his gushing. Robert didn't care.

Friday night arrived. Robert was careful not to show up early. He had to make an entrance. He wanted to measure the crowd to see if, in fact, his presence was as eagerly awaited as Simon made it seem. The address was near the university—a tall condo complex overlooking a roomy pond. He had some difficulty finding a place to park. That, he thought, was a good sign that Simon hadn't misled him. There was a steady stream of affluence heading toward the same open door where a crowd of smokers squeezed together alongside the serpentine walkway.

Robert walked past the front door congestion unsure of the faces or even if he had the right address. Someone was shouting his name above the crowd noise. "Robert! Robert!" A thin man with dark glasses waved at him with a bottle of gin in his hand, pushing through the guests to shake Robert's hand. It was Simon. Robert hadn't seen him in more than a year. It took several seconds before Robert could match the man with his memory of a former legal colleague. Giving the appearance of a physical fitness nut at a slender 165 pounds, Simon was quick to point out his new weight.

"Well?" Simon looked at Robert who had acquired a polite grin. "Whaddaya think? Not the same little fat boy you remember, huh? I've gone on a fitness kick. Up every morning by five. A couple of miles of fast walking—fuck that running shit. Then a light liquid breakfast from the blender and off to the gym for an hour before heading to the office. And look at me!" Simon kept talking and waving the bottle of Sapphire Blue gin toward the cocktail glasses of numerous party goers while patting his hardened stomach through a partially unbuttoned white silk shirt.

Simon wasted little time. As though an afterthought, he deposited the blue bottle in the welcome arms of a guest and led Robert further into the human tangle toward a man seated on the far side of the room in what had to be the only space left with room to breathe. A large, dark man in a black suit stood four feet from the seated man's chair directing partiers away from his charge.

Simon introduced Robert to the seated man and then said something that Robert filed away for later consideration. "Mr. Ramos, this is the man we spoke of earlier." Then, turning to Robert, Simon smiled, patted him on the shoulder and quickly turned away to dive once more into the sea of partiers in search of his blue bottle.

Robert's life found new direction. His grasp on GrowVest was secure and that realization meant he could drive the company in any direction he saw fit. But nowhere in his mind could he have imagined the deal falling into his lap.

Ramos rose to shake Robert's hand. Robert acknowledged the man as a picture of success. His neatly trimmed gray moustache, white hair and dark athletic figure presented a wealthy man late in a successful career. His pin-striped suit and Italian shoes all looked appropriately elegant, tailored to fit his six-foot frame. The full picture included a curiously-colored watch that Robert noticed as the gentleman's hand reached out toward him. Enameled palm trees adorned the watch face. The large, Hispanic man in the dark suit stood quietly beside Ramos's chair continuing to direct traffic away from the two men. Ramos was the definition of power. Robert was transfixed on Ramos's image. It became the only thing he could see or hear.

"I have heard much about you, Mr. Whitney," Ramos said with a slight Spanish accent while firmly shaking Robert's hand.

"Have you?" Robert immediately thought the elegant gentleman was simply being polite. They sat with a small table between them while the bodyguard remained as insignificant as a man of that size can be.

"Yes, you are a lawyer aren't you? And the president of a successful commercial real estate consortium, called GrowVest, I believe. I have heard it is showing great promise under your direction. Is this not so?"

Robert was caught off guard. This was unexpected flattery that momentarily made him dizzy with pride. Then, that unseen light and paranoia alarm ignited inside Robert's head. He immediately ran through a mental rehashing of his phone conversation with Simon. It was a brief discussion that never included anything about Robert's current situation. Simon, he thought, simply congratulated him on once again landing on his feet and then wandered off to boast of his own social recovery. "Caution!" The small hairs on the back of his neck were screaming!

Robert eyed the watch once more.

"I see you enjoy fine watches, Mr. Whitney."

"Well I have a few and like to think of myself as a collector." Robert was lying. He wasn't even wearing one. But he felt the need to elevate his importance in light of the towering performer in front of him.

"Good. Very good. I too collect watches. Perhaps you have seen this one before." Ramos leaned forward and began unclasping the gold buckle on the brown, alligator-leather band removing the watch. "I just acquired it from a business associate who no longer valued it as much as he valued our relationship. We have done business together for years. The watch was his way of showing that my business was far more valued than any of his other associates." Ramos smiled and handed the time piece to Robert.

There was weight and wealth in the watch. "Patek Philippe-Genève" elegantly declared its maker on the dial face. The pink gold case, enameled palm trees, flowers and fruit appeared a bit gaudy for a business man but the watch was superb.

"This is magnificent." Robert stared at the dial face for a moment too long before realizing he was losing his concentration. He had to focus. He handed the watch back to Ramos who casually slipped it back on his wrist.

"I do apologize for showing off a bit, Mr. Whitney. As a collector, I'm sure you understand my interest and appreciation of such things."

"I do. Thank you." Robert composed himself. "I'm sorry but where did you learn of my company?" Robert was really asking how this man knew anything at all about *him* and then it occurred to him that this party, Simon's invitation, was something more than just a former friend looking him up to re-establish a social tie. Robert's hands began to sweat. He was much more wary of Ramos and especially the rock standing in front of him.

Ramos smiled gently and leaned forward reaching for the bottle of single-malt Scotch on the table between them. He splashed the liquid over a glass of ice. Ramos gestured to Robert as if to ask if he would like some and then without waiting for a sign placed the bottle on the table near the ice bucket and eased back into his chair. As the ice chimed against the crystal, he leaned back and apologized once more. "I am sorry. That was a bit rude of me. You see, I have been watching GrowVest for some time and, of course, you as its president. There is genius behind its growth and as an investor in the world's economy, I watch many companies while looking for another place to put some of my wealth. Are you still looking for investors?"

Robert was nearly choking. Too much information was flooding his brain. It wasn't simply the questions. It was what they suggested. What was already known? So much of Robert's activity was kept from Allen and Mac and the investors. So much was just known to Robert and yet here was this man sitting across from him with a comforting, confident smile threatening the secrecy Robert so cautiously guarded. Who was he? How could he know? Robert was overcome by his insecurity. He feared for his life. His impulse was to get up and run through the bodyguard and party crowd and keep going until he outran the panic creeping over him. But the fear for his safety was competing with his conscious greed.

He looked at the gently smiling Ramos and turned toward the bodyguard, then back toward Ramos and the watch. Ramos readjusted his position and then sat back again, crossing his legs. Robert stiffly did the same.

142

Once more Ramos smiled toward Robert then looked up at the bodyguard. "Give us a little more room, Enrique." The big man took two steps to the side clearing bodies on his way. Ramos delighted in Robert's uneasiness. This was clearly his plan. "Mr. Whitney, I think my interest in your company could ultimately make you far richer than you already are.

"I have been involved with other companies like your own for many years. My involvement has always proved lucrative and highly beneficial for everyone involved. I see to all the particulars and provide a guarantee that it is safe, legal and beyond the reach of the tax man."

Robert's fears remained but greed had softened the panic. Greed was listening intently to every one of Ramos's words. "I'm quite flattered that you would find GrowVest interesting," Robert began. "You're correct, it is a great investment. But it is also a closed corporation. Our investors are found through our own invitation versus public knowledge. We keep that . . ."

"Yes, you keep that rather secret, don't you? Let me suggest something to you. I have learned that GrowVest is looking for investors and a buyer. You have your eye on one of the major international banks or some other major player. I know this. It is common knowledge within my circle of friends." Ramos was pushing past Robert's feeble attempt at selling the party line. "It is also a common goal of many fledgling corporations with big eyes set for a quick sales kill. Start small. Sell big and move on. At first, it appears as a good philosophy. Simple. But, it is common and seldom worth the hopes placed in it." Ramos leaned forward still smiling. He reached for the ice tongs on the glass table between them and removed the lid to the ice bucket. He placed three more cubes in his glass. Each cube was precisely placed, one atop the next. His hand was steady and the brief exercise was like a Japanese ritual tea ceremony. It was another of the finer points that defined his confidence, meant to impress Robert with his casual strength.

Ramos was smooth, unexcited by the proposal and very certain of himself. He had done this before. Robert was going to see this and the only thing Ramos wanted to hear was Robert saying "yes." Ramos placed his drink on the table and looked at Robert.

"You see, Mr. Whitney," his words were measured and direct, "while your handling of GrowVest may be genius, your final plan—the sell-out—is predictable. It will be handled by your adversaries in a way that best suits their interests. Not yours."

Robert was irritated. "Genius," yes; "predictable," no, he thought. Robert was certain his plans for GrowVest exceeded anyone's expectations—even Ramos's. Still, it was clear there was a point to this preliminary lecture. For the next several minutes Ramos kept Robert's attention and Robert knew he was stalked. Ramos had stalked GrowVest, too. Ramos listened at the corporate door and crawled under Robert's pillow at night to watch his dreams as they seeped from his head.

"You need to rethink your strategy, Mr. Whitney." The voice re-entered Robert's consciousness tearing him from the thoughts of his sleepless nights and the subtle sounds that had awakened him for the past several months. Ramos, he suddenly realized, might be the answer to all the imagined threats. He could be the justification he needed to redefine the direction Robert had chosen. But, if this was so, Robert would have to realize Ramos was also the newly focused direction for all his fears. Here was the roaring lion asking Robert to lie down and sleep beside him. Trust him. Listen to him purr and believe he wouldn't devour him in the night.

"How do you mean?" Robert heard himself asking the question as an interruption to the panic in his head.

"What you have in GrowVest is not a business in need of a buyer."

"It's not." Robert parroted the response as a statement of fact rather than a question.

"No! GrowVest is a different kind of gold mine. GrowVest should be international and I am certain my investment group could be the investors that take you there." Ramos paused for a moment never interrupting his eye contact with Robert.

Once again, Robert was startled. The GrowVest corporate literature claimed GrowVest was already international. For Chrissake, he told himself, it was called GrowVest International. How could this man know it wasn't—that the title was nothing more than a vague hope and cheap promotional claim to garner more investors?

"Let me suggest something." Again, Ramos hesitated. Robert was too startled to respond. There was no smile on Robert's face. Robert unconsciously wiped his sweating hands on his pant legs then folded his arms tightly against his chest. Ramos started again. "Just to have you present it to your board or whoever." Ramos waved his hand as if it really didn't matter. "An international corporation could easily establish itself offshore for tax purposes, I am certain you are aware of this. Its banking interests are of no one's concern. Profits, in fact all funds, are banked in the offshore accounts. Taxes are avoided, legally, while incomes, private incomes," he looked directly at Robert and waited for the words to register, "are guarded. My investment group routinely channels our cash investments through various companies we have helped reestablish themselves in this way. We are, Mr. Whitney, very interested in GrowVest for those same reasons. I think you may be the person to do this. And, you may be the person to directly reap the rewards for your foresight while making your investors quite happy with their returns."

Ramos uncrossed his legs and placed both feet together on the carpet as he reached for the glass of Scotch now swimming in the water from the melting ice cubes. He sipped it once then drained the contents in a continuous move. The sound of the leather chair creaked softly beneath him and there was the sound of the party that suddenly held no interest for Robert. Ramos lifted his hand above his head and casually motioned while glancing ahead toward Enrique. The bodyguard reappeared. Apparently, he never really lost sight of his charge. Ramos turned slightly to the bodyguard and handed him his empty glass. "Would you like something?"

Ramos knew the impact of his proposal. The only thing left to be measured was the balance of Robert's fear versus his greed. It was a measure only Robert could make. There was silence from both men and then Robert awoke. "No, nothing for me right now," he said turning toward Enrique. "Thank you."

"I'll tell you what," Ramos said reaching inside his jacket and then handing Robert his business card. "I have to be leaving. I have several meetings over the next few days in Los Angeles and Las Vegas. Why don't you visit me next Thursday at *La Nubé* in Mexico City? It's a nice neutral location. I'll have reservations made for you and a limo to pick you up at the airport. If you change your mind and decide to stay with your own business plan, I will understand." Ramos stood and straightened his jacket brushing his pants before reaching his hand out toward Robert. Robert stood immediately grasping Ramos's hand, certain Ramos was noting how wet his palms were. Looking directly into Robert's eyes, Ramos smiled that same comforting smile and slightly dipped his head. Robert said nothing for several seconds until Ramos was several feet away and waiting for the bodyguard to clear his path to the door.

Robert glanced at the white business card that had Ramos's name and an international phone number with a parenthetical area code (52), he did not recognize. "I will consider it," Robert finally blurted as Ramos disappeared into the crowd. "Thank you," he shouted above the party noise as he moved toward the door to watch Ramos enter a waiting limo.

"Nice meeting you," he whispered as the limo's tail lights melted into the city traffic.

CHAPTER 17
Commitment

In the morning's darkness, the black SUV that stopped a few yards from Robert's driveway was invisible—at best, a shadow on an unlighted street filled with shadows. The two dark figures that exited the vehicle were dressed all in black: ski masks, clothes and gloves. They silently made their way toward Robert's car. Hesitating thirty feet short of their goal, at the edge of the lighted floodlight bathing the driveway, one of them pulled a small transmitter from his pocket; aimed it at the car and pressed a button that lit a red light on the handheld black box and—most important—caused the alarm on Robert's new car to beep one quick, sharp note signaling that the alarm system was disarmed.

Immediately, the second man ran toward the car's rear bumper and slid beneath it placing a button-sized magnetic tracking device to the car's frame. It was over in seconds. As the men drove away, Robert rolled in his bed to his back. His eyes were wide open seeing nothing in the bedroom's absolute darkness. Winter put a slight chill in the morning air. The crisp, clean odor at four in the morning should have been refreshing. But it was still dark and Robert hadn't slept well, again. Even though it was more than a year since his car was vandalized, the slightest sounds awakened him.

David was the one to engineer those problems. But Robert's daily self-doubt included a nagging belief that the unnerving events may have included others. Now, the sound, just as sharp as the morning air, had alerted him. Someone, he feared, was in his driveway. He was sure the abbreviated, single, electronic chime of his new silver, Jaguar XJL's security system crept into his dream and caused him the discomfort.

Robert rolled to his right and pulled open the nightstand drawer gingerly searching for the loaded 9 mm Beretta M9 in its holster. Too busy to take lessons, Robert was cocky enough to believe he knew how to use it and was eager to prove it with a full clip of 15 rounds for whoever it was that was causing his sleeping problems. He wanted to see their face when the 5-inch barrel popped out from behind the front door. He switched on the small lamp on the night table and sat up looking at the cold, black pistol. Its weight spoke for its destructive potential. He nervously slid the clip in and out of the grip pulling the hammer back until it clicked. This way the double-action pistol only needed a light squeeze to send the bullet tearing toward his victim. He glanced once more at the drawer's contents of loose 9 mm shells and the set of keys. He pushed the keys out of sight to the back and closed the drawer.

Robert made it to the hallway overlooking the front entry. No suspicious lights were coming in through the glass surrounding the large front door. Faint reflections on the marble floor were from the night sky, brighter than the cavernous house interior. Nothing moved. There was nothing but Robert's fear.

Barefoot and wearing only pajama bottoms, Robert made it to the top of the winding staircase and paused as a chill went through him. He held closely to the smooth plaster wall feeling its clammy chill against his back. Descending the long, spiraling marble staircase toward the elaborately carved front door, he listened for any noise coming from the outside. Robert cautiously approached the door. There was no one in the driveway that he could see through the peep hole in the polished mahogany wood. Besides, he told himself, shouldn't the new security system on the Jaguar have alerted him? What was it he heard? Could it have been another dream? The dreams convinced him to buy the pistol. Dreams are not generated by irrational fears, Robert told himself. They are messages from the subconscious. The dreams were telling him there was a threat. He had to be ready.

Robert crouched and cautiously turned the polished brass dead bolt then carefully pressed the latch on the door's heavy handle. The click was his warning to be prepared. He shook the M9 once more; uncocked it; then cocked it again. He moved his finger to the trigger gripping the gun with two hands. It gave him the strength and confidence he needed. Robert opened the front door pushing the pistol's barrel through the opening. He could see the morning's edition of the *Richmond Times-Dispatch* spilled across the door mat. He edged his way past the opening holding tightly against the building and stepped outside waving the pistol in a 180 degree arc. Robert crouched slightly, still waving the Beretta in front as he stepped toward the Jag. Inches from the car, Robert stood taller and glanced around the vehicle as if expecting a ghost to vaporize with fear at seeing the weapon in his hands. Satisfied with his performance, Robert backed toward the front step, picked up the newspaper and backed into the house. "Maybe it was the paper boy," he whispered. "It must have been. Maybe the sound was the paper hitting the step when he threw it across the lawn and it landed near the door," he said. Then again, maybe it was just another nightmare. Another nightmare. Another day begun with the worry that someone was out there trying to get him.

It was several hours later while sipping his third cup of coffee at his desk that it hit Robert. He had gone outside to look at the car, but the car's motion detector hadn't activated the alarm. Robert got up and wandered to Mac's office. He walked in as Mac was speaking on the phone. Robert fell into one of the high-backed plush chairs reserved for visitors and stared at Mac. Mac watched

Robert walk in with some surprise. This was a first. Robert usually had the receptionist invite Mac to Robert's office if he needed anything. Mac stared back at Robert then shrugged as if to ask what the problem was.

"Listen, uh, Greg, I'm gonna have to get back to you," Mac told the other end of the phone conversation. "Yeah, there's been a slight office emergency and I'm being called away." Mac shrugged again as if looking for confirmation of the statement from Robert. Robert said nothing but continued his stare.

"I apologize," Mac told Greg. "Yes, yes, I will. Thanks. I'll call you right back," Mac said once more as he hung up the phone.

Looking at Robert he asked, "What's wrong? Something wrong?"

Robert hesitated then winced as he softly said, "Something happened last night. I thought I had a prowler. I went downstairs but saw nothing. I even went outside to look. Nothing."

"So . . . , I don't get it," Max said impatiently.

Robert sat up straighter. "I walked outside," Robert said loudly as though Mac should have understood the implications. "The car's motion detectors."

"Yeah, so they go on when you walk near them, right?"

"Yes, right. That's what they're *supposed* to do—but they didn't."

"Oh." Mac still didn't get it. Robert's paranoia wasn't infectious. "Maybe you should look at that as soon as you get home."

Robert didn't seem to hear. "Nothing was out of the ordinary in the Jag when I drove to work," he said confirming his own thoughts. "I walked around it before getting in. I even examined the

151

car's door handle before reaching for it," he looked at Mac. "No smudges, scratches or dents." Robert's hands flinched with the palms moving upward, "Nothing," he said. Staring into the morning's past, he recounted his steps. "The car had hesitated a bit on the first hill but I excused that as a cold engine and the need for another tune up. The AM crackle was more annoying than usual coming in and out several times before I switched it over to FM." Robert refocused on Mac, "No one messed with the car. I just figured the bell that woke me, if it wasn't an imagined part of a morning dream, probably came from the paper boy. But if the car alarm didn't go off, maybe . . ." Robert got up and wandered out of Mac's office still in thought.

Mac was too busy to care and couldn't understand most of what Robert was talking about. "Have it checked," Mac yelled in Robert's direction while reaching for his phone. As the door closed behind Robert, Mac was on the line to his secretary. "Yeah, get him back on the line, right now, will you? Let's hope Robert's little puzzle hasn't blown another deal."

The morning passed with Robert's immediate concerns limited to creating fires for others to put out. He forgot about the sleepless night. Later, just after lunch, Robert called a meeting. He had the authority to do that now having eased his way into the GrowVest power chair. Allen and Mac showed up at two to hear Robert explain the revisions to the work load and financial arrangements. He had the power to do that too. The take-over was uncontested. Allen's resigned demeanor and Mac's willingness to follow had given Robert all the votes he needed.

"I want an updated review of our finances," he said to Mac without lifting his eyes from the most recent report. As CFO, Mac's financial duties only interested Robert as far as cash inflow went. Robert already had a firm grasp on the outflow. Robert's latest raise, loan and expense accounts were lucrative. Allen said nothing. Robert wrapped the meeting in less than ten minutes and asked Mac to leave so he could speak with Allen, "alone." Mac looked startled and offended by the early dismissal from the meeting. He left in a hurry and said nothing.

Robert waited until the office door was closed and then turned to Allen. "I'm considering a proposal by an investor," Robert told Allen. "He wants to push some cash our way in exchange for a percentage of the stock. Mac will see the influx as soon as this all begins. I have to know you are behind me on this before I start getting questions. I don't need Mac questioning the numbers beyond what he is told."

"What kind of money and what percentage?" Allen asked.

"The guy has a business located offshore," Robert said dismissively. "He says, being able to channel some of that cash, on a regular basis through GrowVest accounts could help us all. Let's be honest, the infusion of cash is exactly what we have been looking for."

Allen was silent then softly asked, "Is it legal?"

"What kind of question is that?" Robert feigned annoyance and began rising from his chair. He liked pacing when in these meetings. He knew it made Allen smaller and was sure it helped intimidate him. Getting what he wanted was easy once Allen began shifting in his chair, crossing and uncrossing his legs.

"Look, this guy is big and we need the kind of investor who is willing to pay us to help him channel funds through the company," Robert insisted. "Let's not lose sight of the big picture. Whatever he does, however he makes his money is no concern of ours. This is a legal investment by a funded investor with international credit. The cash infusion will look like product purchase." Robert stopped pacing and looked down at an uneasy Allen. "If anyone asks, we gave him Central and South America as a sales base. We'll open ghost accounts down there and run some cash through them just to keep the local governments happy. The real cash will make its way to the main corporate accounts offshore."

Robert began pacing once more as he sang out a well-rehearsed explanation designed to satisfy Allen's curiosity, all the while hiding the truth behind a dazzling screen of promised riches. "This is the deal of a lifetime," Robert said waiving his hands in the air. "With his contacts we could see a buyer for the company within a few months. Hell, maybe even him. It all depends on us and how this is handled." Robert approached Allen reaching down with one hand to grab his arm and give it a light upward tug. "I'll take care of it. It can be settled in just a couple of days." Robert waved the other hand but now the meaning was a kind of dismissal of any objections Allen might be considering.

Allen said nothing more. The tug on the arm was Robert's demand that Allen leave. The meeting was over. Allen rose from the chair, looked at Robert then dejectedly walked out of the office.

It was done. Allen's refusal to comment further was the confirmation Robert expected. He didn't wait any longer before calling the secretary into his office. "Book me a flight to Mexico City for tomorrow. Put it on Allen's credit card and travel account. I want to be there as early as possible. Check to see that I have reservations at the *La Nubé* Resort. And have the limo driver call just before arriving to pick me up at my home." Robert wanted to be sure the noises in the driveway were recognizable. He didn't want to greet the driver at his front door waving the Beretta. The secretary headed for the office door. "Wait," Robert hesitated, "yeah, make sure I've got about $3,500 in cash. Pull it from the office account. That's all."

CHAPTER 18
First Impressions

The morning's American Airlines flight to Juarez International Airport was uneventful. Mexico City in late November at 75 degrees was cooler than Robert expected. He exited the terminal and walked outside directly to the waiting metallic blue Mercedes stretch limo with the *La Nubé* Resort logo. The driver near the car's front was holding a sign that said: "Mr. Whitney."

"I'm Mr. Whitney."

Without saying a word the driver opened the back door for Robert who found himself, thus far, pleasantly surprised with Ramos's preparations for his visit. The limo's interior was a pale aquamarine blue from the plush carpets to the glove leather seats. Again, the *La Nubé* logo appeared. This time it was hand-embossed into the headrests of the couches that lined the back and sides of the passenger compartment.

The bar was open and waiting for use. Robert decided he needed to remain sharp and ready for any unexpected surprises. There would be no alcohol consumed until after his meeting with Ramos. At their first meeting, Robert was awed by Ramos's display of style and affluence. But for this visit, Robert prepared himself.

155

He wouldn't be thrown from his game again. He slid toward the chromed refrigerator beneath the bar top and reached for a small bottle of pineapple juice. Pouring the contents into a crystal bourbon glass without ice, he settled back into the corner of the limo's rear seat and waited for the driver to return with his bags.

The driver carefully placed Robert's bags in the trunk and then quickly got behind the vehicle's steering wheel. He adjusted his rearview mirror to see his passenger and in heavily accented English asked, "Was your flight agreeable, *Señor*?" Robert said nothing waiving to the driver to move on as he fished through the breast pocket of his suit jacket for Ramos's card. Ramos organized the meeting in what he referred to as "neutral territory." Mexico City neutral? Nonetheless, Robert agreed and now found himself looking outside the limo windows at unfamiliar surroundings.

It was a comfortable though lengthy ninety minute ride to the southwest of the airport, along a six-lane highway. Calling any hotel a "resort" in a city of 120 million means building walls that insulate the guests from the confusion generated by one of the world's largest urban areas. But *La Nubé*'s walls were natural. Elevated above the city in the forested hills of *Los Dinamos*, it had an unobstructed view of the sprawl below. Though the address was Mexico City, it was nestled within a park-like setting that appeared like a clouded oasis after emerging from thickly settled upscale neighborhoods.

The limo driver deposited Robert's bags on a brass cart at the curb near the hotel's entrance. The doorman greeted Robert after opening the limo's door. Robert said nothing and walked through the framed glass entry into the resort's lobby. The lobby was brightly lighted by a massively large crystal chandelier in the middle of its vaulted ceiling. Smaller copies of the chandelier dotted the remainder of the lobby as if spun off from a rotating center. The affect was a blast of softly sparkling point sources that showed themselves on every surface in the room.

An elaborate mosaic design of spiraling black Mexican beach stone against white marble echoed the ceiling's light pattern leading to the center of the lobby. Karabaugh rugs stained in red cochineal were scattered on the floor's stone surface.

A short, dark, well-dressed man appeared at the lobby's center instructing several of the standing bellman to the outside curb. Once the orders were given, he turned to one of the young women behind the main lobby's desk. *"Factúrele y déme el número de habitación."*

She immediately began typing on her computer terminal. She hesitated, then nodded to the man and said, *"De novecientos treinta y dos."*

Now assured, the man approached Robert falling in behind him as Robert, oblivious to the efficiency, walked toward the main desk. Once at the desk the man stood beside Robert and said in crisp, slightly accented English, "Good afternoon and welcome to *La Nubé* Resort, Mr. Whitney. My name is *Señor* Juarez. I am the hotel manager. We have been expecting you."

Juarez took the room key from the counter and exchanged it with the bellman for a package and letter. "These are for you, sir," he said as he handed the items to Robert. Juarez then turned toward the bellman. "Hector will bring your things to your room, Mr. Whitney. It is number 132." Hector was on his way toward the elevators with the bags after a quick nod from Juarez.

"Señor Ramos sends his sincere apologies for his delayed arrival."

Once more Robert was caught off guard. Ramos's delay had Robert waiting versus the other way around. "When is he expected?" Robert's voice cracked.

"I'm sorry, sir. I cannot say for certain. I have a call in to the airport hangar. They will alert me as to when his plane is expected. If you would like to rest a moment, the lounge is ahead and to your right," he continued. "If there is anything at all I or any of my staff can do for you, it would be our pleasure." Juarez bowed slightly and then held out his hand as if presenting the path to the bar to Robert.

Robert looked at the young woman behind the desk who smiled. Robert turned without returning the smile, nodded toward Juarez and walked past him looking at the package. It was unmarked except for his name. He tucked it under his arm and kept walking toward the lounge as he tore open the envelope. Robert pulled a card from the envelope and stopped. In fine block letters in the card's center was "VR." He flipped the card open. "Welcome. I am pleased you have decided to join me. I will be arriving this evening from a late business meeting in Los Angeles. Please accept my apologies for not being able to meet you upon your arrival. Perhaps this token of my gratitude for your attendance will help attenuate some of your discomfort. Meanwhile, *Señor* Juarez has been instructed to see to your every need. Regards, VR."

"So," Robert said softly to himself, "a little power play. Make me wait? And what? Does he expect I might melt in anticipation?" The power, Robert realized, was more than evident in the choice of the meeting place, the limo and the hotel. The delay tactic, if it was part of Ramos's plan, was more like overkill.

Robert entered the lounge and walked toward the elevated bar occupying the room's center. The bar stools brought the patron to the bar's level but the bartender's level was two feet higher making the tall woman behind the bar appear even taller and more imposing as she reached down to present a drink. The bartender approached Robert. Her coarse black hair was pulled tightly back and gathered off of her neck. A form-fitting white blouse pressed hard against her chest. She wore a waisted black apron over black slacks. "Good afternoon, Mr. Whitney. I am Paloma. May I get something for you?"

Instead of being flattered that Paloma knew his name, Robert saw the familiarity as a threat. It was clear Ramos made sure everyone knew him. "Yes, please."

"Single-malt on the rocks?"

"No. I can't stand the stuff," Robert replied abruptly. He was in thought examining the package in front of him and the barmaid's questions were distracting him.

"Something refreshing with a juice and rum, perhaps?"

Robert looked up leaving his suspicions for the moment and focused on Paloma. "Yeah, yeah, that'll be fine." As Paloma left him, Robert looked at the package once more. He picked it up and gently measured its weight, then placed the small package on the bar. He slid the note from the package top and folded it before placing it inside his suit jacket pocket. Paloma returned with the fruit punch.

"Tell me something . . . Paloma is it?"

"Si?"

"How did you know who I was? "

Paloma smiled, *"Señor* Ramos makes certain we know all of his guests."

"He's that important?"

"He owns the resort, Mr. Whitney. He is that important." Paloma placed a small knife on the counter. "You might want to use the knife to open the package," she said as she smiled and walked away.

Robert cut along the top releasing the flap of the box. Nestled within the *La Nubé* blue cotton cloth packing was another box. This one was black leather. Robert was excited as he took the

159

leather box out. The clamshell opening was lined with gold trim. The top of the box had, "For your collection," embossed in gold. Robert opened the box and discovered the Patek-Philippe art watch with the palm trees Ramos had worn to their first meeting. A small, black-and-white card inside the leather box had a simple "VR" embossed on it. Robert removed the watch from the box and buckled the alligator-leather strap to his wrist. He considered taking it off. There were too many distractions. This could all be a plan to take advantage of a weak moment. These were the paranoid cautions of a man cornered, but what a corner. He decided to keep the watch on his wrist. He sipped the pineapple and passion fruit punch then swirled the liquid and cubes while looking at the card with Ramos's embossed initials. Another sip and then Robert collected the box. He shoved Ramos's card into his jacket pocket, fished for a twenty and tossed it on the counter and without saying a word, headed for his room.

CHAPTER 19
A Measure of Sanity

Six months later, when David and the Duster quit wandering, he was as far as he could get from Virginia and the ties to his past. Until David stopped, this trip was a sightseeing adventure along the continental backbone of the Rockies. Nothing more. His funds weren't limitless so he worked odd jobs wherever he could blend in—Wheatland, Wyoming as a short-order cook; Saco, Montana jockeying trucks at a grain silo. He stayed in each place until people became too familiar with him and started asking questions. It was either turn around to head south, or see what was up ahead. Eventually, David made it to Bellingham, Washington and the ferry to Alaska—that was how he ended up in Anchorage. But Anchorage was uncomfortable. As Alaska's largest city, it wasn't the remote outpost he hoped for. There for just a day, David left the car parked at the airport and bought a ticket to Nome. The only way to get there was a two-hour plane ride or eight days of floating on a resupply barge. That, he decided, was the kind of isolation that would help him find peace. Despite a firm belief that destroying Robert was his main reason for living, the sharp mental bruises he carried had him questioning his sanity. It didn't take long before he learned that, in Nome, the cold summers and colder winters afforded abundant alone time—the time he needed for healing.

Over time he forgot about Robert. The venom blew away. David found that the daylight hours no longer included plotting against inflamed memories. Walking the frozen streets, he noticed the same faces each day and gradually learned to greet them with a nod. The nod slowly turned to a grin and though he kept a low profile, David knew he had reacquired a social presence. David was associating with the "haves" once again, even if it was only in the bars along Front Street. That was a good thing. Redefining himself helped him ease his way back into society while the passage of time helped him understand the rage and the real reasons for leaving Richmond.

A year was like six months until David tried to put mental markers down about when important things happened. That's when he realized Alaska could very easily become a permanent thing. He was feeling the need for a different time zone—one that included the rest of the world. There was a growing necessity to seek out the noise that was so foreign to this place. David needed to reacquire his former identity. He was craving the old life like a person who swore off chocolate but day dreamed about the unmistakable taste and smell of a Hershey bar.

It was unlikely David would ever have recovered without the peace Nome offered. He realized the good the town had done for him. The peace he pursued was his recovery. There was no need for more denial. His formerly proclaimed desire to kill Robert was now figurative. The years of murderous dramas that seeped through nightly dreams were enough to satisfy the overt urges. Exposing Robert was satisfaction enough. With that realization, David pronounced himself healthy. It was time to return home. David wanted his old life—the life that Robert took.

Without much more thought than it took to get out of bed, David flew back to Anchorage, paid a 14 month old parking bill and threw the few things he wanted into the trusty Duster and squirmed back to the ferry that brought him there. Landing in Washington,

David took his time skirting as far east as he could before shooting south toward home.

It was nearly two and a half years since the GrowVest fiasco. Anyone looking for David Gere within a friendly radius of Richmond gave up by now. David knew he would have to maintain a low profile and keep his identity as Wayne Brewkowski for a while, at least.

Looking for a place to hide, David found a convincingly lived-in double-wide for rent along the Pictou River in South Harriman, a little town about 40 miles south of Richmond. The property manager insisted on referring to his 28 whitewashed, aluminum-coated hulks as "mobile homes" despite the fact that none was moved in or out of "Riverside Park" since the welcome sign had gone up years before. David's new home was a side-by-side pair of eight-foot wide tubes dating back to the sixties. It came furnished with a polite infestation of roaches and the obligatory pressed wood, glue and stapled furniture repaired with swatches of silver duct tape. Until he could afford it, David's Orkin man was a pair of size 11 Nikes.

There were a few neighbors he avoided along with their polite questions while they tried to figure out who he was. Ceiley wasn't like the rest. Ceiley was a sorry soul—that was David's assessment, not hers—and David's most dependable neighbor. She considered living in an old broken tin-can of a house a step up from where she was. David listened to her stories in politely acquired pieces collected over numerous sunset visits to her porch where they shared their histories. She was right. As bad off as her current life looked, she was still moving forward from a miserable past.

It was a cool Saturday night during one of those collecting events that Ceiley got very personal. Ceiley and David were on the wooden platform outside her trailer door. She jokingly referred to the 4 by 4 foot warped plywood entrance as her deck. David leaned his back against the railing as he sat with one foot on the platform and the other on the next step down. Ceiley sipped coffee from a plastic mug as she sat with one leg bent beneath her in a torn aluminum beach chair. "My father and mother," she told David, "were poor, white-trash migrant farm workers." David flinched at the description. She quickly corrected herself, "Don't misunderstand what I'm saying. That's what I always heard people say—the people we lived with in the worker camps." It did little to ease his discomfort. David knew if he were to describe most of his neighbors, he would use the same expression—and that included Ceiley. David's uneasiness came from believing he was different. He wasn't one of them, he told himself. This was only a temporary thing for him. For Ceiley, it was her life and he doubted that would change.

"One time, I was about six, I remember going shopping at a small store with Mama and three of my sisters," Ceiley said. "I don't know where it was or even what we were buying. But the lady in line behind us came up to us kids when we were waiting for Mama to pay. She gave me a piece of candy and asked Mama where we were from and I said we were from poor white trash." Ceiley started to laugh. "That's what I had always heard them say at the camps. 'We're all a family. All of us from the same place—poor white trash,'" she said quickly as though the three words were one. "The lady laughed and immediately started telling other people in the line what I'd said. I turned to Mama with a big smile on my face for having said something that made everyone laugh. Mama had tears on her face. Mama paid the checkout lady and we hurried out of the store. That's all I remember." David said nothing. For the next minute Ceiley was reliving the moment in silence.

"So, anyway," she quietly said, "now when I say it, the 'trash' part is the way I think of how disposable and easily replaced we were."

David was eager to change the subject. "What kind of work did the family do?" David knew there was no "kind of work." The job description was the title: migrant worker.

"We spent most of our time moving from farm to farm. My parents picked grapes, oranges, lettuce. Anything in season," she quietly told him. David knew she was still walking through her childhood. She sipped from the cup and stared into her past looking up at the towering oaks that hung over the trailer.

"I was a skinny fourteen-year-old with no education or hope," she said as though the thoughts just gained a voice. The words weren't intended for David as much as for the oaks. Ceiley took another sip and looked directly at David. "I was married off to a field boss my father's age," she said with sudden strength. "The man offered my parents guaranteed housing whenever the family returned to the farm and $125." Her voice changed. There was an angry tension in it. "The marriage was consummated after a man claiming to be a Justice of the Peace visited the camp. He said a few words to the field boss. I remember how he looked at me," she said. "He looked at me while he reached out for the fifteen dollars in cash my new husband handed him."

David was feeling the panic now; the fear for her that she must have felt. "The honeymoon was a mid-day affair," Ceiley said. "With everyone in the field returning to work, my new husband and I remained behind for several hours." Ceiley said nothing more for several lost minutes. David whispered an apology as much for himself as her. Ceiley never heard it. She was lost in her daydream nightmare.

Moments passed, and then she said emphatically, "Two weeks later, I was gone. I lived on the streets for three more years before moving in with my second husband. We were together for the next ten."

David wanted to say something, anything. "That must have been difficult. The three years on the street—not the marriage," he forced a laugh. David cringed. He heard himself repeating the comment in an echo inside his head. Each time it repeated he felt a chill. Jesus, he thought, that was incredibly stupid.

"Well, I'm not married right now. I'm 28. I've been alone for more than a year. No kids. No family. Just a cat and the trailer I bought with the life insurance money he left me," she said trying to gain eye contact with David once more. The trance and pain were put away. "And books," she said. "Lots of books." Another sip from the cup.

His comment had him avoiding her gaze out of embarrassment. Ceiley wasn't offended. He knew she sensed his embarrassment. David lifted his head looking at her smile. "I am now a self-educated consumer of anything in print," she chuckled. "Once I discovered what I liked, I spent most of my free time reading." Her reanimation cleared the air for the moment.

David liked her. She was simple, unassuming and smart. Despite never having received a diploma, he didn't doubt she was better educated than most people he ever met, himself included.

Her slight frame looked breakable. Ceiley didn't look like eating was ever a serious hobby. She kept her hair short and finally believed him when David told her she was pretty. At twenty-eight she was still child-like in the way she blushed and covered her mouth when she laughed. During the evening history lessons, sitting beside her on the steps of her trailer, David learned that Ceiley liked to dream.

"I like imagining what might be," she said. "Where I might go or what I might do. The books," she explained, "have become a window for me." She let David share the fantasies. That exercise was one of the joys they shared with each other.

166

Maybe later, David told himself, after this all quiets down, maybe then I'll have the time and inclination to make the relationship something more than talk. Maybe I'll start by making some of those dreams come true.

CHAPTER 20
Contact

Small towns like Harriman are dangerous for someone trying to hide. Few locals means newbies are easily noticed even in trailer parks. But Riverside was a transient's haven. People came and went often carrying everything they owned in 30-gallon black plastic garbage bags. The local city bus stop was beside a telephone pole where a depression in the dirt was worn slick from regular traffic

David was comfortable. Maybe too comfortable—even sloppy. He started visiting old haunts where he thought he might get a glimpse of Allen. David wanted to talk to him; wanted to see if things changed, and whether he was a blip on anyone's radar. This whole revenge obsession could end if Allen told him that Robert was gone.

A late morning need for a beer had David wandering a few blocks from the trailer park on a pilgrimage to the local 7-11. Sitting on the curb, propped up by the shell of an old phone booth, he was sucking on a brown-bagged bottle of Budweiser when Allen appeared. Allen pulled into the parking lot in a burgundy-colored Mercedes S-600 sedan. As he left the car, he pushed his hand into his pocket, retrieved and counted his change without looking up until he reached the store's entrance. David stared in disbelief as Allen walked past.

"You son-of-a-bitch," David murmured as Allen disappeared behind the closing door. "This is unbelievable! Allen is slumming in Harriman," David said as he dropped the bagged bottle to the curb and got up to follow him inside. It was impossible to understand—but there he was. As David hurriedly pushed past the line of gas-paying clients, he saw Allen disappear into one of the aisles. David entered the adjoining row and walked to the end. As he turned the aisle, he came face-to-face with Allen. They both stopped and looked at each other. Allen smiled and excused himself for nearly walking into him then took a step to his left to go around David when it hit him. Allen looked up again more startled than before and gasped, "You!"

David lost a considerable amount of weight in his travels. His face was thinner and tanned a rich brown. The hair that needed cutting had grayed a bit at the temples. Somehow, David looked younger, more fit, more threatening. He smiled at Allen and took a step back.

"Yeah, me. How are you Allen? I understand everything is going well with GrowVest, but still no corporate sale. You promised me it wouldn't be long before that happened. That, I think, was the last time we spoke." David took a quick look around the store then stepped closer to Allen. He had to be quick and forceful. He didn't expect to see Allen but now that the opportunity presented itself, he felt the rage returning—the rage he thought he lost in Alaska. This reintroduction was going to be a fast and terrifying test for both men on many levels. "So, tell me about the progress you've made with all those corporate buyers." David inched toward Allen. Allen moved away until he was pushed against the aisle's shelving. "Just trying to build a sales record I'll bet," David sneered, "or maybe just a better way to take a little extra before dumping the whole game. Is that the idea?"

Very little of what David said sunk in. It really wasn't supposed to. He was simply rattling things off the top of his head in an attempt to keep Allen off balance. If Allen's brain was trying to comprehend anything David said, it was doing so as an afterthought, because the main share of Allen's gray matter was munching on a major surge of adrenalin mixed with a serious case of fight-or-flight.

Allen remained stiffened with his eyes wide open. David inched even closer. "You expecting me to twist your body into a knot?" Allen defensively flinched, bringing his hands up toward his face as David reached toward the shelf to Allen's left. "Or maybe stuff this can of 20 weight Pennzoil down your throat."

"What are you doing here?" Allen said. The question came out the way his brain was asking it—not in a polite or friendly way. It was defensive. Allen heard it and corrected himself. "I mean, when did you get back?" Allen tried regaining his composure acting a bit more relaxed.

"Back? From where, Allen? I've been here all along just watching and trying to understand why you *fucked me over*." For all the nights and days dreamt of this moment, David expected to remain calm. But now he was hearing the words spit from his mouth tinged with fire. "I kinda figured it out," David said leaning with an elbow on the shelving beside Allen. "Or maybe not. Let me try a couple of scenarios on you. Whaddaya say?"

Allen looked quickly over his shoulder. It appeared Allen expected a trap with an accomplice creeping up behind him. Or maybe he was just looking for a quick escape route. David could see him checking out a dented, gray Mercury blocking his Mercedes in the parking lot. One of the two blue-collar worker bees in the Mercury appeared to stare at Allen for a moment but didn't catch the panic in his eyes. The passenger leaned toward the driver as he pointed toward an open parking space, said something, and the driver steered the Mercury into the slot leaving Allen's car unblocked.

170

Allen kept moving cautiously away from David a step-at-a-time. As the one-sided conversation continued, David kept moving too. Each time Allen stepped back for a better focus on David's rage, David stepped forward. Allen appeared ready to bolt for the door and his unblocked car when the opportunity arose. That's when he realized his escape to the door was blocked by stacks of beer forming an impenetrable, chest-high wall decorated with a sign that read "Manager's Special—two for one." Allen was trapped and he knew it and so did David.

"So here we are." David stopped moving and folded his arms. The look of satisfaction covering his face threatened Allen as much as the outraged fury he expected. "You look good," he said showing his teeth with a broad smile. "Nice shoes. Nice suit, tie." He moved in once more reaching for Allen, "A little blue Oxford thing going on there with the shirt collar," he said flipping the edge of the collar with his index finger. Allen cringed expecting more. But David moved back again folding his arms. "Very nice. Very professional." David's relaxed speech and less aggressive demeanor offered Allen a moment to believe David meant him no harm. David simply stood and looked at Allen with the same wide smile as he nodded his head.

"But enough about you," David said shifting his stance and dropping his hands to the back pockets of his jeans. "Let's talk about me for a moment."

Allen responded haltingly with a lowered voice, "Okay, sure. How . . . how are you?" he mechanically asked still pressed tightly to the backside of the Manager's Special barricade.

"Weeelll," David drew out the word as he looked toward the ceiling as if trying to find the right words. He dropped his gaze back toward Allen and with the same toothy smile said, "I need your help."

Instantly, Allen reached inside his jacket for his wallet. Just as quickly David moved a hand toward him. "No, no. It's just the wallet." Allen put his left hand up toward David while he continued reaching inside his jacket pocket with his right hand. "I've got some cash here," he said, finally securing the wallet. Allen opened the wallet, fishing several fifties from his collection. "Maybe this will help a bit." He thrust his hand out toward David presenting the prize as if feeding a hungry animal. "After all,' he explained, "you look like you might be able to use it." Allen's face was flushed. His hands were shaking as he pushed the cash toward David once more. This was the boy David saw in his dreams every time he replayed that haunting day in his mind—the day that put him here. He believed the memories were pushed far back from his conscious life. Now, it was all coming back with an acid scorching the tips of his ability to reason. On that day, Allen sat in his chair fumbling for words to explain why David was no longer needed; fumbling, bumbling and spouting words he had rehearsed quite poorly. That day, Allen's driving emotion was shame. Today, the squirming boy bathed in fear and David was washing his back.

"Look like, huh? You think I look like I need some cash?" David continued crowding Allen. He wanted Allen rattled. He wanted more than just a handful of cash out of this encounter. "Why because you're wearing that nice Valentino suit and I got the old Levis goin' for me? It is Valentino, isn't it? Or, wait, no. Brooks Brothers, yeah. Brooks Brothers. I mean that's what you always wore before. You remember before, don't you Allen? Leaning in David sneered, *I do*."

"No! No, that's not what I meant. I mean . . ."

"You mean what, Allen?" David made a quick jab into Allen's chest with his index finger. Allen leaned back again against the beer cases.

David reached out again to grab Allen by the throat and thinking better of it pounded his hand on the shelving instead.

Behind the cash register, the dark man with the Bengali accent looked up at the parabolic mirror outside his cubicle to see what the noise was about. David quickly picked up a bottle of pickles and waved it at the mirror with a smile. The clerk nodded and went back to ringing the register.

David looked back at Allen holding the jar in his fist like a weapon. "It's been two fucking years of scraping-by just waiting for the opportunity . . ."

"Look, I don't want any trouble," Allen found an opening and some of his lost courage. "You were right to be angry . . ."

"Were?"

"Are. No, are. You *are* right to be angry. You . . . no," he closed his eyes and shook his head erasing the last sentence. "Robert . . . ," he continued. "Robert was responsible for this. He got you out. I had no choice but to follow his demand. He wanted you out. He was afraid you knew too much about his history." Allen looked around as he bent forward. His voice fell almost to a whisper. This was it, David told himself. It was about to happen. This was the confession from Allen he had waited for. But Allen didn't want anyone to hear it but him. There was a pause. Allen said nothing more. At the last moment he held back and David's anger rose once more.

"Yeah, tell me about that history, Allen." David's voice cracked slightly with the tension. The anger was bringing tears that David fought back. "How is the history? Is old Robert still piling the white stuff on the coffee table?"

Allen began looking around to see if anyone was listening.

"Are the blizzards a nightly thing or does it carry on through the day?" David followed Allen's eyes as he continued searching the faces of the store patrons.

Allen looked into David's face and nervously held a finger to his own lips. He moved the hand, placing his palm in front of David's face with the fingers spread and rapidly waved it vigorously polishing the air. "Please, not here. We'll talk. We'll talk," Allen pleaded.

David ignored the pleas. His voice was less forceful but still unrelenting. "Do the nose bleeds ever happen during one of those fund raising meetings he was so fond of chairing?"

"Let me explain, please. But not here"

"And how about you, Allen? How's your position?"

"All right! All right!" Allen tore open his wallet again and counted the remaining cash. "Look, here's . . . five-hundred and . . . 12 dollars. That's all I've got on me but it's yours. Here take it." He reached for David's hand and shoved the bills into it then quickly closed David's fingers around the money.

"Why, Allen? I haven't asked you for anything."

"You don't have to," Allen said waving his hand and shaking his head. "You're owed this and a whole lot more."

"Hold it. Slow down." David stuffed most of the cash into his pants pocket. "I want to know some things. I searched my mind a long time trying to understand why you fucked me over so quickly and without any regret. I figured you knew there'd be noise among the investors if you canned Robert. You could have claimed he was being retained as council or said he needed to get back to his profession. But, whatever you said, it would be read that you canned the bastard. You couldn't do that. OK, I got that."

David looked at Allen and saw him relax slightly. "But why," David spit the last sentence at him, "why did you throw me away the way you did when you knew the truth?"

174

Allen was silent.

"No. No more talk," David said emphatically, shaking his head from side-to-side. The quiet hovered in the air over Allen for a moment. Then, slowly with his teeth grinding, David leaned forward. "I—want—Robert." The words were spaced as if each was a sentence of its own. "I want to see that son-of-a-bitch burn in somebody's car wreck." The rage was back. "I want to stand five feet away, close enough to have the hair on my balls singed, and I want to watch him reach out for my help and be able to piss on his hand. And I'm still not certain I don't want to see you in the back seat."

Allen leaned against the stacked boxes. Maybe the image was too real. David gave him some room backing away. Maybe Allen still wasn't certain the jar of pickles wasn't going to end up crushing his skull.

Allen was nervously inching toward David, looking around as he spoke. "First, let's see, yeah, Robert's bout with the drugs had to be covered to prevent a loss in stock value. That could cause ICF."

"What the fuck is ICF?"

"Investor confidence failure—I call it investor confidence failure."

"Jesus, it's beginning to look like you've been playing with your marbles on the edge of a cliff and too many rolled over. This is beautiful," David laughed. "What the fuck are you talking about?"

Allen held his hands up once more and took a deep breath as he looked at the floor. "It was all about the money. It meant millions." Allen lowered his hands as his eyes searched David's face for a response.

"So," David said slowly, "This . . . means you literally sold out our friendship—plain and simple—for a buck."

But it wasn't a buck. It was a lot of bucks and David knew it. Maybe it was millions of bucks which, as a stock holder, he had a stake in. David was given the stock in lieu of the promised salary compensation years before. It wasn't much but if the stock went for the speculated $100 per share, David would have enough to buy something small like maybe Rhode Island. Of course, Allen and the rest of the triumvirate would have the choice of entire continents. Still, David didn't care. His whole point was that the money wasn't worth what Allen . . ., what they had done to him.

David stood looking at Allen. One hand was still grasping the remaining cash that hadn't made it into his pocket, while the other hand held a glass bludgeon with eight kosher ounces of baby gherkins. David looked down at the cash. This was more than he had seen in months. Then he looked back at Allen.

There was silence and then . . . "There's more." Allen said. "I'll meet you somewhere later this week and have a check for you. Anywhere you want. How much? How much do I make the check out for?" Allen reached inside his jacket and pulled out a piece of paper and a black enameled roller ball, then looked up at David like he was ready to take a letter.

Sure, David thought. Why not? He owes me the money. "I want my two year's severance. The amount we agreed on. And interest at ten . . . . No, twelve per cent. And, what the fuck, cash. I want it in cash."

"Cash? No, that's not possible. Cash is no good."

"No," David said slowly. "Cash is great. Whaddaya think. I'm going to go the bank and cash a check in my name when half the county is still looking for me? I want cash."

"David, think for a moment," Allen spoke slowly as if speaking to a child, "That's a lot of money. I'd have to deliver it in a suitcase. You'd have to hide the entire suitcase. Is that what you really want?"

It pained David to admit it, but Allen was right. If he was going to remain inconspicuous—as inconspicuous as a man with a suitcase full of money can be . . . It couldn't happen. Impossible. "All right, a check. Make it a cashier's check to Wayne Brewkowski."

"Who?"

"Brewkowski! Here give me your pen." As Allen handed over the pen, David grabbed his hand and turned it palm-side up writing the name on Allen's hand.

The look on Allen's face was pure puzzlement. He looked at the name and said it once, "Brewkowski."

"Yeah," David said, "Wayne Brewkowski and don't ask."

Allen didn't. He placed the pen back in his pocket staring at the scrawl on his hand. "Good. Good! I'll have it for you by Friday. Same place?"

"No. What are you nuts? Meet me downtown at Willy's in the back. Ten o'clock before any of the noon crowd starts showing up."

Willy's was the locals-only burger and beer spot. Truckers and lonely women were his clients. He sold barrels of beer and about six burgers every day. No one would see them as long as Allen didn't park the Mercedes out front.

Allen was too eager. But, he knew enough to dangle filet mignons in front of a starving man. David bit big time. This steak was worth about 250 thousand plus interest. It was going to make things a lot easier for David.

David left the store after Allen and watched as Allen squeezed between his Mercedes and the gray Mercury with the two ham-and-eggers inside eating lunch. In a moment Allen slid into his car and was gone before David rounded the corner of the store and began walking back toward the trailer park. But, as he looked back, he saw the Mercury pull out behind Allen's Mercedes. The Mercury's passenger looked like he was talking into his sandwich. David realized it was a radio! Allen was being tailed by cops!

CHAPTER 21
The Proposition

It was Friday. About twenty minutes before ten. David wanted to make sure he arrived at Willy's before Allen. Allen's suit and car were enough to draw curious flies and David didn't want any company near them while they talked. He was thinking about the Mercury that tailed Allen as he left the 7-Eleven. He might have been overly suspicious but now he wondered if the tail was cops, or a suspicious partner, or nothing at all. Maybe the guy only looked like he was talking into a radio when it really was his sandwich. David was beginning to doubt what he saw. It didn't matter. Without windows in Willy's place, the only way anyone could follow Allen was to come in.

David let Willy know about Allen and the possibility of unwanted company. Willy put up a yellow plastic rope and scrawled a "closed section" sign on the back of a greasy menu. David sat in the back behind the rope. The dim lights created silhouettes. No one coming in from the street could see him. By the time their eyes adjusted to the darkened atmosphere, David would be gone.

The side door opened. Allen wisely parked in the back—out of the street. As he walked in, he was instantly recognized by Willy as more than a usual customer. The clean clothes were probably the first clue. Willy pointed to the roped off area. Allen weaved his way past the tables and juke box to the yellow rope and sign bumping into chairs as his eyes readjusted to the darkened room. David called to him from the shadows as Allen ducked beneath the rope and walked to the corner where he sat in a chair propped against the wall balancing on two legs. Allen came casual. For him that meant a shirt with a horsey logo, pastel pants and his favorite Italian-made Moreschi shoes with no socks. "No socks" was his definition of dressing down.

"Sitting in the dark—that's a good idea." Allen hoarsely whispered. There was no need for secrecy at the moment. If it wasn't liquid and within reach, no one at Willy's was interested. Allen stood beside the table and looked around once more. Even in the shadows there was little difficulty seeing him. His bright pink shirt made him an obvious curiosity.

"Yeah, good choice," David said sarcastically as he assessed Allen's choice of clothes. "I guess you figured being less than five-and-a-half feet tall, Asian, and dressed like a golf professional would make you inconspicuous enough, huh?"

Allen grabbed a chair next to David and looked back nervously at the front door. He leaned in, and asked, "Is it safe here?"

"Safe from what? I'm the most dangerous thing in your life right now. I wouldn't worry about much else, if I were you."

As it turned out, Allen came more prepared than David gave him credit for. Just then the front door opened and a flood of light washed in scattering through the airborne dust. A backlit figure of a man drew Willy's attention as someone new. Willy turned and looked toward David. Allen looked toward Willy and shouted, "It's OK. He's with me."

180

David was more than surprised. It appeared Allen had a new toy and this one had everyone's attention. David nodded to Willy who cautiously went back to polishing glasses as the man slid into a table seat near the front door.

Allen looked away from the door to David and weakly smiled.

"Wait. Just wait a minute. Who or what is that?"

"That's my protection," Allen said and then quickly added, "Not from you. Not from you. I trust you. I know I can trust you," he said reaching out to touch David's hand for reassurance and then quickly withdrew the attempt as David pushed away from the table. "That's my bodyguard. His name is Michael Daly. He's Irish. Been here for a few weeks. He's sort of hiding. Something about trouble in the old country. I don't really care. All I know is that he comes highly recommended and I'm safe with him."

"Safe from what?"

"That's what I was trying to tell you the other day. But we kind of got sidetracked . . . saying hello and all." Allen wasn't trying to be cute. It was another gentle attempt at reconciliation. The only thing David was interested in was the check . . . and Daly.

It appeared Allen had entered a darker zone. That was where Mike Daly came in. Daly was the special secret Allen held onto— the one that legitimized some of his riskiest chances and insulated him from Robert and his cohorts. Daly was a broad-shouldered man. His sandy hair had a reddish tint that complemented his dull olive-green tweed sport jacket, gray vest and rust-colored tie glowing beneath the Budweiser carousel circling over the table. Daly nestled in and stared in Allen's direction.

This guy was another luxury—the kind Allen collected when he could afford one. He was something not to be used but to have— like a beach house that's too far away for weekend visits or a mistress in San Francisco that's available only on the rare visit when Allen was in town—which was nearly never. David dismissed Daly as a toy; something a younger brother buys because he can and wants his older brother to know he did. Daly was status. Nothing more. After all, bodyguards were used as protection against threats. As far as David knew, he was Allen's only threat and Daly was too far away to help his client. So, why did Allen think he needed him except as a status symbol? But David was wrong. Just like that younger brother trying to impress, Allen had to tell his story. David decided to listen.

"I originally hired him for his security skills," Allen said with a smile. He glanced back at Daly then turned to David and raised his eyebrows with a broader smile. "Daly's a killer."

That caught David's attention. Allen's cat dragged in something lethal. There was reality sitting by the door sipping a pint of Guinness staring back into the darkness at them as though he could see through walls like some mutated Superman. David felt a chill as the thought ran up his spine. All he had pissed and moaned about was there. Right there in front of him, just a few tables away. This wasn't David's idle ranting. This was a trained attack dog waiting for a command. Toy or no toy, Allen had bought a shiny, new weapon.

"He was an active member of the IRA," Allen said looking back once more at Daly. "Daly did the impossible. When someone needed killing in Ulster, he got the job. His reputation was quick and accurate. That's what they said. And lethal." Allen chuckled as he explained. "Professional," was how Allen put it. That meant few mistakes and even less collateral damage—one quick bullet to the head. His resume included 17 British officers, three Ulster politicians and one beautiful, young woman from Belfast.

Allen was feeling cocky. He settled into the bar chair pulling it closer to the table. He had another story and this one would legitimize Daly, and Allen as the owner of the ultimate possession.

182

"The woman is why he's here instead of back in Ireland," he said. David said nothing but it was clear to Allen he had an audience. He inched his chair still closer to David and kept his voice low as he explained Daly's history.

Maggie Arnold was well-known in Belfast. She managed a small pub that had become a local hangout for Catholics and military types. Every other man that walked through the door had fallen in love with her bright smile. So had Daly.

It didn't last long. Word came down of a security leak that gave numerous IRA details to the British. Through a plan where bad leads were planted throughout the district, Maggie was identified as the leak. Another bit of false information was passed to Maggie alone, this time with directions for a meeting. When local British troops were seen staking the place out, it was conclusive. Maggie was working for the hated English and Daly was given the job of taking her out.

Daly was visibly troubled by the idea. He never killed women. It would have to be a very special job for his involvement. When the job was complete, Maggie was found wrapped in her shawl gently placed beside the river near the Milltown Road and Clement Wilson Park. Her arms were folded over her chest and a bunched cluster of flowers picked from the surrounding grasses was thrown near the body. There was one shot to the back of Maggie's head with a low caliber pistol. The next day, Daly was gone. No word as to where, though many figured they knew why. The Brits knew only that Daly had killed their spy. The reward was set at six figures; an accumulation based on his dark portfolio with emphasis on his last crime. It didn't matter. No one would try to collect.

Daly made his way to New York through some old connections and was absorbed by the city. Soon, he was working again in a much bigger arena—as a private consultant. This time there was no purpose, no cause, and no reason other than the money. It paid well and as before, it was quick, clean and he was in demand.

By the end of the story, Allen was giddy. Leaning on the table with his chin nearly resting on his arms he stared, smiling at Daly like an admiring five-year-old boy. David stared too still leaning on two chair legs against the wall. He said nothing.

Allen fidgeted with his own chair trying to make it fit better and, after a moment, as he realized David would say nothing, Allen said, "I got your check." He reached for his back pocket.

David whistled softly and looked toward Willy holding up two fingers on both his hands. "Two and two," Willy announced. He wiped his hands on the soiled white apron that covered his t-shirt and said, "Got it," then disappeared into the kitchen.

"Now, let me see the check."

Allen reached back once more and pulled his brown leather wallet from his back pocket. He pulled the light blue personal check out and put it on the table. As David placed all four chair legs on the floor and leaned in to take the check, Allen put his right hand flat on top of it.

"What's this? What are you doing?"

"I've got a proposition for you," Allen said. The childlike smile he wore since he arrived disappeared. Allen the boy with the toy was replaced by Allen the worldly businessman.

"I don't want any propositions. Last time I listened to your proposition it cost me several years of my life, my wife and a couple hundred thousand dollars just to mention the more noticeable losses." David reached over and grasping Allen's hand pulled the check away. As David looked at it, he couldn't help thinking how nice the 314 looked but the three zeroes that followed made him want to yell "drinks on the house" to both of the drunks at the bar.

"Listen to me. Just listen for a minute," Allen said excitedly.

"No, first you listen," David said folding the check. "I want a couple of answers. The one's you didn't answer in the store." David took a quick breath to keep Allen from finding an opening to speak. "Maybe," David told him, "there is another scenario for the way you fucked me. We'll get to that in a minute but personally I'm hoping I know the real reason. The repercussions are much weightier. You know, possible jail time. Ruined reputations. That sort of thing." David stared at Allen as if trying to burn a hole through his head with his stare. "I'm figuring it's blackmail. How am I doing?"

"Listen, please . . .,"Allen had something important on his mind.

"See, the way I figure it, during what you took to be Robert's ass-kissing stage . . .," David kept going mindlessly ignoring Allen's objections.

"If you'll let me speak . . ." Allen's interruption wasn't something David was willing to deal with. He kept going.

"Robert took you to a party or two. And during the course of the evening as you sipped on one-too-many cranberry cocktails, he introduced you to the happy powder, yes?" Allen's lack of objection had David believing he was on the right path.

"You liked it and had one hell of a great time that you didn't remember the next morning. Oh, you knew you hit the coke but not much else." Allen was sitting back in his chair with his arms hanging to his side.

"Next time you saw Robert your sheepish greeting was answered by a man with uncharacteristic confidence. Robert had you by the balls and you and he both knew it. It was your secret with him. Something special the two of you would share." There was a squeak from Allen as he tried to interrupt. David kept going. "Nothing had to be said but you both knew Robert could crush you as easily as you might want to crush him. Kind of a Texas stand-off." David nailed it—dead-on. All the time alone, lost in thought led him to the truth and now all that remained was the confirmation he was seeing on Allen's reddened face. David smiled with too many long years of satisfaction, ignoring what sounded like an impending plea for mercy.

Allen leaned in. His hands were fists pressed against the sticky glass table top. "You've got to understand something," he said. As he pleaded for David's attention, his voice cracked under the pressure.

"You see," David interrupted, "that story makes the most sense. That one says the decision wasn't yours and that it was not about money as much as self-preservation. I could almost accept that excuse. Respect it and even forgive. But what you didn't see was that Robert wanted and would get more than just a 50-50 split of responsibility. He wanted more and took it. Your push, your ability to direct this business venture was suddenly taken from you. Robert acquired the control. So, you went along with whatever he wanted and when he told you to get rid of me before I found out about his coke history, you said yes because now his history was your history."

David paused and stared at Allen, but Allen said nothing. David's need to sear through Allen's skull tapered off. Allen was quieting too. His fists relaxed and his reddened face paled. David was looking for something more in Allen's eyes, his body attitude. Sweat. Anything. But, there was nothing. And then it was Allen's turn.

"Robert could have destroyed you," Allen said in a slow, rational voice and normal volume. "He claimed there were witnesses that would gladly swear to seeing *you* as the user. There was nothing," he said slowly shaking his head, "you could have done." Allen was convincing. As he spoke the nervousness left him and his

186

own anger began surfacing—a long-hidden anger brought on by Robert.

"Robert began demanding things." Allen stopped and eased closer to David. As he nervously looked over his shoulder toward the bar he said, "He has brought in another investor." Allen looked directly into David's eyes. "This guy is trouble." Again he waited, then, sat back. "That's why I have Daly," he said tilting his head toward the bar and the man sitting next to the door. "I'm fucking scared! You've got to listen." There was urgency in Allen's claim. "Robert is using GrowVest as a front of some kind. They funnel money through our accounts. It makes it look like there is some major revenue being generated in South America."

It was obvious David was not Allen's prime problem anymore, if he ever was. There was a change in Allen as he spoke about the problems at GrowVest. Allen   prepared his presentation and the facts were ready to roll just as Willy delivered the "two and two" burgers and beer. David pushed his plate aside more interested in Allen's story. The aroma of the freshly grilled beef and onions only came to his consciousness when he saw Allen lock his hands around the pile of bun, lettuce and pink, dripping beef and take a bite.

"Robert made him Vice President for Central and South America," Allen said muffled through the burger. His facial expression changed from frustration at not being heard to concentration. He was excitedly telling David what he came there to say while absentmindedly stuffing the burger in his mouth. "But it wasn't Robert's idea," he mumbled.

Allen had just peeled off 314 big ones from his personal bank account and was sitting across from an astonished David scarfing down a burger and beer. To David, it appeared Allen was at any old business luncheon with a trucker. Allen looked like an animal that hadn't eaten raw meat in a week. It was impressive. It was also very unlike Allen. Fear has a way of changing behavior. Allen, it seemed, was trying to eat his.

"This guy," he said with his mouth half full, "has something on Robert and makes plans that Robert is expected to execute. I have no control." Allen raised his voice and waved a free hand. "He has taken it all." And then another bite and a sip of beer.

David was in absolute awe as he watched and listened to Allen. He couldn't eat or drink. He just sat watching. The circus came to town and David was in the trapeze lady's dressing room watching her barely cover her sinewy body with a skin-tight, sequined costume. It was far more than David expected.

"GrowVest is lost in a much larger shadow corporation. Drugs, gambling, I have no way of knowing." Allen was quiet for a moment as he stared at the grease in his plate.

The feds would love this information, David thought. But that was too easy. He played that dream years before and saw little satisfaction in its conclusion. "Why are you telling me this?"

"I told you," Alan looked at David with his eyes wide open. The hamburger dripped from his hands and a small stream of grease ran toward his chin from the corner of his mouth. "I need help if I'm ever going to regain control." He reached for a paper napkin and wiped his face.

"I've heard enough," David said as he pushed his chair from the table ready to leave.

"Robert is afraid of this guy," Allen said pushing his chair back. "He's always on edge looking like a little push will put him over." Allen was hurriedly making his case, trying to capture David's interest before he walked out. "You could push him just by showing him you're still in the picture," he said dropping the burger to the plate.

David waited, tempering his impatience. He listened to Allen ramble on for another five minutes. Then, without waiting for Allen to clear the fries from his plate, David got up to leave. After grabbing a smoke from the counter near the register, he nodded to Willy and motioned that "the short guy with the pink Polo shirt is paying." As he passed the table near the door, he nodded to Daly. Daly raised his index finger of the hand pressed to the glass table top. The other continued cradling his Guinness. David walked away from lunch hungry and very confused.

Allen never stopped talking as he passed Willy at the bar. He reached into his pocket and peeled a fifty from the stack and tossed it on the counter. While David continued for the door, Allen kept talking in hushed tones trying to keep up with David's departure.

Willy looked at the fifty as though it was foreign currency. "Uh, wait a minute," he said. Allen stopped and impatiently turned in Willy's direction. Willy picked up the fifty. "Got anything smaller?" he said supplying a quizzical look and a shrug of his shoulders. Allen waved a "keep the change" and stuffed his cash roll back in his pocket squinting in David's direction as the bar's open door exposed the cavernous room to daylight and the welcome aroma of fresh, diesel-tinted city air. The change blinded Allen for a moment. He dipped his head and quickened his step to catch up to David. Daly was immediately behind him.

"I need to take some time and figure this out," David said loudly enough that Allen could hear over the light street traffic. Certainly, the information was exactly what David needed to destroy Robert. That meant Allen might take the hit as well. But, David figured, Allen wouldn't be giving him information that was self-destructive. No matter how guilty Allen might feel he was no fool.

David was on the sidewalk chewing off eighty cents of a dollar-fifty White Owl corona with Allen right there still yammering through the cheap cigar smoke faster than David's mind could process Allen's accent. He tossed the pale brown cigar stub to the curb and began walking away.

"Where are you going? We have to do something," Allen shouted. "You are in a perfect position to get him out of here. Think about it. Robert thinks you're dead. It's been two years. He's consumed by this new guy," Allen continued shouting as David crossed the street leaving him on the curb with the bodyguard looking both ways like a lethal crossing guard. "Two years since I left," David said to himself. "But four years that I invested in you and your company," he shouted back across the street. "That's four years of wasted time and all of it is on your head—you and Robert."

Allen didn't hear him. He was shouting back and for a moment their words clashed like the traffic sounds coming from the street between them. "He spends his entire day on the phone or taking three and five day jaunts to Costa Rica and Venezuela and Ecuador," Allen shouted.

Near the opposite curb, David stopped and turned to see Allen dodging cars, scurrying in his direction. Allen caught David's attention. "If I see him at all," Allen yelled, "he's on my door step long enough to push by me and make some demands about transferring funds from one account to the next. He is distracted all the time and wound so tight he could snap at any minute. You could push him," Allen was anxiously waiting for a reply. Then, quietly he added, "You could be the one to end all of this."

His fading voice sounded like a plea. David realized that, if he was right and not just piling on one more piece of shit, this could be the perfect set-up to destroy Robert. David still wanted Robert. He reminded himself to keep his eye on the goal. The whole situation, he thought, might be working toward an end without his help. "You know, there is the argument that my best position is to stand back and watch it happen," David yelled toward Allen. "Getting involved in any way could only get me in trouble." He looked to see any reaction from Allen as the words carefully spilled from his lips. "Maybe killed," he said. "I know nothing of this investor. The amount of money running through GrowVest's accounts is motive enough to have me sent on a vacation that ends as soon as I get to my hotel room. I'm not interested in becoming part of anyone's plans for destruction. I just want to be the voyeur." David turned from Allen, "I'll catch you later." As he walked away, Allen followed still talking with Daly several steps behind watching the traffic and the roof tops.

"I'm not listening anymore," David said as he hopped onto the bus. "Gotta get to a bank. We'll talk later."

CHAPTER 22
Kiss the Corvette Goodbye

Mac was in a hurry. The GrowVest building was dark except for the lights that burned in the CFO's office and the front lobby. It was late—sometime after 1 a.m., Saturday. Mac was emptying file cabinets while the computer dictated more files onto a small, red and black, 4 GB flash drive. He haphazardly piled the paper files on the floor. One stack of yellow manila folders mixed with the next. The calculated confusion would take clerks hours to reconstruct. In the end, no one would notice if any files were taken. All the files they believed that should be there were there. This, he hoped, would add more days to the search as the team of harried clerks was forced to refile the mass of documents looking once more for any missing files. Mac believed Robert and Allen would conclude that something was missing but would never know what. It would take days. The confusion would help Mac delay his pursuers. That was, of course, the plan.

Satisfied with the beat up condition of the room, he stepped back and turned to the desk directing his attention to the computer. "Come on!" he growled. Mac's mind was working at a much greater speed than the machine. The download ended and he pulled the finger-sized collection of files out of the USB port and stuffed it in his vest pocket beneath his pin-striped suit jacket. Once more Mac
192

typed directions into the computer. This time he commanded an erase of the copied files typing in a code that encrypted the files multiple times before erasing them. That completed the job so that no one would be able to trace its ghost in the company's computer bank.

"Gone, ha!" he said in triumph. All files were completely gone except for the flash drive. He grabbed his gold-tinted Haliburton brief case and threw it on the desk. He fumbled with the latches briefly and in his haste pushed the case causing a stapler and glass paper weight to crash to the floor. The molded aluminum case was open. His passport was visible in the upper compartment. There were three stacks of twenty dollar bills and one of hundreds pushing against the case's upper liner. Mac moved to the wall of file cabinets. He pulled his ring of keys from his pocket. There was a key for each of the twelve master drawers. He fumbled for the black-coded key and inserted it in the cabinet lock marked "correspondence." The key turned and the oval lock popped toward him with a resounding click. Opening the top file drawer, he went immediately to the back and hurriedly pulled out an unmarked yellow, clasped envelope. Opening it, he was presented with a one-inch thick stack of government bearer bonds with interest coupons still attached. The colorful collection was diverse representing several countries. He checked the numbers in the upper right corner as he flipped the pages and then moved to the last bond and glanced at the final number. Because the buyer of the bonds was never recorded, the bearer was the owner. The stack of certificates was as good as cash—a very large sum of cash. The bonds were essential to his plan. Without them the stacks of money represented were impossible for Mac to hide or carry away so easily. Being able to escape with the envelope's millions in a golden Haliburton, he told himself, was one more ironic stroke of genius.

Satisfied with his collection, he tucked the envelope under his arm. Mac was a busy boy creating a very special collection while counting the money that came in through GrowVest's investor doors. He grabbed the remaining files and threw them to the floor. He opened two more drawers and carelessly emptied them, also distributing their contents over the disarranged pile.

Satisfied that he had it all, he tossed the bonds into the Haliburton, then reached for the flash drive in his vest and threw that in with the bonds closing the case. Mac hurried to the office door, hit the light switch and closed the door without regard for the bang that accompanied his haste.

A moment passed. The lights were flipped on as the door opened again. He had forgotten something. He was muttering, swearing. "Idiot! What are you thinking? Why do you think you came here? Hurry, you son-of-a-bitch! Hurry!" He threw himself down into the black leather swivel chair behind his desk, slapped the case on the desk once more and opened it. He leaned to his right and pulled out the bulky key ring from his pants pocket. Flipping through the collection of keys he found a small brass key for the locked desk drawer to the right of his chair. He inserted it in the desk drawer lock and turned it, then yanked at the handle. Too much haste. Too much fury. He jiggled the key in the lock and turned it once more. This time there was an audible click. He yanked at the handle again and the drawer slid effortlessly open.

Inside was a lock box and another key was required. Once again he fumbled at the key chain selecting a smaller, silver-colored key that he inserted and turned. The box opened. A coarse, white cotton cloth bag was pulled from the box. It bulged with heavy contents. Mac placed the bag in the palm of his left hand and bounced it once and then again. The heavy gold coins had a rich sound as they clanged together. Mac smiled and then turned once more to the box. His left hand moved to deposit the bag of 15 gold coins on the desk while his eyes and right hand plunged once more into the box. He pulled out a second bag. This one was smaller, made of smooth, shiny, black silk. There was little time and Mac had to hurry. He pulled the draw string open on the silk bag and poured a few of the diamonds out into his left palm. There were more, many more, in the bag. The diamonds were pushed back into the smooth bag. The top was folded over, tied with the draw string tightly around the bag. It and the coins were dropped into the open Haliburton. Mac again closed the case snapping each chromed latch and twisted the combination lock shut. Dragging the aluminum case from the glass-covered desk, Mac headed for the office door one last time.

Bold. Mac was bolder than he ever was in his life. His confidence had him avoid the side entrance that might mask his departure time the guards were required to post in the lobby's log. Instead he walked back through the main lobby on his way to the front entrance. He walked past the security desk where the night crew sat watching monitors. He said "good night" as he passed the two men. One waved while the other made the required log entry of the time of Mac's departure, then, commented, "I wonder what that was about."

"Yeah," the other answered. "What was that, fourteen minutes?"

There was still a degree of purpose in what Mac was doing. He was not safe yet. He hadn't wiped away his tracks. He wanted to be in the air before sunrise and lost to the world by the time the damage to the office was discovered at eight o'clock, Monday morning when the rest of the office began funneling in.

He walked through the front door toward his reserved space where his bright red Corvette C7 was parked. He opened the car door and slid into the body-formed leather seat. He carefully aimed a finger at the starter button. Six-hundred and thirty-eight handcrafted horses screamed back and Mac smiled once more. This was it. His plan looked complete. It was more than a year since he realized Robert was the perfect fall guy for this game. Everyone hated Robert. Even he had grown to hate him until he realized that Robert's ignorance of what Mac did and who he really was, was the perfect way for Mac to take what he wanted and leave Robert to cover it up. Robert had to or risk being accused of embezzling the funds himself. Allen would, once again, have to agree that public knowledge of the affair might threaten the company's position. If Mac's treachery was ever discovered, Robert would look like an idiot; Allen would look like the fool; and Mac would be too far away to care.

The 6.2 liter 'vette cruised at an easy 80 as Mac headed toward Richmond International Airport. He drove into the long-term parking garage and parked in GrowVest's reserved space. Grabbing the brief case from the adjacent seat, Mac exited the car. He rubbed his hand over the satin-smooth red finish as he walked past the car. Mac turned once more to look at the car one last time as a tall black man emerged from behind a concrete pylon and raised the suppressed gun for Mac to see. It spit once. Mac fell face down. The aluminum brief case skidded across the parking lot wedging beneath the tire of a silver SUV. The gunman walked to Mac and fired twice more at point-blank range into the back of Mac's head then casually walked to the SUV. He bent and picked up the scratched case and walked to the stairway door.

There was no mention of Mac's murder in the press. The office mess didn't exist. Nothing was noted as missing. Mac was the last person noted in the log—1:27 a.m. It was assumed Mac was looking for something at a very late hour. Mac often worked late— even though this was his latest venture. Allen was disturbed. Robert was not. After that, no one spoke of Mac again except for Allen who said he received a typed note of resignation in the mail from Mac and an attached note that said he would not be returning. The postmark was blurred. He could only make out the letters CA and a date that coincided with the day Mac disappeared. Shortly thereafter, Robert hired another private firm to look after the books. The firm Mac hired was dismissed.

CHAPTER 23
Made in Germany

The next couple of weeks were dangerous for David. He spent more time in town—usually close enough to get a peek at Robert. Nothing more. He just wanted to see him. He wanted to know what he was dealing with. He wanted to know if Robert was focused on the game he was playing. If he was, then Robert might be oblivious to everything else and David might go unnoticed.

Things seemed to be on David's side. From all that he was able to see, Robert was definitely breathing rarified air. The custom clothes, new house, and luxury car were obvious assets and so was the way he flaunted it all. Then, there was the flashy new watch. It was often the first thing people noticed when speaking with him. If they didn't, Robert usually made a point of telling them what time it was turning the conversation toward the timepiece. Robert didn't wear it every day, usually reserving the expensive jewelry for Fridays or special meetings meant to impress.

David listened as a pair of street associates left Robert's side and walked in David's direction. The conversation was about the watch. They described it and guessed its value. This, David thought, was a prize. This was one of the few items David had ever seen or heard of that Robert coveted. He made up his mind. He wanted the watch and somehow, he would get it.

Suggesting Robert's wealth was not entirely derived from his legitimate efforts at GrowVest was a lot like asking if the last fourteen items you bought at WalMart were all made in China. Both were guarantees. Both should have been obvious. But even the obvious needed documentation, if he expected to convince anyone. There was too much opulence in Robert's new neighborhood and too much in what he wore. There must have been proof hidden somewhere—a defining collection that could tell David everything about Robert's activity. He needed to find the hidden documentation.

Robert's house contained the proof. He was certain of it. Keeping it at the office was too risky. David concluded that he had to get into the house. But it was undeniable that David's experience at breaking and entering lacked a history of success. This "prank" was more than popping tires or scratching car paint. He had to find someone with more experience.

The most likely source for finding the expert was the neighborhood bar. The large red metal "Polly's" parrot that hung over the sidewalk identified the place. The sign swung gently in the late afternoon breeze giving a momentary illusion of life to the faded, paint-chipped bird. The bar's interior was bright with windows near the front that wrapped around the building to the parking lot. Years of nicotine stained the walls and other wooden surfaces a sticky, walnut-like brown. A lonely speaker vibrated on the back wall thumping out an unending array of Eagle's songs at a dollar per juke box selection. The sound flowed out to the nearly empty parking lot through an open back door that acted as an escape for the thick layers of cigarette smoke. The door belched clouds like a dying dragon whenever the draft created by the opening of the front door allowed the air to flow.

There was nothing glamorous or trendy about Polly's. People came there to drink, smoke and socialize. Mostly drink. It was a private club where membership was immediate and friends were just as easily acquired. It had its contingent of "regulars," and established life-long patrons—men and women whose names were riveted to the backs of the short-backed bar stools they occupied until their livers retired.

Polly was the owner, though she seldom visited anymore. Years of cigarette smoke contributed to her early departure and emphysema. Riki was the bartender on duty that afternoon. She was an attractive, 30-something dressed in black tank top and jeans that matched the color of her curly hair. The deeply cut tee revealed a Suicide Girl mural of tattoos that covered both her arms. The art work carried across her chest continuing beneath the tee decorating all that could be seen of her breasts. Riki was a hard worker moving the length of the bar, visiting each person to fill or refill their glasses and always with a comment that elicited a smile from the patron. If anyone could steer David to his expert, Riki was the one. She knew all of the regulars by name.

"Hey Wayne, how's it goin'?"

David was barely through the door when Riki saw him. "All is well, beautiful. Hey, I've gotta ask you a couple of questions. You got maybe five minutes?"

"Sure, just let me finish with Kevin down there and I'll be right back." She finished the pour and slid it toward him, then grabbed a second glass, filled it and walked to the bar's other end to deliver it to Kevin.

There was time for one sip from the mug before Riki returned. "OK, what's up?" she asked.

"I need some help with a special project and I thought you might be able to steer me toward someone who could help me."

David pulled out a twenty from his shirt pocket and placed it on the counter.

Riki looked down at the twenty and frowned. "Project! I need a little more information."

"I need someone," David hesitated looking for the right explanation without giving too much away.

Riki laughed, "Anyone I know is gonna want more than twenty no matter how quick you are. You better put that away."

David pocketed the twenty. "No. Not that," David said laughing. He placed his elbow on the bar, covered his mouth with his hand and said quietly, "I need someone who might be able to open a door . . . or two."

"Uh oh. That sounds like something I don't want to know anything about. But if I did want to know about that kind of thing, I think I might talk to Barry." She turned and looked down the bar. "You know Kevin," she said. "Barry's to his right talking with him. Need an introduction?"

"No, no I'm okay." David walked toward the other end of the bar, then turned back toward Riki and said, "Send down a couple more of whatever they're drinking and one more for me too."

Riki nodded and went to work filling glasses.

Kevin was one of the regulars and was David's connection to Barry. Kevin was perpetually friendly. Know Kevin for five minutes and he considered you a friend. Buy him a beer and you were related for life. It turned out Barry was just as easy to know. Both men spent the better part of each day warming their bar stools and emptying glasses. The rest of their day was an interruption reserved for earning a few bucks as day laborers. After fifteen minutes and a few strategically placed, veiled questions, Barry gave David a solid lead for a future interview.

200

"But the real expert you gotta meet is Leonard," Barry said with his eyes half open. A vigorous shake of Kevin's head in agreement had David interested.

"Leonard," Barry said, "spends some time here."

"You've seen him," Kevin assured David. "You've probably even met him. He's usually here on Monday or Tuesday nights. He'll never admit it, but everybody knows he's a thief. Nothing big. Just little break-ins for TVs and stereos."

"Yeah, nothing big," Barry echoed as if size mattered.

After a few more minutes of explanations about Leonard's bar attendances, David began to understand that Leonard visited the bar early in the week and saved his mid-to-late weekdays and weekends free for his preferred hobby. David subsequently decided to extend his Monday beer-side visit into the evening when Leonard was expected.

True to form, Leonard glided in and grabbed a seat at the end of the bar near the front door. Leonard was wiry and in need of a shave two days ago. He was average height with tightly-cropped, brown hair mixed with gray. Slender but clearly muscular, he wore Nikes, his usual blue sweat pants and a gray Washington Redskins hoodie. David had already mentioned him to Riki and asked her to point him out when he came in. David had to be sure.

He watched as Riki walked over to Leonard. She delivered a long-neck and said something to him. Leonard took a side glance in David's direction and nodded to the bartender then he looked at David and nodded his head once more. David did recognize him. He remembered that Leonard was always pleasant usually sharing a moment with various people that stopped by. He drank little, nursing one or two beers for several hours before slipping out of the place, mostly unnoticed. Knowing now what he did about Leonard made David think he was there just long enough to establish an alibi.

Leonard picked up his beer and walked to David's end of the bar where Don Henley's voice and guitar were just a bit louder. He took the stool beside David. Riki introduced them and smiled at Leonard to indicate that David was okay. The two men shook hands. David noticed Leonard's hands were very small, smooth, and uncallused. David ordered two more beers before Leonard had even sipped the first. "No, no. I'm okay, thanks," he said. David turned to Riki. "We're good," he told her. The bartender left and for the next fifteen minutes while they talked, kept patrons away from the area.

Leonard asked no questions, at first. Just sat and listened with one curiously small hand cradling his chin. Soon, Leonard was talking too. Ten minutes of listening to Leonard had David convinced this was the man he needed. David had to work out some conditions. "The rules are very simple," David said, "You get into Robert's house and find out if there is a safe or likely place where important papers might be kept."

Leonard smiled and said, "Papers? That's whatcha want, papers?"

"Yeah," David explained, "the papers are proof of something more. Anything else you find, you keep. I want nothing except the watch and the papers," David said. He described the watch to him and Leonard smiled once more.

"That sounds like a major piece a work," he said before taking a short tug on the beer.

David stressed once more, "You understand? You keep everything but the watch and the papers" He had to be certain Leonard understood.

"Why? Why you doin' this? If it aint for the money, why?'

"The reasons are personal."

"If it's just for the watch," Leonard reasoned, "you wouldn't need the papers and if it's just the papers then what's with the watch? Is it some kinda family heirloom?"

David's jaw tightened as he clenched his teeth. "Let's just leave it this way." David took a sip from the sweating brown beer bottle in front of him then put it down on the uneven bar surface and crossed his hands trying to keep them and his anger under control. He turned to Leonard and calmly said, "I want the son-of-a-bitch dead but before that happens I want to see every fucking thing he's ever done exposed."

"Dead" was the wrong thing to say. Leonard straightened up and turned away from David toward the bar. He grabbed his beer and nodded toward the bartender. There was a momentary pause before he shook his head. He turned to David and said, "Maybe this ain't for me. I don't get into hurtin' people. No physical shit. If you wanna kill the guy, I'm out." Leonard slid from the stool ready to leave.

"Whoa, wait!" David said it too loudly and quickly looked to see if anyone heard him. "Wait," he said again, softly. David leaned in and placed a hand on Leonard's arm. "I said I *want* him dead. I don't intend to kill him or even have him killed. I want to destroy him. The papers, if they exist, will help me toward that end."

Leonard moved back toward the bar. "You're sure 'bout that?'

"Absolutely. No funny stuff."

"'Cause if there's even a hint of violence, I'll scream so loud there'll be cops from the next city comin' over to help."

"No, it's all good," David assured him. "Nobody is going to be hurt. Nobody."

"OK."

"The watch," David explained, "is just salt in the wound. It's a prize of his. Apparently it represents his success. I get the watch and I hurt him—especially if the papers don't pan out." Then, as if to reassure him, "As I said, you keep anything else you find in or out of the safe. No one is physically hurt. No violence."

Leonard edged his way back to the bar stool and sat down once more. He stared ahead without saying anything. David wasn't certain he had convinced Leonard but he was clearly considering the proposal. Turning to stare off at the same imaginary object, David said nothing waiting for Leonard's response. Leonard dropped his head and without looking at David turned as if speaking into his shoulder. "I keep the rest, that right?"

"Yes everything but the watch and papers."

Leonard hesitated, drained half of his beer and said, "Awright, here's what I'll do. I'll check into this guy and the house. Lemme see what there is. By that I mean, sometimes there aint no need to break in if the guy clearly has nothin' of value."

David began to interrupt. Leonard raised his hand, "Wait. I know you said he's got a watch. Maybe he does, or maybe it's just some piece of shit worth a couple hundred bucks. Either way, if it's not worth my time, I'm not takin' this any further. You understand?"

"Yeah, got it."

"One more thing. If I get caught, I'm not protectin' nobody. There's nothin' noble about this gig. I get caught and you go down too. So, tell me once more. Is this worth it?"

David smiled. This was Leonard's confirmation. He would do the job. David told him, "If you don't think this is everything I've promised you after checking him out, I'll agree to let the whole thing go. No strings. No regrets. This is all your game." That wasn't true. If Leonard walked away from this after casing Robert's house, David knew he would have to find someone else.

Leonard promised to check the place out over the next few days. They agreed to another meeting the following Wednesday before any final decisions were made about the job

A week later, David was waiting for Leonard at the bar. Wednesday night came and went without Leonard and now, at 2 a.m. it was Thursday morning. David was worried. Maybe he gave Leonard too much information or the "dead" thing had him rethinking the job. Maybe Leonard would go ahead with the plans and keep David out. Then David realized he knew who Leonard was and could easily kill any chance he had of fencing whatever he took, especially if that included the watch. No, Leonard hadn't skipped. Something was up.

It was 3 a.m. when David left the bar and hit the sack exhausted and worried. At 8 a.m., the same morning, the phone rang. It was Leonard.

"Where the fuck were you last night? We had a meeting." David was tired and instantly pissed.

"Yeah, yeah. Listen, I'm sorry but I think you'll be happy to hear what I've found out. Be at Polly's at noon."

David arrived and stood in the doorway. He scanned the bar looking for Leonard. At the opposite end of the bar still wearing the same sweats from the week before, he saw Leonard smiling back. As David approached, Leonard got up and moved toward a table farther away from the few people talking nearby.

"You ever change those clothes?"

"What this? This is kind of a signature thing," Leonard said smiling. "People see me and recognize me immediately, just by the clothes. It gives me credibility with the cops. If anyone asks, people always say they saw me and always describe what I'm wearing. Besides, they're baggy enough that I can wear other clothes underneath." He pointed to his head and winked. "Always thinking, ya know?"

David still wasn't smiling and was still a little pissed for being stood up the night before. "OK. What have you got?"

Leonard was excited with his news. They pulled up chairs at the table. Leonard started. "I've got this buddy, Leon," he said. "He's a legitimate businessman. Been in the lock and safe business for years." David suddenly realized why Leonard had such a glowing reputation as a B&E man. Know your subject, reap the rewards. It was all about who you know. "This guy, Leon, he knows about Robert," Leonard told him. "About a year ago, your best friend was shopping for a special safe." David winced at Leonard's reference to Robert as his friend. Leonard saw David's expression, smiled and said, "Whatever." Leonard laughed and shrugged. "He asked every freakin' locksmith in the state about it. Funny thing is that no locksmith knew about the safe so they're all callin' each other tryin' to get information for the guy. Pretty soon, it's common knowledge that this Whitney guy has pulled out all the stops lookin' for this safe."

"Ok. So, the safe is very special, I got it." David was still fighting off the morning fatigue and had no patience. He wanted this story to move on but Leonard was too pleased with his discovery to let it out too quickly.

"Of course! But no one can help him 'cause no one even knows what it's called. All Whitney could tell them was that the safe was German made and very high end—so high end that Leon had never seen one. But Leon is an old pro. He's one of those collector freaks—always stashin' away information in a file. He's sure he's read about the safe once before. Several years ago in a trade magazine, he thought.

"So, we start pawin' through his magazine stash. Page by fuckin' page," Leonard laughed. "We spent most of that night diggin' through stacks of old magazines Leon saved. Leon's got magazines that go back to the early 80s. He never throws anythin' away that might have information he can use. So, we finally found the magazine—some obscure German copy from the late 90s with lots of photos. Neither of us could make out what the article said. We got the company name, model number and the basic idea of what made it so special from the pictures. One thing I can tell from the pictures is that the safe is always custom made for the client. We also made out that fewer than 20 had ever been installed back then." Then Leonard said, "So, I figure this guy's gotta have some heavy cash in that safe." He smiled and said, "The safe cost nearly a hundred-fifty thousand twenty years ago."

David frowned as if he didn't believe what he was being told. This story didn't sound right, he thought. Leonard may have gotten his information wrong.

Leonard went on describing the safe. "The safe has no handle on the outside. No tumblers, no hinges. Just the door with a kind of inset or depression to pull it open." David was slouching in his chair losing confidence as Leonard described the safe. Leonard saw David's frustration and laughed. "It gets better," Leonard said. "If we figured this out right, the safe is made of two-inch thick carbon steel around a one inch thick liner of magnesium! Magnesium, get it?" Leonard continued to beam at this discovery.

"No. So, it's made of magnesium on the outside. Is that something special in a safe?"

"No, not on the outside. Inside." Leonard stressed it once more and continued smiling to the point that he started to giggle.

"That's special," David said it hoping that Leonard would think he understood.

"Ohhh, yes it is. Magnesium," he explained, "is a special metal that burns when it gets to a certain temperature. Once on fire it's almost three times hotter than the cuttin' torch trying to cut through it."

It was starting to make sense to David as to why the safe cost so much. "The last thing," Leonard said leaning toward David and pushing a pointed finger into the table, "anyone tryin' to torch the safe open sees is flames shooting outta the safe toward their face." Leonard smiled and leaned back in his chair locking his hands behind his head. "Of course, all the shit inside is toasted to ash if it's not in some kinda fireproof case, so ya gotta ask why anyone would want the safe to begin with. Your buddy must have some items he never intends to share."

David was so intently listening to Leonard's story about breaking the safe that he nearly forgot the obvious. "How do *you* get into it?" David was annoyed. "How does Robert open his own safe?"

Leonard was still smiling. "It's a sound activated lock." Leonard waited for the information to settle on David's already confused brain. Then he added, "There's an ultrasonic key that you point at the safe. It can't be heard by the human ear but when the safe hears the sound, it pops open." On cue, David's mouth popped open. There was a little drool on the table pooling in front of him.

"Fantastic!" he whispered.

Leonard kept chuckling while David thought about the safe. He quietly considered the 20 years of undiscovered improvements that weren't in the aging magazine article. He thought they should have Leonard justifiably worried. He wasn't.

"Yeah fantastic. But there is a catch," Leonard smiled. "The direction that the key is pointed in is so exact that if it's off by even a small amount, the key won't work. Incredible huh? It's got a one degree angle for sensin' the sound to open."

"What the fuck? This is no confidence builder you're painting here," David said, frustrated by Leonard's apparent loss of
208

direction. David believed Leonard's admiration for German engineering was misplaced. "I need some idea from you that you're going to be able to open the safe, not stand in admiring awe once you go back to crack it."

Leonard kept smiling. The smile broadened as he chuckled and presented a clenched fist in front of his face.

"What? What have you got?"

Leonard was hiding something but it was small enough to be completely hidden in the grasp of his small hand. David could see nothing but the Cheshire cat grin behind the fist. Leonard lowered his hand to the table and opened the fist showing a small key chain with two keys attached and, what looked like a small, square, flat flashlight about an inch and a half long and an inch wide. Leonard pressed the button that covered one of the flat sides and a small, powerful light shined a very narrow, bright green laser beam on the table's surface.

"You think I wasn't workin' all this week, Wayne?" Leonard chuckled, turned off the light and left the keys on the table. David picked them up and shined the light on a nearby wall. The light was pin-point accurate with no intensity fall-off. At eight feet the lighted spot on the wall was smaller than a pencil's point.

"How? How did you get this?"

Leonard took the keys and began playing with the beam. "I stopped by the house the mornin' after we spoke last week. I got there and waited for Whitney to leave for work," Leonard said. "I've got a construction helmet with the water company's name on it and a clipboard I carry with me. If anyone sees me they think I'm the water meter guy."

"You got into the house?"

"Yeah sure. Popped the back door and walked right in. But it didn't go as smoothly as I figured." His giddiness toned down but the smile was still there. "There's an alarm system. I've never seen one like this, Wayne." Leonard leaned in, "Once I realized I couldn't do nothin' with it, I decided to give myself six minutes. That's about how long it takes for a police response in that neighborhood." This was a man that knew how good he was and took a distorted sense of pride in his work.

"So, I got in. Silent alarm. Very cool. I head upstairs to the bedroom. That's usually the best place for these things. Sure enough there's the safe behind a painting. Very cliché. But then I notice there's no tumblers, no locking lever, just that half-sort-of-hole big enough for the tips of two fingers. I pull. Nothin' happens, of course. So, I decide to make the most of the moment and I begin goin' through the dresser drawers. I got about two minutes, I figure. Beside the bed is a night table. The top drawer has a 9 mm pistol, a couple of loaded clips beside it and the remains of a box of shells rollin' around beside the gun and . . . ," Leonard held up the keys and dangled them in front of David, ". . . these."

"What about the gun? You didn't take the piece, did you? Anything out of normal could tip Robert off. He's a paranoid son-of-a-bitch. If he suspects anything, ANYTHING, it will ruin any hope of getting what I need."

"No, relax. It's OK. At first I figure, grab the gun and the loaded clips. So, I do and start headin' for the bedroom door to leave. Then I figure, if I want to get back in the keys might be useful. So, I go back and get the keys and leave the gun and magazines. I'm thinkin', maybe he won't notice the keys are gone if it looks like nothin' has been touched. Then, I got the hell out of there just before the cops showed.

"Okay. So, last night, as I said, I'm over at Leon's to ask him about the safe. When we find the article, there's a picture of the key chain—just like this one—with a diagram of the light and the

210

sound. Leon don't read German but he figures out from one of the picture captions that there's a one degree arc at two-and-a-half meters. That's just about eight feet. One degree for the light and a directional matchin' one degree sound emitted along an intersectin' axis. The light is a visible guide to aim the sound at a spot just below the handle depression on the safe door. Hit the spot with the light and you hit it with the directional sound and "pop," the safe opens by itself. No two safes have the same frequency. Each safe comes with two of these little beauties. This must be the spare."

"How do you know this?"

"What? That it's the spare?"

"Yeah, how do you know this even works?"

"Well, as for workin'," Leonard says. "I don't."

Again, David was sinking. This was going from one high to the next with deep valleys in between. This, he hoped, was the lowest drop and the last.

Leonard saw David's expression and rescued the moment once more. "I didn't try it because I didn't know what it was. I only took it for the attached keys, remember? But as for the spare thing, I've been tailin' him since last Thursday. I see the keys. He's always playin' with 'em. He shows everybody his little flashlight."

The next two hours they both nursed along a beer or two while David listened to Leonard's plan on how they were going to re-enter Robert's house and find out what was in the safe.

CHAPTER 24
Awakening

Robert was notified at work by the alarm security service that the home alarm was tripped. They told him there were police on the scene. Nothing else. Robert ran several lights and arrived at the house in record time.

There were numerous cruisers outside Robert's house when he arrived and several cops—one unrolled yellow police line tape threading it along a path from the front door to an, as yet undetermined, anchor; another was directing neighborhood traffic. A cop searched outside the home with a German shepherd sniffing the ground for clues. Still another was asking the neighbors to stay out of the area and "let the police do their work." It resembled a murder scene more than a burglary, but then, one had to consider the neighborhood and the importance of the people living there to know why the police had turned out in force.

The quiet neighborhood was alive with activity. Neighbors wandered over Robert's lawn trying to get rumor-based answers to questions from neighbors who knew next to nothing but swelled the event and excitement with speculation. Robert pulled up on the road opposite his driveway. A cruiser blocked the view of the front lawn.

The Jaguar came to a jerked stop as he slammed it into park and exited the car all in one motion. As Robert crossed the street he was shouting, immediately demanding attention.

"Who's in charge here? Who's in charge?"

An officer walked up to the advancing Robert as he made it past the curb and onto his lawn. "Just a moment sir. Are you the owner?"

Robert sidestepped the officer and marched past him toward the front door saying, loud enough for the cop to hear him, "Damn right I am."

Inside, Robert was greeted by two more cops with flashlights in hand. The first was young and wide-eyed. The morning's excitement was providing the kind of rush more experienced cops found in their morning coffee. The other cop wore sergeant stripes. He was considerably older with a late middle-age spread that had "donuts" written all over it.

"Mr. Whitney?"

"That's right, you in charge?" Robert never looked at the cop. His head swiveled from side-to-side looking over the room.

"Yes sir, I'm Sergeant Merris, This is Officer Simmons. We answered the alarm. Your back door appears to be open. Nothing was forced so it was either someone who knew the lock or the door was open when you left."

Robert jerked his head turning his attention toward the cop. He angrily dismissed the cop's analysis. "Sergeant Merris?"

Yes, sir."

"Sergeant, the door was *not* open when I left." Robert pushed past the cops into the living room and did a quick 360 of the walls, tables and then looked at the two cops standing at the front

213

door. Simmons was scribbling something on a notepad. Sgt. Merris was talking into the microphone attached to the epaulet on his left shoulder while he watched Robert bully his way through the room.

"Was anything destroyed or taken?" Robert demanded.

Sgt. Merris took a few steps toward Robert. He was holding his own pad and pen in his right hand at the ready. Without looking at his notes Merris got within two feet of Robert and with a smirk said, "Well, that's kinda what we were hoping you could tell us. See anything out of place?" He looked at Robert as the smirk turned to a sarcastic grin. "What about the upstairs area?" Merris looked up motioning with his head. "Are those the bedrooms?"

Robert broke his angry stare at the officer as he suddenly realized there were more important things to consider than a few items stolen from the living area. He turned and hurriedly headed for the second floor. Charging the stairs two-at-a-time, he rushed into his bedroom. Robert quickly glanced around the room. Other than the unmade bed and a towel still-damp, draped over a chair from his morning shower, nothing looked disturbed. It was all as he left it that morning. The ageing cop took a little longer to arrive. Standing directly behind Robert he huffed, "Well?"

Though nothing was disturbed, Robert was not relieved. He turned and made a second, slower scan of the bedroom. Seeing the bed table, he walked toward it and pulled open the drawer. The holstered, unlicensed gun and both clips were there. The loose bullets scattered and rolled inside the drawer. The magnified, hollow, drum-like sound of the moving ammunition on the drawer's wooden surface caused the sergeant to look up from his pad. Robert quickly closed the drawer concerned that the cop may have recognized the sound. He turned and made a step toward the painting covering the wall safe, hesitated, then turned to the cop and said, "Thank you officer. It appears nothing has been disturbed."

214

"Yeah, well that's not as unusual as you might think. Broad daylight and all. It is more likely the back door was not closed tightly and the wind blew it open enough to set off the alarm."

Robert was certain that that was the cop's way of rubbing it in a little more. He was right.

"We've seen it before," Merris curtly assured Robert as he made another note on his pad. "This sort of thing happens at least three or four times every month around here." Without looking up, the officer continued writing and said, "Just in case, be sure all windows and doors are secure before leaving." The cop looked up, smiled broadly, clicked his ballpoint once and slid it into his uniform shirt pocket without removing his eyes from Robert. He turned and walked toward the stairs and said to his partner, "We're all set." Robert followed and stood at the top of the stairs as Sgt. Merris flipped his notepad shut and walked down toward the front door. At the bottom, he turned and looked up once more at Robert. "We'll file a report on this and list it as a break in. Nothing taken. If you do find something missing, give me a call at the station. I'll put my card here on the table next to the door. Anything else?"

"No. I think everything's fine," Robert said in a cool tone. Mustering a socially correct smile he said, "Thank you officers." Robert muttered as the front door closed, "You stupid son-of-a-bitch." He turned and reentered the bedroom. He didn't want to uncover the safe with the cop standing there. Now, he removed the painting and saw the safe door was closed. Examining the safe's surface for any signs that an attempt was made to pry it open, he found no scratches. Satisfied everything was in its place, he walked away from the safe after rehanging the picture. There was no doubt the back door was closed when he left this morning, he told himself. As he walked downstairs to the kitchen area and the still open backdoor, he knew the wind did not blow it open. He grabbed the door knob, locked it, and closed the door jiggling the knob as if in needed assurance that the lock still worked. Robert stared at the door, in deep thought, wondering who and why, when the front door bell rang. It was Robert's elderly neighbor from across the street grasping the front of her checkered, cotton house coat with one hand and a mug of coffee in the other. She must have bolted from her kitchen window as soon as she saw the police leaving. She was still wearing her bedroom slippers. "I just wanted to check in with you," she said. "Make sure everything was all right. I saw the cruisers." Now she was expanding the conversation and Robert didn't have the time to play neighbor.

"We had a break in just a couple of months ago too," she said. With that acknowledgement, she made Robert a member of her exclusive club. "Nothing of any value was taken except a laptop from my husband's study." Her voice trailed off as she leaned past Robert for a view of the house interior.

Robert didn't need this. "No everything is all right. It appears it was just the wind blowing the back door open. I appreciate your concern," he said as he slowly exited the house, turned, locked the front door, and headed for his car.

"I would appreciate your keeping an eye on the place, just in case," he said as he got in the Jaguar. He smiled at the neighbor, waved, and drove off leaving her standing on his front lawn weakly waving goodbye.

Robert was worried. As he weaved through the neighborhood, he reached into his coat pocket for his phone. He hit one button. The phone stoically addressed him through the car's sound system. "Say the name of the person you wish to call."

Robert barked, "Office."

"Calling office," the mechanized voice answered.

Robert's secretary, Melanie, answered the phone and began the standard greeting: "Good morning, this is GrowVest INTERNATIONAL. How may I . . ."

"Yeah. This is Mr. Whitney."

"Oh, good morning sir. I have no . . ."

"Hold on. I want you to call a locksmith and send him out to my house. Tell him no one will be home. Make sure the son-of-a-bitch is bonded. Tell him to replace the backdoor lock with something substantial. I don't want anyone getting in without a key. Is that clear?"

"Yes sir, a locksmith and secure lock." Robert could hear the scratching as Melanie wrote down his demands.

"No! Not just a secure lock. Tell him to make sure no one can get in without a key. I want fucking Ft. Knox assurance. Is that clear?"

"Yes, sir. Secure lock. Fucking Ft. Knox assurance. Yes, sir. I'll take care of it immediately."

"When he's done, have him stop by the office and leave the key with his bill." Robert ended the call. The car voice notified him, "Your call has ended."

"No shit."

CHAPTER 25
Check the Water Meter

David needed to be certain that Robert would not be home when the next break-in occurred. He enlisted Allen as his eager inside accomplice. Allen gathered the needed where, when, and why. David told Allen he feared Robert might figure it out—that he was the one who recently broke in. "Is it possible?"

"Robert," Allen said, "thinks you're dead lying in a shallow grave somewhere behind a mall." The thought made David laugh.

After three weeks of twice-weekly meetings to share information and modify the plan, David and Leonard met for the last time in the Parrot's parking lot on a Monday morning at 6:30. The lot was empty except for an abandoned car. Leonard insisted they go over the plans several more times before considering the break-in. "This is how I earn my living. I don't make mistakes. I can't afford 'em. You're my liability. If you're gonna do this with me, I gotta know you can do it. Clear?'

Three weeks and Leonard was more nervous now than at any time before. "Clear," David said emphatically nodding his head as he replied. It *was* clear. David went over the plans most of the night getting very little sleep. On his way to the meeting David played several unscripted scenarios in his mind. In each one things went wrong and Robert discovered David in his house. There was a secret delight for David in each scenario. Even a failure had an emotional benefit for David but he knew he couldn't share that with Leonard. His day dreams always included a shocking surprise as Robert discovered David was alive. Each daydream ended in a fight, or death—Robert's. None of the fantasies were logical but they served the purpose for David. He was ready—even excited about the break-in.

When they got into the house, Leonard would scan Robert's office for the quick score—find things of value, snatch them, and leave. The desk was his main target. Leonard was certain David's prize was in the safe. "The safe is the obvious target for the papers you're after," Leonard said. "That's yours. Get in. Go upstairs. Take the painting down. Use the laser. Get what you want and get out." After 20 minutes of review, Leonard's summation was brief.

In their weeks of planning, they went over the plan a hundred times or more. David said the watch and papers were his prize from the very beginning. Standing there in the parking lot for their final review, David began to question Leonard's resolve. For a pro, he seemed far more nervous than David. Maybe he had reason to be.

David hoped the papers would show Robert's new-found power changed the worm's lifestyle. With the money flowing into GrowVest, Allen was certain that Robert was collecting some part of that for himself. If David could find any indication of that kind of activity, he would have what he wanted and what Allen needed, too.

For most of the three weeks they planned the job, Leonard staked out Robert's house noting Robert's procedures for leaving the house in the morning. Robert was prompt—always the same time: leave the house; lock the door; get in the car and go. He never stopped to pick up his paper, look at the lawn, or check out a neighbor. He was all business and always in a hurry.

Allen corroborated Leonard's notes. On the Friday before the break-in, Allen produced a copy of Robert's schedule for the week. "The morning schedule only varies on Mondays," he told them.

"Yeah, he leaves home 15 minutes earlier than the other weekdays. About 7:15," Leonard confirmed.

"His schedule is blocked for "weekend data entry," Allen told them. "It's the time Robert reserves for work-related information he gathers over the weekend. Monday is the day he spends the most time in the office, too—nearly a guarantee," Allen told them. "He never schedules any meetings. No clients come in for appointments. As far as anyone outside the office knows, Robert is not in on Mondays."

"So, this is the day when the watch is in the safe at home." David wasn't asking a question. He was stating what he considered fact. "He only wears it when he's hoping to impress a client. No one is there to see it on Monday."

"Yeah, I guess so. I mean, I never noticed. But I can tell you he always mentions it whenever we have a client meeting. He'll take it off and pass it around. He shows everybody that watch."

It was 7:30. The sky was overcast, and the neighborhood was as quiet as usual. Leonard parked several blocks away. The two men weaved through the neighborhood houses to Robert's street. Both men wore white, short-sleeved shirts opened at the collar, tan pants, and dark shoes. A bright, yellow construction helmet with the water company's logo completed the uniform.

David walked the lawns stopping at each house appearing to record something on a shiny aluminum clip board. Both men were conspicuous. "Sure, we'll be conspicuous," Leonard told David.

220

"We want them to know immediately that we're with the water company. Once they know that, they won't pay any attention to us."

Leonard followed the same procedure on the other side of the street. As he walked from one lawn to another, the house's front door opened behind him. "Hey. Excuse me. Sir?"

David stopped, and watched and breathed a warning that only he could hear. "Ignore her, man. Just keep walking," The woman came out of the house still calling Leonard. Leonard stopped, turned, and walked back to the woman. His left hand held the brim of the helmet. His right hand pulled the aluminum pad to his chest. David couldn't hear the conversation. He could see that Leonard was smooth.

"Yes, Ma'am. What can I help you with?" The rest of the conversation was a hum of the two voices. The woman pointed to the house. Leonard opened his pad and scribbled something. Then tipped his hat and walked away after receiving a brief wave from the satisfied customer. David also moved on.

As he approached Robert's house, David saw the car was still in the driveway. Robert was late. Still at home. David froze. Three houses from the goal and the plans were in jeopardy. There was no backup plan. If they couldn't get in now, it would be another week before the opportunity returned.

Leonard was still canvassing homes on the other side of the street when he saw David standing motionless looking toward the house.

"Shit!" The sharply declared word echoed. Leonard nervously looked around to see if anyone might have been outside to hear him. The comment was enough to snap David from his trance. He turned toward Leonard holding both hands with the palms up. "What now?" he silently mouthed.

Just then Robert's front door opened. Leonard immediately walked toward the side lawn of the house he was canvassing, away from the street. With his head down and nose buried in his pad, he waited until he was hidden before turning to watch Robert. Startled by Robert, David also retreated, hiding behind shrubs, then watched as Robert hurriedly walked to his car. Robert got in the car and backed out of the driveway. Moments later, he was gone.

Leonard quickly emerged from across the street and walked up the block past Robert's house still writing on his clipboard with his head down. Not wanting to attract attention, David took another minute to catch up. No one other than Leonard's customer and Robert had emerged from their homes. If the two were spotted, the neighbors would consider the water men harmless.

Leonard walked two houses past Robert's and crossed the street. He wandered into the back yard of the nearest home doubling back to meet David at Robert's back door. It was locked, and a plate with the words "burglar proof" was applied to the outside near the door knob. David nervously fumbled with the keys. "No go," he said.

"Yeah," Leonard answered. "He did just what you'd expect. Robert called a locksmith and installed something a little more difficult to open." David was beginning to hyperventilate but Leonard was showing his expertise. The tension he showed in the parking lot was gone. He was in his element.

"Are we going to have to change our plans?"

Leonard looked at the seemingly impenetrable lock once more. "Naw. Piece of cake." Leonard laughed as he reached inside his back pocket and pulled out a small bar. He inserted it above the plate. Leonard leaned into the bar. There was a crack as the wood splintered around the newly installed brass plate. Leonard's bar easily ripped past the burglar-proof security lock popping open the door.

222

The plan called for a six minute window. They had to expect cops would show up after six minutes. It was the same plan Leonard had used before with one big exception. Leonard was smooth the first time leaving no trace of entry. This time there would be no doubt as to what happened.

David ran upstairs headed for Robert's bedroom. Leonard broke for the study. Running as fast as he could for the upstairs safe, David was carrying nothing but the clipboard notepad, a telephone and the laser key. The plan was to photograph everything in the safe with the phone and leave any valuables. In that way, it made the first burglary look like an exploratory attempt that concentrated on the downstairs study. Robert might believe both entries were common break-ins that never made it upstairs.

It took Leonard less than a minute to turn Robert's study upside down. Books were pulled off the shelves. Drawers were pulled from the desk and the contents dumped on the floor. Leonard suspected that there was a cash box in a locked drawer. He split open the desk's locked, lower right-hand drawer pulling out several stacks of banded twenty and hundred dollar bills. He hurriedly stuffed the cash into his pockets. But the piece that had Leonard giddy was the handful of 15 Krugerrands neatly clustered in a white bag made of coarse, heavy cotton fabric. A folded paper with a key taped to it was tucked in the bag's bottom. Leonard had enough. This was far more than he expected. He was ready to leave and shouted, "Wayne! Time!"

While Leonard was ransacking Robert's study, David was standing in Robert's bedroom staring at the painting on the wall. A pale, worn, ghostly face dominated the scene. The man in the painting walked in a fiery, non-descript landscape holding his face. His mouth was wide open. His terror was real. The painting was only a copy but the impact given the circumstances was startling. Robert chose Munch's _Scream_ to hide his trophies. David was convinced the details of every larcenous moment that elevated

Robert to this point in his life were in the safe behind the screaming man. If David was right, the safe closeted all the anguish, all the twisted dreams Robert collected since capturing his position at GrowVest.

David removed the painting, pulling it from the wall. He was in high mode. If he remained focused, he told himself, this uncontrollable shaking that had taken over his body would help him get what he wanted and get out in the allotted time. The clock was moving. David dropped the painting to the floor. His nerves were winning the control game. He lacked the stone-cold professionalism Leonard was showing while dissecting the desk in the study. As David drew the electronic key from his pocket, it slid from his latex gloved hands and landed next to the painting. As he reached for the key, he took a deep breath hoping for control. He fumbled for the laser finally managing to grasp the small rectangle and point it toward the safe. With the laser beam of green light tracking its way up the wall, David aimed for the spot beneath the finger hole where the sound lock was supposed to be. He heard a slight click and the safe glided open.

There was no time for any disappointment. The clock was ticking away the seconds too rapidly. But, except for a small stack of papers, the safe appeared empty—mostly envelopes and from the looks of things, nothing special. There were three different bank statements. Robert was banking some money but from the looks of the quantities involved, this was just a part of his salary. "No time to analyze. Keep moving," David told himself. The second bank had three envelopes that were mostly records of checks from more than a year before. The third bank was one envelope—a letter advising him that his safe deposit box was coming up for renewal. "No, this couldn't be anything," he said, softly. "This is too open."

The bank statements are the first place the IRS would look for a lead. This stuff was almost public knowledge and easily used in an investigation. FBI-101: find the bank, find the assets.

224

"This means nothing. This can't be anything more than things he can afford to lose." David was losing it.

He took a quick photo of each account number and bank address. As he replaced the papers into the safe something fell to the floor near his foot. He nudged it into sight. It was a small red and black, flash drive. David picked it up and rolled the two-inch-long drive in his hand wondering what to do. He suddenly realized he could download the drive's contents to the phone. He set the phone on the table next to the safe; plugged the drive into the USB port on the phone's side, and began the download. With the download progressing, David replaced the safe's contents.

As he reached in he felt a small box. David pulled the black leather box into the light and saw "For Your Collection" embossed in gold letters on the box top. David opened it and . . . there it was! "That is what I want! The watch!" But he hesitated. "No, I can't take it. But, I want the watch! I have to take the watch." His hesitation made no sense. If the purpose of the break-in was to make it look like the safe had never been discovered—much less opened—the watch had to remain!

"Fuck it. Reason will have to wait." David took the watch dropping the pink gold and alligator leather bundle into his pants pocket. He closed the box and returned the empty case to its position in the safe.

Looking at his phone, he saw "Download complete 105 Kb." in red letters. "Small file." David hurried to place the drive inside the stack of papers and close the safe. He quickly hung the picture. There was still one more task to complete. He turned toward the nightstand where Robert's pistol was supposed to be. It was there. David picked it up rolling it over checking for the clip and then cautiously discovered there was one in the chamber.

The safety was off. This was a strong testament to Robert's continued paranoid state. He shoved it and both clips farther back in the drawer and placed the keys and safe laser in with them, then pushed everything to the back of the drawer, "Robert will check this drawer," he whispered. "After a second break-in, Robert will examine every inch of the house down to the lint in the dryer." David was hoping that with the gun and keys at the drawer's back, Robert would see them together, untouched and believe the safe was never discovered.

David scanned the room once more. Nothing was out of place. He told himself again, Robert's review of the damage might have him conclude the burglary was isolated to the downstairs where the mess was. But, what if Robert opened the safe? A sudden rush of doubt overcame him.

Just then David heard Leonard's call. "Wayne! Time!"

Time was up. He decided he would confront Robert, just as he had Allen. He wanted to see Robert's face when he discovered him wearing the watch. It wasn't the stone-cold push David needed to send Robert over the edge, but it would help.

The bedroom window overlooked the backyard. As David crossed the bedroom hurrying toward the door he saw Leonard scurrying through the back yard gate. He also saw the reflection of flashing red lights on the neighbor's garage. The cops arrived! They came with sirens off. David feared they would be just as quiet climbing the stairs. He edged toward the bedroom door. Two cops with guns drawn entered the front foyer creeping in from the kitchen. As they crossed the foyer one stopped and pointed back toward the adjacent hallway. The second nodded and both men cautiously headed, once more, toward the back of the house. David knew he had only a moment before the cops saw the first floor was clear and turned to look upstairs.

Edging his way down the stairs, David continued watching over the banister for any sign of the cops. With a sudden rush, David bolted for the front door. Immediately outside, he turned, rang the

226

doorbell, and began writing on the clipboard note pad. Instantly, both cops appeared at the door with guns drawn pointing to the ground. David saw the guns and jumped back.

"Who are you?" one of them asked.

"Here to check the water meter," David said pointing to the logo on his hard hat. "Figured I should let the people know I was here. Is there a problem, officer?"

"No, no problem. Gonna check the water meter?"

"Yeah, that OK?"

"Do it some other time, we're kinda busy, at the moment."

"Oh, all right. Thanks." David continued jotting notes on the pad until the door closed.

Back at the trailer for less than a minute, Leonard opened the door without knocking. He was smiling and clearly excited. "Wow, what a rush. I was afraid you didn't make it past the cops," he said.

"Come on in," David said as he poked his head outside and quickly scanned the neighborhood. "Yeah, well it's my own fault. Spent too much time trying to cover my ass," he said quietly closing the door.

"So, how'd *you* make out? Didja find what you were after?" Leonard was being cagey.

"I got what I needed and maybe a little more." David turned toward the refrigerator and reached inside. "Beer?" He took one for himself and grabbed another for Leonard who already found the soft spot on the couch.

"Yeah, well, Wayne that's kinda what I wanted to talk to you about." Leonard popped the top on the can and took a sip. There were several more audible gulps before Leonard came up for air. The smile was still there but David thought it seemed sheepish, almost apologetic.

"I was able to pick up a few things but nothin' of much value." Leonard wasn't going to tell him what he found. But from his animated behavior, it was obvious he found enough to make the morning's party worthwhile. Leonard wasn't taking any chances that David might change his mind about their agreement.

Leonard reached inside his jacket, "I did find these." He dropped the bag and the unmistakable sound of coins hit the glass-topped coffee table. "They're gold," he said.

Reaching for the bag, David felt the weight. He poured 15 shiny gold coins into his hand. All had a picture of an antelope on one side and the words "Krugerrand" above and "one ounce fine gold" beneath it. David looked back at Leonard startled by the find and figured this should make Leonard very happy. But he wasn't.

"What's the problem? These things have to be worth about $1,500 a piece."

"*That's* the problem. I can't get rid of 'em."

"What are you talking about?" David couldn't believe what he was hearing. "Anybody would be glad to buy these from you. It's gold, man. Basic currency and you've got, maybe, twenty thousand dollars' worth. I don't get it. Why is this a problem?" David dropped them on the glass table top and began stacking them into two piles.

"Twenty-two, five," Leonard corrected. "Look, I don't do big stuff," Leonard said almost apologizing. "One of the reasons I'm still around is because the cops have bigger things to look after than some bicycle bein' stolen or somebody's wallet disappearin' overnight. I make out 'cause I'm below the radar." Leonard stood

228

and began pacing. "Shit, man, there are nights when I'm drinkin' with some of these off-duty cops at the bar and they know who I am and what I do. I'm smalltime and I wanna stay that way. I show up with Krugerrands to fence and word gets out fast that I've graduated to a higher clientele." Leonard stopped and looked at David waiting for a reply.

"What do you want to do." He knew what the answer was.

"Buy them from me. Twenty-two thousand? I'll let you have them for . . . fifteen. That's a good profit for you and a good nights' work for me. No one is the wiser."

"I'll have the cash for you in a day or two," David told him. He had to pull it from his recently opened account. "It won't be a problem."

"Thanks, Wayne." Leonard gathered the coins and dropped them back into the white cloth sack; downed the rest of the beer in an uncharacteristic, hurried style; belched; waved, and left.

David was alone still coming down from the day. "For the first time since being back," he said looking around at his surroundings feeling lost, "I can see this mess isn't me." David felt like celebrating. "After seeing how Robert is living, I can see I've been camping out at the dump." He looked around and saw cluttered newspapers, dishes from a breakfast a week old and a couple of boxes of clothes he picked up at Goodwill. "What a hole."

He glanced at the wall clock, "11:30 and I haven't eaten breakfast. This is as good a time as any." On his way toward the bathroom he grabbed two slices of bread from the loaf on the kitchen counter. A quick look at both sides of each slice told him they were still okay to eat. Nothing green or black had grown yet. David threw them into the toaster and pushed down the lever. He was hungry but still had too much to do to take a break. "Business comes first."

Remembering the watch, he pulled it from his pocket. "Incredible!" He couldn't stop looking at it. He strapped it to his wrist. "A shower would be perfect right now." He settled for the kitchen faucet dipping his head under the cool flow. David reached for a towel on the sink counter and began drying his head.

The phone was the next item of business. He pulled the laptop from the couch where he had thrown it the night before after a marathon solitaire session that lasted until 3 a.m. He placed it on the counter next to the wet towel. "You know," he said talking to the machine, "sometimes you are the only way I can get tired enough to fall asleep." The excitement of the next day's job would have had some guys pacing the floor all night. Not David. He played solitaire.

He opened the computer and turned it on. In thirty seconds it was ready. Taking the cell phone, he configured it for an infrared download. When ready, David pointed it at the computer. The button was pressed. The file downloaded instantly. "Ah, good, wait what's this?" The computer asked if he would like to see the file. "Oh, yeah sure." David hit "enter." There was only one page with a series of numbers listed in several columns scrolling on the screen. The file was named "Mac new." The heading at the top of the page was a number—"127." David was intrigued and scrolled to the bottom of the page. The entries were all numbered with cash amounts beside each date. One number for each entry and the last one was 127. "Mac? Why Mac? Maybe these are copies of files Mac generated. Maybe they're business accounts. Robert knows exactly how many accounts he has and how many deposits have been made." David mumbled. "Maybe they're not business accounts at all. There are too many and why would they be hidden in the home safe? Numbering the deposits suggests that more are expected." David took the laptop and phone and walked toward his office—the coffee table in the living room. He rearranged a pile of papers looking for his flash drive. Plugging the drive into the computer's side, he downloaded a copy of the files from the computer, then, dropped the drive into his pocket for safe keeping.

Once more, David glanced at his wrist. "Nice watch," he laughed. "Robert must be making some nice money to be able to throw this much out just to see how late he is." David gladly held onto it as a spoil of war and when the time was right, Robert would know he had it. There was a strong sense of accomplishment tied to the watch. It was like something he hadn't felt since leaving GrowVest. Life was so much sweeter with the watch on his wrist and not on Robert's. David walked toward the bedroom at the back of the trailer. He removed the watch and buried it in a cabinet among stored winter clothes. David turned back toward the kitchen and breakfast. Glancing at the toaster, he saw the toast hadn't popped up. David reached for the chromed appliance. The toaster was cold. "Damn thing works like everything else around here— when it wants to or not at all," he said as he slammed the useless piece of metal into the wall at the end of the counter. Time to catch some food at the local diner.

Thirty minutes later David was sitting at the counter enjoying the aroma of his first cup of coffee as the eggs and hash arrived when he heard the sirens from the fire trucks. As he walked outside, the smoke dusted the streets with a light fog that burned his lungs. The flames rose above the trees in the direction of the trailer park. When he reached the park, the firemen were pouring water from three sides onto his trailer's fallen shell. David saw through the steady spray of water and charred ruins that the only things remaining were a few water-soaked boxes of clothes in a corner of the living room. The bedroom appeared wet and gray but mostly untouched. Everything else in the middle was either charred or melted. Nothing appeared salvageable. David stood looking at the smoldering mess when a fireman in a yellow helmet approached. "You Brewkowski?" the chief asked.

Dazed, David just looked at him.

"Yeah, you gotta be him. Mr. Brewkowski, I'm sorry for the mess. We did our best. These things are made to burn," he said as he turned toward the smoldering mess, "though this one seemed to take its time before making itself known." The fireman was speaking of the fire as if it were a living thing—something he admired for its ability. "They're only waiting for the opportunity."

"Who?" David only heard part of what was said.

"What?"

"Who's waiting for what opportunity." David thought the chief was suggesting arson.

"Oh, yeah. Sorry. No, uh, I meant the trailers. These things," he said making a large swing of his arms toward the rest of the trailers nestled tightly together. "They're a fire trap. You wouldn't believe how many times we've come to one of these fires and found people dead inside." There was that admiration thing again. The fire prevails. The fire wins. Then as an afterthought, "There wasn't anyone inside, right? They told us you lived alone."

"No. Nobody else."

"We can't beat these things. It's more like we try to keep it in its cage. But, every once in a while—too often if you ask me—it gets out."

David stared at the chief shaking his head in disbelief.

The chief noticed David's reaction. "Yeah, I know. It's a damn shame," he said misunderstanding David's amazement. "Preliminary thought is faulty wiring in a kitchen appliance. Right now, through the rubble, we can't tell which one." The chief patted David on the shoulder and walked away. David took a solemn oath at that minute never to eat toast again. If he did, it wouldn't be without remembering that damn toaster and all it cooked for him.

David watched as one of the two fire trucks rolled hoses preparing to leave. The second continued spraying smoking areas of the burned out hulk. Some of the residents left leaving a much smaller crowd. As David turned to see who was watching, he saw Ceiley standing beneath an oak at the edge of a nearby driveway.

"Got any marshmallows back at your place? I think we might be able to convince the fire boys to leave us a small flame," David said as he walked toward her. He could see she was crying. "What's wrong? You all right?"

"Yeah, I'm fine but what about you."

David shrugged. He walked to the trunk of the tree and sat down with his knees up to his chin. Ceiley slid down beside him.

"It's no big deal. There was nothing in there I couldn't replace, if I had to." He smiled and looked at Ceiley. She frowned and tipped her head.

"Come on, no big deal? Are you kidding?"

"No really. I'll get by." Though she didn't know it, his bank account guaranteed that.

"You need a place to sleep? I've got a couch."

Any other time that kind of an offer would be gold for him. "No. But thanks. I'll probably stay here until the firemen leave then grab a couple of hours sleep before I see what has been left behind. I don't want anyone getting there before I do. If I don't see you in the morning, don't worry. I'll be fine and I'll be back."

The rest of the afternoon and into the evening David stayed near the burned trailer wandering along the edges of the lot where it melted. Several neighbors saw him and brought coffee and an occasional sandwich that he ate beneath the tree. Ceiley walked by several times but said nothing. More than once they looked at each other. David gave a weak smile and Ceiley dipped her head and walked away.

After spending the night in the car, the sun was up before he was able to walk through the charred remains. Still, no one beat him to it. He could see the fire spread from the kitchen and left the bedroom end of the trailer mostly untouched. In the corner where the watch was hidden the cabinet's outer door was scorched. Thankfully, the watch was still hidden inside wrapped in some clothing—apparently no worse for wear. David peeled it from the smoke-filled clothes and slipped it onto his wrist.

Where the kitchen should have been were remnants of the white porcelain sink shattered and lined in soot on the melted linoleum floor. David waded through the mess, crunching through heat bonded bits of glass and plastic into the charred living room. He kicked the crispy refuse looking for his laptop. There, merged with a melted red and yellow plastic plate, was a deformed, gray lump and the recognizable green of the mother board and computer contents. All that was left of his cell phone was the deformed 8, 9, and O keys that withstood the intense heat though they now joined to resemble a single three-digit number. David consciously reached into his pocket searching for the flash drive. Satisfied that the only remaining copy of his work was saved, he confirmed for himself what he told Ceiley the day before. Nothing of value was lost.

CHAPTER 26

The Scream

It was Tuesday morning. Not a good one for David after the fire but a whole lot worse for Robert. He just didn't know it yet. There was no news of Robert's burglary in the morning papers. Robert showed up for work at the usual time; ordered his coffee from his secretary, Melanie as he blew past her—"black, two sugars;" entered his office, and closed the door.

". . . and maybe a little rat poison," Melanie whispered sarcastically.

Robert still didn't know the watch was gone. According to David's break-in calculations, Tuesday was not a day for Robert to wear his prize. Though the leather watch box in his safe was empty, Robert was still unaware that the contents were missing. It could be several more days before he discovered it.

After being summoned by the alarm company, the day before, Robert drove home quickly. He immediately saw there was a great deal more activity than at the previous break-in. The same policemen that were at the first event were there and so were several others with more arriving as Robert pulled into his driveway. Having upper echelon neighbors with connections in upper echelon

235

positions was a peripheral benefit to living in this neighborhood. There was no shortage of highly placed concern. Knowing that was little comfort for Robert after the first break-in—the one no one but Robert took seriously. This time the neighbors could hear Robert's yelling shortly after he entered the home.

"What the fuck! Look at this. Look at this," Robert yelled as he pointlessly searched for eye contact from any of the men in blue. Papers and a broken lamp Leonard had knocked to the floor in his haste to leave were laying in the hallway near the study. Even without seeing into the room, the destruction that spilled into the hall guaranteed chaos just around the corner. "You bastards wouldn't listen to me before. Look at this!"

"Mr. Whitney?" a dark, black detective in a darker suit said as he walked up to Robert. "Mr. Whitney, I am Detective Barile. You are Mr. Whitney, aren't you?"

"Yeah, that's him." Sgt. Merris, the lead cop from the previous break-in confirmed. Both men hurried to Robert from different parts of the house as soon as the shouting began. Robert ignored them both pushing past to stand in the hallway for an unobstructed view outside the open study. He looked at the mess and saw his desk opened. The Krugerrands and cash were gone, he was certain. Robert hesitated long enough to assess the barricade of policeman and yellow tape that crisscrossed the entry to the study.

As Robert lifted a strand of the yellow plastic barrier, a patrolman warned him, "Uh, sir? Please do not step inside . . . the . . . . yellow . . . tape." Robert ignored the warning and ducked beneath the tape without losing his stride. Merris looked at the detective shaking his head and shrugging his shoulders.

"Mr. Whitney, I am Detective Barile with the Richmond police," the detective said loudly as he slid beneath the yellow tape into the study. Both men slowly circled the damaged desk. Robert watched the policemen dusting for prints, taking pictures and

236

scribbling notes on their pads. He also scanned the ravaged room while the rage built inside him.

"Mr. Whitney we need you to tell us if you see anything is missing. Write it down," Barile told him. "I'll need it for my report and you'll need it for your insurance company. You'll be able to go through everything as soon as the lab guys have finished."

Robert heard nothing. He turned from the study as a thought electrified his brain. Robert quickly ran from the room rushing upstairs to the bedroom where he stood for a moment looking at the wall and the artist's expression of anxiety and fear that guarded his safe. Robert saw the painting was undisturbed; seemingly untouched. Still, it screamed at Robert. The mouth was open and the image silently screamed to Robert that it had failed to hold onto his secrets. But Robert couldn't hear anything except his own heavy breathing.

Robert went to the nightstand; pulled out the drawer and then pulled it out farther. The gun and clips were pushed to the back. There beside the gun was the key chain with the safe's laser. He grabbed it and walked to the wall removing the painting. As he pointed the beam at the safe, it popped open, just as it had done less than an hour before. Robert looked inside. Nothing was disturbed. The papers remained stacked as he remembered he left them. He shuffled through the short pile of envelopes and located the flash drive. Hurriedly thrusting his hand deeply inside past the papers, he felt the watch box where he left it. Nothing was touched. Everything was as he knew it had to be.

Robert replaced the picture over the closed safe, tossed the keys on his bed and walked downstairs dazed by the adrenalin rush, still lost in thought. There was something residual to Robert's anxiety over the burglary. His most important assets were untouched. Still, his suspicious nature told him he was a target. This was no coincidence. He was now certain that the first break-in was a fishing mission. Someone knew Robert had secrets and wanted to know what they were. He was certain the blame for these events rested with his new partner. Yes, there were items taken, but he believed it was only a cover for the real reason. They were looking for the contents of the safe—or more specifically, the information on the flash drive. Robert knew he had every right to be concerned. If Ramos was the connected live-wire Robert thought he was, the people who chased people like him for a living already had an eye on Robert's flashy new friend. That meant they had an eye on Robert and Allen too.

David came to the same conclusion. But he believed there was city, state or federal involvement. His own participation was one more confusing element in the mix. He told himself it didn't matter. He wasn't going to wait for anyone to make up their minds as to when or how this would all come to an end. David considered it a guarantee that Robert would fuck up somewhere and either be erased by his new-found friend or latched onto by the law. An arrest was the least desired alternative for David. He didn't want to see Robert caged on some legal foul-up that might end in his release.

There was a third possibility. It was the best one. Allen said it at their lunch meeting as he chased David across the street to catch his bus. David could push and Robert would self-destruct. David decided on driving Robert over the edge. It sounded less merciful. Thanks to Allen's perverse sense of generosity, David had a checking account and cash to burn.

First thing he bought, after paying Leonard his fifteen thousand dollars, was a box of black, 30-gallon plastic bags. Back at the rental property, David peeled off one bag; then another. He placed the first one inside the second and proceeded to empty the water-soaked cardboard boxes on the living room floor. The remaining bags, still in the box, were tossed on the piled rubble of empty boxes. David scribbled something addressed to the management on a piece torn from one of the boxes—*Gone Fishing.*

"This is going to be a monumental fishing trip for trophy game," he said propping the note.

Walking away from the ragged trailer shell, David carried an overstuffed black plastic bag knowing, one way or another; this was the last he would see of his transient lifestyle. From now on it was all the marbles or nothing. "Nothing" meant Robert won but Robert would have to kill him for that to happen.

At the bus stop, David left the bag and its wet, smoke-soaked contents near the curb on the bare piece of depressed ground beside the telephone pole. Maybe someone could use them. David walked away from the bus stop and more than two years of hiding. It was time to reappear and see where it had gotten him.

CHAPTER 27
Right This Way, Sir

By Wednesday, David was staying at the Hilton in a roomy, one-bedroom suite with a spacious living room and a furnished, mirrored bar with sink. A glass-topped coffee table stretched along the front of the striped satin couch between stiff French period chairs just opposite the suite's door. Another, larger chair, softer and roomier occupied a corner between the living room and bar surrounded on both sides by climbing wooden bookshelves that stretched to the ten foot ceilings. A polished chromed floor lamp reached in over the chair and a half-sized table hugged the chair's right arm where a book and the prized watch were deposited along with pocket change. A small, mahogany desk had a brass library lamp with green glass shade casting a soft incandescent glow in a corner near the curtained living room window. The view from several stories up displayed the city and the river below. The manager accommodated David's request for a quiet area away from nightly replacement guests. He intended to stay for an extended visit, David told the manager, and preferred not to be disturbed. There was no one else on this wing of the floor.

After seeing the barber, he did some shopping for shoes and other necessities, along with an assortment of shirts. A couple of high-end suits found their way into his closet too. A few more days would pass before the credit cards showed up, but the bank was on it and David knew he didn't have to worry.

David contacted Allen by phone. When the answering machine took over, David left a message. "Allen, let's meet for lunch at the Green Grocer's. I'll see you there. Tomorrow at noon." The Green Grocer's was the local businessman's yogurt and salad shop. After the call, David spent the rest of the day planning the game.

David arrived first at the restaurant taking a table near the front just past the maître d's position. David was wearing the priciest suit he could pull from a rack. At $3,000, the light gray, vested Ferragamo was perfection. A lightly starched white shirt and yellow, silk tie with narrow, lime-green stripes nearly completed the presentation. There was only one more element needed. David would wait for the proper moment before making certain it was seen.

Allen was right on time. Looking around, he found David immediately and quickly rushed toward him, his face flushed. "David, we can't stay here. Are you crazy? Robert eats here just about every day. He's bound to see us."

"Good. That's the whole idea."

"No! Robert's going to think I've been working with you and if Ramos gets wind of this . . ."

"Ramos? That's the VP? The investor? Ramos?"

"Yeah. He's not in town right now but he's already placed someone in the company to keep an eye on things." Allen was fidgeting, constantly looking over his shoulder. He moved closer and held onto David's right arm with both hands and squeezed. "If you thought Robert was paranoid before, you won't believe what he's like now," he said while scanning the restaurant entrance for any sign of Robert. "Why are we here? Is this some kind of final plan?" Allen sat down with his back to the entrance.

"No. There is no plan." David was smiling as he watched Allen squirm from one side of his chair to the next looking over his shoulder from the left, then the right.

"We have to go. You deceived me to get me here just so you could ambush him. Look, we need some time to discuss this. We can come back tomorrow *with a plan.*" Allen included pleading with his growing panic.

"There is no deception; no intended ambush. I realized last night that playing this game was going to cost some money. So, I decided to play."

"At the rate you're spending your resources this could be a very short game."

"Relax, Allen. I'm playing with house money." David threw the comment away as he searched the entrance. He knew Allen wasn't listening.

"Why are we here," Allen shouted while banging both palms on the table.

The maître d' looked over and signaled a waiter to the table.

Allen took a deep breath and sat back in his chair straightening his tie as the waiter came to the table. "I'm so sorry to keep you waiting. Would you like to order something to drink to begin with?"

"No. We're not staying." Allen said as he pushed his chair back ready to leave.

David interrupted, "Yes, why don't you bring us some wine. Something red and three, no, four glasses. We're expecting company." David watched the waiter leave.

242

"We have to . . ."

David held up his hand to quiet Allen as he waited for the waiter to disappear. He lowered his hand and looked at Allen. The smile was gone. Allen could see David's resolution in the color of his flushed face. "I believe I have found a way to lean on Robert the way he leaned on you," he said. "I am going to make Robert aware that I am back and then let Robert's anguish and confusion drive him toward a cliff. The final play won't have to be mine. Not directly. That will belong to this mysterious money man already haunting Robert. We'll use that mystery investor as the weapon. It begins with this meeting."

"What? Do you expect him to shake your hand and welcome you back? 'Hi David. How the hell are you?' That kind of surprise? Or the kind where he grabs a butter knife from the nearest table and stabs you in the throat? That kind? 'Cause that's probably what he'll do to you and then to me!"

David remained calm. "I want the perfect unexpected face-to-face. I figure if Robert sees me back in town, looking prosperous and with you, it will be enough to have him relapse into his paranoid fantasies."

"I'm telling you the paranoid part has already been triggered by Ramos." Allen was pleading, again. There is no telling what your little gambit is going to do."

David turned his attention to the maître d'. Robert had just walked in.

Robert was talking to his guest showing him the keys to his new Jaguar XJL. He smiled and shined the green beam from his key fob flashlight onto the floor and laughed. Allen leaned in toward David. "The dark, Hispanic guy in the blue suit with him is Enrique, one of Ramos's new hires."

David stood. Allen quickly stood beside him while David untangled Allen's arms from his jacket and gently pushed him aside. Robert took a few steps past the maître d' before he lifted his eyes to look up and see David standing directly in front of him.

"Hello Robert," David sang in a cheery greeting. Turning to Enrique, he continued, "How do you do? I'm an old friend of Bobby's. My name is David Gere. Perhaps Bobby's mentioned my name once or twice?" After purposely murdering Robert's name, David didn't wait for an answer thrusting his right hand forward toward Enrique. Robert's guest reluctantly extended his own, slowly shaking David's hand. "How do you do?" Enrique responded in a deep, hushed voice. It was then that David purposely glanced down at their clasped hands. Enrique's eyes did the same. There, shining on David's right wrist was the pink-gold, Patek-Philip palm watch. Enrique quickly turned to Robert as if to say, "Isn't this like yours?" The fear in Robert's eyes was overwhelming. No one could hear the screaming and noiseless explosions inside Robert's head scrambling his thoughts. Here he was, *David.* It was clear that Robert believed David was dead. At best, he thought he might be wandering the streets alone, broke and homeless. But here he was, apparently rolling in cash and even more troubling, David was wearing *his* watch. He knew it now. David was the one. David was in his house. Robert was in an enforced state of panic, a kind of survival-self-denial.

"You couldn't have been there," Robert mumbled.

"What's that?" David said leaning in and turning his head slightly. "I'm sorry I didn't hear . . . Say it again for me."

Robert was thinking out loud. "I checked the safe. It was never opened." *Boom!* Then another crashing rationalization. "You took the watch from the desk or found it in the study or beside a book on one of the tables in the living room."

That comment, David heard. He smiled and shook his head slowly from side-to-side.

"No one could get in the safe. No one!"

In a slow-motion nightmare, Robert glanced past David to Allen and then refocused recognizing David once more. Robert was about to choke. He gasped for air.

"Enrique, maybe you and Bob might stop by the Hilton this evening. I have a suite there and can usually be found in the hotel's bar after a late dinner. Maybe you'd like to stop by for a drink." Then turning to Robert, he added in a sing-song delivery, "It's the perfect spot to sit back and talk about old times. Whaddaya say, Bobby?" Bobby wasn't talking. Without saying a word to Enrique, Robert turned and hurriedly moved for the door stumbling over the maître d' and into Enrique. Robert never stopped and was gone before the maître d' and Enrique had a chance to pick up the padded, red menus that flew from his hands on impact. Enrique bent to collect the folders. David crouched down to assist and said, "You know, he's awfully touchy about nicknames. Absolutely hates the 'Bobby thing.'" Enrique and David stood without losing eye contact. David never lost his smile. Enrique handed the collected stack of menus to the host; turned to look quizzically at David once more; then, left in a rush only slightly less important than Robert's.

David watched him leave. "Fucking priceless!"

Allen was nearly as shaken as Robert. As David turned to him with a broadening smile he said, "That went well, don't you think?" Allen immediately excused himself and exited for the men's room. At least, that's where he said he was going. After a few minutes the waiter came to the table and leaned over. "Mr. Gere? Mr. Nguyen has said he has an important meeting and won't be joining you for lunch." David rose and reached into his pocket handing him a fifty dollar bill. "Thanks," he said and left.

CHAPTER 28
Laura

Robert ran. He hit the front door of the restaurant with both hands slamming it open so that it bounced off of the exterior wall and back at him hitting his shoulder. On the sidewalk, he pushed through the gathering lunch crowd and into the street. Robert was blind with rage. He just saw a man he thought was dead—a problem that blew away with the wind years before. His mind was racing as his paranoid streak widened and began talking to him. The adrenaline rush, fueled by an incomprehensible sequence of unexpected events, had him running away without direction.

He was near his office's building—several blocks away. "Go to the office. GO TO THE OFFICE," Robert shouted as he crossed the street. He was cutting across mid-day traffic without waiting. There was a squeal of tires as brakes were slammed trying to avoid his blind rush. Robert alternated between fast walking and running over the next couple of blocks. He stopped abruptly as he stood across the street from the GrowVest offices. "This could be a trap," he whispered. "They wouldn't send someone here." Robert cautiously crossed the street purposely mixing with the crowd. He wasn't running anymore. He studied GrowVest's front entry. The address included several large legal firms, investment companies and a popular first floor sandwich shop. The traffic at the front

246

entrance was nearly constant. Robert stood beside a light pole and watched the lunchtime crowd entering and exiting. He looked up and began counting windows. Robert's office was on the 27th floor. He leaned back counting until he came to his office window. A reflective dot against the building's smooth gray stone façade was all he could see. "I can't go there. That's where they expect me to be."

The parking garage adjacent to the building was where he kept his car. Robert avoided the garage front entrance ducking into the truck-wide alley that separated the two buildings. The cobble stoned path was swayed with two grooves from years of overweight delivery trucks squeezing past dumpsters. Robert had traded fading traffic sounds for the odor of stagnant puddles where rusted trash containers squeezed their liquid refuse into the tire ruts. GrowVest reserved parking spaces were on the first level near the garage's side entrance. He hurried toward the entrance. As he approached the vehicle, his heightened sense of danger reminded him how David created his previous car problems. Though that only amounted to a couple of flat tires, it might now be a proper time for something more personal, destructive and permanent. He stopped 15 feet from the Jaguar. "Get out of here," he said his voice echoing off the concrete walls. "Run!" Robert awkwardly jogged to the street waving his arms wildly at the first cab he encountered. Before the cab stopped, Robert opened the back door and jumped in. "Drive. Go. Go!" Robert knelt on the back seat watching out of the cab's back window as his office disappeared in the distance.

Panic still squeezed his heart and pounded against his brain. It was coming out as tear-stained, squeaky-voiced anger. Defiant curses spewed from his lips into the cab's back window in a limitless string. His mind was racing out of control as his eyes catalogued each item in the road behind the rushing cab. "Faster. We have to lose them," he shouted into the back window.

The cabbie stared at his rearview mirror wondering if he should pull his concealed pistol from beneath the front seat—just in case. He listened to Robert's psychotic ranting and watched as his passenger leaned into the back window. The bellowing continued. "Fuck you! Fuck you, Ramos!" Robert wiped the window clean of the humid fog he barked in the window's direction. Robert never turned away from the rear view and though the driver hurried as he was instructed to do, he kept a close eye on his mirror and one hand free to reach for the pistol if needed.

"There's no one following. We must have lost them," Robert said gasping for air. He turned toward the front of the cab and slumped exhausted into the back seat.

The driver continued his stare into the mirror at Robert. "Where we goin'?"

Robert's tie and collar were pulled open. His jacket was torn at the upper sleeve on his right arm where the restaurant door hit him. He noticed it and fussed with the tear cursing as he stuffed the lining back into the sleeve. "Shit!" Robert looked up at the staring eyes in the rearview mirror. "They won't find me. Take me anywhere. Anywhere that's busy. Lots of goddamned people." Robert's voice trailed off as he picked at the jacket tear. "Best place to hide is in a fucking crowd." He turned to look at the back window once more, "Anywhere."

"District's up ahead," the cabbie loudly suggested hoping to convince Robert he needed to leave the cab. The district was the section of the downtown area that the city zoned for adult businesses. It was a place where prostitution, though illegal, was ignored. The city fathers realized there was no eliminating the biology involved. Men wanted sex and would do whatever it took to find it. In a move to finance an already bleeding economy, the city council created the district where adult businesses crowded together and collected the late night wanderers while the city raked in the taxes. What the city never expected was how the area became a full-time moneymaker reserved for more than just horny insomniacs and nighttime visits. As the largest city south of D.C., the district became a tourist attraction filled with farmers, locals and out-of-state parties that made plans months in advance and spent big even when the sun was up.

"Busiest spot is probably the Valley even in the middle of the day," the cabbie told him. Door men along the sidewalk club entrances shouted their flesh menus like side-show barkers at a small-town carnival. The cab pulled up to the curb. A doorman opened the back door for Robert who handed the driver forty dollars. "Forget you ever saw me."

"No problem."

The Deep Valley was the largest of the strip clubs. "*Totally Nude*," the red neon sign flashed above the canopied entrance casting a flush, embarrassed glow over the passing crowds. Robert ducked under the canopy and followed as the doorman rushed by to open the club door. Once inside another equally large man stood behind a wooden dais demanding a ten dollar entrance fee. Robert quickly slapped the bill into the man's hand as the hulk pulled a silk rope aside. Robert walked through into the darkness bumping through the crowd of topless waitresses, wide-eyed farm boys and beer-soaked truckers toward the darkest corner table. He sat down with his back to the wall. A mirrored ball dangled from the ceiling near the bar. It scattered the red and blue gelled spotlights over the guests giving little time to make out faces. Robert was certain he was safe. More colored lights splashed over eager partiers gathering around the stage edge. The men fondled their stacks of dollar bills and sipped watered drinks as the naked dancers moved past them collecting the money and rubbing breasts against their grateful faces.

"Ten dollar, two-drink minimum. What'll you have?" The topless waitress wiped Robert's table purposely swinging her tits in front of him while waiting for his reply.

"Nothing." Robert ignored her and threw the ten on the table.

"For ten you can get at least something. Wanna Coke?" She stood up straight and took a deep breath performing one last time before Robert's dismissal. "No, nothing. Go away." Robert wasn't interested. She took the ten and moved on.

Robert continued searching the crowd. Still, no one he knew. A good thing. And no one was looking his way. The dark corner away from major activity was safe enough.

"You look lonely." She spoke loudly above the noise. Robert turned to see the tall, naked brunette standing beside his table. Most of her height came from the three inches of spiked red heels.

"I'm not. Go away."

"You know, I don't really care." She pulled out the chair next to Robert and dropped down into it, exhausted. Robert pulled back.

"Don't sit there. I told you I'm not interested."

"Relax. That's all I'm trying to do. My fucking feet are killing me in these damn heels. The only way we get to sit down is if we're invited. You gotta buy me a drink or I have to leave. Buy me a drink and I'll make it a pleasant moment for us both."

Robert pushed his chair back hitting the wall. He was trying to leave but the table in front and the naked woman sitting next to him were making it impossible. He was trapped and began fighting the table, and pushing the woman's chair. It was enough that he caught the attention of the club's muscle. Wally was the floor manager. He was responsible for whatever passed as polite behavior in a room full of sweating, naked women and horny men. He watched the guests and girls and got a small percentage of everything sold. Keeping order made the club happy and profitable and made Wally a nice pile of cash too.

Robert saw Wally moving toward him and immediately calmed down sheepishly sliding back into the chair while watching the big man move quickly toward the corner where Robert and the startled woman were sitting.

"OK, OK, fine. We'll have a drink," Robert realized the woman's reasoning was better than anything he could expect from Wally.

The woman also saw Wally coming toward them. To avoid any problems she reached for Robert's arm and wrapped hers around him. She took Robert's hand and placed it between her legs then turned and smiled at Wally. At about the same time Wally became distracted by another disturbance and quickly left Robert and his newest best friend tangled in the dark corner.

"What's your name, honey? I'm Laura." It wasn't her real name, not that it mattered. Laura would do for the moment.

"Yeah. Right. What do you want from me?"

"I told you. I just want to sit down for a while."

Laura let go of Robert's arm. He quickly pulled his hand from between her thighs. Laura leaned forward to slip off one of her shoes and rubbed her foot. A naked breast purposely rested against Robert's leg moving with the motion of the massage. She was working as hard on the sale as she was her foot. Robert moved his chair out of nipple range while Laura looked for any sign that Wally was wandering back to her area.

As the waitress walked past, Laura reached out tugging on her apron. "Hey honey, two champagnes."

"Twenty bucks."

Robert hesitated then reluctantly reached back into his jacket pocket and peeled a twenty from his dwindling fold. The move wasn't lost on either woman. Laura slipped the shoe back in place and leaned forward onto the table with a hand beneath her chin.

"I haven't seen you in here before, have I? You look like you don't belong. None of the hypnotic stare at all the tits that most of the farm boys have. And you don't smell like sheep shit, either." Laura paused looking at Robert and added, ". . . but your jacket's torn."

Robert stopped scanning the room long enough to look at Laura. He glanced at her face then down at her breasts and the piece of white gauze cloth wrapped around her waist meant to resemble a skirt.

"You're not here for the ladies, are you? What? Are you hiding? That's usually why guys take the dark corners. They're afraid someone will recognize them. That means your local but since you aren't looking for women . . ."

"That's enough." Robert didn't need to hear any more. Just then the waitress returned with the champagne placing the drinks on the table while blocking Robert's view of the room. She stood staring at Robert.

"What the fuck? You want a tip now?" It took a moment before Robert was reminded that making any kind of fuss here would bring unwanted attention. He pulled the roll from his pocket once more and dropped a five on the table. As he was putting the fold away, Laura reached over and casually peeled two tens from the fold and gave them to the waitress. Laura smiled at the waitress. She looked at Robert and sang, *"She works hard for the money."* She laughed as she slid her hand into Robert's lap, "Come on, loosen up."

252

The joke wasn't lost on the waitress. "That's right," she said as she pushed the bills into the pocket of the short white apron that covered her panties and walked away.

"You know," Laura said, "if you're really trying to hide, this is not the best place to be right now. The first place anyone is going to look for you is in the darkest corners and with this kind of a crowd you might not even see them until they're right next to you."

Robert knew Laura was right. Both the waitress and she had gotten too close before he realized they were there. Once again, Robert was nervously adjusting his chair.

"I got an idea. Come with me. We've got these private dance rooms. Nobody is allowed in as long as you're in there with a woman."

Robert looked startled.

"Really. As long as I'm with you, they'll leave us alone. Come on," she said grabbing Robert's hand as she stood. "Come on, I'll show you."

Robert reluctantly followed her through the crowd to an area where the tables were pulled away from softly lit doors. Gaudy red velvet and brass rivets covered the doors. The number "3" was stenciled in gold paint to the one Laura walked toward. A small red light over the number blinked off and the door opened as a short naked woman pushed past Laura counting a few bills in her hands. "Room's yours."

Laura pushed past and into the room dragging Robert with her. A startled man stood near a stiff clear plastic-sheathed couch stuffing his shirt into his pants. With his head down, as if trying to hide his identity, he hurriedly walked past Laura for the door.

"The fly honey. You gotta zip up before you get back out there or they'll ask you to leave." Laura chuckled and Robert froze. This wasn't what he was after.

"Relax. What we do in here is our business. No one watches us and no one comes in as long as the light is on. It goes on when you sit down." Laura patted the couch and Robert sat. "It goes out when you get up or I open the door from the inside. See?" Laura closed the door. "No one will bother us here. Now, you sure all you wanna do is sit and hide? 'Cause you gotta pay for the room and since we're both here, we could use it."

"How much?"

A quick smile came to Laura's face.

"No. I mean for the room," Robert added.

"Oh. Fifty bucks for 15 minutes."

Robert reached into his pocket and took a hundred dollars from the fold. Laura took the cash and walked to the wall where she pushed an intercom button.

"Yeah?" A harsh male voice blurted back.

"It's Laura," she said slowly as if to be certain the voice on the other end recorded it correctly in the ledger. "Thirty minutes."

A responding click of the speaker acknowledged the time.

Laura walked back and sat beside Robert.

"You have to stay?"

"Sure, honey. Why don't you relax? No one will bother you. At least not for the next 29 minutes." She paused, "Who you hiding from? Your wife that vicious?"

Robert sank into the couch as best he could. The stiff, thick plastic cover squeaked beneath him. He said nothing.

"Ohhhhhh. Somebody else, huh? Business?" She looked at Robert scanning him from top to bottom.

Robert nervously stuffed the lining back into his torn sleeve.

"Yeah. Business. Must be pretty serious," she said.

Robert shifted on the couch and it spoke back creaking with a dry, irritating sound.

Laura looked away and began fussing with the cash and the tissue-thin, white cloth around her thighs. The cloth fluttered in response to the humming air-conditioner duct that poured stale, musty odors of sweat and sweet cologne. As she retied the garment she mumbled as if talking to herself while concentrating on tucking the cash into a cloth fold at her waist. "Hiding is no good. It just makes you the victim. Best way to get out of this is to attack. Go after the son of a bitch before he finds you. If nothing else the surprise will throw him off balance." Laura's voice trailed off. As she stood up, she heard the creaking plastic and turned to see Robert sitting up straight and looking at her with a surprised look on his face. "What's wrong?"

"You're right!"

"I'm right?"

"Yeah. You're right about the attack."

Oh, that. OK." Sensing an opportunity, Laura moved closer. "You want some more advice? I bet I can bring him to you, if you can tell me who we're looking for. And then, you could do whatever you want with him."

Robert paused, looking at Laura's face, trying to size her up. "Is this a joke? Can you deliver? All I need is to isolate these guys,

255

one-by-one." The wheels were turning. Robert could see a way out of his problem. "You might work. At least on Allen and Gere. Ramos is something else but we'll consider that later," he said. "Right now, at this very minute, two-thirds of this problem is solved." He looked at Laura hoping to see the same excitement in her face that he felt.

"How? How will you bring them to me?"

Laura began moving her hips in time with the club music seeping in through the padded door. As her hands cupped her breasts, she leaned in toward Robert. A broad smile and a tongue that curled toward her upper lip was enough. Robert smiled. This was exactly what he needed. Laura could get them to him. That would be the start.

It took another 20 minutes of more relaxed discussion while Laura proved her point. When she walked toward the padded door at the end of Robert's paid stay, she had a job and Robert had his plan. Laura explained that she would meet David at his hotel bar where, according to Robert, he spent every evening. She would tell the bar tender who she was looking for. Slip him a hundred and then sit and wait. When David showed up, she would take the cue from the bartender and meet David then convince him that she needed to see his suite. Once upstairs and inside the room, Robert would take over having entered the room with his men to await David's return. Laura would get a chunk of cash for her trouble and then disappear. It was set. Robert was delighted. He thought he would have David all to himself and completely harmless while he pumped him for information about Allen.

Robert left the Valley, side-stepping the burly doorman busy collecting his cover from the next lunch-time patron. Robert moved to the curb and hailed a yellow cab inching its way through the crowded street. For the first five minutes of the cab ride, Robert instructed the driver to drive randomly around town. All the while Robert kept his head turned and eyes glued to the back window looking for any sign he was being followed. Assured no one was behind him, he instructed the driver to take him home. The cab dropped Robert at the end of his driveway. His suspicions were still high; his mind on full alert. Robert walked slowly toward the front door looking to see if there were any signs of another person waiting for him in the shrubs. Convinced the coast was clear, he hurried to the door, pressed the numbered key combination, and stumbled inside.

"They won't try anything in broad daylight," he reasoned and then quickly shifted to the offensive. "Strike first. Now is the time!" he told himself. He began by running upstairs. In his bedroom he retrieved his pistol, checked the chamber and put both clips into his pocket. Then he scooped as many loose shells as possible and put those in the pocket with the clips.

Robert, still hurrying, moved downstairs and into the kitchen. "The plan," he said. "The bitch will make this right. She is *perfect*." He paced waving the Beretta all the while conducting an audible conversation with himself sometimes yelling questions and then whispering answers. "How? How could Gere be here?" Then, "How long has he been here?" he shouted. That question started him on a whole new track. "Why was he with Allen?" he whispered the question and followed it with a logically paranoid follow-up. "Does Enrique know too?" His reasoning was beginning to come to a wonderfully logical point—"If Enrique and Allen know, then Ramos must know. That's it! Ramos wants control," he said slowly realizing the imagined danger he now faced. The world, he reasoned, was once again falling into line to hate Robert. "Ramos must have learned about me from Allen," he said. "Allen wants it all back so he's made a deal with Ramos." It all fit in a distorted illogical kind of way. Everyone was out to get him. Now, Robert had to attack before he was attacked. He was certain that the attack on him must be coming soon. "That," he reasoned, "was why Gere showed himself. That's why Allen and Enrique were there," he said. "But they showed their hand too early."

Robert carelessly threw the pistol on the kitchen counter, got to the phone and hit a few keys. "Get over here now. Both of you. No, you idiot," Robert shouted. "The house. Get here now!" Robert slammed down the phone.

In less than ten minutes after Robert's abrupt call for help, a blue, two-toned Chrysler with Michigan plates pulled into his driveway. Two large black men occupied the car's front seats. The driver had a large diamond stud in his left ear. A fine gold chain lay against a white cotton t-shirt covered by an open-collared white dress shirt and blue silk tie. His dark blue suit jacket bulged beneath his left arm. The big man opened his door and took a moment to untangle his long legs from the car's grip. He turned and placed both size 14 shoes on the pavement before leaning forward to unfold his powerful frame. He stood straightening the blue tie. "Next time I rent the fuckin' car, you stupid son of a bitch." As he stood he added something unintelligible to the passenger. At six-six, he towered above the car and the car's other occupant, a smaller, rounder man having difficulty finding the seat belt buckle buried beneath his untucked orange shirt and overhanging belly. Once out of the car, he snapped back, "fuck you." The fat man made a passing attempt at fixing his tie and buttoning his shirt while tucking it into his pants. His undersized black suit jacket remained unbuttoned as they both walked up the driveway to Robert's front door. The fat man rang the bell. Robert's voice echoed a command for them to come in. Robert met them standing at the top of the stairs that overlooked the foyer.

"You have a job to do," his words bounced off of the marble floors and large empty walls.

Walking confidently toward the stairs, Robert began explaining his plan. "It has come to my attention that our Mexican partner has decided to play a different game. This has gone too far. We will remove him!" Robert's words echoed throughout the house with a clipped finality. "I want you to eliminate Nguyen too," he said as if the order was an afterthought of little value. "But first, there's one more." He stopped midway on his descent of the stairs. His right hand released its grip on the stair railing and turned to a white-knuckled fist as he slowly pounded rhythmic emphasis on the polished rosewood. "Gere. David Gere. I know he is staying at the Hilton. We have work to do. Find out his room number." Sneering through his teeth, "I want to be there when he is killed." He continued pounding out each word with his fisted right hand. "I want to see his face and have him know who is pulling the life from his body."

CHAPTER 29

Meet Señor El Grande

After the lunchtime fiasco, David left the restaurant just short of one o'clock. The lunchtime crowd was at its peak. He figured he could head back to the Hilton and get a quick couple of hours rest before trying to contact Allen. When David checked in the day before, he used the alias. The bank issued him a temporary debit card and the bank manager's business card to use as a reference, should he need one before the account was available. As far as anyone knew, David was still Mr. Brewkowski. There were no problems so far and he didn't expect any.

The suite was roomy and comfortable. More comfort than he felt in years. On that first trip to the room, he handed Clarence the bellman $200 with orders that the bar was to be replenished with a fresh bottle of Scotch every evening. "I'll leave another couple hundred at the desk every morning before I leave. Be sure the bottle is there when I return."

"Yes sir."

"Hey Clarence," David called to the bellman as he was leaving the suite, "Make sure it's something worthwhile. You keep the rest for yourself."

Clarence nodded. "Yes sir, Thank you, sir."

It was afternoon. David was tired and just wanted to relax. He could see Clarence made the liquid delivery. There was a bag on the bar. Taking the TV remote from the glass coffee table, he began flipping through the channels. David took a handful of shirt and pulled the tucked cloth from his pants; removed his shoes, and fell on the couch's firm cushions grabbing a small pillow for his head. He slept for several hours before the phone rang. Allen was in the lobby and needed to see him. "It's late man, and I am tired. I'm not getting off of this couch."

"What are you talking about? It's just after eight. I need to see you. It's no formal meeting. You don't need to get dressed." Allen was whining, again. He needed something.

"All right. But be grateful, at least, I still have my pants on." David hung up the phone and ran his hands through his hair as he sat on the couch edge. "For a rich man, he sure does beg a lot," David said, then chuckled.

A few minutes later, there was a knock. David got up and walked to the door in his stocking feet. As he opened the door David saw Allen wasn't alone. The first of the two men to enter he recognized as Enrique. The white-haired, elegant-looking, mustached man in his sixties with the friendly smile, he knew, had to be Ramos. Allen crawled in last looking like a beaten dog. He whimpered a hello and was about to introduce everyone when Ramos took over. Allen quietly moved to a stool by the bar.

"Mr. Gere, isn't it? Or should I call you Mr. Brewkowski?" He extended his hand and David took it without hesitation. "I apologize for the late hour. I can see you have already settled in for the night."

"No, no. Please come in and make yourself comfortable. There is no need to apologize . . . , and. David will do."

"My name is . . ."

"Oh, introductions aren't necessary, Mr. Ramos. I know who you are. It's a pleasure to meet you."

"How very kind of you. I have heard a great deal about you also, Mr. Gere, from your former associates Mr. Nguyen, here, and of course, Mr. Whitney." He paused and smiled.

Okay. A sense of humor was a good thing even when it was gallows humor, David thought as he walked away from his guests toward the couch and his shoes. He stuffed his shirt back into his pants and moved to the mirrored bar. David removed the Scotch from the bag and began twisting the corked top on the single-malt. Meanwhile, Ramos moved to the large, soft chair nestled near the white, floor-to-ceiling book shelves. He stood looking at the few prop books supplied by the hotel's interior designer as if reading the titles; he turned and settled into the chair.   Enrique remained standing a few feet away with his legs spread and hands folded in front of his body resembling a towering granite guard blocking the entry to King Tut's tomb. David walked behind the bar and reached for a glass. As he looked up into the back bar mirror, he saw Ramos looking back. "Can I get you a drink?"

"Yes, thank you. I see you have Macallen. That will do fine."

"Yeah. Macallen." David was surprised. He read the label out loud. "Eighteen year-old, single malt." He looked at the room reflection in the mirror. As he twisted the cork on the Scotch he made small talk, caught off-guard by the unexpected guests.

"I've got a deal with Clarence, the bellman downstairs. I give him cash and he presents me with a grab bag of goodies."

Ramos nodded, "You'll have to compliment him on his good taste."

"Ice?"

"Yes, and just a little water, if you please."

David dropped two cubes in the glass and poured the Scotch splashing it with some water from a newly opened bottle. He crossed the room with Ramos's drink and was intercepted by Enrique who reached for the glass and then carried it the remaining few steps to the man. "Thank you, Mr. Gere. Please forgive Enrique, he takes his job very seriously and is quite good at it too."

"Since he's working, I don't suppose he wants one for himself, then." David was slightly startled and trying to be cute under the mistaken impression that he was on home turf.

"No, Enrique is fine," Ramos said never losing his smile. Ramos took the glass from Enrique and sipped. "Mmmm, very nice," he said as he rolled the glass between his hands. "Mr. Gere, I asked Mr. Nguyen to bring me here this evening for a very special reason."

As David finished pouring his own drink, Enrique leaned in and whispered something in Ramos's ear. Ramos glanced at the table near his right arm where the contents of David's pockets were deposited for the night along with the watch.

"Please, we're all old friends here, or should be. Call me David. That makes it easier than trying to explain how to pronounce Allen's last name. Everyone butchers that one. Isn't that right, Enrique?" Again the attempt at levity. No one was amused and the only one that counted was Ramos who never lost his warm smile.

Ramos looked at David and squinted slightly as if about to present the circumstances of an unexplained mystery. "Mr. Gere . . . , David, I learned of your surprising reappearance this day from Enrique. Actually, Enrique tells me, Robert showed some discomfort after seeing you with Allen at lunch. Allen says you were discussing old business. Just catching up. Is that accurate?"

Ramos was being very direct; moving fast in the direction of an interrogation where David thought he would have to cover Allen's ass as well as his own and for the first time, in a long time, he wondered if there was any benefit. David edged his way to the corner of the bookshelf near Ramos and leaned against it, a more conversational distance from his guest.

"Mr. Ramos, I am flattered you would find me or my life interesting enough to wonder what Allen and I were discussing much less to come here to ask me."

Ramos smiled, and laughed slightly without taking his eyes from David.

"The truth is Allen and I were discussing you and your involvement with GrowVest and how I might become involved in any project you might have planned for the company."

Allen groaned.

"Ah good!" Ramos put his glass on the table near the watch. "As I had hoped. I understand your involvement with GrowVest ended abruptly after some difficulties with Mr. Whitney."

"Mr. Ramos, I can see you are a diplomat as well as a businessman."

"One and the same, sir. But my interest is in wondering if you think you could work with Allen and Robert again, if I were able to convince them that you might hold some value to my interests."

264

David's face flushed at the thought of working or even talking to Robert. His polite attempt at banter was going to have an edge the next time he opened his mouth. He would have to be careful. "The truth, Mr. Ramos, is that I have no problem working with Allen. He is a long-time friend who stumbled on his way. I have forgiven him for that and feel as close as ever before."

"But . . . ," Ramos interrupted.

"But, Robert . . . well, Robert I would prefer to see in chains in a very small box hanging from a tree that leans over a cliff where the weather is wet and the chain rusts and weakens on a daily basis, and the blowing wind elicits a creaking sound from both the chain and the son-of-a-bitch wrapped up inside the box. Realistically, I would be able to forget about Robert if someone like Enrique, here, were able to let me know just before the chain were to break so I could be there to watch him fall and listen to the crack and splat as the box and his head burst on the rocks below. Not too graphic I hope. I was only hoping to make a point." David walked to the bar and filled his glass once more drinking several gulps before placing the glass on the bar.

"And you have made your point quite succinctly. So, I can safely assume Robert's panic was genuine."

"I'd say Robert wasn't panicked enough."

Ramos laughed and David smiled back then took another gulp from the nearly empty glass.

"As I mentioned," Ramos said, "I have heard some very good things about you."

"Actually," David interrupted, "you said you had heard *of* me. It's nice to hear they were good and even nicer to hear it from a gentleman such as yourself." David smiled again and raised his glass in a mock toast before taking the last sip. The eighteen-year-old Scotch was beginning to loosen his tongue at a time when David

265

figured it was already as loose as it needed to be. By the looks of his chalk-white face, Allen must have felt the same way.

Ramos laughed again and moved forward in the soft chair to stand. "I think I have learned something new about the man tonight." He stood up and took a step toward David. "And I like what I have learned. I'll contact you in a day or two. I have to be out of town until next Wednesday on business. I travel a great deal. My work requires it. But when I return, perhaps we might enjoy a late evening dinner together. I believe I may have a proposition for you . . . " he hesitated and then smiled once again adding, "David."

Enrique opened the suite's door, then, stood back. Ramos reached into his pocket and produced a white business card which he handed to David. David took the card glancing at the name. Ramos reached out once more to shake David's hand. "Well, thank you for allowing me to interrupt your evening. It was a pleasure meeting you." Ramos dipped his head slightly, turned away and stopped. "Oh, by the way, I noticed your beautiful watch on the library table," he turned to look at David expecting a reaction. There was none. "I collect watches," he added, "and believe that one may be quite valuable," he said nodding toward the small table where the watch sat. "Perhaps you can tell me how you acquired it."

"Well, that is a rather lengthy story. Maybe we'll just say it was a down payment at settling part of an old debt, for now. Next time, if you've got a moment, I'll tell you the whole story. I think you'll be amused."

"I am certain I will be. I'll look forward to it," Ramos said. He dipped his head slightly once more never losing the perpetual smile. "David. Goodnight sir."

"Goodnight," David looked at the card then casually said, "Victor."

Ramos, still smiling, chuckled and left with Enrique close behind.

Allen stayed for a moment, looked at David, then craned for a look down the hotel hallway to make sure Ramos was out of earshot. "You crazy son-of-a-bitch. What the fuck do you think you're doing?"

Gently pushing him into the hall, David said, "Good night, Allen. Thanks for stopping by," and closed the door.

Finally alone, David wandered to the bedroom shedding clothes along the way and climbed into bed. It took several hours of tossing before he gave up on sleeping. The late afternoon nap had freed his mind for unwanted activity. He wasn't going to get any sleep for several more hours. The thought of lying in bed, watching TV had no appeal to him, either. He decided to get dressed and wander to the hotel's lounge to warm his favorite chair. It was midnight.

CHAPTER 30
Leave It Where You Found It

David sucked down a couple of Johnny Black's sitting by himself at the far end of the lounge bar where he could watch anyone coming in from the lobby. It was his favorite spot. He knew it and the bar tender, Freddie, fairly well after several visits on a nearly daily basis. Most of the regulars found their favorite spots too. It was easy to find new faces that way. Once you knew the faces that were usually there, you just had to look in the places where they weren't. Tonight, the collected balance of visitors was about right. There were the expected number of hotel guests—usually businessmen working a client or one of the ladies that frequented the hotel.

At the other end of the bar, David noticed a lone drinker clutching a glass of whiskey. As he lifted his glass for a final sip, he caught David looking at him and nodded. The man said something to Freddie; reached into his pocket and threw twenty dollars on the bar. As he got up to leave, David watched him, thinking he had seen him some place before.

The next hour was uneventful until Freddie wandered down to David's end and leaned in to tell him there was a woman at one of the tables who was asking about him. "She claims she knows you,"

Freddie told him. "She asked me to pass on an invitation to say hello back," Freddie smiled and motioned toward the woman with his head. The very attractive brunette was wearing a blue dress nursing a tall Vodka martini. She reached in for the olive and holding it by the toothpick waved it in David's direction.

David asked Freddie about the guy at the end of the bar. "He looks familiar. Is he a regular?"

"No, first-timer. Good tipper, though. Had one Jameson—that's it."

As for the brunette, David didn't know who she was either, but she sure recognized him and who was he to argue with a beautiful opportunity. So, he figured he would get close enough to see her reaction when she realized David wasn't who she thought he was.

When David approached her table a chill went through him. He realized this was his truck stop interruption.

"Remember me?"

"Of course I do," he said. "But not the pretty hair. Last I knew it was red."

She smiled and brushed it from her face.

"I think the last time we saw each other, I was catching a ride north and you were thinking about breakfast," he told her.

"Yeah, about the breakfast, next, time, I buy and we enjoy it together. Sound fair?"

"Next time," he said.

"What are you doing here in Richmond," she asked.

What was he doing in Richmond? David had a list of questions of his own. None of which he expected to ask. What was she doing in Richmond? Who was she? What affiliation was there with today and him and would this affiliation carry on into tomorrow? David thought this was beyond coincidence. His mind was racing for an explanation while the suspicions grew frantically in Ramos's direction and a little voice kept saying "Leave this one where you found it." David wasn't listening. This was a good time waiting to happen. At best, he decided to stay alert and see if anyone else might be watching them.

"You know," she said, "I have to get up early in the morning and really think I should be getting to bed shortly. Maybe one or two more and then you can show me your suite, hmm?

"I think I've heard that story before," he said. "I like old stories that involve beautiful women." David signaled the bartender and sat down.

A couple of hours later and David was stumbling toward his room after drinking himself into a near stupor. His jacket was thrown over one shoulder while he leaned heavily on the female guest he hoped might turn this night into a pleasant morning.

As he fumbled with the room key, the door swung open. David was immediately greeted by both of Robert's hired friends. The fat man dragged him into the room to meet Robert. The second man with the diamond earring overshadowed David's date. He reached into his jacket; retrieved an envelope and handed the cash-stuffed gift to the woman who turned and left without closing the room's door.

Robert kept his distance. He watched David sway after being released by the fat man. "I think I have to sit down." David stumbled to the couch.

"He's drunk. Too drunk." Robert was shouting. His disappointment at David's lack of participation made his anger swell. Robert's fury took over as he hovered over David and began swinging hitting David hard enough that he passed out sliding to the floor hearing and feeling nothing else. The fat man walked to the television; turned it on while maximizing the volume. His partner reached for the radio volume and maximized it too.

Robert continued barking out words as he swung wildly at David's limp body. One curse followed a violent strike. Another shriek from Robert was accompanied by a punch or kick. Robert was a man possessed verbally and physically, exorcising demons with each slamming fist. He screamed, "Who are you working for? Is it Ramos?" David wasn't answering. He was off in an alcoholic Never Neverland as the television's Cartoon Network collided with a Queen rhapsody blaring from the radio. David was out, gratefully feeling none of the kicks to his ribs and face.

Just about the time Freddy Mercury was wishing he'd "never been born at all," Allen reluctantly crept into the room unannounced, expecting the worst after hearing shouting muffled by the blaring radio and TV. Shocked at finding Robert and his entourage, Allen hesitated as if ready to leave the room in a hurry. But, when Allen saw David on the floor, he discovered the courage that prevented his departure. Allen began shouting at Robert mixing his voice into the chaos of the TV, Queen and Robert's sputtering tirade.

"What are you doing? Stop this! You're going to kill him!" Allen was nearly hysterical. The towering black man dwarfed Allen who received a silver-hammer blow from a six-inch, leather-covered, lead club the big man pulled from his jacket. Allen crumbled to the floor. As Allen's body laid twitching in convulsive spasm's, the assassin reached down and with a swift slice ran a straight razor across Allen's throat. The execution brought Robert to the body's side where he began kicking Allen's now lifeless form.

While the blood continued flowing from Allen's throat, Robert's kicking spattered his pant leg and those of the big man with the bloody razor. All the while Robert kept up his verbal tirade. Robert didn't care that his efforts elicited no response from Allen other than the steady red flow from his neck. Robert was feeding the paranoid monster cleaning up the mess that threatened his life.

The fat man dragged Allen's body into the suite's bathroom hallway leaving a red trail over the living room's blood-smeared carpet. He was deposited on the cold tile near the bathroom door. Robert ordered David's body carried to the bathroom too and followed as the smaller fat man wheezed under David's weight. Robert cared little if David was still alive. The original plan included David breaking down to lead Robert to any undiscovered accomplices. Robert no longer cared.

David's lifeless body was dumped on the floor. His head slammed against the tub's side before resting on the bathroom tile. The fat man struggled to bend over and pull David closer. He gripped David's belt and lifted, pouring him into the empty white porcelain tub while Robert stood shouting and swearing. David lay on his side with his back to Robert. His head was propped against the sloping end of the tub. His face was swollen, cut and bruised. Blood trickled from his ear. His lips and nose blended together leaking a red wash that colored the white porcelain. A gash and lump on the back of his head were the latest contribution resulting from his fall from the fat man's arms. Robert continued yelling as he stood over David. The fat man slouched seated at the tub's edge gasping for air. He looked to his side and watched in disbelief as Robert tried unsuccessfully to reach his foot over the tub's side for one more kick at David.

In the outer room there was a crash and a hard slap as the suite's door was broken open and swung hard against the wall. Allen's bodyguard, Mike Daly, bulled into the room too late to protect Allen—his sole reason for being there. His eyes furiously searched the room followed closely by the muzzle of his gun. He didn't know that Allen had already departed the room and the rest of the earth. Daly saw the tall black man in the middle of the room turning toward him, pulling a gun from his shoulder holster. Daly popped a single, two-handed, .32 caliber shot to the big man's brain from his silenced Walther pistol. The black man stiffened, his eyes wide open, and fell backward crashing through the glass coffee table sending glass chunks onto the floor near the couch where he lay draped over the table's frame.

Robert and the fat man were still in the bathroom when they heard the melee in the adjacent room. Robert immediately pressed hard against the bathroom's mirrored wall while his accomplice pushed past him fumbling for his holstered gun and stumbling over Allen's body. Daly saw him. He fired twice embedding both silenced shots in the bathroom door's frame near the fat man's head. As his unharmed target fell, Daly saw Allen lying across the bathroom's doorway and knew it was time to leave. He disappeared into the hotel hall.

Robert remained glued to the cold, glass-covered wall, a pool of his own warm urine at his feet. The television and radio continued their audio competition preserving the confusion. The fat man jumped to his feet, then, gasping for air, stumbled over Allen's body once more while entering the living area where his partner lay across the broken table's frame. His arched back thrust his belly upward. Both arms were flung to his side. A large portion of the broken glass table top protruded painlessly from his left leg. The sliced artery had already stopped its flow. His head was awkwardly propped against the couch's shiny red, satin-striped fabric. Both eyes were open, blankly staring upward at the ceiling. A small trickle of blood followed the curve of his nose trailing to the side of his head ending as a drying drip at the end of the diamond piercing his ear. The fat man turned to Robert, mouthing silently beneath the pounding music, "What the fuck?"

Robert had no answer. "We've gotta get out of here," Robert yelled. "Now!"

Robert edged his way toward the door. Tears began streaming down his face as he gritted his teeth and restarted his swearing rant. There was no sense or definition to his words just a stream of Tourette-like frustrated obscenities.

The gunman impatiently pushed past Robert and with his pistol boldly leading the way, entered the hallway. Robert waited; looked into the hallway, and fell in, crouching behind his bodyguard. He followed as both men weaved through the hallway to the elevator and the hotel's ground floor garage. They hurried to Robert's car. Robert remotely unlocked the car as they approached and quickly slid into the driver's seat immediately starting the Jaguar leaving the fat man wrestling with the locked passenger-side door handle. Robert lowered the passenger window a few inches. "Stay here," he shouted. "If anyone comes down here, kill them. Then, call me when you've finished."

He put the Jag in reverse and left the angry fat man standing in the empty parking place with his jacket open, shoulders drooping and hands by his side. For a moment he thought of raising the one hand still holding his pistol and placing a couple of shells into the back of Robert's car, just to let him know how pissed he was. He decided instead to redirect his anger at anyone entering the garage.

CHAPTER 31

Fly Me to Your Room . . .

Things started out fuzzy. This had to be a bad dream. On the edge of consciousness, David's awareness slowly increased. He only knew his eyes were closed and he was cold. Each second was adding to his memory of what happened before he blacked out. The bad dream was blossoming into a full-fledged nightmare. People were speaking very loudly in the next room—confusion mixed with music. Then, he realized it wasn't a dream. He thought the loud noise could be a TV or a radio blasting through the fog and suddenly, he was very conscious of the pain. The pain was bringing him back with every twitching muscle spasm. Memories were coming into focus while his eyes didn't want to do the same. Even with all David's effort he couldn't open them. The thumping in his head was accompanied by an inability to take a deep breath. A searing pain clutched his chest as if to warn him against any thought of breathing. It was encouraging David to pass out once more to his previously comforting dream state.

The talk mixed with music. It was the radio *and* the TV. They were both blasting in the outer room. He was uncertain if there was anyone else in the suite. There couldn't be. No conscious person could take the noise. David managed to peer through his swollen eyes. He was lying in the dry bath tub. That explained the doubled-up position with his knees in his chest. Except for the badly torn shirt and the lack of shoes, he knew he was fully clothed with his belt loose and fly unzipped. David managed to turn over and pull the knees up beneath his body. There was the sound of water dripping in a half-filled sink and through the flaring glare of the lights multiplied in the mirrored walls David could see the bathroom door slightly opened. The blur was showing him a foot with a black shoe and sock. It laid between the door and the jam. It didn't look like it wanted to move any more than he did. The foot was on its side. There was blood pooled around the shoe's toe. Maybe it wasn't blood. It was so hard to see through the mist. Given his state, the foot didn't seem like much of a surprise. At this point nothing did. Adrenalin pulsed through David as his heart reacted to the pain and the realization that the pool by the foot had to be blood. And the rest of the body connected to that foot didn't feel any of the pain David felt.

A sudden wave of nausea swept over him. He turned his head and vomited blood and alcohol-soaked bile toward the tub's drain. The rib-searing pain amplified with each wretch of his stomach. He told himself he had to get to his feet. He had to get out of the bathroom—out of the hotel room.

David lifted himself to the edge of the tub and flopped onto the cold tile floor. It was slippery from what smelled like urine. David's legs wouldn't work. The pain in his head competed with other pains in his jaw, ribs, stomach, and knees. Even in his semi-conscious fog, David thought *they* must have considered him dead when they left. They finished him and left him in the tub, out of the way. They? He had no idea and didn't care.

"Fuck!" Even shouting against the pain hurt as he pulled his body up. David used the toilet and then the sink counter to slowly gain access to the sink's mirror. The clouded, pulverized mess looking back from the mirror between the lids of two nearly closed eyes was barely recognizable in spite of the fact that he had stared at it under better circumstances for years.

David was standing but having trouble moving and even though it appeared nothing was broken, his breathing problems suggested cracked ribs. He grasped the sink with both hands. Still fighting the urge to pass out, David fumbled for the faucet handle and heard the welcome sound of running water. There were involuntary spasms from his stomach. He vomited again. Choking, David looked down into the white porcelain bowl and through the blur saw the colors of his pain washing past the chrome drain. The curve of the faucet guided his hand toward the running water. There was the tangy taste of blood and vomit mixed with the water that he sipped from cupped hands. The cold water refreshed. As it washed away the flavors of his beating, it also awakened the painful cuts that slashed the inside of his mouth. Pulling a cloth from the towel rack, he ran it beneath the faucet; soaked it, then stuffed it into his mouth. It helped soothe the jagged fleshy area where his teeth had sawed into his cheek.

Nothing was coming back to him. None of the beating. The pain, the tub, the foot at the door, it was all still a mystery. The pain was the distraction that prevented his recall. It hurt to think. He couldn't remember anything beyond the pain.

More water on the towel pressed this time against his eyes. The cool darkness helped. He remembered taking a walk downstairs to the lobby and then over to the bar after the meeting with Ramos. Nothing else. He needed more water. He wasn't sure if he remembered being in the bar or was recalling one of several other nights that ended in alcoholic amnesia. He tried to remember anything. Reality check. David reached for another towel for his neck as he turned toward the door. His eyes were beginning to open a little wider now. He could see the foot wedged in the doorway was bloodied and definitely male. David stumbled into the door forcing it open. He recognized Allen lying on the cold tile with his other leg bent at the knee and raised high up toward his face. Allen's head was bent down with his arms stretched above his head. The pool of blood coming from his neck coagulated after running down to his foot. His eyes were open and unmoving. Allen was very dead. David was startled as Allen blankly stared back. There was a moment of surprise, then regret. Despite their recent history, David remembered Allen as a friend.

"Why is he here? What happened?"

David's memory was returning. He remembered drinking with the woman from the truck stop, or maybe that was a trick his mind was playing to make him stop thinking?

Leaning against the bathroom door jamb, David cautiously stepped over Allen's tortured body and stumbled toward the living room. The noises from the TV and radio were louder out there. His head pounded as he tried to focus through the slits in his swollen eye lids. The room parts closest to him looked torn up. Lamps on the floor and Allen's blood spread across the thick beige-colored carpet leading to his final stop by the bathroom door. David lifted his head slowly to focus on the rest of the room. His heart leaped. He stumbled backward toward the bathroom door. His first thought upon seeing the body that laid fifteen feet away near the window was that he was alive. The gun with the suppressor laid on the floor near his limp hand. It was not what David expected to see. He walked toward the man lying face-up, draped over the shattered table. The dead man's eyes were wide open as if surprised. This kill was clean. One shot to the black man's forehead. David remained propped against the wall as he ran the face through his memory. It was no one he knew. Except for the blood near the wound and the jagged piece of glass embedded in his thigh, the body was clean. The pant leg was saturated making the fabric appear black as it dried.

"He's not the one that did this to me." David was disappointed. "But he could be the muscle that sliced Allen." This didn't fit. It didn't feel like Ramos had done this.

David reached out for the dead man's jacket and found his wallet. He opened it and held it close to his face to read the license. "Claxton. Jerome Claxton. Looks like Michigan. Yeah, Michigan," David was suddenly convinced. "This wasn't Ramos." He knew the only one left was Robert. "Crazy fuckin' snake. I never thought he had enough guts to try something like this." That meant there was, at least, one more . . . and Robert. Moving a little better, David slowly walked toward the TV and turned it off. He reached for the radio and welcomed the silence. The noise was gone replaced by an eerie sense of fear. The sounds were gone but the pain was louder.

David looked back at Allen once more. Allen should have had some protection. Then David remembered Daly. "Daly! It was Daly in the bar. He was the Jameson. That was why he looked familiar. So, where was he?" David looked outside at the city. There was a faint glow on the horizon. It wasn't dawn yet but now he knew he spent much of the night unconscious. "He was supposed to be here to protect Allen. If he was in the bar, then he should have been nearby when Allen came into the room."

David figured the single, well-placed shot to the forehead was Daly's work. Then what? There was no more blood that suggested Daly got anyone else or that anyone shot him. Still, why was Allen there? Was he there after something? No, Allen knew better. Lately, they were working more together than apart. But no one was supposed to know that. Maybe Allen's murderers thought he had something. It looked like Allen stumbled in expecting to find David alone.

"Maybe so he could bitch about my being too familiar with Ramos."

That explanation was more likely. Allen was an unwilling part of the plot. David wanted to believe Allen tried to stop the beating of an old drunk friend before they turned on him.

"But then I might be giving Allen too much credit." He limped back and slowly bent down beside Allen's twisted frame placing the wet towel from around his neck over Allen's face. Maybe he should call the manager and then the police. Or, maybe he should just get the hell out of there as fast as possible. Intentional or not, it appeared David could easily be set up for Allen's murder. After all, this was his room. Allen was dead and everyone knew Allen and he had issues. That was putting it nicely. That was motive and opportunity enough. But it also appeared that his attackers didn't care whether David lived or died. That too was possible.

"They could have killed me but they didn't. What's one more body?"

David couldn't create any scenario that made sense except that they left too fast without the time to clean up or kill him. "If framing me for the crime was the intention, then why haven't the police arrived?" No. No one reported this.

"Get out! Fast! This isn't anyone's plan. This was an interruption. They meant to kill me too. That explains why the cops aren't here; why they left one of their own behind."

David had to make a logical decision before taking another step. Truth was he was in too much pain for clear thought. He and his mind were both wandering. David was in the bedroom. He grabbed a shirt from the closet. Tearing off the bloodied, tattered remains of the one on his back, he threw it on the bed. As he slowly buttoned the clean shirt, David walked into the living room toward the dead man. He found the dark suit jacket he wore to the bar laying on the floor near the sofa. David reached inside. Good, he thought, the wallet and contents were still there. He wrapped the jacket around his left shoulder and looked back once more at Allen feeling sorry for the stupid son-of-a-bitch.

"He started all of this. One simple idea to make a million. The million became less important to me over time. Probably meant little to Allen before the end came crashing down."

David stuck his head outside the suite's door into the hallway looking for any sentry. "If they're waiting for me, they'll be watching the elevators in the lobby and probably the stairways too. Best bet is the service elevator," he whispered to himself. It looked clear. He slipped into the hallway and quickly limped to the stairway. Getting to the service elevator meant walking down several flights of stairs to the 30th floor. That elevator went no further up, but it also dropped down to the basement laundry running adjacent to the garage. David used it more than once as a short cut from the parking garage. Now, he was hoping to get into the garage unseen, and then out to the street to hail a cab.

As he got into the stairwell he could hear a dull mumble. It sounded like someone talking in a very low voice. Removing his shoes, David slipped his jacket sleeve inside the door to muffle the noise as it closed. Hugging the wall, he worked his way toward the stairs and began easing down the steps while grasping the railing for support. The shooting pains in his side made each step so painful that he feared an involuntary squeak of pain might give him away. David also realized one voice suggested at least one more person. He had no plan to surprise two men. He wasn't that foolish. Still, he had to know. This might be his only possibility of escape.

The first landing was clear but the muffled speech was getting closer. David could see a shadow on the wall of the next landing—only one shadow. He waited, listening, hoping he could learn something more. If there was a second man, he would have to work his way back up the stairs. But if the shadow was talking to itself . . . .

David cautiously ducked to the side for a clear view. There was the blur of one man—young, skinny and very unthreatening despite the gun tucked in his belt, wearing a denim shirt and jeans.

David figured the kid couldn't have been more than one hundred thirty pounds. This was not what he expected. Somehow, David believed, if anyone was waiting for him it would be a carbon copy of the big, black, dead man he just left in Allen's care. This guy looked small enough that, even in David's battered condition, he was certain he could take him down. Surprise was the key. The blue-denim voice continued talking David could hear that he was muttering a song. There was a wire in his ear. The idiot was listening to an IPOD. This meant David could move a little more swiftly without worrying about the slight increase in noise. He made it half-way down the next flight before the blue man turned to see David barreling down the stairs in his direction. Clearly surprised, IPOD man backed toward the wall reaching for the gun in his pants as David jumped the final five steps and hit him hard. Both bodies slammed against the gray concrete wall and fell to the landing rolling down the next flight.

Lying tangled at the bottom of the stairs, neither of them moved. Then, wedged between the wall and the motionless man in his arms, David fought against his crippled muscles to stand. Rolling to his side, David climbed to his feet using the cold concrete wall as a brace. He readied himself, expecting to swing at his victim hoping the weight behind the punch would be enough to put the guy down once more. But he didn't have to worry. The blue man's head looked like a plastic toy that split along a seam. The bright red blood trail started at the top of the previous landing. It was spattered and smeared high on the wall and followed their ragged tumble to the bottom with more shiny red pools on each stair. Apparently, the jump slammed his head against the concrete wall hard enough to crack it open. Blue boy was dead the instant David's lunge crushed him against the stairwell's wall. The roll to the next landing was a freebie. He was already dead. David stood over the body panting and wincing from the exertion. "So much for getting the information I need."

Once more David folded his aching body, kneeling beside the corpse to go through his jacket. He took the IPOD, blue boy's wallet and a few papers. There was no time to look at anything now. "Just grab it and hope there is something I can use later," he said to the echoing walls. David weakly retraced his steps upstairs and gathered his shoes and jacket leaving the dead man's gun swimming in the blood near the body. Walking back down again to the elevator and through the garage, he was awkwardly straightening his jacket and shirt while dusting off the pants as best he could when he heard shuffling feet approaching from behind. As David turned, he saw a short, fat, expressionless black man close enough that he could hear his labored breathing. Fifteen feet from the outside and freedom when suddenly David was face-to-face with what must have been Allen's killer. He was frozen in place by fear as he watched the man raise his arms and point a pistol. There were two muffled pops. Instinctively, David ducked as the fat man fell dead at his feet. Thirty feet away, David saw someone fade back into the shadows followed by the sound of jogging back into the garage and the dark. Still shaken, David crouched next to the nearest wall and looked back at the body until he was convinced the assassin was dead and David's savior was gone. A deep sigh of relief accompanied by the adrenaline rush eased much of his physical pain. There was little doubt someone did him a favor—intentionally or not. Looking in all directions before rising, David cautiously headed for the street. There, the hand slowly went up and the cab pulled over.

David needed answers.

CHAPTER 32

Regroup

The cabbie headed for the police station. The cops were the logical choice. It was his best bet for more protection and for getting untangled from the mess. There was less of a threat to his freedom in turning over the whole problem to the police than there would be if his attackers decided to rearrange his life once more. The next time, if there was a next time, would be the last and David was not willing to take the chance. He wanted answers but did not intend to get killed trying to find them.

A light rain was falling as the yellow cab hurried through the city streets. David nervously gave every car that passed a close look. The constant thumping of windshield wipers and flashing pattern of the early morning street lights were not racing as fast as David's heart. He began thumbing through the things taken from the humming, dead man in the stairwell. If he brought the items close to his face to read them, he could make things out through his still badly swollen eyes. The money was easy to see—a few hundred bucks in small bills. There were a couple of credit cards for "Larry Hopkins," a folded piece of yellow paper alongside the driver's license and a receipt from a drug store for $12.23. That was it. Nothing more. David rolled down the window and tossed the IPOD, the wallet and most of its contents out the window. He pocketed the cash and looked up to see the driver looking in the rearview mirror at him. "Just trash nothing important."

The yellow paper folded in the wallet was a little more interesting. It looked like a receipt. David unfolded the copy of an apartment lease with an address: Oboaa? No. Odessa. Odessa Apartments, 1237 Odessa Way. David's eyes were coming around. From the address and the first and last on the lease, this place looked pretty good. "Forget about the cops," he leaned on the back of the driver's seat handing him the paper with the address. "Know where that is?"

"Yeah but you look like you might need a hospital."

"I'm all right," David told the driver. He was hoping the apartment was empty. He might be able to stay for a few hours. Hopkins wouldn't need it. This could be his safe house. By the time he got up, something else could happen to make all of this go away. It was wishful thinking and David knew it. But there was a steadily growing fear inside him. It was cornering him into a belief that there might not be anywhere he could hide and maybe, just maybe, there were still elements to this he hadn't figured out, yet.

The cab took a quick left and 15 minutes later David was standing in the drizzling, early morning darkness on the wet curb in front of Hopkins' apartment trying to figure out how to get in.

Sliding glass doors were always a good bet. Hopkins' was open—broken lock. David slid the door open wide enough to wedge through, then entered the apartment through the parted vertical blinds. He was alone and didn't expect any visitors—certainly Hopkins wasn't going to return any time soon. Even in the morning darkness, the apartment looked nicely furnished with a collection of rental items. All still had the red and white "Owens' Weekly Rental" tags plastered to the bottom of cushions and the backsides of furniture. Hopkins poured a little money into the place and then must have stayed somewhere else because the cupboards were empty. The answering machine on the counter beside the kitchen wall phone was blinking.

David began an orienting search of the other rooms. The bed was without sheets, blankets or pillows and the dressers held no clothes except for a few pairs of socks and some underwear. The bathroom was empty too—nothing, not even towels or toilet paper. He walked back to the kitchen and played back the lone message on the answering machine. Playback was a delightful surprise. David recognized the voice as the mystery bitch with the newly colored brunette hair. It was the same sugar-sweet voice seeping through his clouded memory that walked him back to his suite and the beating that found him waking as a bloodied, tortured pile of pain in the bathtub. "Laura," she said her name was Laura. From the tone of her recorded voice Larry and Laura were pretty good friends.

"Hey baby. I'm still walking a little bow-legged from the last midnight ride. Maybe the horse needs another rub down. I'll be seeing you tonight right after we complete our little adventure. Can't wait. Bye."

David concluded he was the adventure. He also figured that since the adventure was complete, Laura might be on her way—if she didn't know her boyfriend was collecting dust in the hotel stairwell. David began going through Hopkins' closets looking for something to defend himself with beyond a kitchen knife. Only the bedroom closet had anything in it. It resembled the contents of an emptied suitcase. There were a few shirts and pairs of pants. In the top of the closet, beneath some sweaters, lover boy's Glock box was empty. That had to be the gun Hopkins was carrying. The second box said "Smith & Wesson." The small caliber automatic with the word "millennium" occupying most of its length just became David's newest best friend. The pistol looked like the perfect toy to push into the back of someone's head. There were two .40 caliber loaded clips and one more shell that Hopkins must have ejected from

286

the piece before dropping it in the box for storage. David pushed one clip into the pistol and pulled back the action loading a round into the chamber. He gently uncocked the hammer and flipped the safety into position. Shoving the weighty promise into his pocket, David headed for the sliding glass door. He would rather not be there when Laura showed up. She could have friends with her. He was not going to test his expertise against any more professionals.

David slipped out the door and pulled it closed. Just then headlights passed over the back entrance from the street. He could hear the car engine turned off and the car door open and close. There was no haste in any of it. If it was Laura, she was alone and in no hurry. David was hiding in the wet bushes with the millennium sweating in his right hand waiting with a partial view of the living room through the glass door and the slatted blinds.

Laura came in, apparently expecting that no one was there. She hesitated, looked around and then pulled a small caliber pistol from her purse and flipped on the light switch near the door.

"Hello?" She took a couple of steps forward to the answering machine. She hit playback; heard her voice; then hit erase. Using her sleeve, Laura erased her prints from the machine. Sliding the pistol into her purse, she turned and hurried toward the door. The lights went out. David waited to hear the car door and the engine. There was a flash as the headlights passed over his hiding place—and then she was gone.

Slipping back through the glass door, David decided to stay in the dark. With Laura's visit over, he assured himself there would be no further interruptions. There was probably no one other than Laura that knew of Hopkins' connection to the night's events. David figured Laura's visit to the apartment was an early breakup notice. She must have decided she had all she was going to get and didn't want to share it. It was just as likely she was sufficiently frightened by the violence that leaving town was the best idea. As a ghost without ties to anyone or anything, Laura stood a better chance of surviving. Hopkins was just one of those ties. She might already know Hopkins was dead. Hanging around as a witness and accessory to murder put her in a vulnerable position. The police might help but as deeply involved as she was in the whole mess, there was little hope she could go to them without some consequence because even Laura had something to hide.

The morning rain increased. The sun was hiding too. David realized the apartment was the best place to stay to wait out the rain and the delayed sunrise. Sleeping in the living room near the slider offered David a quick escape if he needed one. But he didn't want anyone walking by and seeing him sleeping on the couch. He took the cushions from the furniture and spread them on the floor behind the couch. Now, there was an empty room and furniture between David and anyone who might take advantage of the sliding glass door. In about five minutes, David was asleep with a firm grip on the pistol lodged beneath his pillow adding to his comfort.

The sound sleep seemed like minutes when the blaring police siren and flashing lights awakened him. David stiffly lifted his head and pulled the pistol from beneath the pillow. The earlier beating was having the painful effect that comes with not moving the body for a while. His first moves were like revisiting the beating— stiffness and unbearable pain. David looked around the room. The vertical blinds weren't blowing against the glass door. That meant the door was still closed. The siren and lights disappeared in an instant. The sudden, sharp noise startled him enough to get the adrenaline pumping once more. David checked his watch. The watch! It wasn't on his wrist! This was the first time since leaving the hotel that he looked at it. It must have been taken during the beating. The red blinking digits on the answering machine said "Thursday, 8:14 a.m." Two hours of sleep would have to do. He couldn't stay any longer and take the chance he might be seen sneaking out. Rummaging through the kitchen once more, David saw the cupboards were empty but the refrigerator had an apple, half of a deli-turkey sandwich still partly wrapped and a couple bottles of

Heineken. He collected the beers—one for each pocket—and took one pain-filled bite from the sandwich before heading for the door.

Slowly weaving his way along a side street, David got back to the main drag where he hailed the first cab that didn't have a lighted, red, "off duty" sign. The cab dropped him three blocks from the Hilton. He wanted to see if there was anything happening—if the bodies attracted any attention. As David turned the corner toward the hotel, he saw everything was quiet. Through the hotel's glass doors he saw the hotel lobby's glittering interior busy with early morning checkouts. The rain slowed to a light drizzle as patrons gathered at the curb beneath the blue and gold Hilton canopy filing into waiting cabs.

"I don't get it," David said as he stared at the unexpected activity. "Normal. It all looks normal."

The doorman, Bruno, was outside directing bellman, hailing cabs and opening cab doors while shielding departing patrons with a large blue and gold umbrella. Bruno's uniform echoed the corporate blue tones. Wearing a long Hilton-blue overcoat with gold epaulets, gold-trimmed blue cap and white gloves, he was the beacon that drew David's attention. "Bruno will know what's going on. He always does."

An arriving cab's tires squeaked on the wet pavement. Its headlights, faded in the clouded sunlight, swept the hotel lawn and the curved driveway approach to the hotel entrance. Bruno hurriedly opened the umbrella once more, adjusted his hat and pushed past bellman jockeying for position with their luggage carts. He walked to the curbside beneath the canopy and opened the taxi's rear door greeting a tired guest and his female companion still in evening attire. Bruno apparently knew them. There was a pleasant exchange. As Bruno closed the cab door, David heard him say "Goodnight, sir." Bruno waited a moment watching the guests as they walked across the lobby then turned back to the curbside action and saw David crossing the street walking toward the hotel entrance.

Surprised to see David, Bruno left the canopy and walked rapidly toward him beneath the blue umbrella.

"This can't be good," David whispered. He considered turning around and walking away as fast as he could before the imagined flashing lights and sirens of a hundred police cruisers encircled him and the uniforms poured out of the cars and into the streets with guns drawn.

But Bruno wasn't running away in fear. The rain stopped but the immaculately landscaped lawn between the weaving entrance to the Hilton and the street was soaked. Bruno unexpectedly walked across the wet ground to meet David as he limped up the driveway. There was a white envelope in Bruno's gloved hand. "Mr. Brewkowski, this was left for you about seven this morning. It must be important," Bruno said then pulled abruptly back as he saw David's beaten face. "Are you all right, sir? Should I call for help?"

"No. No, it's all right, Bruno."

"What happened, sir? Was there an accident?"

"No. No accident. It was completely intentional." David took the envelope from Bruno as they walked toward the hotel's doors. Under the lighted canopy, David stopped and tore open the envelope. Inside was a business card. *"Hope you slept well. Call me as soon as you can. I think I may have some news about your friend that left town. VR."* David turned the card. It said: *Victor Ramos, Continuity Investments.* The rest of the information had a line of ink through it and beneath was written a local phone number and an address. David stuffed the card into his shirt pocket then crumpled the envelope.

"Who left the note? What did he look like?"

"A tall, white-haired gentleman. Neatly dressed," Bruno said. "The driver pulled up and he got out and gave it to me with a fifty-dollar bill. Said to make sure you got the note as soon as you got home. That it was very important. Are you certain you're all right, sir? I can get . . ."

"No, I'm fine. Listen, did you tell him I wasn't in?"

"No sir, he seemed to know you weren't. Then he got back into the front seat and nodded to the driver and they left."

"Ramos himself huh?" David said out loud.

"Sir?"

"Oh. No. Nothing."

The fact that Ramos knew David wasn't in his suite had him shaken. This was more information for an adrenaline-soaked brain. Loose ends and hanging questions were coming together, fast. The answers were there but they must be put in some kind of order. The clearest and most frightening answer for David was that Ramos *had* looked for him. That seemed clear.

David looked up blankly at Bruno. "Maybe he found me. He must have or he wouldn't have known I wasn't home when he left the note. He must have walked in on me at Hopkins'."

"Sir?"

David looked down and kept talking. "Finding me at the apartment means he probably knows about the kid and Allen too."

Bruno shook his head slowly as he listened to David. There was a quizzical look on his face. Bruno backed away as more hotel guests arrived. He began greeting people leaving David by himself. David was lost once more in his thoughts. This time, only he heard them.

David reached for the business card in his shirt pocket. "He could have eliminated me while I slept. That he didn't is another part of the message. He found me, let me alone and then sent a message to tell me he had. I guess he's telling me I am supposed to trust him and believe he had nothing to do with my beating or Allen's death." That was it! The real meaning of the note. David turned to Bruno as he closed a cab door and tipped his hat.

"That's it! The 'friend who left town' remark must refer to Allen." His words were mixed with the noise of busy guests, bellmen and cab tires splashing through the wet streets. Though they made eye contact, Bruno could see David was talking to himself. He directed hurrying bellman away from David unsure of the situation.

"Ramos knows Robert killed Allen and wants me to believe Robert is working on his own. It *was* Robert! But just because he wants me to think that, doesn't mean it's true." David stuffed the card back into his pocket and walked toward Bruno.

"Has anyone else been here looking for me, Bruno?" He was fishing for the obvious—where the hell were the cops and the forensics guys and the ambulances and police tape?

Bruno stood very straight as David walked closer. Bruno was unsure of David's next move. He watched David while directing guests and bellmen. "No, Mr. Brewkowski. It's been very normal this morning.

"Nothing out of the ordinary?"

David's question was heard by a bell hop lifting the last bag onto the brass hotel luggage cart. "Yeah, nothing if you don't count that weird party on one of the upper floors," he laughed as he caught Bruno's disapproving glare, and hurriedly pushed the cart toward the hotel entrance.

"There was a party?"

"Yes sir. Short one at about five this morning. That's not that unusual. We get people coming in at all hours from late parties."

292

"Weird. The kid said weird."

"This one looked like it was moving from one place to the next. They were pretty busy but left within an hour." Bruno opened another cab door for a departing couple; accepted a tip, smiled and closed the cab door tapping on the roof as he pocketed the money. "Must have been pretty good," he said as he turned to David.

"Why. Why was it pretty good?"

"There were probably 20-30 people and they were all carrying things." Bruno hesitated again –"before and after," he added. "I didn't recognize anyone but they must have had a key. They took the side entrance."

"Ramos." David mumbled. "He sent in the cleaning crew—the reasons there were no cruisers with lights flashing or cops stringing yellow tape outside the hotel."

David was dead-on-his-feet tired. "Hey, take these," he gave Bruno the two green bottles in his pockets as they walked back toward the hotel entrance. David threw the turkey sandwich in the door side ashtray. "Give me a half-hour then call a cab and let me know when it arrives."

Bruno nodded. "Yes sir, 30 minutes."

David made his way to the lobby elevator and pushed floor 35. As he stepped from the elevator he could smell a strong odor of pine scented disinfectant that got stronger as he approached the suite's door. The door was closed and locked. David unlocked it quietly, half expecting someone on the other side with a gun. As he stood to the side, he removed the millennium from his pocket and cocked the pistol while flipping the safety off. David gently pushed open the suite's door and peered around the corner. No one was there. Still cautious, he entered the room with the pistol in front gripping it with both hands. The place was immaculate. The carpet was still damp. There was no sign of Allen or the blood in the bathroom, either. Lamps were replaced. The smashed glass table and the accompanying body were gone. Without looking, David expected the stairwell probably experienced the same thoroughness. Wherever Allen, the dead, black Cyclops, and Hopkins were taken, David didn't want to know and probably never would.

Despite his relief at seeing a large part of his problem gone, David still wanted answers—at best, all of them or at the very least the "why" that got Allen killed. Ramos had the answers that was certain. From the note left with Bruno, it was clear Ramos had something to say. "If Ramos was responsible for all of this terror, he would have killed me while I slept at Hopkins' apartment. If it isn't Ramos; if Robert is working on his own; then I have to hope Ramos will be there when I need him—hopefully, before the bad guys got close."

Walking into the bedroom, David removed his clothes dropping the shirt and then the pants. He limped toward the master bathroom and turned on the shower. Five minutes of stinging water was all he could afford. One look in the bedroom mirror after emerging from the shower gave visible evidence to this pain. A mixed palette of blues, reds and purples covered nearly all of his body. If he hadn't believed the fury of the attack before, this sight confirmed it. Clean shirt, socks, underwear and a clean suit. "I have to give the appearance of being unruffled and ready for anything Ramos can throw at me." He slipped Hopkins' gun into his suit jacket pocket. He picked up his wallet and Braun electric razor sitting on the dresser; ran a comb through his hair and walked quickly to the door as the phone rang. "Mr. Brewkowski? Your cab is here, sir."

"I'll bet your timing gets you some nice Christmas tips."

"Christmas sir?"

"Yeah, never mind. I'm on my way."

On the way down in the elevator, David shaved, finishing as he walked through the lobby. At the door he handed the razor to Bruno with a twenty. "Hold on to this for me, will you?"

David brushed off the razor dust that fell on his suit and jumped into the waiting cab. After giving the driver the address on the card, he leaned back and reached for the gun hidden in his jacket pocket giving it a reassuring tap. Just the same, David doubted very seriously that he would get anywhere near the man while still in possession of the millennium. "But I have to show intent, if nothing else."

The driver looked in the rearview mirror. "What's that?"

"Uh yeah. How much farther?"

It was close to 10:00 a.m. The streets were wet and traffic was slow. Ramos would be up. David knew he wouldn't be waking him.

CHAPTER 33

*I'll take "Surprises at the Bottom of the Barrel" for $1,000,
Alex.*

The address could only be described as upscale. "Nice!" The cabbie
was impressed as the cab approached the gate.

The first impression wasn't lost on David, either. "Who
would expect anything less?"

The cab pulled up to the large ancient, weathered wooden
gate. "Don't get too excited," David told him. "It's not mine." David
handed him a hundred dollars for the ten minute ride. "Wait. There's
another hundred if you're here when I leave."

As the driver pulled out to the street, the cab's red brake
lights illuminated the driveway's large, tree-shaded, oak gate and
the smaller, pedestrian-sized, barred, iron gate that guarded the
walkway. Pressing the illuminated button on the intercom, There
was the click of an immediate pickup. "Please come in, David." It
was Ramos's voice. There was another click as the iron gate
electronically unlocked. It was accompanied by a slight whirring
sound as the overhead camera mounted above the oak gate panned
with his movement.

The brick-paved circular drive nestled against a Tudor, ivy-covered, stone mansion looking like something Hugh Hefner or Henry the Eighth might have created. The sprinklers scattered water over the lawns, despite the recent rain, and spritzed a fog through the tightly manicured shrubs surrounding the entry. There was an earthy odor of rich, damp soil mixed with camphor chips that laid thickly beneath the shrubbery. The large wooden doors with sturdy black iron hinges resembled the front gate and came with an equally aged, freshly-pressed butler and Ramos's bodyguard, Enrique, two steps inside. Enrique motioned David to the side and led him to a room just off the front entrance. Ramos was seated inside the walnut paneled room still in his pajamas wrapped in a Chinese-red silk robe. A small fire crackled behind him in the Victorian tiled fireplace bathing the room in a warm complimentary light. The orange wash was custom made to enhance the colors of the large painting of a French Impressionist hayfield hanging above the mantle.

Enrique's hand fell firmly on David's shoulder after they made it far enough into the room for the butler to close the door behind them. Then, with far less formality, Enrique firmly pushed him toward the paneled wall and pulled his arms up to check for weapons. "It's in my jacket pocket." Enrique had it before the words left David's lips and continued looking until Ramos stopped him.

"That's enough, Enrique. I think Mr. Gere has more questions than a need to kill anyone."

"Anyone here, maybe," David said while walking slowly toward Ramos readjusting his clothes.

"Please sit down, David. Let me see if I can answer some of those questions for you."

David carefully lowered his body toward the cushions trying not to betray the pain from the beating. Still, Ramos noticed the effort. The soothing milk chocolate leather couch was next to one of several softly glowing lamps that made the Chinese red of Ramos's robe seem as if it was on fire. David was trying to look comfortable but his still swollen eyes and facial cuts couldn't be ignored. Enrique placed a cut crystal whiskey glass with ice cubes on the table next to David and poured several inches from a bottle of David's favorite, Johnny Walker Black. "You don't miss much, do you?" David said while looking up at the man's cold stare. Either he or Ramos made the note.

Ramos smiled, "We'll have some breakfast out by the pool a little later, if you like."

David was impatient. He came for answers and wanted Ramos to know it. "What's going on, Victor? You had nothing to do with making the mess so why did you take the time to clean it up?"

"Slow down David. First, I had nothing to do with your beating or with Allen's death. I'm pleased you figured that out. My people arrived shortly after you left. And, yes, they cleaned up both the mess in the hotel and the one on the staircase. I received a tip about the event from an anonymous voice with an Irish accent. The tip included details about the fat man in the garage. I think it is safe to assume that we both know Mr. Daly was responsible. I think that might be the second thing you'll have to thank him for, if you ever see him again."

"So you know about everything?" David said it with unmasked surprise and shifted uneasily as the couch's leather cushions crunched beneath him.

Ramos stood and walked toward a small mahogany table near the fireplace where there were two white, silver-rimmed, china coffee cups with saucers and a tall, matching coffee pot. He began pouring as the permeating aroma of hot coffee filled the room. Ramos finished pouring the first cup. "I assume you are content with your drink or would you prefer a cup of coffee?" He made a gesture as if offering the saucered cup to David, then pulled it back.

"No, thanks. I'm fine." David took a stinging sip of the Scotch and placed the glass on the table.

Ramos slowly turned once more to the coffee table dropping two sugar cubes in the cup and gently stirred the liquid with a small silver spoon while he walked back to his chair. "Yes, I am aware of both assassins. I am also familiar with your removal of Mr. Hopkins. That was unnecessary but effective. You should have realized the fool in the stairwell was supposed to be watching for you. He meant you no harm." Ramos stopped before sitting and looked at David without saying anything. He smiled and glanced back at the chair before easing in

"He had no intention of hurting you," Ramos repeated. "But killing him was probably the best thing to do. Now anyone who cares thinks he ran away with his new girlfriend. Laura yes?"

"Who killed Allen? That's why you asked me to come, wasn't it? Who killed Allen?"

"David, you and I are involved in this together beyond just being the victim of a beating and the cleaner of nasty deeds," he said with his congenial half-smile. "You see, Robert Whitney has become quite the entrepreneur. Initially his interest in money was nothing more than an interest in his personal cocaine habit." Ramos sipped from the cup and then placed it and the saucer on the table beside his chair.

"He needed cash to keep the habit pure and ongoing. But the same greed that pushed him for his next envelope of powder is the same greed that channeled him to me. I made sure of that." Ramos reached across the same table for a collection of white papers stapled together and began flipping through them. "I first learned of his need for investors in GrowVest, then, realized he was skimming from the company as fast as the investors could pour the money in. The more investors he could gather the more money he could bank

299

and the more reliably he could fill his nose." Ramos looked up at David and leaned forward handing him the papers.

The papers were filled with numbers in columns under the bold heading: **"GROWVEST-Robt. Whitney."** Beside each entry was a date, address and amount. "Mr. Whitney," Ramos said, "if this is accurate, and there is no reason to believe otherwise, has acquired much more than a simple nasty habit." It wasn't clear if the entries were for expenditures, collections or both. There was no need to ask.

"He wasn't very good at keeping the secret," Ramos added. "In fact, he was just plain sloppy. Stories began filtering out of the parties he frequented and before long, I recognized his greed as an opportunity for my own businesses. I began banking with GrowVest, funneling funds from one account into those set up by Mr. Whitney.

"My business, what I do, is not important. It is not what this is about. I paid him directly for his service and watched as he began stealing from me just as he had all the others." Ramos crossed his legs and sank further into his chair.

"No," David said shaking his head and looking up from the white pages. "This isn't right. You are twisting the truth just a bit." David threw the pages on the table. "If Robert was taking *your* money, your credibility in the business world would be lost— painfully damaged at best. By rights, Enrique, here, should have rearranged Robert's life for him and dropped him in a hole—a little Darwinian confrontation, a modified survival of the fittest." David emptied the Scotch pulling a shard of cracked ice into his mouth to soothe the pain. He cradled the glass with its melting ice between his hands in his lap and edged forward in his seat. "So, you've just been sitting back with business as usual watching Robert? Why? You already know he's making you look pretty stupid, if you'll pardon the interpretation." Ramos listened without seeming troubled. "And now you know he probably thinks he killed me and did kill his partner. This makes no sense at all."

David looked for a reaction. Ramos raised his eyebrows and tipped his head. He casually reached for the coffee cup; took a sip and replaced it on the table. Nothing! Not even a squeak from him. Ramos rested each elbow on the arms of his chair, folding his hands with the index fingers touching and extended. He touched the fingers to his lips and audibly exhaled as if he just exposed a primary part of the puzzle.

"Wait a minute. If all he wanted was a little dope to feed his habit, why would he go so far into this whole money laundering with you? And why murder Allen? You can't make me believe this is just a series of missteps on his part." And then it hit him. David's epiphany must have been obvious because a wide smile replaced the perpetual grin on Ramos's face. "There's someone else. Is that what you think? Someone else Robert is working with?" David rearranged his thinking.

"Exactly David. Exactly!" Ramos leaned forward. "There is a whole lot more going on here. Our friend Mr. Whitney is working for, not with, someone else. Someone much bigger with more at stake than my money laundered funds. Mr. Whitney's interests stem from his love of the powder. Those with whom he is connected sought him out for their interest in GrowVest, just as I have."

David was having trouble keeping up with Ramos. Ramos was eagerly leading him in a particular direction and David wasn't certain he wanted to go there. At least not until he had a chance to figure all of it out a little better than the story Ramos was shoving at him.

"They also launder through Mr. Whitney," Ramos continued, "but their product seeps into the equation as well. The cocaine that attracted Mr. Whitney to his supplier is the link that generates the cash to be cleaned. Mr. Whitney and GrowVest together have created an outlet for the quick reintroduction of cleaned cartel cash. I think that may have been what Allen was coming to tell you when he walked in on Mr. Whitney and his friends beating you. You were just too drunk and by then, too beaten to hear or see much of anything. They were convinced you were working for the police. They wanted to know what you were telling them." Ramos stopped talking as if to see how much of this revelation David would accept. "And then there was Laura." Ramos reached for his cup; took a sip and cautiously replaced the cup. "She said she knew you."

This sounded more like a question than a statement of fact. "Knew me? Yeah, she knew me if one night at a motel counts as knowing," David said it without giving the question the thought it deserved.

"David . . .," Ramos said slowly with rising inflection and a lowered voice. He was preparing to ask David a question that would help him fill in one of his own missing puzzle pieces. There was a hole in Ramos's understanding of the situation. "David, Laura was a very low level leach. Until her productive evening working for Mr. Whitney, her occupation peaked at frequenting rest stops along the interstate servicing truckers. Though her talents were mostly physical, she did have a primitive sense of survival that could keep her alive if she didn't spend too much time at the same venue. To call her a con-man or woman, if we are to be politically correct, is to elevate her position. She said she ran into you several years ago and remembered you when Mr. Whitney showed her your picture and described you as the mark. If we are to believe her, then her entire involvement in this was fortuitous. Nothing more. Is that what you would have me believe?"

"Believe it. I met her at a motel off the interstate about two years ago in Colorado, I think. We shared a Biblical moment and I left. Last night I thought she worked for you."

"All right." Ramos paused several seconds digesting the information. "Well, she was employed by Mr. Whitney. Apparently, nothing more than a pick-up off the street with a promise for some cash if she could produce results." Ramos dismissively reasoned. "Whitney hoped she would find out what he wanted to know the

302

easy way. She collected her fee and left before you were beaten. Laura figured once you were dead she would sneak back into the hotel room and take whatever cash you had. She had the boyfriend wait in the stairwell, telling him to block your escape. It is likely she intended to leave him there."

David impatiently redirected Ramos. "But in the middle of the party Allen decided to walk in. Allen must have realized he came in at the wrong moment when he saw Robert."

"Yes," Ramos added, "and the last thing he felt was his skull caving in. But it all got a little more complicated when Mr. Daly arrived. He assessed the situation and seeing Allen dead, must have decided his work was done. He was responsible for the body they left behind. He shot at but missed the other gunman with Mr. Whitney before escaping. All-in-all, he could have easily remedied the situation by himself. Apparently, Mr. Daly was not harmed in the exchange. I doubt we will see Mr. Daly again. Too bad. I think he could have been useful."

Ramos looked at Enrique and casually waved his hand and nodded. Enrique opened the door to the room and the ageing butler came in to remove the coffee and cups. "Can I interest you in that breakfast now, David?"

"No, no thank you," he said softly, David was detached and still trying to make sense of Ramos's interpretation. Ramos was telling David inside things. Things that only someone who was there could have known. Laura was there. According to Ramos's story, she left before the excitement began. His interest in Laura consistently referred to her in the past tense—like she wasn't around any longer and that he had the information as to why and where she might be. David suddenly interrupted his own thought and blurted out, "What happened to the girl?"

"Laura?" Ramos stood and casually slid his hands into his robe pockets as he walked toward the French doors that opened to the pool-garden area and a breakfast table set for two. The butler was pouring orange juice into the glasses while an attractive uniformed maid arranged the covered silver tray that contained the meal. "Ah yes, after the exchange of gunfire, after all parties left the room, Laura came out of her hallway hiding place and left as well, and in her haste left the boyfriend in the stairwell. It is likely he never even knew she was gone. Never knew anything about the beatings or the murder. But no matter. He was a small-time vulture expecting to skim off a small amount of cash and spend a couple of lusty weeks with Laura before moving on. He got what he deserved." Ramos was avoiding David's question.

Ramos stopped before entering the pool area. He turned and looked back at David. "As for Laura . . . ," he said removing his hands from his pockets. He added a slight shrug while turning his palms up showing his hands were empty. "I suspect she is running." Ramos turned redirecting his attention to the breakfast table walking slowly into the garden's light. "The murder was unexpected. She was a hapless witness. I doubt anyone wanted any of those. It won't be long before some jogger finds her in a bundle beside the road somewhere." He was dismissive of her as if she was not worth the trouble of considering. "Why do you care?"

"The information you just gave me about Laura was more than conjecture, wasn't it? You spoke factually suggesting that the information came directly from Laura." Ramos looked back toward David, smiled and kept walking.

"You want me to think that you know the roadside Laura is already occupying," David said. "Is that it?"

"More importantly David, who put her there."

The threat wasn't lost on David. Ramos was still in control. With his back to David, Ramos proceeded to sit while still talking. "You, you're probably bruised and angry but . . . healthy. Anyway, you may now believe as I do that before Mr. Daly interrupted the event, they didn't want you dead. It is my belief that they were hoping you would run to your fictional police contact and they would be able to acquire one more link in the chain. They would discover one more person they would have to annihilate before coming back for you." Now seated, he looked up again and smiled. "Or maybe they did intend to kill you before Mr. Daly interrupted their plan."

"Robert is pushing some buttons in this game and you're certain someone else is pushing Robert's, is that it? Well, I'm not as certain." David was suddenly angry. These weren't the answers he came to hear. He wanted to hear about a bumbling thief who had finally committed the ultimate error where all his vulnerabilities were in the open. Instead, Ramos had a story that portrayed Robert as the clever assistant to a much larger untouchable cartel. David's face flushed. His heart was beating faster. "Why me?" David was yelling as he started toward the table. The move was sudden and his anger was evident. Enrique quickly caught up. David was looking down at Ramos seated only a few feet away. Ramos looked past David to Enrique and waved him off.

"Why did you include me in this? I would have been content just to harass Robert for the rest of his life. I was just trying to drive him nuts and hope he would kill himself. But you're telling me there's a much bigger picture, that Robert Whitney is somehow connected to something or someone much bigger." David looked ready to kill. He turned to face Enrique daring him to come closer.

Ramos put his hands up as if trying to calm the situation but he was just as excited. He began talking over David—louder, until nearly yelling. David turned toward him and Ramos blurted, "David, you included yourself in this. You injected your person into the story when you decided to reintroduce yourself to Allen that day at the convenience store." Almost as soon as he said it, Ramos shut up.

There was silence. The wheels were turning in David's head. He remembered that first meeting with Allen. He left and the dark-colored Mercury parked in front of the store left too. "The men in the car, they were what Allen was interested in all the time we were talking," David said revisiting the moment. "Allen kept edging his way forward. I thought I cornered him. I thought Allen was trying to get to the door. But that wasn't it, was it?" David shook his head acknowledging his own question. "He was moving toward the window and glancing back toward the car. I saw it but never thought anything of it. I was enjoying Allen's shock. All the while Allen was covered." David looked at Ramos, "Allen was being watched. No! That wasn't it! You said that I jumped into the middle and screwed the plans for the day. *You were there.* That was *you*," David exclaimed. It was the perfect explanation. David's immaculate fairy tale collapsed. He never believed he was in control of most events surrounding Allen and Robert. But he believed he was the one that started the ball rolling. He believed that first accidental meeting with Allen was the beginning. Now, he believed that nothing about the fiasco was his to claim. Ramos *allowed* that first meeting.

Ramos was quiet. The perpetual smile was gone. Enrique shifted his stance and backed toward the garden's French doors. David glanced back and saw him staring at Ramos. "Wait a minute. That isn't right, either. Is it?' David's brain swirled trying to catch up. "What the fuck? *You* were following Allen?"

"David . . . "

"But it wasn't you. It was the police. Right?"

Ramos shifted in his chair and leaned back.

"This is all one big joke, isn't it? You're working this, all right, but not for any mysterious cartel laundering money," David said as he looked at this new person sitting in front of him. "God, what an idiot I have been. There is no Ramos. No mystery investor." David turned away ready to leave. He stopped with his back to Ramos and, slammed his hand on the table. "This was all a set up by the cops trying to have Robert lead them to the real "Mr. Big."

306

Ramos stood and walked toward David with his hands out. "You were never supposed to be a part of this," he said. "We learned about Whitney when he started asking around for investors. His interest in major funding was finding its way into the darker circles that we normally monitor."

"Monitor? Dark circles? We? Who the hell are you guys?"

"We work for several agencies . . . as actively participating consultants," Ramos said.

"Fucking mercenaries. That's what this is. Somebody, somebody official, doesn't want to play by the rules so they hire you guys to play on the fringe, just outside of legal. Is that it?"

"David, *David!*" Ramos shouted. David stopped speaking. Ramos began again in a softer voice. "David, the agencies have their own people but occasionally they need outside help, someone who cannot be recognized. We are a private firm. Our people are highly trained and trusted. We are not regulated by any laws and no senate sub-committee is ever going to hear about us. Our job, David, is to locate the major funders involved in Whitney's illegal transactions. These connections are transient. The laundry pathways are very short-lived. That much cash, no matter how prosperous the company appears, never goes without notice."

"How much?"

"How much?" Ramos asked with a quizzical look. "How much . . . money?" Ramos threw out a number without hesitating. "We're figuring 40-50 million in the first eight months. But that changes fast. Soon, the operation is uncovered and while people like Robert Whitney are prosecuted, the real money makers, the ones running the operation simply move on to their next outlet. They find another GrowVest —another Robert Whitney. Even with a small percentage of the take and all he has skimmed from GrowVest investors, Whitney is covered in green." Ramos raised his eyebrows,

"Do you understand? The small army at his disposal undoubtedly works for his handlers, but Whitney has to feel the power associated with the money and the guns."

David was sure this was a gross exaggeration. Ramos was still talking while David's mind moved in-and-out of the moment. Robert never showed signs of having unlimited resources. There was no "army" small or otherwise. The most Robert's muscles flexed was in the last twenty-four hours and even then one lone gunman—Daly—was able to alter Robert's plans. David recognized that Ramos was still telling him only part of the truth and expanding on the rest.

"Do you see? To get closer, we have to become a part of the process," Ramos reasoned. "We have to appear to compete with the cartel." This was a sales job—probably the same line of reasoning the Feds used to enlist companies like Ramos's. This was the sort of convincing fear tactic thrown at a prospective draftee to get him to sign a contract. The next step was to let him loose on the world with all the money he needed and none of the required responsibility. It was done by Ramos's handlers to get Ramos on the job. Now, Ramos was practicing the routine on David. This was Ramos the salesman, the corporate CEO protecting his own interests. This was David's recruitment speech. God and country trumps all reason. It was an appeal to his patriotic sense of valor. Ramos believed he could have him. But the look on David's face showed Ramos that he wasn't buying the pep talk. One hand went back into his pocket and Ramos turned toward the pool with his back to David. The sale didn't work.

Ramos shifted gears. Truth would have to compensate for failure. "You were never a part of the scheme. You injected yourself into this plan and threatened to make it a very large mess." He turned again and walked toward David. In a soft voice he explained, "We thought of removing you but then realized you might be just what we needed—a visible thorn for Whitney. If he had any suspicions, we were counting on your furnished paranoia to have him think you were responsible."

"Yeah, well that part went pretty well. But not for Allen."

"No, that is unfortunate for Allen, but it may have been fortunate for us. Allen knew about our involvement. He knew who we were and what we were doing. We included him in the plan early, once we discovered the friction between Robert and Allen. To his credit, he never said a word about it." Ramos walked back into the study. He reached toward a lion-crested humidor on the bookshelf near the fireplace and removed a black maduro cigar. "But, of course, his intention that night was to let you know about it. He walked in expecting to find you alone. Apparently, he tried to stop your beating but Mr. Whitney turned on him." Now that the frenzied discovery was over, Ramos was falling back into character. "Robert must have decided he no longer needed Allen." Ramos ran the handmade cigar across his nose. He reached back to the shelf retrieving silver cigar scissors.

"Wait, wait. If Allen knew, why was he so jumpy at our last meeting? He was telling me I wasn't showing you enough respect and that it could threaten my life."

"And he was right." Ramos looked up gesturing with the cigar in one hand and the cutter in the other. "You were becoming too familiar. Between us, without a third party involved, there was no problem, but to speak as you did with Mr. Whitney or one of his people present could show weakness on my part. Allen was there to tell you the whole story. Allen wanted you in or gone—and by gone, I mean out of the country. He was looking out for you." Ramos waited for David's reaction. To break the silence, he snipped the end off of the cigar and placed the cutter in his pocket.

"Allen's conscience was working after all. The insensitive prick who left me out to dry a couple of years before, must have had enough time to realize what he did." David was quiet for a moment.

"His last contact with me cost him his life." As cold as it sounded, David knew they were even.

There was more. There had to be more. David quietly asked, "What do you want from me?"

Ramos retrieved a red enameled butane lighter from the mantle. He methodically toasted the maduro's tip before grabbing the rolled tobacco with his teeth. Quick short puffs produced flames at the cigar's end while the aromatic smoke clouded David's view of Ramos's expression. Ramos stopped puffing; turned his head and exhaled. He walked toward David holding the cigar as if inspecting the dark leaves. Closer, Ramos extended his hand and rested it on David's shoulder guiding him back to the pool's open air. "You are a part of this," he said. "Mr. Whitney sees you as someone trying to ruin his deal. We have every reason to believe you will be his primary target once he discovers you are still alive and there's very little we can do to help you." Ramos shifted purposes once more. This was Ramos the recruiter, again. "The truth about all of this is out. There is nothing left to hide." Now, he was offering David the "join-or-die" option.

"So, maybe I should move in with you. Stay out of sight and enjoy the room service. Is that what you're suggesting?"

With hands in the air as if presenting the estate to David as his own Ramos said, "It's all government funded. *Mi casa es su casa.*" The smile was returning. "It all goes on the final tab. Besides, we like you. *I* like you. I don't see the need to remove you from this," again he made a wide-armed gesture and turned slightly as if he suddenly became a realtor selling a palatial estate. "With you close by, we can better script your moves to keep them within our plans. It's your chance to repay Allen for your life."

David heard enough. "The thought of being the guest of the government or some clandestine organization that is above the law is a lose-lose for me." David stopped walking and turned toward Ramos returning a plastic smile then walked away.

"Where are you going, Mr. Gere." Ramos's demeanor changed. His cheerful, lilting speech melted along with his smile.

"I'm going to find Robert and kill him. See how that fits into your plans."

CHAPTER 34
Reason for a Future

It was tough maintaining his anger after the butler insisted on getting the door for him to charge through. There were no stamping feet or fiery words to accompany his false rage. Just the same, it was worth a chuckle as David followed the sidewalk past hissing sprayers dousing the shrubbery. He could see the red light on the gate mounted camera. He was being watched as he left.

Despite the false bravado for Ramos's sake, David had no intention of running out to find Robert. Not now, anyway. The pivoting gate mounted camera watched as David jumped into the cab. "Let's get the hell out of here." As the cab sped off, the driver told David, "Doesn't look like anyone is following."

The cab dropped him a couple of miles from the trailer park he once called home. He handed the driver the promised hundred and told him, "If anyone asks about where you dropped me, just tell them you're not sure."

There were several low-end hotels in the area. It was early afternoon. They could spend the rest of the day and night knocking on doors and never figure out where he was. Now, David hoped an old friend might have room on her couch for a long safe nap. Tomorrow morning he would try catching up to Robert.

As he walked, David spoke softly. "Ramos's description of Robert's alliances and army of assassins is bullshit. There is no sound reason to believe Ramos, or whatever his name is. He just wants to increase his importance to me as my protector and ally.

"There's also no reason to believe Ramos is letting me walk away. But he did." David searched for some sense in Ramos's move. "The slip where Ramos exposed the operation should have been reason enough for Enrique to shoot me on the spot. Instead, they let me leave." David was in the middle of a war and both sides targeted him for attention. "It's getting harder to tell who the dog is and who is the wagging tail."

His voice was getting louder as he fought the traffic. He decided to get off of the road and walk some of the back streets. It would take longer to get where he wanted, but it was safer and quieter. "Being with Ramos is safer than being without him. That's what I have to consider. It is more than a little disturbing, however, that Ramos relishes explaining that he isn't regulated by any laws or the consequences that breaking those laws might have. Bottom line is that I have to watch my own back. I have to be careful not to expect anything from a bunch of strangers whose monetary motives define their loyalties." David stopped talking. He was satisfied with his conclusion.

When David left the trailer park the last time, he told Ceiley his real name and a little bit of the confusion that surrounded his circumstances. She said nothing but insisted on calling him David, from then on. He also told her he would be back to take her anywhere she wanted to go. "Kind of a vacation," he said.

At the time, she just smiled. "I've never had a vacation so, I wouldn't know how to handle it." It didn't matter. She didn't believe he would ever return.

He knocked on the hollow, chalk-white aluminum door of the trailer and felt the tremors and dull thuds of footsteps inside as she approached. There was the mechanical clank of the door handle with the squeak of metal-on-metal as the door opened.

"Hey! How you doin'?"

Ceiley was a hard worker—always doing something. She didn't like to admit it but, it was probably a part of her childhood lifestyle as a farmer's kid. She was barefoot but fully dressed in jeans and a flannel shirt wiping her hands on a dish towel when she recognized him. Genuinely surprised, she fell from the doorway into his arms wrapping hers tightly around his neck. "You came back!"

"Of course I came back. Told you I would. Hey, got room on your couch for one night?"

"Oh, I see. Just passing through?"

"No, no. I've got some business in town and can't go back to my hotel just yet. But maybe tomorrow, when I come back, maybe then we can spend some time planning that vacation we talked about."

She smiled and hugged him once more then pulled back and looked into David's still swollen eyes trying to decide if he was lying or not. "OK, maybe tomorrow when you get back," she said dismissing the probability. "You OK? Looks like you've had a few recent problems."

"No, I'm fine. Nothing time can't fix."

"Eaten yet? I was just cleaning up but I'll have a cup of coffee with you while you eat. Eggs OK?"

"No, nothing for me except maybe that coffee. I'm beat and need a few hours' sleep before taking care of that business I told you about."

Ceiley took a pair of cups from the cabinet over the kitchen sink and filled them both with coffee. She carried them to the table where David was sitting and placed one in front of him then sat across the table. "Let's see. Black, right?"

"Yeah. Great. Thanks. Listen, I've got something going on tomorrow morning. It's pretty important and may have some consequences attached. I'll tell you the rest in the morning but right now," he sipped the coffee, "I just want to rest."

"Bedroom's in there. Need company?"

"Maybe for a while. Just until I nod off."

He followed Ceiley to the bedroom. She pulled back the blankets on the freshly made bed. David pulled off his shirt and turned to see Ceiley taking off her flannel shirt. She wore no bra. Her small, round breasts were pleasing to see. She was staring at David's bruised body. Her mouth was open as if caught in mid-sentence. She looked up at his face clearly shocked by what she saw.

"Is this a part of the consequences?"

"Long story. Like I said, I'm tired. I just need some sleep."

"I'll get some ice," she said as she stepped toward the kitchen.

"No!" David said sharply. It stopped and startled her. As she turned to look at him once more, he said softly, "No, wait, please. It's all right. I just need some rest and maybe a gentle hand."

Ceiley stepped out of her jeans and panties. She walked to the opposite side of the bed and pulled back the sheet.

"You know, I really did mean I needed some rest." He was apologizing. "I know I'll probably be sleeping moments after my head hits the pillow. No matter how gorgeous you look and despite

315

the desire I have to please you. Did you think this was just a ploy to get you in bed?"

"Did *you* think it wasn't?" She laughed.

"I'm not going to be any use to you. I swear I am absolutely beat."

"Shhh. Get in bed and close your eyes. I promise to behave."

Once in bed, the soft sheets and pillow soothed him. David relaxed and drifted. Ceiley took his arm and wrapped it under her head. She lay against him gently stroking his bruised skin as if her hands could eliminate the pain and neutralize the varied hues that covered his body. Her warmth was soothing. David was asleep in moments.

Somewhere around eight in the evening, David rolled over toward Ceiley and sensed she was gone. Startled, he opened his eyes and looked up at the doorway where Ceiley was standing looking at him.

"Well, you really were tired weren't you?" Ceiley was once again wearing her flannel shirt and jeans but she was still barefoot.

"You just get up?" he asked.

"No. I never went to sleep. I just stayed until you were snoring. And you do snore; don't let anyone tell you differently. Lucky for me it's not going to be an issue."

He got up; showered, and with a yellow towel wrapped around his waist, he wandered into the living room where Ceiley was reading with the TV mumbling softly in the background.

She looked up. "Wanna go out for dinner or order in?"

"I think for now, staying in will have to do. Besides, we need some time to talk. Actually it's more like I talk and you listen.

It's that important. I need to explain a few things to you. I can't tell you everything but there is something I want you to know." David sat beside her on the couch.

"You don't need to tell me anything. I saw the bruises," she said rubbing his shoulder.

"Hard to miss"

"Yeah, but I can also figure they didn't happen washing a car. Someone has hurt you and you're hiding from them. I can see that. I'm just very happy you decided to come to me."

"Listen, I have to tell you some things. Not everything, not yet anyway. But some things, right now. They are very important."

Ceiley sat back on the couch; pulled her legs up and crossed them under her. She looked into David's eyes. She was going to listen and see if there was any way she could help. "I want you to know you can count on me."

David looked back at her and then slowly began listing the items she had to remember. "First: if anyone comes by looking for me in the next couple of days, you don't know me that well. We just met and you haven't seen me in more than a week. Second: Trust no one. If they're asking for me there's a good chance what they plan is not going to help me in any way. Last thing: I made a check out to you and signed it. It's dated for last week that way if anyone sees it they'll believe your story about seeing me a week ago. It's in the other room on the dresser. It's yours. Wait for a week. If I don't come back, cash it and leave town."

"What kind of trouble are we talking about?"

David looked at her and shook his head slowly. Nothing more was said for the rest of the evening. They spent the next couple of hours making dinner together. Ceiley found some candles and a bottle of wine. By eleven o'clock she was lying with her head in his lap watching television.

"I think I could get used to this," she said.

"What? Watching TV or putting your head in my lap. Either way, I think it could work but I especially like the head in the lap part."

She sat up and turned to him. "No, I mean it. This has been nice. Easy. Like we have done this before a hundred times. I'm comfortable with you." She moved closer and kissed him. David reached around and pulled her closer. She moved to his neck and kissed him again. Ceiley took his hand. "Come," she said. He followed her to the bedroom. The bed was unmade as he left it. Ceiley removed all the top blankets and sheets and threw them in a pile in the corner of the room and then began removing her clothes. David said nothing. He did the same. She lied on the bed and held her arms out to him. Sitting beside her, David leaned forward to kiss her breast then moved to her belly and thigh before returning to her lips. As he kissed her he lay down beside her. She pulled him over her body. David was mapping her body. Touching everywhere. Kissing everything he touched. He wanted to know her completely. She was soft, warm and smooth. He knew he could never be happier than he was at that moment with her. He was beside her and she began her own search. David felt her fingers and lips and heard her sighs. Time didn't matter. They held each other. Loved each other. Much later, as David was drifting off to sleep in a warm glow, Ceiley was beside him in his arms. He heard her whisper, "I think I love you."

CHAPTER 35

Fatal Wishes

Robert left his home and went into hiding at about the same time David returned to discover his sanitized room at the Hilton. At the back of a small out-of-town motel, Robert hid his car and burrowed into the motel room. Inside, Robert propped a chair against the double-locked door and placed his pistol on the bed in plain sight. When the rain stopped and the sun finally showed itself, Robert was still wide awake, bouncing around his prison after taking a handful of something that promised to "keep you awake, without lingering side effects." Sleep was out of the question for several hours. Robert paced waiting for the fat man's call. By mid-day, unable to fight the fatigue, he fell asleep lying across one of the beds. When he awoke it was well past midnight. In his dreams, he decided his next move.

Robert never knew about Daly being employed by Allen and assumed the gunman was sent there by Ramos to eliminate him. Robert figured Daly left after concluding he wasn't in the room. Daly never saw Robert pressed against the bathroom wall. He was more concerned about the armed fat man coming his way. He could see his employer, his sole reason for being there, was lying at the fat man's feet. No matter. Robert's thought only reinforced his belief that Ramos must be eliminated before he had the chance to regroup.

Believing two of his problems were out of the way, he reasoned that Ramos was the only thing that stood between him and his success.

Leaving the motel Friday morning, about 1 a.m., he drove to the GrowVest offices and parked the silver Jaguar XJL near the main entrance. Before exiting the car he reached beneath the seat. The small gray plastic box Robert grabbed had the Jaguar logo and the word "tools" on its top. Robert opened it removing a six-inch-long, black-handled screwdriver. He pushed the tool box to the side and hid the screwdriver in his sleeve. Robert walked briskly through the corporate doors as the guards recognized him. Though it was very early, they were unconcerned with Robert's presence. There was a polite greeting from one of the guards that Robert ignored as he walked purposefully for the elevator to the office floor.

At the top, Robert exited the elevator and walked past his own office for Allen's. He pulled the concealed screwdriver from his sleeve and attacked the door lock popping the door open with little effort. Rummaging through Allen's desk papers, he was looking for any kind of reference to Allen's association with Ramos. He used the screwdriver once more to jimmy the lock on Allen's desk then pulled each drawer open emptying the contents in turn on the desk's surface. Again, he plowed through the collected contents without finding his proof.

Robert moved to the shelves surrounding the office, maliciously sweeping them clean. There was no regard for the contents. He was no longer looking for evidence. His purpose was altered. Now, he simply wanted to destroy. After six raging minutes, Robert left GrowVest, storming past the guards.

The streets downtown were empty. It was nearly 2 a.m. Reflected light bounced off of the puddles from a recent shower. The sound of an occasional car passing by in the rain-soaked streets was the only noise breaking the morning's silence. Robert unlocked his Jaguar and buckled himself into the black leather interior. He looked in his mirror and saw no one. This was the city's business

320

district and there were few people here for several more hours. Robert pulled out onto the street and started for home.

Three blocks away from the office the large white Lincoln Navigator in front of Robert abruptly slammed on its brakes. Robert saw the intense glow of the inflamed red tail lights too late and slid into the larger car submerging the hood of the smaller Jaguar into and then beneath the Lincoln's rear end. Robert's head whipped forward toward the steering wheel. There was the explosive sound of the air bag opening as the fabric enveloped his head and upper torso. A second white Lincoln immediately hit the Jaguar from behind. The Jag's trunk folded from the second aggressive strike. The back seat wedged tightly behind Robert. His involuntary motion reversed bouncing him away from the rapidly deflating airbag; throwing him hard against the leather seat as his head crashed into the head rest. He was dazed. Next, his side window was smashed. Dime-sized shattered glass pelted his left shoulder as a black-gloved hand reached in for his throat. The door was pried open and Robert was dragged through bits of metal and glass across the gasoline and puddles to the lead car. The rear door of the Navigator opened. A black cloth bag was hooded over Robert's head. There was the sound of duct tape peeled from a roll. The tape tightened the hood's grasp of Robert's neck while his arms were simultaneously pulled behind him. The locking grasp of heavy-duty electric cable ties secured his wrists. Robert was pushed into the car. Several doors were slammed. Not a word was spoken. The twin Lincoln's sped away leaving Robert's silver luxury vehicle compressed with a single yellow flasher hanging from the car's front blinking its message as steam escaped from the car's crushed radiator.

David was awake with the sunrise. Ceiley helped him forget Robert and Ramos for the better part of a day and throughout a comforting night. Through the night he awoke several times in a half sleep—the kind that allowed him to regain his dreams a moment after verifying where he was. For David, the verification was Ceiley beside him.

It was very early Friday morning. The sun was only just beginning to turn the eastern sky pinkish-orange. With the exception of the hacking cough from a neighbor sucking on his morning cigarette, it was very quiet. David tried not to shake the bed figuring he might be able to leave before Ceiley woke up. He collected his clothes and walked down the narrow hallway past the bathroom and into the kitchen. Finding a pen on the kitchen counter, he kept it simple writing on a paper towel, "Be Back Tonight." He stepped into his pants; slid his feet into the shoes and while still carrying his socks, threw the shirt and jacket over his shoulder.

"You sure are in a hurry." He turned to see Ceiley's naked form standing in the doorway to the kitchen. "Afraid I would ask you to stay for breakfast? Looks like you already paid for the lodging. Breakfast is included," she said waiving the check David left on the dresser the night before.

"No, no. I just didn't want to wake you. I promise I'll be back tonight. I'm good on promises, you know that."

"Yeah, I'll give you that." She gave him a half-smile and walked toward him wrapping her arms around his waist and pushing her head gently against his bruised chest. "You're good on several things. Me included." She looked up at David and smiled. He kissed her and patted her warm behind then held her tightly. "Thank you, for everything," he said. "Everything." David walked outside. A few feet from the steps he heard her.

"Hey."

He looked back and saw her standing naked in the doorway for all the neighbors to see. All David could do was laugh. "Don't worry," she whispered while she looked around, "They're all still asleep. Come back tonight, please. We still have to discuss that vacation." She never asked for anything before. This request was her first and David realized its importance. After last night's abbreviated conversation on what this day might bring, he knew she was concerned and may not have completely believed him when he told her he was coming back. There was doubt in his mind as well, but not for the same reasons. David raised his hand to wave and moved it to his mouth instead touching his lips. As he turned toward the bus stop, he stuffed his socks into the jacket pocket and wrestled with buttoning the shirt.

The bus arrived at its usual five minutes behind schedule and directly behind it was Ramos's limousine with Enrique behind the wheel. David walked past the bus to the limo driver's side. As the window was lowered, he looked in to see if Enrique was alone. "Where's the boss?"

"Get in. He has a present for you."

David walked in front of the car to the passenger side and saw Enrique reach into his jacket pocket. This didn't look good. David hesitated. "C'mon, get in," Enrique shouted. David opened the door and sat on the black leather seat staying as close to the door as possible. "I said he has a present for you. Well," he reached into his pocket, "it's actually two presents. This one first." David was ready to bail out the door until he saw Enrique had the palm watch in his hand. Not a gun. *The watch!* Enrique handed it to him and immediately shifted the car from park.

Nothing was said as they drove to the warehouse district and pulled into a yard cluttered with shells of cars and piles of scrap metal. Enrique parked beside an inconspicuous, long, white metal building with numerous businesses claiming identities over a series of adjacent doors. The car was parked in front of an open bay door. David saw a collection of tools and machinery, tires and a soiled, green, serpentine air hose hissing its way quietly across the entrance. Outside, there was a constant neighborhood noise. The sort of noise hard work makes—an early morning din of scraping and pounding mixed with the whining of sanders, drills and the metallic thumping of air hammers. It was the kind of constant irregular hum that absorbed other noises without attracting attention. It appeared no one was working inside the bay as they walked toward a door to the right that said "Office. No Visitors."

David was unarmed, and despite the return of the watch, he remained seriously worried. As they walked toward the door he kept looking for some kind of club, anything he might use as a weapon. He knew he would have to hit first and then dive for any dropped gun to have a chance. Enrique saw David checking everything out. "Relax. You're going to enjoy this," he said. That was exactly what David was expecting him to say.

"I expected something a little bit cleaner—less dungeon-like from you." His nerves were getting the better of him. They were inside and walking toward the offices and still, there was nothing he could find to use as a weapon.

"You take what you can get. Besides, this is a great place. I get my oil changed here all the time and never have any complaints," Enrique said grinning. Grinning! Enrique! This definitely did not make David feel any easier.

There was a strong odor of oil, grease and gasoline. The grime-soaked floors had a slippery texture that transferred to the soles of shoes so that even after leaving the area the shoes slid.

Enrique and David walked past the boxes of canned oils and transmission fluids and weaved through several large oil drums while ducking the elevated front wheels of a two-toned, white and powder blue, '57 Bel Air missing its rear axle. Ahead of them was a door with a large fogged glass window and "Office" neatly stenciled in black, block-letters like something left over from the same year as the Chevy. A hum from a florescent light sang in monotone while a chorus of mumbled voices moved with the blurred shadows generated by a flickering bulb behind the frosted, crackled window glass.

Enrique reached for the knob and pushed the door open waiting for David to go through. David hesitated, looked at Enrique and forced a smile. Enrique's smile was gone. He was back in character. There was no expression on his face. He just jerked his head to the side motioning David in.

David turned his attention to the open door. As he walked in he saw Ramos standing beside a table that stretched from one side of the room to the next, ending in front of the doorway. There was only one chair at the far end of the table. A beaten and bloodied Robert had that one. One other very large man in a sweat-stained white shirt with rolled up sleeves loomed over Robert with his back to the door. As David entered the room the hulk turned his head. The man's bright red face was contorted with seething anger. Here was a true specialist. White knuckles and club-like fists were wrapped in blood-stained cloth.

Ramos was in character too—the same slick grin and perfect appearance. He was wearing an expensive suit and tie with no hairs out of place. Robert, on the other hand, looked like a rat in a trap heavily marinated by a severe pounding. Robert's left eye was nearly shut and the purple color that adorned his cheek and jaw brought warmth to David's blackened heart.

"Come in. Come in, Mr. Gere. How good of you to come on such short notice. Let me introduce to you one of my closest companions." He gestured toward Enrique. "You know Enrique of course."

Looking at Robert, Ramos said, "Well, this large, uncouth character is Geraldo." Ramos stopped and turned toward David with a very broad smile. He looked back at Geraldo and lost his smile. They both turned to look at Robert. Robert understood the threat and stiffened in the chair.

"Geraldo," Ramos continued still looking at Robert, "is a bit of a communication specialist. If I have difficulty understanding someone, I often ask for Geraldo's help. And he's very good at translating." Ramos was playing this right to the end. "And you remember Mr. Whitney, don't you?" Though he addressed the remark to David, his direction was Robert's. "Mr. Whitney, you see, was a partner of mine. We had an agreement that Mr. Whitney has recently decided he wants to change. But, word on the street is that Mr. Whitney decided to tell me in a rather unique way. He was going to send several of his employees to find me to deliver the message. Unfortunately, as I have been explaining to Mr. Whitney, those employees must have decided to look for work elsewhere. We are all wondering if perhaps, Mr. Whitney might consider the same idea for himself." Ramos never interrupted his unsettling stare at Robert.

Giddy with delight, David chuckled as he asked, "*This* is the surprise?"

"Yes David a very special surprise. One you may never see again." He leaned in slightly toward Robert. "Would you agree, Mr. Whitney?"

David glowed with satisfaction. Robert was completely at the mercy of a room filled with people who cared little if he lived or died—and David who relished seeing him bruised, battered and captive. Every day, every minute, every sleepless night, every nightmare, every teeth-grinding thought ever associated with seeing this bastard in a situation just like this one was being realized. David hated this son-of-a-bitch with all his rotting soul and now the hum of the florescent light was a choir of avenging angels serenading them all at this wonderful moment. There could be no mercy in David's heart. The only concern David had was for what was next. His heart beat faster as he gasped for air like an overheated puppy. This was tail-wagging fun! There were no consequences to this. David was part of a group that was above the law. *No consequences.*

David was knee-deep in a green, slime of hatred. He happily bathed in the filth.

Robert contracted a hit on Ramos and Ramos knew it was coming. "I wish I had been there to see Robert's face when Enrique showed up at Robert's and invited him to the garage." David's excitement bordered on hysteria. Ramos had Robert but David knew Robert was his. David came closer. Ramos motioned Geraldo to let him by and the big man moved to the side of the table beside Ramos. Reaching out toward Robert, David hoped to touch his face and bring him a little torment of pain. Robert cringed and brought both untied hands up as if protecting himself from another blow.

"It appears he fears your touch, Mr. Gere," Ramos remarked. Enrique chuckled while Geraldo's expression still bordered on unbridled fury. If this was an act, Geraldo had it nailed. He resembled a salivating, angry pit bull on a short leash.

Sitting down on the table with one leg on the floor, David looked down at Robert. Ramos continued his monologue. "Mr. Gere, it is our belief that Mr. Whitney has been stealing large sums of money from me and, incidentally, from everyone else he has fooled into becoming a part of his GrowVest scheme. But I don't believe Mr. Whitney is doing this just for himself. I am convinced there is someone else involved. Perhaps several people for whom Mr. Whitney works."

Ramos wasn't giving up on the story he related to David the day before at his home. True or not, it remained that if Robert hadn't taken out the hit on Ramos, everyone might still be dancing. Instead, Robert's decision to kill Ramos was responsible for bringing the entire puzzle to light. Ramos considered it unfortunate that he had to pressure Robert but realized there was no longer any other reasonable way of finding out who Robert was working for. The only remaining choice was to hear it from Robert's own swollen lips.

Robert watched Ramos pace back and forth with his one good eye as Ramos explained the situation. "I have promised Mr. Whitney a position in my own company if he might help me track down the money and those responsible." Of course, that was a lie. "But Mr. Whitney refuses to tell us anything more than that the plan was his." Ramos stopped pacing. He looked back at Robert and then toward Geraldo. Robert stiffened once more at the visual suggestion.

"Geraldo has tried several arguments but none has worked. We thought you might like to speak with Mr. Whitney. Perhaps, by yourself. I would be pleased to commission you on all funds that find their way back to their rightful owners."

And there was the real present! That was it! David's arms got lighter. His heart quickened again. Robert really was his. He was going to get his time alone with the greasy bastard! It was the ultimate showdown with the odds firmly on David's side—one badly beaten, frightened, paranoid bastard and one bruised man aching to hurt the son-of-a-bitch some more.

Ramos uncharacteristically broke character. His voice changed and his accent faltered. Ramos lost the smile. He became that mercenary David met twenty-four hours before when he learned who Ramos really was. "I cannot convince him the truth would be best. If he does not become an employee, he serves me no purpose. But, my hands are tied. And the flexibility of my position is no longer what it once was. I cannot take care of this my way." His expression was blank as he stared at Robert. Then Ramos motioned Enrique and Geraldo toward the door. Geraldo removed a black-handled, double-edged knife with 8-inch blade from the scabbard attached to his belt and thrust it into the long wooden table. Robert's good eye widened staring at the brightly polished blade.

Ramos moved toward the door and David followed. Ramos turned and with David blocking Robert's line of sight, handed him a pistol, the one Enrique confiscated from his jacket at their last meeting. Ramos said nothing more and turned closing the door behind him.

The sound of the door closing was the opening bell for round two. Robert wasn't waiting. His chair crashed to the floor as he leaped to his feet. Pushing the table forward, it collided with the back of David's legs. David faltered toward the door and felt a searing slashing pain run through the triceps of his left arm, then a stinging numbness as the knife severed the arm's ulnar nerve.

David turned with the gun at his side. Blood freely flowed from the sliced arm. Robert raised the knife once more and lunged toward David. Without lifting the pistol, he fired in Robert's direction hitting him in the thigh. Robert stumbled taking two steps back then came at David once more. Again, he fired, this time hitting Robert in the lower abdomen. Robert dropped the knife and fell backward toward the wall sliding to the floor.

David was losing blood fast. He was light-headed—on the edge of passing out. He leaned on the table and then fell to his knees. Crawling toward Robert, he turned against the wall and propped himself up beside Robert. There was the knife between them and a pool of comingled blood around them both. David's slashed arm was useless. He used all his strength, fighting to remain conscious.

There was a sign of resigned relief on Robert's face, or maybe it was the look that comes with the realization that these were his last earthly moments. "I did this. I created GrowVest and all its success," Robert calmly said. Then, as if realizing his failure, he yelled, *"I did all of this!"* He turned his head toward David with his teeth clenched. "I had this planned for the last couple of years. Mac was supposed to be a part of it. But Mac got greedy before I had the chance to dispose of him." He turned away to look blankly at the wall in front of him. "No matter. In the end, he only made it easier. He didn't get very far." Robert exhaled and dropped his head to look down at his stomach wound and the blood soaking his clothes.

"I'm dying but I still win because nobody will find the cash. You can look for the next hundred years and you'll never find it, never find it all." Now that it was over, Robert was claiming victory. It was his final reminiscence—a final bit of peace and comfort reviewing his accomplishments. "Allen was an idiot. Allen thought he could still be part of the whole thing. Allen believed GrowVest was *real*," he turned again to David, "*was his!*" Robert yelled, "GrowVest was gone more than a year ago and Allen never knew it."

Placing the gun in his lap, David reached into the left breast pocket of his blood-soaked jacket. Searching for a moment, he extracted the flash drive copy of Robert's bank files. "This is your money. All of it," he told Robert. "And I have it all. Not Ramos or the cops or anyone else. Just me. I have every stinking dime that you ever stole. You're dying you stupid son-of-a-bitch and everything you have done, every deal you ever made is mine and I'll be spending it before your body is cold. You know what that means, Robert? It means you lose."

Robert lunged for David's hand knocking the computer drive into the pool of blood between them. In the scuffle, the pistol fell and laid two very long feet to David's left. Robert slid a hand through the blood and grabbed the drive. He fell to his side and reached for the knife. He was very weak but managed to sit upright. His one eye closed as he gasped for air and exhaled. Opening the eye, Robert looked at David once more. "Ramos," he said haltingly. "Ramos tried . . . to muscle me out. I knew about him . . . all along. As soon as he figured out . . . there was more money in GrowVest that he could . . . take, he'd get rid of me. I knew that. But you can't count on anyone. I should have killed him myself."

As David looked at Robert, the face went in and out of focus. David was getting weaker. "You still don't know," David said. His voice was soft. He was losing all strength. Robert still had the knife in his hand. He was feeling the handle—trying to get a better grip on the knife. "Ramos," David said, "wants the money because he works for the feds." The gray veil was falling over David's mind. He turned his head away from Robert and stared blankly to the front. "His whole scheme," David said, "was to get you to show him who else was involved."

David felt sleep overcoming him. He was losing the battle to stay awake as he lost his blood. He looked down at the blood-red floor. "He still believes you aren't working alone."

Robert groaned.

"Let's face it Robert, no one ever believed you were smart enough to make this happen. In the end you proved them all right." David forced a smile and turned his head to look at Robert's empty expression. Robert stared back and said nothing. Robert's breathing was a gasp of air and quick exhale, a hesitation and then another gasp and exhale. His body was demanding oxygen but he was only able to get it in short bursts of energy.

"You never suspected Ramos, did you?" David's zeal for revenge was gone pooling on the floor around both men. While Robert felt defeat, David felt satisfaction. Both men were dying.

"At this moment, for me," David said, "this is what makes it all worth the pain. The creeping sleep is the price of admission. This might even be worth dying for."

Robert blankly stared at David. With his hands drenched in blood Robert made a last lunge toward him. Falling face down only inches from David's thigh. He hadn't the strength to lift his arm from the floor. David fell to his left crawling the few inches needed for him to reach out for the pistol. His fingers stretched to the grip scratching the gun toward his open hand. David took the bloodied, sticky grip into his right hand and turned to see Robert's battered face emerging from the pool of blood where he landed. His eye was wide open in a final moment of panic. David lifted the pistol and

Twisted Dreams, Fatal Wishes

placed it against Robert's forehead. He let it rest there hoping to feel something, some kind of accomplishment knowing what he was going to do. He looked for the final satisfaction of seeing the fear in Robert's face. He wanted to feel it channel from Robert's brain up the pistol to his hand. He wanted to hear Robert beg.

There was nothing. There was nothing there but the one-eyed stare of a man about to fade into death. This wasn't the way David wanted to see Robert go. This wasn't falling to a skull-crashing end or squirming behind the wheel of a burning car. Robert had to die knowing David was killing him. He had to see the joy in David's face. David needed that. He needed that from the very beginning. "You won't steal that from me." David squeezed the trigger. The gun's recoil blew itself from David's hand and back to his left skidding once more through the blood on the floor. Robert's head snapped backward toward the wall splattering bone and brain in a gray and white pattern worthy of a Jackson Pollock creation.

Robert was dead.

There was silence. Now, it was David's lungs that were aching for air and he could hear himself gasping. The door clicked and opened slowly. Enrique cautiously came in with his gun pointing the way. Ramos was right behind. "Get an ambulance," Ramos said with no apparent alarm or hurry. Enrique quickly disappeared. As Ramos walked toward David, he scanned the floor and saw the large pool of blood, the gun several feet away and the knife still clenched in Robert's hand. He pulled a white handkerchief from his jacket and pried the knife from Robert wrapping it in the handkerchief and placed it on the table. Then he noticed the flash drive. "What's this? Should I know about this, David?"

David was capable of a few words. A gasp for air. "Bank accounts." Another labored breath, "Everything."

"By rights," Ramos said, "I should just leave you here. I figure without help you might last another 20 minutes. The upside is mine; I get rid of a loose end. You get blamed for the murder and I don't have to explain anything, just present the prize," he said waving the drive, "collect my check and move on." Ramos stooped to the floor beside him and lifted his eyelid as if judging David's degree of consciousness. "The downside? Well, that's the funny part. The downside is all yours. You die. But here's the thing, I figure you know something . . . and besides, I sort of like you. You might even say I admire you."

David heard and saw nothing more. There was a blurred face in front of him, a hollow echoing voice and pain. Lots of pain.

CHAPTER 36
The Motion of Tides

My latest lifestyle is a conscious choice. I made my plans a year ago, after realizing the flash drive in Robert's safe was the pot of gold at the end of Robert's rainbow. It listed more than 15 numbered accounts in the Caymans and 12 more in Switzerland.

A second surprise was the safety deposit box—the same one noted in one of the bank letters found and photographed from Robert's safe. The box held bearer bonds and a few thousand carats of diamonds. I only became aware of the possibility that it was something more when I read the note with the bank key taped to it left in the bottom of the bag of Krugerrands taken the night of Robert's burglary. The box's contents were an eye-opening inventory—minus the intended deposit of coins Leonard liberated in our raid.

The feds never learned of the bank box or the gold coins. I didn't feel the need to tell them after they tried to open the safe with a torch. Turned out the safe's designer was correct. As soon as the flame's heat cut through the outer steel casing and hit the magnesium inner shell, the safe burst into a very hot flame that turned the safe's contents to ash.

I figured they had enough to worry about.

Besides, the government was very pleased with the printout of the accounts from the flash drive. I figured Ramos got his percentage—several million. My reward arrived as a tax-free, green, government check with Lady Liberty along the left border and the treasurer's signature at the bottom right—an equally sufficient amount.

Ramos appears to have vanished. I am glad to keep it that way not having seen or heard anything from him since the day in the garage. I stopped looking over my shoulder when I became convinced the entire affair was done, half-believing it never happened. In the interim, as you already know, I wrote an account of the entire event and labeled it fiction—not hard to believe when looking back on it now. More than just fiction, it was a catharsis, a way to iron out the residual hatred. Now, I can bury them all— Allen, Robert and Ramos. I can forget the reality and heal while enjoying the fairy tale.

There is a river here—bordering the backyard of our home. It flows at varying speeds into the convergence with the bay depending on the more powerful mass of the bay and whether the tide is coming in or going out. The mouth is where we sit near the shore line. From here we watch the river inhale as the tide pushes it back and then exhale as the tide recedes and the bay accepts its breath of fresh water. Each cycle fills me with a necessary rebirthing of a portion of my life. I collect the energy, purpose and renewed enthusiasm from the water's flow.

This is a weekend I intend to spend by the shore. After more than a year, the arm is better, though there remain some "dead" areas as the severed nerves regenerate. There is a green-bottled Rolling Rock in one hand while the other hand swats any mosquito that tries to share my slowly beating heart and the byproducts of the beer bottle it pushes through me. That is the intention.

I got as far as the aluminum chair and the sloping shore line's bank before Ceiley asked, "Do you really think you can get away with anything remotely like a day off." Ceiley is part of my reason for seeking this salt water refuge. Too full of energy and things to do, Ceiley is the bane of any procrastinators existence and she is doing a hell of a job helping me redefine my lifestyle. I am grateful for it.

The pair of chairs has worn a well-earned groove into the shore line where I sit waiting for Ceiley. Behind me, she cautiously moves from one overgrown clump of grass to the next to avoid sliding down the slope to her folding chair. She balances holding a handful of mail and brochures.

"I see you already found the mail," she has to speak loudly to overcome the noise of the gentle surf lapping at my feet. She stops on a large green clump of sea oats beside a small sapling. I opened the day's mail collection glancing at each new contribution to our travel fantasies and then threw them on the kitchen counter for her review. She grasps the small tree tightly as if on a slippery ice-covered ridge overlooking a frozen ocean. "You know, at some point these travel agencies are going to give up on you," she warns me while looking down at her footing. "You're ordering lots of brochures but don't go beyond that," she says. Then smiling and looking toward me she says, "I got all this STUFF." She emphasizes "stuff" as if it has no value and she needs to dispose of it before the crowding gets to be too much in our shared double-wide. Then she pushes her left hand filled with mail toward me waving the newly acquired diamond ring as if the burden is too much for her. "This whole collecting brochures thing is beginning to get messy," she says with her voice fading as if losing interest while she negotiates the trail toward the chairs.

Revenge has a way of changing who you are. You become one-sided lacking any other dimension than the one dominated by hate. But bits of hatred dissolved daily for me with each cycle of tides and Ceiley's help. I have remained close to Ceiley. She is growing toward me, trusting as each sunset presents us with a night of mutually generated peace. She knows little of Ramos or the money. She was there in the hospital when the agents visited. Though she undoubtedly overheard some of those conversations she never asked and probably never will.

"Hey, you there," Ceiley shouts above the tide's rhythmic noise. I look back at her half turning in my seat. Ceiley is still negotiating the shore line bank with a death grip grasp on a small oak tree. She gains her balance and lifts her smiling gaze toward me. I can see the child in her eyes. "I have your stack of bills," she says waiving them once more with her free hand. "You know, the ones you like to avoid," she says. "You really ought to let me handle these things if you're going to ignore them."

Getting up and taking two steps in her direction, I gently take hold of her hand and guide her to the chair next to my own. She slumps into the chair and hands me the envelopes. As I thumb through the stack, I find everything I expect. She was right, mostly bills. But there is one more official-looking, long envelope that I don't recognize. There is no return address. I turn it over and look again for a recognizable mark. Nothing. I tear at the envelope's flap. Inside is a hand written note on a Mexico City hotel's stationery: "Book was great. Maybe a little too much information, but nothing I can't live with. Congratulations." It is initialed "VR."